# the BEST GOOD TIME

## A Nostalgic Journey for Baby Boomers

# the BEST GOOD TIME

## A Nostalgic Journey for Baby Boomers

MIKE SCANLON

Aventine Press

© 2010, Mike Scanlon.
First Edition

THE BEST GOOD TIME
A Nostalgic Journey for Baby Boomers
is a work of fiction, and as such, any resemblance between the characters
herein and real persons living or otherwise is purely coincidental.

No part of this book may be reproduced or transmitted in any form or by any means, electronic, or mechanical, including photocopying, recording, or by any information storage, and retrieval system without written permission from both the copyright owner and the publisher of this book.

Published by Aventine Press
750 State St. #319
San Diego CA, 92101
www.aventinepress.com

ISBN: 1-59330-664-4

Library of Congress Control Number: 2010928096

Printed in the United States of America
ALL RIGHTS RESERVED

For
Paula Bartlett Roane
and
Elizabeth Ann O'Neill.

# ACKNOWLEDGMENTS

I wish to acknowledge the valued assistance of Paul Gallagher for his willingness to read the early manuscript and for his many suggestions that improved the work. Any weaknesses that remain are the result of my having ignored Paul's excellent advice. In addition, the kind words early-on and encouragement of Bill Harlow, author of Circle William, have been much appreciated. Last and never least, I express many thanks to Gay Rothe and Bill Rothe for their editing skills and keen eye for detail.

I thank the late Bob Johnston, my good and dear friend of long-standing and former beach house colleague for providing me with the original stimulus for this literary effort. Also, I want to express my appreciation to my close friends Gary and Linda Milliken, Pete Roussel, the late Jim Tasse and Karen Tasse, Beau Bouthillier, Chris Cobb, Troy Mashburn, and Rick Thornburg for providing inspiration along the way.

Lastly, I refer the cross-country traveler to several texts which helped me to refresh my memory of roads traveled many years ago: the "Frommer's America on Wheels" series, the "National Geographic's Guide to the Interstates - Crossing America" and its "Guide to the National Parks of the United States," as well as "The Smithsonian Guide to Historic America series." I commend these excellent books to those who seek the open road.

Mike Scanlon
Easter, 2010

"It is not necessary to imagine the world ending in fire or ice.
There are two other possibilities: one is paperwork,
and the other is nostalgia."

-- Frank Zappa

# INTRODUCTION
## March, 1978

AS TIME GOES by, thirty-something years ago is but a quick glance over the shoulder.

Many people would have to stop and think long and hard about what they were doing during a given week way back in 1978. However, that year remains fresh in Mark Stanton's memory. A particular week in late March sticks out -- seven days that had a profound effect on him. That was the week Mark drove cross-country with his good friend, Bill "B.J." Jackson.

Short of the abhorrent terrorist attacks on the World Trade Center and the Pentagon on September 11, 2001, and the Mount St. Helen's eruption in 1980, there have been few other earthshaking alterations to the American landscape these last four decades, but lives have evolved. Like a river that naturally changes direction when dammed by storm-created sandbars and rockslides, personal lives are forced to take new twists and turns upon encountering unexpected incidents and episodes, ever meandering toward the ultimate delta of life.

Each person marks the passing of time differently. Certain stimuli have a way of triggering remembrances. For some, a particular song or melody takes them back in time to a specific moment, years before. For others, the mere mention of a bygone incident, a sporting contest, a hit motion picture, a political crisis, a human tragedy, or an uncommon event jogs their memory banks to a certain date or place. For Mark Stanton and Bill Jackson, it is the songs -- particularly the rock'n'roll music of the '60's and '70's -- that bring on waves of baby boomer nostalgia.

In retrospect, and for those not of age at that time, the early spring of 1978 was part and parcel of the pre-terrorism, pre-Saddam Hussein, pre-"Dubya," pre-Bill and Hillary, pre-Ronald Reagan, pre-Pope John Paul II, pre-space shuttle, pre-cellular phone, pre-ATM machine and pre-personal computer era. There were some 216 million persons living in the United States (some 100 million fewer than today).

In March of 1978, Jimmy Carter had been residing in The White House for only fourteen months. Tip O'Neill held sway in the U.S. House of Representatives and Howard Baker managed the U.S. Senate. Leonid Brezhnev was in control of the Soviet Union. Since the death of Mao Zedong, the so-called "Gang of Four" led by Mao's widow, Chiang Ching, had been attempting to maintain the status quo in Red China. As always, Fidel Castro just kept on "keeping on" down there in Cuba.

In the news, the great national debate during the first several months of 1978 was over the proposition: "Should the United States turn over control of the Panama Canal to the Panamanians?" In California, taxpayers were on the warpath, revolting, trying to pass something called "Proposition 13," an action that promised to slash property taxes (and did a year later). The Dow Jones Industrial Average was bouncing around between 750 and 800. What a country we were.

For people of Mark Stanton's generation -- the seventy-eight million baby boomers -- late 1977 and early 1978 was an era in which very familiar names were doing extraordinary things. Muhammad Ali reigned as the undisputed world heavyweight boxing champ. Ted Turner, on his yacht *Courageous*, successfully defended and retained the America's Cup, besting Australia, 4-0. Just seven weeks prior, the Dallas Cowboys captured the Vince Lombardi trophy at Super Bowl XII, defeating the Denver Broncos, 27-10, at the Superdome in New Orleans. Seattle Slew proved himself worthy in the sport of kings by running away with 1977's Triple Crown, in 1978 he was happily out to stud. A.J. Foyt held the Indianapolis 500 title. And the "damn Yankees" took the most recent Fall Classic beating the Dodgers in six.

"Annie Hall" won Best Picture the previous April, but "The Deer Hunter" and "Coming Home," two post-Vietnam era films, were sure to vie for the most coveted Oscar, to be awarded in just a few weeks. Although critically acclaimed, neither motion picture was likely to unseat 1977's box office mega-hit, "Star Wars," which -- at that time -- was the all-time highest-grossing movie in history at $322 million.

The top-grossing movie in 1978 would be "Animal House." When circumstances became untenable at Delta House, the solution for Bluto and the Delts was to yell "Road Trip!" load their six-packs into the car and head for an adventure on the open highway. And when they did, gasoline was an average of 67 cents a gallon. "Road rage" was not a familiar term -- and why would a road get mad at you anyway?

In March of 1978, America was suffering through the silly symptoms of disco fever. The Bee Gees, from Australia, topped the popular music charts. "Laverne and Shirley" was the top-rated network television sit-com. Cable television was a relatively new phenomenon for Americans -- only 16 percent of Americans were wired. Today's "fax" machine was still in its embryo stage, known simply as a telecopier.

NASA's Voyager I was well on its way to Jupiter and Saturn, and Voyager II was right behind it, headed for the planets Uranus and Neptune. A new version of the Boeing 747 had just set the speed record flying around the world, over both poles, from and to San Francisco, in a time of 57 hours, 25 minutes and 42 seconds.

March of 1978 existed in a relatively calm period before a nuclear reactor at a place called "Three Mile Island" went up in a cloud of green smoke -- before the government agreed to bail out Lee Iacocca's Chrysler Corporation -- long before a swarm of unshaven, unruly Iranians, followers of Ayatollah Khomeini, took sixty-three Americans hostage at the U.S. Embassy in Tehran, triggering our nation's second energy crisis in just seven years.

If you can imagine, it was a time before political correctness, or "P.C.," was in vogue or considered a theology by the liberal or progressive sets. Young people enjoyed drinking beer and driving fast cars -- sometimes, at the very same time. In those days, few people even considered fastening their seat belts. They should have known better, but in those days they didn't see drinking a beer and driving as such a big deal. That was before Mothers Against Drunk Driving (MADD) woke the nation to a serious and deadly problem. Baby boomers had been drinking 3.2 (% or lower alcohol content) beers since college days and no one had ever even heard of the National Highway Safety Council. "Baby on Board" signs hadn't even been thought up yet.

Also, in the '70's -- believe it or not -- young people actually viewed one another as sex objects. Casual sex between consenting adults was not such a big deal. Those were the days before Americans ever heard of genital herpes, and HIV-AIDS was not even in the vocabulary. Male baby boomers had been chasing female baby boomers since high school and only recently had a few of them been catching any. As a matter of fact, most young people considered themselves lucky to be living in the 1970's -- the decade of the birth control pill and rather liberalized sexual mores. In their minds, it helped make up for having had to live through the nasty Vietnam era of the 60's.

In particular, Mark Stanton's good friend B.J. didn't see casual sex as a big deal, but then he was the one always living with a good-looking woman. It was still a big deal to Mark.

At the time, Mark Stanton was a 30-year-old baby boomer, full of ambition, yet quite distressed because he had recently been diagnosed with cancer. He was frustrated because the disease clouded his hopes and planning for a future career. In mid-spring of 1978, he decided to take a leave from his job to get away for a time and enjoy life to the fullest before taking on exploratory surgery.

That year, things began to change for him. During a specific week in late March, Mark arrived at a definitive fork in his road of life. Looking back years later, he holds no regrets about what happened to him, nor about the path he chose that week.

During the coast-to-coast trip with his good friend B.J., more than thirty years ago, Mark finally cut loose and gave himself a much-needed change of scenery. That week gave him a few precious days to think things over on the open road. He experienced his first true adventure -- exciting incidents and episodes that he will always remember. That likely "once-in-a-lifetime" cross-country journey provided Mark Stanton with the time he needed to reflect upon what was really important to him -- and what rightly should be next in his life.

# CHAPTER ONE

## Tuesday, March 21, 1978

### Someone in the City.

THE PORSCHE 924 barreled off the highway ramp into the Presidio Heights section of "The City." Its radio was blaring "That Old Time Rock'n'roll" by Bob Seger and the Silver Bullet Band.

The San Francisco skyline at 6:50 a.m. looked like a postcard scene with wisps of billowy fog airbrushed over the orange towers of the Golden Gate Bridge.

A few minutes later Mark Stanton wheeled the sports car into Arguello Street and stopped at the curb in front of the address B.J. had given him. It was an old, but well-kept Victorian house, yellow with white trim. When the car came to a stop, Mark lunged to turn down the radio, which was playing way too loudly for such an early hour in this peaceful neighborhood.

As he removed his sunglasses and looked about, Mark spotted a familiar lanky figure topped with a curly-perm. His good buddy B.J. was standing in the side driveway surrounded by piles of clothing. His frizzy head was bobbing up and down, as he scooped up an entire wardrobe scattered all over the yard. At first Mark thought his friend might be sorting the laundry. *But, in the driveway? At this early hour?* Then he noticed that clothes were fluttering down on B.J., one piece at a time, from a second story turret window.

From behind the steering wheel, Mark leaned back and looked up through the open sunroof. He spotted a woman halfway out the window, obviously irate, tossing garments and screeching, "you no-good shit-heel... you bastard... you dickhead..." a verbal barrage of epithets from the young woman accompanied the hurling of each article of clothing.

From the unfolding spectacle, it quickly became clear that B.J. had not told his girlfriend -- at least not until bright and early this morning -- that he and Mark were leaving for the East Coast. When B.J. looked up from his laundry and recognized Mark in the shiny new car, he dropped an armful of clothes, turned his back on the laughable scene, and headed for the curb.

Trying to suppress a shit-eating grin, Mark took the initiative, "Jackson, my man, it doesn't look like you're quite ready to depart." Mark and B.J. -- and most of their friends -- had acquired the habit of referring to one another by just their last names. It was a baby boomer thing. Mark, trying to be diplomatic while maintaining a straight face, said, "Do you want me to circle the block and come back in a half hour or so?"

"No Stanton. Just give me a couple of minutes with Laurie and I'll be ready to roll." With that, B.J. turned and headed up the front steps two at a time with a determination to have a face-to-face confrontation with the woman of the household. In this instance, B.J. was the live-in boyfriend.

Mark settled back in his bucket seat and lit up a Salem contemplating the moment. B.J. was one of those enviable guys who always seemed to have his way with the ladies gliding from one torrid relationship to the next -- all with gorgeous women -- without any thought of commitment. His life seemed like Easy Street to guys like Mark who spent their lives tip-toeing down the rocky road to romance. Among their beach house friends B.J. was the undisputed expert on single women. However, the nasty little episode that was taking place this morning reminded Mark of some unsolicited but sage advice, *there are no real experts.* Perhaps this advice included Bill "B.J." Jackson, the man every lady eventually referred to as "Sweet William."

On the other hand, Mark Stanton always had the reputation of being the storyteller in their beach house group. And this morning, unfolding right before his eyes, was a real doozy of a story line. *Wait until the guys hear this one*, he thought.

Mark already had a complete anthology of B.J. stories committed to memory, but with some people one just never had enough.  Like vintage French champagne, with enough time and constant turning, he would hone this storyline and save its debut for just the right moment, back in Washington, D.C.

Eventually B.J. emerged on the Victorian front porch with his arm wrapped around the shoulder of a disheveled beauty. She was draped in a powder blue silk robe that left very little to the imagination.  With her head down and ear up against his chest, she clung to B.J. with both arms as he eased her down the front steps.  The revealing robe fluttered teasingly in the crisp breeze coming off the Bay.  Despite the awkward embrace and the juxtaposition of their bodies, somehow they moved in unison down the walkway toward the car -- a bizarre tango not unlike the movement of a hostage and gunman in the telescopic crosshairs of police sharpshooters.

Mark was certain that the scene would provide theater for the entire neighborhood for some time to come.  Also, he sensed that he would not have to embellish this B.J. story much when he got around to telling it.

Arriving at the car, B.J. said, "Stanton, I want *you* to fill-in Laurie on our travel plans... while I collect my things."  B.J. left her and wandered off with a duffel bag, no doubt, to select what would be a wrinkled travel ensemble.

Still seated in the Porsche, Mark tried with every fiber of his being to focus on the tearful face above him, and not to peek at the barely-concealed, ample bosom poised right at eye level.  B.J.'s friend, Laurie, whom Mark had not met before, was a natural beauty with spaniel eyes and thick sable hair.  Here it was, daybreak.  And from all the laundry lying around, it was Mark's guess she'd been ranting hysterically for good while.  She wore not a trace of make-up, and, obviously, she'd been crying.  Despite these less-than-favorable conditions, Laurie was absolutely stunning.  In fact, she was so beautiful that Mark found it nearly impossible to maintain contact with her penetrating pale green eyes for more than a few seconds at a time.

What was he supposed to say to her?  B.J. is going to ride shotgun with him for a week and then probably remain in Washington, D.C., until he wears out his welcome with some other star-crossed beauty.  Knowing B.J.'s *modus operandi* by heart, Mark's most optimistic guess was that his friend might return from the Nation's Capital to see young Laurie in two or three months' time -- if at all.

*But was that what B.J. had told her? Probably not.*

Mark maintained constant eye-to-eye contact with Laurie lest he give away his thoughts. *God, I wish someone in the city who looked half this great was clinging to my thorax this morning, pleading, trying to keep me from going away.*

Giving her his best job-interview smile, he said, "Good morning Laurie... I'm Mark Stanton." He spoke somewhat haltingly, stalling for B.J. to reappear and take him off the hook. "I'm looking forward to a nice trip with Jackson. It will give us a chance to catch up with each other while we drive to Washington," he babbled. "I didn't really want to ship my brand-new car... so I thought I'd break it in with a road trip. When I mentioned to B.J. that I planned to drive, he insisted that he come along..."

Laurie interrupted, "*William* says he'll be back in a week or two." She was searching to locate B.J. as if to acquire some sort of visual confirmation. As she turned, the front of her silk robe inched open, even wider. "Do you know where you two will be staying?"

"Well, I don't have a phone in my new place yet. But I'll remind B.J. to call you when we arrive," Mark said, thinking quickly, yet trying to maintain some flexibility and plausible deniability for his friend.

"The 'rat' just told me about the trip this morning," she muttered in a soft voice, still on the threshold of tears, "I'm not mad about him going... I'm really not. It's just that he isn't anywhere near finished with the remodeling job on my house. The bathroom is a total mess... it seems as if every bit of plumbing in the house is torn up. My hot tub isn't hooked-up yet... and now he's gallivanting off to *Seattle* with you."

*Seattle?* Mark had the right to remain silent, and he did. At this point, he was not prepared to split continent-wide "hairs" about East Coast versus West Coast destination points. Mark recognized that most California people actually view the entire world from the left coast perspective, so he presumed that it's only natural that Laurie would assume that "Washington" meant they were headed for Washington State... *ergo*, Seattle, he supposed.

Despite his Ivy League education and Masters degree in philosophy, B.J.'s chosen career specialty was rehabbing fashionable upscale homes -- almost always owned and occupied by stunningly beautiful, fashion-conscious, wealthy single women.  Where did he find them?  That was one of the things Mark hoped to learn during this weeklong trip.

After what seemed an eternity of false departures, hugs and releases, and several good-byes, punctuated at one point by a spiteful single-digit salute from Laurie, B.J. was finally ready to depart.  It wasn't exactly a Frank Capra finale, but B.J. seemed satisfied that he'd pulled it off  -- without either losing the girl for good, or losing face in front of Mark.

## Continental Drift.

MARK HAD ARRIVED at B.J.'s temporary abode at Laurie's in "The City" a few minutes ahead of schedule, even though he'd stopped to pick up a jumbo coffee during the drive.  It had taken the blistering-hot java a full fifty minutes to cool before he could sip it without self-cauterizing his soft palate.  But now the caffeine was beginning to kick in.

He had driven north, along the scenic San Andreas Valley, up the San Mateo Peninsula from Palo Alto.  And after one hour in the briskness of Pacific Ocean air at 70 mph with the sunroof open, and sixteen ounces of coffee, Mark Stanton had never been more wide awake, felt more alive, or been more eager to take on a given day

Seven o'clock this morning was "Zero Hour," and today was "D-Day" -- departure day.  Today's 573-mile trip to Las Vegas would be the first leg of a weeklong, 3,600-mile, cross-country journey that would take Mark and B.J. all the way to Washington, D.C.

Mark Stanton was moving back east, leaving the Golden State behind; and he was not unhappy about it.  The moving van had departed from his Palo Alto apartment for the Nation's Capital the day before.  Now he had an entire week to kill before he was due back east to meet up with all his worldly goods.  What few possessions that weren't already aboard the moving van were jammed into the hatchback of his just-purchased Porsche.

The German automaker had just introduced its brand-new "924" line to the United States.  It was designed to appeal to upwardly mobile males in their thirties -- guys like Mark, who were ready for the first booster shot of testosterone that a new sports car provides. The 1978 Porsche 924 was the hottest new car in California. Fewer than 7,500 of them had been sold in the U.S. Only a handful was available outside of the populous East Coast and West Coast markets. In the weeks since Mark bought the 924 he'd put fewer than 1,000 miles on it, so the upcoming drive to Washington, D.C., would be its true maiden voyage.

In light of a sudden change in his health and his subsequent decision to take a sabbatical from work and head back east, Mark thought that he probably should have re-thought buying the Porsche, but "Stanley" -- as he called the car -- seemed to be just what the doctor ordered -- a stress reliever. Besides, the sports car stood for everything that *is* "California." And more to the point, it seemed that he didn't want to return home to D.C. after two years without some sort of trophy to show for his time out west.

The cross-country itinerary was well thought out. A clipboard wedged next to the driver's seat held detailed trip maps. Mark had already spent two weeks calculating mileage segments between stops, overnight cities, and estimated driving times. It was mid-March and snow continued to blanket much of the Midwest and the major east-west corridors, Interstates 70 and 80. So he plotted a more circuitous route. His southerly route would improve chances of driving the whole way in decent weather. Also, it would enable him to keep "Stanley"-the-Porsche's sunroof open, stowing the portable hatch top in the trunk.

If the schedule held up, Mark and B.J. would arrive in D.C. on Monday, March 27th, with a mid-season tan, or at the very least, two very conspicuous cases of sports car windburn. Unfortunately for Mark, two days after arriving in D.C., on March 29th, he was scheduled to be at Johns Hopkins Hospital in Baltimore for exploratory surgery. No one -- not even B.J. -- knew about Mark's impending operation.

This adventurous fellow who'd volunteered to ride shotgun with Mark all the way to Washington, D.C., was Bill Jackson. Most people knew him as "B.J." However, Mark always called him "Jackson" -- kind of a one-syllable "Jcksn" -- sort of snapped-off when said, just as a Parris Island drill instructor might yell at a Marine recruit he wanted to step up, front and center. The ladies -- and there were many in B.J.'s life -- would describe the 30-year old Jackson as a tall, slim, handsome sort with hazel brown eyes. Since moving to California, B.J. had grown a scraggly beard to cover the remnants of teenage acne scars, and opted for a blonde Art Garfunkel-like hairdo -- the white man's version of the 'fro. Mark considered B.J. sort of a John Lennon look-alike especially when he sported his raspberry-tinted granny glasses. Needless to say, with his never-ending collection of stonewashed denim outfits, B.J. didn't look very Republican, and he didn't vote that way either. B.J. had a brilliant mind sometimes hidden by his very laid-back personality. He wasn't lazy; it's just that he thought things over a bit before he got involved.

Mark and Bill Jackson had met and become fast friends six years earlier at an East Coast resort, Dewey Beach, Delaware. It's a spit of hot sand on the Atlantic Ocean where randy singles from Washington, D.C., go on summer weekends to spawn in the sun. The two men, along with several other single guys and gals, shared a rambling seaside house on weekends from Memorial Day to Labor Day during the 70's. All these folks were known as the "beach house crowd."

Socially, Mark and B.J. had a lot in common.

Politically, they couldn't see each other's stance on a given issue due to curvature of the earth. When they first met in Washington in 1972, B.J. was working for a Democrat Congressman from Illinois. According to Mark, B.J. was a "we-can't-spend-enough-tax-money-on-the-downtrodden    one-worlder," like his boss. His tendencies toward largess, Mark suspected, were attributable to gilded guilt. Also, he felt that B.J.'s Princeton University yearbook photo should be in all the political almanacs beside the term bleeding-heart-liberal.

It wasn't his fault that B.J. was a bleeding heart; Mark was sure it was his blue-blooded upbringing. B.J. probably never really had a choice. He was born into money, lots of it, and he was smart enough to know how fortunate he was. All his life, B.J. wanted for nothing but undivided attention. To him, hard knocks were something cheap unbranded gasoline caused in a "Beamer." If you didn't know that B.J. came from money, you would never think that he had any. He certainly didn't flaunt it. Always clad in denims, he certainly didn't wear it. He never talked about it. And God knows he never had it on him when a waiter brought the tab. Mark respected B.J.'s low-key style; he was not sure he could handle having money the same way B.J. did. However, Mark loved to tweak B.J.'s knee-jerk liberal sensibilities. So he referred to their impending cross-country itinerary as his "Southern Strategy" just to piss B.J. off -- knowing that every Nixonian reference elicited a partisan whine. And Mark loved to hear a liberal whine.

If you asked B.J. about Mark Stanton, he would think for a moment and say Mark's one of those Type A, alpha-male Republicans, but not a total nut case. He considered Mark to be a middle-of-the-road Rockefeller-type Republican -- not too intense and way too squishy on the cutting edge GOP issues of the day to be full-blown, Bible thumpin' right wing crazy. B.J. would add that Mark came from Ohio roots, the state that served up seven nondescript U.S. presidents -- all conservative Republicans.

What with his impending rendezvous with the surgeons and their scalpels, Mark truly relished the idea of spending the upcoming week driving cross-country, talking politics with B.J. It would take his mind off more serious matters. Over the last six years their clamorous debates on current events were legend among the beach house crowd. Although they were opposites on many levels, they never, ever, let it get in the way of a good time. And when B.J. and Mark got together they always seemed to have a good time.

Logistically, Mark Stanton was a total time freak. He functioned as a fine Swiss clock. To the contrary, B.J. didn't even own a watch. That's why this particular morning Mark had hoped -- probably against all hope -- that B.J. would have been ready on-time to leave on their cross-country journey. Just to demonstrate to B.J. -- and perhaps to himself -- that he was not totally anal retentive about time, Mark had built-in some slack into each leg of the week long trip so they could stop and see some of the country along the way. As an American history buff, Mark wanted to absorb some of the antiquity of the Old West, get a feel for its geography, and hopefully meet some interesting people along the way. He'd already warned

B.J. that that might involve a few stops at roadside historical markers. At least that's how Mark had planned out the week on the road.

B.J., "Stanley" the car, and Mark were setting out this morning for the Nation's Capital. Little did Mark know how his concept of a well-planned, crisply-executed itinerary was about to come up against B.J.'s idea of a cross-country ramble -- usually a barely moving pace best described as "continental drift."

## Reflections in the Rearview Mirror.

TEN MINUTES AFTER departing Laurie's home, with B.J.'s lone duffel stowed in "Stanley's" hatchback, Mark and B.J. rolled onto the open road via the Route 101-South ramp. It was now 7:45 a.m. England Dan and John Ford Coley were wailing "We'll Never Have to Say Good-bye" on the radio.

B.J. stretched and gyrated his neck awkwardly -- as was his habit -- until he heard it pop; he let out a guttural growl and rubbed his stomach. "Stanton, my man, where are we stopping for breakfast?"

"Breakfast? We're not -- at least not right now. We've got to get back on schedule. Thanks to your departing-is-such-sweet-sorrow scene at Laurie's, we're already forty-five minutes behind schedule," he said firmly, not wanting to let the situation get out of hand during the very first hour of a seven-day marathon.

"Maybe I'm late Stanton... but that Laurie, you gotta' admit, she sure is something..."

"I'll give you that," said Mark, shaking his head. "She's got the best profile I've seen west of the Grand Tetons."

As they continued south, on their left, San Francisco Bay sparkled in the low-angled morning sun. The northbound lanes, opposite them, were filled with thousands of cars in bumper-to-bumper rush hour traffic -- Bay area commuters creeping into "The City" for another day of work.

"Are you going to let me get behind the wheel of this new Black Beauty you're driving," B.J. asked.

"It's not black. It's pearl gray. And it's not a 'she.' It's a 'he.' And *his* name is 'Stanley.'"

"Well, first of all Stanton, you're color-blind. This car is *black*. And second, why would you want to call your new car Studley?"

"It's 'Stanley'... and it's a long story. I'll explain it some other time. But for now, just remember, you'll *not* be driving 'Stanley.'"

"You know... I used to race Porsches back in Illinois."

"How would I have ever guessed that a limousine liberal like you grew up racing expensive foreign sports cars? Gee... it must be my Republican intuition. All I can say is... this is one sports car you're not going to be racing. I'll be doing the driving, thank you very much."

"Suit yourself, Parnelli, if you want to drive all 3,000 miles..."

"It's 3,600 miles the way we're going," Mark corrected, "but who's counting."

B.J. folded his arms behind his head and leaned back in the tan leather seat, "I'd rather sleep than drive... I was just trying to be polite, offering my expertise with these German babies."

They passed the entrance to Candlestick Park, the home of the Giants. One thing all Mark's friends knew about him was that he's a true dyed-in-the-wool baseball fan. Candlestick was a ballpark he wished he could have been more enthusiastic about visiting. At one Giants' game the previous June, it got so cold in the upper deck that shivers shook a cup of coffee right out of his hand. In Mark's mind, baseball was meant for ice-cold beer on a hot, humid day. Coffee, even if amply laced with Jameson's Irish whiskey, was something one smuggled into a football stadium, not something you needed to survive a night baseball game. It was just another bizarre reason why California and Mark didn't seem to get along.

B.J. studied the inside of Mark's new car. He examined the clipboard with the itinerary, trip maps and routes attached. "Stanton! The Presidential advance man! I must say, I'm impressed with your scheduling prowess, but I don't think this-here travel agenda is going to hold up under the pressures of the open road."

"It's all been thought-out..."

"Not by me it hasn't. But I'll look it over and let you know later what I think," B.J. said with a smirk, knowing that the comment wouldn't sit well. Mark's passenger then pulled out his ever-present harmonica and blew warbled strains from "Do You Know the Way to San Jose?"

Prior to bailing out of his political position in 1976 before the oncoming rush of the Carter Administration, Mark had held a plum assignment in the Nixon and Ford Administrations as an advance man for The White House. An advance man travels in advance of "The Man" and arranges for the scheduling of all the President's moves and political stops. Thus, as a professional traveler, Mark was quite proud of the more than one million miles of globetrotting he'd done since graduating from college. It had been stressful work but stimulating excitement for a young man in his twenties.

So, like anyone with advance training would, Mark had viewed the upcoming transcontinental trek as a logistical challenge. He figured if he could plan a trip for "POTUS" -- the President of the United States -- on a minute-by-minute schedule, surely he could arrange for an hour-by-hour, cross-country trip for B.J. and him. *Some advance man*, Mark thought. *They'd been on the road a total of twenty minutes, and they were now forty minutes late. The advance man must be losing his touch.*

They continued down the San Mateo peninsula; on their left was San Francisco International Airport. Mark had come and gone through that buff-brick, boxy terminal building so many times during the last two years that he'd lost count. In fact, last week he had returned from Baltimore after appointments with his doctors at Johns Hopkins Hospital. The job that he had held for the last two years, as a lobbyist for a forest products company, required him to fly to Washington each week the U.S. Congress was in session. A quick guess was that he had made some eighty round trips, more than 500,000 air miles, to and from D.C. since he'd moved to California. To his mind, the job and all the travel had been killing him, physically as well as socially.

Seeing the airport jogged Mark's memory banks. "Say Jackson. You remember Tony Masterson from Dewey Beach days?"

"The airline pilot guy? Sure."

"He was in here a couple of weeks ago for a layover and we got together. He's been flying back and forth from Dulles

Airport to Frankfort, Germany, for a couple of months. Over dinner, he told me the weirdest story. He's a co-pilot and was assigned to work with an old-pro Captain who'd been flying in and out of Europe for years. Catch this! Tony says that on their first flight together, just as they are coming into Frankfort's airport, at the outer markers, he's landing the plane and he hears the Captain say, 'Geez'us... will you look at the giant tentacles on that thing!'"

B.J. sat up. "Giant tentacles on *what* thing?"

Mark laughed, "That's exactly what I said. Anyway, Tony meant to ask the Captain what he was talking about, but was so busy landing the plane at the time, he forgot. On the return trip to the States, the exact same thing happens. Tony is landing the plane at Dulles and when they reach the outer markers the Captain says to no one in particular, 'Geez'us... will you look at the giant tentacles on that thing!' Later, as they were riding the crew bus into the terminal, Tony makes it a point to ask the pilot what's with the 'giant tentacles' routine every time they land. And the Captain says, 'Oh, that's not for you Tony. That's for the voice cockpit recorder. If I ever crash, I don't want it to be attributed to 'pilot error'... so I'm just giving those bastards at the National Transportation Safety Board something to think about when they listen to the tapes from the black box they find in the crash debris!'"

B.J. had an incredulous look on his face, "You gotta' be kidding me."

"Swear to God..."

They both had a good laugh. B.J. continued to shake his head while watching a plane hang low in the sky on final approach into the airport. "I always wondered what kind of weird and perverted stuff goes on up there in the cockpit. After that story I'm certain that I really don't want to know."

A few minutes later they sped by the familiar Palo Alto exit, Mark's usual point of departure from the U.S. 101 freeway. He could see the neon sign in the distance advertising the Porsche dealership where he'd recently bought "Stanley."

He recalled the eerie day when he first heard the word "cancer" in a phone call from his doctor. That very afternoon he drove into that auto lot to trade-in his fire engine red 1970 Cougar convertible for the brand new 924. Upon hanging up the phone with the doc, he had decided it was time to start enjoying life a little more.

One small problem -- Mark hadn't driven a car with a stick-shift transmission since drivers-ed class in high school, some fifteen years prior. Driving a new, four-speed Porsche for the first time was an intimidating prospect. No one wanted to embarrass themselves by crunching gears as they pulled out of the dealership in front of the entire service staff -- especially with all those blond-haired car-Nazis clad in their white lab coats with names like "Hans," "Gunter," and "Leopold," embroidered on the pocket flaps. As wary as he was of the car dealer's staff, Mark was even more petrified of the thought of steep streets with stop signs. The night before he picked up the new car, he lay awake all night. Not being able to shift "Stanley" away from an uphill stop sign was his worst nightmare -- the dreaded thought of rolling backwards, slamming into the car behind him, before he could get the damned thing in gear.

However, it seems as though this had become the time in his life to address certain fears. So before buying the 924, Mark made himself a pledge. He would begin to overcome trepidation and stick-shift fears, one at a time. He knew that the streets of San Francisco were the most precariously steep on earth. So, if he could master stick shifting away from a stop sign atop the steepest hill in "The City," he could just as easily stick shift his way up Mount Shasta. He vowed to master a dead stop shift-away from the stop sign at the fabled Gough Street hill. He would practice until either he bettered Gough Street, or he rolled backwards and drowned in the Bay. So, the Sunday after Mark bought the Porsche he drove it up to San Francisco at four o'clock in the morning. The day after he bought the new Porsche, in those foggy, pre-dawn hours while confident drivers were abed, the insecure Mark spent the wee hours stick-shifting his way up progressively steeper and steeper slopes. He felt sorry for the poor denizens of those lovely homes that cleave to the city's steepest inclines. He was sure they planned on sleeping-in that Sunday morning. However, up at the corner of the street, much to their chagrin, a flaming ass in a shiny new 924 was revving his engine, rasping the gearbox, and laying rubber in a jerky staccato. What they heard in the foggy dark that morning was an obsessed individual, endlessly rehearsing stop sign get-a-ways like some Navy pilot gone-mad practicing night carrier landings. At last, around 8:00 a.m. that portentous Sunday -- four full hours after he began -- Mark declared himself ready for the ultimate test. He approached the gut wrenching Gough Street summit -- the near-vertical pavement with the stop-sign-from-Hell perched precariously at the pinnacle. He'd seen this exact scene, over and over, in his sweaty nightmares. The Gough Street hill was generally considered, by stick-shifting San Franciscans, to be the worst. Mark worked for another hour on that precipice until he'd perfected the art of peeling away from a dead stop, at the worst stop-sign, on the steepest hill, on the most treacherous fog-slicked street, in the most hill-riddled city in the world. He got so damned good at it, and got so cocky, that he purposefully stalled the car, restarted it and shifted away, barely rolling back an inch before he left Gough Street and the first of many impending fears in "Stanley's" rearview mirror.

Now, just a few weeks later, as the tree-lined streets of Palo Alto disappeared behind them, Mark said a silent goodbye to his neighbors and the handful of truly nice people he'd gotten to know while living there. Initially, he had anticipated that life in Palo Alto, in the shadows of Stanford University, would be rather exciting. In reality, he couldn't have been more wrong. Unfortunately for Mark, most of the Stanford women he'd met looked like they were related to Jerry Garcia of the Grateful Dead. To make matters worse, they tended to wear their black truck-tire retread sandals with white anklet cotton socks, the penultimate turn-off in Mark's book. He was sure that all the Stanford coeds were as smart as whips, but finding one that caught his eye turned out to be like trying to find a ferret, without the ferret-face.

They continued driving south at 75 mph. The last familiar surroundings -- the stagnant and pungent salt ponds at the southern tip of San Francisco Bay and the massive blimp hangars of Moffett Naval Air Station slipped past on the left.

At just after eight o'clock, they drove through Sunnyvale, the emerging capital of the high-tech area, now being referred to as "Silicon Valley" -- *a rather stupid nickname*, Mark thought.  He was sure that such a silly label wouldn't stick. They continued past the burgeoning City of San Jose, toward the agricultural community of Gilroy -- the garlic capital of the U.S.

The two were officially on their way -- coast-to-coast -- and at that point in time, only thirty-five minutes behind schedule.

"Fly Like An Eagle" by the Steve Miller Band was on the car radio.

## California Dreaming.

CALIFORNIA IS A present day Garden of Eden.  Without a doubt, its extremes in physical terrain are unmatched for beauty anywhere in the world.  Mark Stanton loved the Golden State's scenery -- the rich textures and the unique colors so unfamiliar to easterners when encountered for the first time. He'd always loved the low-lying, fast-moving clouds and the aquamarine color of San Francisco Bay.  He wished he had the talent to paint landscapes that could capture the coloration, especially the undulating golden hills with the dark-green stands of eucalyptus and live oak.  Then there was the imposing Coastal Range, fog-topped mountains with blue-green crests of Douglas fir and redwood.  Unsurpassed were the awe-inspiring vistas overlooking the Pacific from anywhere along the Coast Highway.  Photographs never captured the real beauty.  No, despite any misgivings about leaving, he was pretty clear on one point: Mark loved California, the state. Even after living there for two years, the incomparable blend of fog, sunshine, surf, and mountains never lost its allure.

Mark's first months in California were spent exploring the whole coastline from as far north as the tiny logging village of Orick, not far from the Oregon border, to the breath-taking Monterey peninsula, its windy neighbor, Big Sur, and famous San Simeon, farther to the south.  At one point during his first year in California Mark seriously explored the possibility of buying a seaside parcel of land at Bodega Bay -- just north of Marin County -- the very hamlet where Alfred Hitchcock shot his eerie film, "The Birds."  He asked a local representative of California's Coastal Zone Commission, would he ever be able to build his dream home on a particular plot of land?  The bureaucrat's only reaction was to say, "You know, Mr. Stanton, the English language is the only language in which the words, 'fat chance' and 'slim chance' mean the very same thing." At that point, Mark abandoned any hope of a picture window overlooking the kelp beds and sea otters.

For the last two years, Mark had been working for a forest products company headquartered on the San Mateo Peninsula. In 1976 he'd accepted the company's offer letter -- perhaps a bit too quickly. He rationalized it by saying that he'd been trying to avoid the unshaven unpleasantness of unemployment during the transition between the Gerald Ford and Jimmy Carter Administrations. However, his move out west and time in California had been more stressful than he'd ever expected, what with all the weekly coast-to-coast commuting during Congressional sessions. Just last month after serious conversations with his gastroenterologist -- a fellow he had known for years in Washington, DC -- and the specialists the doctor had recommended at Johns Hopkins, Mark made a decision. He asked his employer for an unpaid medical sabbatical, with pre-paid health insurance benefits, and decided to head back east to face the "demon cancer." This was very much unlike him -- doing all this without a specific understanding as to future employment.

For several reasons, both health-related and social, Mark wasn't enjoying his present state of affairs, but he was determined not to have second thoughts about his decision to head back east. He felt he was not prepared to face the challenge of an uncertain medical outcome all by himself, in a state where he knew virtually no body.

If Mark had a specific problem with California it was that he never came to understand the incomprehensible inhabitants of this paradise. Professionally, he found them to be a lackadaisical lot, spending much of their time meditating about where to drive on the weekends. And when it came to their cars, Mark considered Californians to be flat-assed weird. Golden-staters' have this peculiar habit of heralding anyone who drives the same model of car they do. If identical car models pull up beside one another at a traffic light, the drivers will honk horns and exchange waves. When this first occurred to Mark, he suspected that they merely wanted to acknowledge the uniqueness of his new Porsche. His first instinct was to blow them off. But he usually waved back, feeling like a total nebbish. The whole car-wave thing became contagious. Over time, he even picked up the annoying habit himself. After growing up in the Midwest and living and working in Washington, D.C., it was very difficult to adapt to the distinctive California way of thinking, talking and doing things.

Now he had his brand-new Porsche. But he also had an impending date with destiny at Johns Hopkins in Baltimore, and no job. *I must be nuts,* Mark thought.

His inner musings were jogged when "Dance, Dance, Dance (Yowsah, Yowsah)" by Chic came on the radio and B.J. sat up, broke the silence by trying to play back-up musician on his "Bluesband" mouth organ.

Between harmonica blasts B.J. said, "Stanton, what with all the travel and everything, I guess I can understand why you want to leave your job, but you've never explained why you're so happy to be leaving such a beautiful place," he said with a sweeping gesture.

Mark puffed on his cigarette and bought himself a moment's time before answering, "Right now I want to spend my time where I know people. One reason I'm leaving is that I never really hit it off socially out here on the West Coast. I never found what I was looking for," he said.

B.J. scratched his sideburns and pondered the statement carefully. "So, in essence, what you're telling me is that you couldn't get laid in 'Paly-Alty' with hundred dollar bills sticking out of your pocket?"

Mark mumbled, "Yeah, well, something like that."

B.J. had a maddening way of cutting right to the chase. Next came his philosophical pontificating. "With so many homosexual guys living here in the Bay Area, and so many single women working in 'The City,' you'd think a decent-looking straight guy like yourself, with a good-paying job... you'd assume a fellow like you might be in some sort of demand."

*Decent-looking? If that's how a friend describes me, I can just imagine what others might say, trying to describe me to a blind date*, Mark thought.

Mark realized he was no more than average in many ways. His five-foot ten-inches in height was average. He was still somewhat stocky, at his usual 180 pounds, but had recently experienced an unexpected 15-pound drop in his weight. Women relatives always described Mark's ruddy looks by saying that he had the map of Ireland on his round face. Most women his own age seemed attracted to his clean-cut preppy appearance and thick shock of sandy-brown hair. The precious few women who stuck around long enough to notice often commented favorably on his baby blue eyes. Mark always believed that each person has a little something going just for him or her. They merely have to figure out what it is, and then decide how to use it to best advantage. On the down side, he certainly didn't have B.J.'s handsome physical assets for attracting women, but on the plus side, Mark's outgoing personality had usually helped him do all right for himself. Although, he had to admit, his recent romantic drought in California had begun to rattle his confidence about dealing with the opposite sex.

"That's what I'll never understand about this state," he said to B.J., keeping his eyes on the road, "the whole time I've been out here, Californians always seemed to be zigging, when I was zagging."

B.J. grinned and added, "What they really know how to do out here is *burn* Zigzag papers."

At the town of Gilroy they headed due east for the first time, on state route 152. As they turned into the strong morning sunshine, B.J. and Mark both reached for their sunglasses at the same time. It was 8:50 a.m. They were now thirty minutes behind schedule, catching up slowly.

B.J. fiddled with the dial of the Blaupunkt radio. He finally settled on a San Jose station just as the deejay was premiering a song from Paul McCartney and his new band, Wings, called "With a Little Luck."

Mark puffed on another cigarette, still reflecting. *It wasn't California... it was me*, he thought. *I just didn't fit in with the left coast lifestyle.*

"Stanton," B.J. interrupted. "When are you going to give up on those coffin nails?" He was fanning away the cigarette smoke. "And how many of those damned things do you smoke a day? I hope that someday they get around to banning those things. Only prisoners on death row should be allowed to smoke them."

Mark purposely directed a jet of white smoke from the corner of his mouth right at B.J. "Cigarettes, my friend, are as American as red meat. No way are people going to turn against smokes or steaks."

"The only smoke I want to see this week should be coming from a barbecued chicken... soon," B.J. retorted.

The only shred of enjoyable social life Mark had found during his time in California was the Palo Alto Jaycees. After joining, he learned it was the only Jaycee chapter in the nation to be banned from the 1977 national convention because it admitted women members. The Jaycees met one evening per month at a restaurant and bar on the El Camino Real nicknamed "L'Ommies." He signed up for every committee that met on weekends, trying to meet singles. The Palo Alto Jaycee women tended to be rather attractive professionals. After just one meeting, he figured that the national organization should consider women for membership in all the clubs. Hell, it increased volunteerism -- at least so from his perspective. Before he'd discovered the Jaycees, Mark frequented all sorts of local haunts trying to meet single women -- the kind of places he would never even consider entering back in Washington. He even became a regular patron of a small bar tied into an awful Mexican restaurant after he noticed that attractive women regularly frequented the place. It got to the point where he even stopped into several San Mateo peninsula jazz clubs. For an old time rock'n'roll guy like Mark, that was really scraping the bottom of the barrel.

In California when good-looking single women came into a place unescorted, they would purposefully stroll right past open barstools next to guys in order to take seats at an empty table in the far corner of the room. The local male yokels seemed content to sit all by themselves at the bar all evening putting up with such nonsense. It drove Mark nuts! On several occasions, after a few Jack Daniels, he summoned up the nerve to walk over and say hello, with little success. He ended up many an evening muttering *how did couples in California ever get together*?

The California bar ritual was clearly the reverse of the East Coast scenario. Back in Boston, New York, Philly and D.C., one could visit any singles bar on a Friday night where people stood elbow-to-elbow, talking and drinking. People bumped into one another; it couldn't be helped. That's how you got to meet and talk to members of the opposite sex. Striking up a conversation with a woman back east was a cinch. On the San Mateo peninsula just trying to get within striking distance of delivering a pick-up line had all the fun and excitement of snipe hunting.

## The Things We Do for Love.

LESS THAN AN hour east of Gilroy, along the right side of route 152, the twosome passed Diablo Mountain and the beautiful San Luis Reservoir, said to be the largest off-stream lake of its kind in the country. The water accumulated in the lake ended up irrigating the crops in California's lush Central San Joaquin Valley.

"Stanley" cornered like an Indy car as Mark downshifted into third gear and rounded the Interstate-5-South ramp; now they were pointed in the general direction of Bakersfield. The Porsche slipped easily into the light midday Tuesday traffic. He shifted back into fourth gear and the speedometer climbed past 90 mph. The radio was belting out "Baby Hold On" by Eddie Money. Maybe there was hope after all -- of getting back on schedule. As they turned south again, the blinding sunlight shifted to their left. They removed their sunglasses in unison -- as if on cue. "You know... we look like those two guys on Saturday Night Live... John Belushi and Dan Aykroyd. You know, the 'Blues Brothers,' doing their shtick," Mark said.

"Yeah, I've seen them... pretty funny stuff. Those guys should make a movie."

The Central Valley terrain flattened out and the Porsche picked up speed.

"So there's not one woman you're going to miss from here?" B.J. asked incredulously.

"Not really."

"Besides your irritating personality, what seemed to be the biggest problem?"

Mark ignored the gauntlet. "Well..." he paused, "when I first moved out here... and met a girl, invariably she would ask, 'What do you do?' I'd say that I'm a 'lobbyist for a timber company.' She would immediately turn on her heel and be gone in a second."

"Your worst nightmare Stanton... there are a lot of card-carrying Sierra Clubbers out here... total tree-huggers."

"Well, after striking out a dozen times, I finally got smart. I caught on to the game... the 'What Do You Do, Voodoo' game, I call it. Jackson, I went so far as to lie about what I did for a living."

"How *low* can a grown man go for sexual gratification?" B.J. said, shaking his head in mock disgust.

"Even lying didn't work. For a while I said I was a travel agent... but then I was always afraid someone might call me looking for a discounted ticket. Later, I claimed to be a landscape architect."

"Good move, Stanton... that whole ecological thing. 'Save the Baby Whales' has a lot more sex appeal than chain-sawing and clear-cutting trees," B.J. said with a nod.

"Jackson, it got so bad I even asked a woman the 'what-do-you-do' question first, but she dodged it and wandered off, realizing I didn't know how to play the You-do-Voo-Doo game. Then I began listening to how other guys answered the question. A girl would ask, 'What do you do?' And a fellow would say something like '...well, Buffy, I'm into mountain rappelling at Yosemite... or body surfing at Santa Cruz... or wine tasting in Napa... or camping in the high Sierras!' Jackson, when I locked onto the real deal, it was like discovering the Rosetta stone. I finally figured that California women didn't care a whit what a guy did for a living, or what kind of money he made. The only thing they wanted to know was 'what do you do on weekends!' Can you believe it?"

"Yeah," said B.J., unimpressed, "I would guess that eventually even a horseshoe crab could figure that one out."

To the contrary, in Washington, when a woman wanted to play the "What Do You Do Voodoo" game, and she asked what a guy did, she didn't give a damn about his sailboat in Annapolis or his golf handicap at Congressional Country Club. She wanted to know where he worked. Was he wired politically? What was his job title? Was he in a position to help her career? Was he upwardly mobile?

"It may have taken me a while to catch on, but after a few stops and starts I got the hang of it."

Mark's real difficulty with California, it seemed to B.J., was that Mark had been spoiled by Washington's career-oriented social life. With all the available women living and working in

Washington, the simple fact was, the odds were about 3-to-1 in favor of single men. "So, how'd you get past the Voo-doo test?" B.J. asked.

"I'd say, 'Actually, Matilda, I'm into wine country.' Now that wasn't a total lie, I love red wine. It was a safe answer for me. Anyway, if some young honey took me up on it, I figured I could learn all I had to know about wine in a couple of days.

"But to my sheer astonishment, the female responses were always off the wall. They would respond by saying something like, 'Well, that's nice. I'm into hiking the Coastal Range... but it was real nice meeting you.' Or, 'Well, Mark, I'm into yoga, but it was so nice talking with you.' Or, 'I'm into saving the baby seals Mark, but it was swell of you to buy me a drink.' Then they would turn and go.

B.J. grinned from ear to ear, listening intently to what a mere amateur had to say about meeting women -- what he considered to be his area of expertise. "I'm still pullin' for ya' Stanton, keep going... you're almost there."

Mark prattled on, "I discovered that the secret was in sizing up each potential target from across the room well before you approached them or spent any money on drinks. From then on, I would lean against the bar and analyze my surroundings. I would try to guess what each woman there did on weekends. Then, all you had to do was match-up your 'whopper' of a lie about how you like to spend Saturdays with their favorite hobby. If, by some chance, there was a hit, then you prayed they didn't ask you too many questions, lest one look like a total jerk.

"Jackson, I wound up talking to myself. I'd say, 'That one over there. Does she look like an indoor or an outdoor type? Could she be a skier, a camper or a hiker? What is the give-away? Did she have countless mosquito-bites on her arms and legs, or the smell of Calamine lotion? If some chick staggered around at a party or looked as though she had a buzz-on after a couple of glasses of Merlot, did that mean she was a wine country freak? I began to lose hope.

"Then one evening at a cocktail party, I came up with a new approach. I fell into an animated conversation with a stunning airline stewardess with sturdy set of legs. When she asked me the inevitable question, I responded... based on my prior across-the-room assessment... by saying, 'hiking in the redwoods.'

"She responded, 'Mine is hang-gliding at Big Sur, but, gee, it was awfully nice meeting you, Mark.' The same ol' – same ol'.

"Later on, I met an auburn-haired beauty. Based upon the way she swirled and longingly gazed into her Chardonnay, I assumed that she was into wine country. So that's what I told her when she popped the $64 question. She came back with, 'Well, I'm into smoking hemp up at La Honda.'

"'Hemp at La Honda,'" B.J. smirked. "Heavy. That's a new one even for me. Okay, okay... so get to the point. When did the breakthrough occur, or did it ever?"

"At what was, for me, the very nadir of my West Coast social life, toward the end of that evening I turned around and bumped right into a dynamite-looking blonde who looked as though she belonged in a Hawaiian Tropic TV commercial. I did a little 'shtick' and said, 'Hello there, cocoa-butter-cup.' She giggled. I was on a roll! We talked a while, and eventually, Megan... that was her name... asked me, 'Now, Mark, what exactly do you do?' I hadn't had time to scope her out from across the room. But she had a beautiful tan. So I took a wild stab at it and told her I was into visiting the beach at Aptos. One of the guys at my company had a weekend place there and I'd heard him talking about. Guess what? My cocoa-buttered Megan says she loves the beach! She shares a place with friends every weekend... right on the ocean, at Rio Del Mar... the next village down the coast from Aptos!"

B.J. beamed. "The things we do for love... I knew you could do it."

"Jackson," Mark blurted out, "I was so freakin' excited, after months and months of hang-gliding, mountain-hiking and para-sailing bullshit-excuses, I dropped my beer and bear-hugged that poor broad. I gave her a dip and planted a kiss on her like it was V-E Day in Times Square. Hell, I was so turned on I told her, right then and there, that I wanted to have her babies."

B.J. doubled over in laughter and, in the process, smacked his head on the dashboard. "Well, Stanton my man, so that's when you finally earned your membership in the Pacific Time Zone 'Club.' Congratulations," he said.

"Yeah," Mark turned and smiled. "Eventually..." he muttered. Then he leaned a little harder on the gas pedal to the strains of Jackson Browne's "Running on Empty."

B.J. had a one-track mind. He cried out, "Hey Stanton, you're killing me... show me some food!"

### Slick the Slash.

IF KANSAS IS America's breadbasket, then the San Joaquin Valley is the nation's victory garden. On both sides of I-5 for a stretch of 125 miles between Stockton and Bakersfield, and for as far as the eye could see in any direction, grew every conceivable agricultural product known to man. In some places, you could smell the crops, even at 80 mph. The twosome passed miles and miles of fields and orchards with almonds, apricots, artichokes, broccoli, celery, lettuce, oranges, peaches, potatoes, strawberries, sugar beets, tomatoes and walnuts.

At one point Mark noticed B.J. rubbernecking and asked, "What are you looking at?"

"I'm thinking about how hungry I am," he said with a sigh.

Mark had grown up in rural Ohio and B.J. was from central Illinois. Both were from agricultural areas. They'd seen a lot of farmland in their respective political travels, but they agreed they'd never seen anything like the Central Valley. It was the first time that either had traveled through it. The soil was so rich, B.J. said that farmers could grow three crops a year if they could find enough water.

B.J. and Mark spent the next half-hour or so trying to impress each other as to what they knew about California water rights. The daily regimen of reading West Coast newspapers provided Mark with all he needed to know about the various interest groups competing for a spigot off the water pipeline.

At one point B.J. flashed a mischievous grin, "It's Gitties, not Gittles," he said with a sinister accent.

"What?"

"No wonder L.A. is so dry. All the water is being pumped out here to the valley, at night."

"What the hell are you babbling about?" Mark asked.

B.J. kept at it. "Hey, don't let it get to you, Jake. It's Chinatown..."

Belatedly, Mark realized that what he knew about California water rights came from newspapers. What B.J. knew must have come from the Jack Nicholson movie "Chinatown."

After they evaporated all they knew about water rights the twosome moved on to a discussion of other ecological issues. B.J. wanted to know what it was like working for a timber company involved in environmental controversies such as harvesting redwoods and clear-cutting forests.

Mark explained that before he'd accepted the job as a timber company lobbyist he wanted to see how things were done in the woods. Company lawyers assured him that the firm operated only on its own private timberlands, cutting its own trees in an environmentally conscious manner. For example, Mark explained, the company planted as many as five saplings for each and every mature tree that was harvested. And that the company was harvesting *coast* redwoods, not the protected giant Sequoia trees -- the kind you see on a postcard with a car driving through a carved arch in the tree. Mark thought that he'd better see things in the woods for himself, before he had to raise his right hand and testify under oath before a congressional committee about the company's logging practices. So he took his three weeks of accumulated federal government vacation time, and with the help of his new boss, he was assigned to work as a grunt in a company logging camp near Arcata, California.

"No one in camp except my crew chief was to know that I was in line to be the parent company's new Vice President for Government Relations," Mark said. "I was supposed to be just another minimum wage gopher."

"Not knowing exactly what to do, I showed up in camp the first morning wearing a plaid wool shirt, Levi's, a pair of brand-new work shoes that I'd rubbed dirt on, so they'd look worn. I was carrying a battered-up black lunch box, the kind with a rounded top for the Thermos bottle. I kicked it around a bit the night before so it would look used.

"I sat there at 4:30 a.m. on a split-log bench in the dense fog outside the foreman's clapboard shack until my crew chief showed up. Just before five o'clock, the loggers began arriving in their pickup trucks. To a man, they wore white thermal underwear tops, bib overalls, tall rubber boots and colorful hard hats. Each one carried a large picnic cooler instead of a lunch box – a cooler so big you could hide a litter of Chihuahuas inside. I was already self-conscious. Compared to their work outfits, I was sitting there like a male model for the Abercrombie & Fitch catalogue. The first two loggers walked by, looking right through me. Neither said a word in front of me, but as they headed for the cookhouse, I overheard one ask the other, while pointing a thumb in my direction, 'Who's Slick?'"

B.J. squinted, stifling a laugh.

"Jackson, until that morning, I'd never seen a man eat twenty pancakes in one sitting," Mark continued. "The piles of food in the company cookhouse were something you had to see to believe. You could find anything and everything you would ever want for breakfast. Going through the food line, the loggers used whole cafeteria trays as though they were plates. These loggers were big strapping men with stupendous appetites. When they finished downing a heaping tray of breakfast, they got in another line and filled up their lunch coolers from mountains of pre-wrapped sandwiches, cookies, fruit and sodas.

"Then we all piled onto the company buses and headed for the hills. After a short drive north on the paved highway we turned east and bounced up and down on gawd-awful logging roads for miles until I was ready to lose my flapjacks. Just as I was about to retch, we reached a clearing in the forest and stopped.

"I started out that first day in the woods as the 'slash boy,' collecting wet tree branches, known as widow-makers, for burning. Theory is that if one of these huge limbs falls on you, as the saying goes... your wife's a widow. It was filthy, backbreaking work. By noon I was all scratched up and bleeding from a dozen places. I had accumulated enough pine tar on my clothes to be declared a National Forest, all by myself. My *stickiness* was quite ironic because everyone, for some reason, kept calling me '*Slick.*'

B.J. snickered, "I guess you could say that you were... 'Slick, the Slash.'"

Mark continued, "When the lunch whistle blew, I just slapped my sap-covered work gloves onto the trunk of a tree and they never moved. There was nowhere to wash my hands.

Everything I touched stuck to me. That first day my fingers were so sticky I could have palmed a weather balloon.

"I sensed that my crew chief, Pierre, and the other loggers were watching me like hawks. I guess I didn't look the part of slash boy. That first week, no one said a personal word to me, other than 'Slick, get that... or, Slick, drag dat widda-maker outta here.'

"A few days later, after an unfortunate accident involving a member of our crew who was taken away in an ambulance, I received a battlefield promotion. Within three days, I'd moved from 'Slick the Slash' to become 'Slick, the Slash-cutter.' Along with my new job title I was awarded a 30-inch-long paddled chain saw. Also I got a pair of metal-covered spiked boots with metal wings coming off them, at the heels... I looked like a cross between a medieval knight and the guy on FTD flower ads. I was a hybrid wing-footed god... the 'Mercury' of the redwoods.

"My career advancement consisted of getting that nasty, long-paddled, gasoline-powered chain saw started, and then clomping down the spine of a felled tree, cutting off all the slash, all the while trying not to sever any of my own extremities. Newly felled, never-quite-lying-horizontal tree trunks were always wet from the constant fog and slippery with bark moss. My greatest fear was slipping off a felled tree still holding a whirring chain saw. I had nightmares about it... afraid that if I lost control I would cut myself, or someone else, clean in half."

B.J.'s eyes narrowed in horror at the thought.

"After work each day, I was so dead tired I never even bothered with dinner. My bleak room at the 'Bates' motel had no television reception to speak of, anyway. So I would hit the bed and fall asleep within minutes, dreaming about those awesome breakfasts. By the time the Friday night whistle blew during my first week, I was craving the sack and an all-day Saturday sleep-in. But that night on the way back to base camp the company bus made an unexpected stop, at some rustic roadside saloon. Everyone on the old school bus piled off and went inside, so I followed along. The entire work gang was drinking boilermakers, 16-ounce draft beers in hourglass-shaped mugs with shot glasses full of Corby's Whiskey dropped inside, like depth charges. The most popular diversion for these guys was trying to guzzle a boilermaker without the shot glass sliding down the inside of the beer glass and knocking out their two front teeth. When I looked around, as far as I could tell, I was the only guy in the work gang with an original God-given set of enamel choppers.

B.J. listened with arms folded.

"Jackson, a half-hour after we arrived at the bar a thirsty busload of boisterous loggers from a competing timber company came into the same forsaken saloon. I was sitting all alone, at the front door end of the bar, quietly working on my second boilermaker when ice hockey broke out in the back bar. It was an old-fashioned logger brawl. Apparently, one guy from our work gang had a score to settle with a fellow in the other crew.

"Personally, I was not looking forward to, or completely ready for, a bar fight involving forty brawny loggers who'd been avidly downing snorts, and the smallest of whom was *me*. All I really wanted to do was go back to my miserable little room and sleep. When the melee began, I got off my stool and backed over to the wall where fresh cases of beer were stacked. Behind my back, I reached into the nearest case and retrieved two full long necked bottles. I grabbed them around the necks, in case needed. With one bottle in each hand, still hidden behind me, I backed into a corner and waited for the fight to come to me. The growing scuffle tumbled toward the front of the bar.

"Pierre, the massive crew chief from my logging gang must have noticed what I had done. A wicked smirk crossed his face. He raised his muscular forearms, held up his ham-sized hands and yelled out: 'Sacrebleau! Shut *zee* fuck-up!' The biting, pushing, shoving, punching and wrestling came to an abrupt stop. There was a hush as everyone inhaled. Then big Pierre turned and pointed right at me. He said, 'you come here.' He waved me to the middle of the room. I reluctantly came forward with the two bottles of beer still clenched in a death grip behind my back.

"Pierre said, 'Show 'em what you got there, Slick.'

"I held them up, still gripping the beer bottles by their long-necks. Then Pierre pointed to the two slobs who started the whole fracas. 'Listen up you two coon-asses... knock it off... or Slick here and me... we'll bash the shit outta' bot'-a-you!'

B.J. threw his head back with a laugh, "You and Pierre, I can picture it now... red-necks with longnecks."

"Well, Jackson, that announcement pretty much wrapped up the bar fight. Loggers on both sides started laughing, and I mean laughing hard. I vividly recall that one guy laughed so hard he puked all over himself."

All B.J. could do was slap Mark on the shoulder.

"From then on, for some really strange reason, I became one of the guys. I didn't have to buy another drink that night... the beers just kept coming over to me. I guess that in some bizarre way my willingness to fight, if it came to that, instead of running out the door, passed some logger litmus test. Somehow, the mere act of arming myself for the worst, instead of bolting, made me an official member of the work gang after just five days in the woods... not bad, eh?"

B.J. nodded in silent agreement.

"The following Monday morning, during breakfast at the cookhouse, Pierre and the boys, with great ceremony, awarded me my own red and white "Playmate" cooler, to replace my lunch box, with the slogan 'Slick - a very dangerous man,' scrawled on it in magic marker. It was a used cooler that had belonged to a guy who had fallen out of a tree a few weeks prior. But in the woods, it's the thought that counts.

"A week later, following yet another unfortunate incident and the second visit from the rescue squad in two weeks, I was promoted to the lofty position of choker-setter. I gladly surrendered my 30-inch chain saw and spiked metal boots with the wings to a lanky guy named Caleb in exchange for a pair of bizarre-looking metal gloves with pointy fingers... like an armadillo's claw.

"My on-the-job training in forestry continued. I learned that once a tree is felled, and its slash is cut-off, the tree is then bucked... cut into log-sized lengths that fit on the trailer bed of a truck. Once bucked, each log section must be dragged or lifted from the muddy hillside by the winch line up to the logging road where it is loaded onto the truck trailer. Coast redwoods, which can grow taller than 350 feet, thrive on very wet, always foggy, steep and slippery hillsides. Thick metal cables must be fastened to each bucked log in order for the diesel-powered crane to drag or lift it up to the logging road.

The logs are lying deep in the soft loam. So how does one fasten a metal cable around the log? That, sir, is a job for 'Slick, the choker-setter.'"

"So what are you choking? Your chicken?" B.J. wanted to know.

"The choker-setter's job is using those metal claws to dig a hole under the log, slide the 20-foot long thick metal cable under the log, and then take the eye-loop into the C-hook and lock the cable together atop the log, like setting the choke-chain on a dog's collar. Having done this and then signaling the crane operator, the heavy cable is tightened and the log is half-lifted, half-dragged up the steep hillside to the logging road.

"If there is any finesse to the choker-setter's job, it is to dig the hole and to thread the cable underneath without triggering the log to roll over on top of him. The very first lesson they teach a new choker-setter is to claw out his own 'grave,' a man-sized hole in the dirt into which the choker-setter can dive should a log get loose and decide to roll back down to the creek. The grave is dug just in case the log begins to move downhill before the choke is set. Also, there are exciting occasions when the log 'hit's a snag' -- catches on a stump -- while the cable is moving it up to the road. Choker-set logs have been known to hit a snag, snap the cable, and bounce downhill, right on top of the poor choker-setter. So, you see, whether the choker-setter actually sees the log coming at him, or not, a pre-dug grave always seems to come in handy.

"Jackson, during my third and final week as 'Slick the choker-setter' I believe I turned in my personal best. I'd found my calling in the woods. I was a diggin' fool. No self-respecting dog was a better digger than I was with my funky metal digging gloves. In the 'head-down-between-my-knees position,' I could move a ton of dirt through my legs, like a terrier gone mad, digging my own grave. A good man can choker-set 'twelve or ten' logs before lunch, as my Cajun boss Pierre used to say.

"Stanton... at least you didn't choke like a dog," said B.J. with a smirk.

"Before I said good-bye on my last day in the woods, the word leaked out that I was a 'suit'... a white collar guy from headquarters. And since it was my last day, Pierre let me fell a tree. By the way, Jackson, they don't yell 'Timber!' when they cut down a tree."

"What do they yell?"

"'Overhead!' if you can believe that.

"Sounds like something a pissed-off bean counter would holler, doesn't it?" B.J. said with a puzzled look.

Mark related that months later, when he was on a trip to the company sawmill with a bunch of corporate executives, he had breakfast at the cookhouse. He was only "suit" the loggers would come over and talk to. They cut off his tie at mid-belly, mussed up his hair, and they called him "Slick." They ignored all the other executives; and the other guys from corporate noticed that. "Damn, I was proud," Mark said with genuine emotion.

"Stanton, I never knew you did all that. Now I know why we're always at loggerheads," B.J. enjoyed the story and reveled in his own pun at the same time. He never expressed his personal opinion on redwood logging after the "Slick" story, but Mark could imagine B.J.'s ecological view of it.

## Panning the Panama Giveaway.

A HALF-HOUR LATER, at 11:00 a.m., Mark and B.J. headed due south again on California route 99 into Bakersfield for refueling and lunch. James Taylor's "Handy Man" was playing on the radio. B.J. stirred from his nap.

They passed over an irrigation canal. That simple act led to a discussion of various canals, which ended up in a rather heated political debate about President Carter and the judiciousness of the United States deeding the Panama Canal back to the Government of Panama.

The U.S. Senate, just five days earlier, on March 16th, had given approval to a treaty guaranteeing the neutrality of the Panama Canal Zone all the way to the year 2000 -- twenty-two years hence. But the big vote on whether or not to turn over the Canal to Panama would not be taken until the middle of April, some three weeks away.

The Panama Canal issue split Americans not so much along political party lines as it did along the liberal-conservative axis. It was the perfect issue for B.J. and Mark to argue.

Mark's personal position on the canal issue was akin to former Governor Ronald Reagan's: "We dug it. We built it. We stole it fair and square."

As a liberal, B.J. could not bring himself to admit that the canal was ever America's property. "Teddy Roosevelt," he said, "created Panama by setting up a puppet government and telling them to declare independence from Colombia. The whole U.S. Navy just happened to be holding massive training exercises out in the Caribbean. What a coincidence... our U.S. Navy, just sitting there, was waiting for Columbia to object to losing Panama."

"Yeah, and ol' Teddy didn't care if we was fighting Colombians or fighting Panamanians," Mark rebutted. "That's true big-stick 'gunboat diplomacy.' Hell, most of those people down there would still be picking coffee beans for a living, if we hadn't built the damned canal."

"Typical American leather-neck bravado," B.J. said. "But Senator Howard Baker and even your idol, that right-wing John Birch nut, John Wayne, have been doing television commercials asking Americans to support giving the canal to Panama."

"That's because the Duke's wife is from down there somewhere. He's probably afraid she'll cut off his pecker in his sleep, if he doesn't support it."

B.J. was getting riled up now. "We don't need the damn canal any more, anyway. It's an albatross around our necks. It can't even handle those extra-big super-tankers."

"Listen, if I built a canal on your land, with your permission, and I paid you plenty of rent each year, and I guard it, and I employ half of your otherwise banana-picking economy, then I'd say, legally, the canal was mine."

B.J. was getting disgusted with Mark's argument. "We forced the whole issue with battleships, and you know it. But you're right about one thing Stanton. We do pay rent, because we don't *own* it. We can do without paying that $2.5 million tab each year, thank you very much. And when we're gone, the Panamanians can employ *all*, not just half, of their population."

"Well, I predict that if we ever give it to them, they will screw it up. No maintenance... not enough security. Hell, they'll probably lease it out to the Chinese Commies. The government there is more corrupt than the District of Columbia, and that's saying something.  Just wait and see... the damn canal will probably dry up, right after we pull out.  Why don't you liberals just go 'all-the-way' and get it over with... ask some third-world country to guard our gold in Ft. Knox.  Or maybe it's not our gold, maybe we should give it back to the Spanish, because they used to own California."

"Stanton, that nonsense makes you sound like a reactionary, and don't try to tell me there aren't any rednecks from Ohio."

"Well, there aren't any.  We're referred to as Taft Republicans."

It was no use.  Neither one was going to budge on the Panama Canal issue.

Somewhere along this stretch of road, listening to Crystal Gayle's "Ready For The Times To Get Better," the two began to relax and get into the rhythm of the open road.

B.J. wanted to stop at every exit and eat, but by now he knew it was futile.

"You'd better soak up all of the scenery you can," Mark suggested.  "We may never get a chance like this to drive cross-country again. You see, Jackson, this truly could be an once-in-a-lifetime experience."

"Hell, if I don't get to Bakersfield pretty soon and eat some lunch, I might never finish *this* lifetime experience," he groaned.

B.J.'s hairy look-alike, Art Garfunkel, and James Taylor were singing "Wonderful World" on the radio.

Just when they finally caught up with Mark's original schedule for the day, at high noon, they pulled off the road and stopped for the first time.  Due to some medication he had taken along the way, Mark had an upset stomach and did not feel much like eating. He was more concerned with what the car might need than he was about B.J.'s appetite.  After all, he was still breaking-in his new baby, "Stanley."

"How many miles you got on this thing," the fellow filling the gas tank wanted to know.

"As of this moment, it just clicked over 1,600 miles," Mark said checking the car's odometer.

After dropping the hood with a thud, the fellow pronounced everything to be "okie-dokey."

The attendant pointed at the hood. "What color is that paint job?"

"It's called pearl gray," Mark said.

"I thought it was black when you pulled in, but it kind-a' looks a tad green here in the shade, don't it?"

Mark hunkered down close to the hood, but couldn't see what the guy was referring to. Meanwhile, B.J. kept asking everyone in sight for a recommendation of a local restaurant. He finally landed one.

The route to B.J.'s restaurant selection took them way off Route 99. Ten minutes later they settled into a well-worn booth at "Mom's, Home of the Deep Dish." "Can't Help Myself (Sugar Pie Honey Bunch)" was coming out of the ancient Wurlitzer.

"What are you going to have?" the matronly waitress asked. It could have been *Mom...* as in 'Mom's'... herself, from the looks of her. "Make sure you boys save some room for dessert, got a Dutch apple crumb coming out any minute."

They survived a nondescript lunch and a slice of crummy homemade pie. Before they paid the waitress, Mark watched as B.J. tried a liberal's method of rubbing shoulders with the little people. He asked the waitress, "What do you think about the Panama Canal... do you think we should give it back?"

She bent over the table and whispered, "Honey, do you really think they even know it's missin'?"

### Plane and Simple.

THE ROAD BETWEEN Bakersfield and Edwards Air Force Base took them southeast through the Mojave Desert. They passed through the village of Keene then successfully navigated the Tehachapi Pass. About 2:00 p.m., at the little town of Mojave, they made a left turn and headed due east again.

After lunch, B.J. nestled in the passenger's seat for his afternoon siesta. He was soundly asleep before Mark hit the first stretch of open road.

B.J. and Mark were good friends, not necessarily best friends; but they knew each other pretty well, having roomed together at the beach house on summer weekends at Dewey Beach. A person really can get to know what another is like over three summer seasons of weekends. Then one day, some four years ago, Mark heard the rumor that B.J. had fallen in love. Four years earlier, back in 1974, Bill Jackson picked up and moved west to San Francisco to live with a gorgeous jet-set debutante. It wasn't until Mark moved to Palo Alto in late '76 that the two of them really bonded. Outside of B.J., Mark Stanton didn't know any other person in California when he moved there.

B.J. would call from time-to-time, or drive down from "The City" and stop by Mark's Palo Alto apartment for Sunday afternoon chats, usually in the company of his latest flame. Each woman B.J. brought by to visit during Mark's time in California was traffic-stopping attractive. But, then again, he was always known to have the best eye in the beach house crowd for a well-turned ankle.

During one of these Sunday chats at Stanton's place, just after Christmas, Mark first mentioned to B.J. his problems adjusting to the California lifestyle. What he failed to mention was that he had been experiencing health problems and was seeing a specialist back east. However, he did say that he was considering taking a few months off from work and driving back to Washington. B.J. wouldn't leave Mark's apartment until he promised that B.J. could come along on the trip cross-country. That's how this whole trip thing got started.

So now here they were -- tooling down Route 58 some seventy-five miles to the east of Bakersfield, grooving to "Rocket Ride" by Kiss, on the radio, when -- *WHAM!!!*

The concussion from the explosion hit the car like a staunch gust of wind. The cigarette Mark was smoking flew right out of his hand.

B.J. was jolted awake. "What in the Sam Hill...?"

Mark's first thought was that he'd lost a tire doing some 75 mph, but "Stanley" was handling all right. Luckily, there was no one coming toward them or behind them for that matter; they were the only ones on the desolate stretch of road. Mark slowed the Porsche down, without skidding, and pulled onto the shoulder of the road beside a cyclone fence line. They both jumped out of the car to see what was wrong. Just then, a second, smaller blast came from behind the fence. The fence, with barbed wire strands atop it, was covered with dark green plastic fabric -- one couldn't see through it. However, they clearly noticed thick black smoke spiraling upward about a mile or so behind the fence. A few moments later they began smelling the acrid odor of burning petroleum.

Mark grabbed the road map. All the empty land to their south was labeled "Edwards Air Force Base."

Jumping up on the car's rear bumper B.J. said he could make out what looked like a plane crash off in the distance. "Whoa," he said, "there's a parachute coming down."

Mark shimmied up through the open sunroof hatch and knelt on the roof of the car. He too could see some fire, a plume of black smoke and a red and white parachute drifting down.

"Some poor bastard done lost his plane," B.J. said with a grimace.

"Is that what you think happened?" Mark asked.

"I think the damned thing just fell out of the sky."

"Jesus... I hope the guy's all right."

Based on what they heard, saw and smelled, there was one hell of a crash at Edwards Air Force Base that afternoon. It was maddening not to be able to know what was going on. They stayed there trying to look over the fence for about ten more minutes, until other cars came along. Then they got back in and continued heading east toward Barstow.

"Now that was exciting," said B.J. "We'll have to read the Las Vegas papers tomorrow and find out happened. That, sir, was at least a $20 million pile-up. Someone just 'screwed the pooch,' as they say."

"You know, I've read that there is this secret base around here somewhere. Some former military people say they're testing planes without wings and flying saucer kind of things... you know... secret stuff."

"Right. And they have three little green men in a hangar at Wright-Patterson Air Force Base in Dayton, Ohio, who eat strawberry ice cream and broccoli," he sneered. "Stanton, surely you don't buy all that grocery store tabloid stuff about UFO's and spacemen, do you?"

"Maybe I do. Hell, even Perry Elam reads those gossip sheets all the time looking for leads on Washington insiders."

Perry Elam was a mutual friend from Dewey Beach days who worked as a political writer for the Washington *Evening Star* newspaper.

Mark figured that if the newspapers in Las Vegas had a plane crash story tomorrow morning, it was probably just a routine flight screw-up. But if there were no coverage, it would be clear to him that something mysterious was being tested and that something had gone terribly wrong.

What are the chances? You're driving cross-country and a plane crashes right next to you and nearly blows your car off the road. Does that mean you're lucky? Or is that an omen for unlucky? Either way, they had to figure it out soon. They were only about 180 miles from the gambling tables of Las Vegas, a place where luck can come in handy.

Tonight Mark planned for them to be gambling in "Lost Wages" with Jerry Mulligan, his oldest friend from high school days. "Mully," as he preferred to be called, and Mark had grown up together during the '60's in northern Ohio. Mully had moved to Nevada several years earlier and landed a fancy front office job in one of the major casinos. Although the two kept in touch by telephone, Mark hadn't seen him for a while and he was looking forward to catching up with Mully and the latter's long-suffering live-in girlfriend, Janet. When Mark called two weeks before, to pin-down his trip to Las Vegas, Mully said he'd arrange for a "comp" room. *What a great guy*, Mark thought. Even though they didn't see each other as often as either would like, Mully and Mark were friends for life who always seemed to pick up right where they left off. Years before they made a high school pact and agreed that, "they'd stay in touch, just like the thunder thighs on a sweat-hog."

Mark and B.J. stopped in Barstow to fill-up on gas and buy some beer. Mark wanted to make sure that the car would be all right through the next long stretch of desert. B.J. returned with two six-packs of ice-cold Olympia beer. They asked the elderly station attendant if he'd heard about a plane crash at Edwards on the radio within the last hour or so.

"Nope," he said with a spit into the dust, "but I wouldn't be surprised if they totaled another one. They're always crashing something over there." He paused. "Funny thing 'bout Edwards... you can hear 'em fly over all the time, but you never, ever see 'em," he said. "I believe that they's a-testin' an invisible plane."

"Invisible plane... no shit," Mark said, nudging B.J. with his elbow.

B.J. shook his head at the notion. No way.

"Good lookin' car, Mister. Never seen one. What is it?" the attendant asked. He had a "Matt" name tag affixed to his oil-stained blue shirt.

"Thank you, Matt. It's a new Porsche 924," Mark said proudly.

"Paint job's kinda' got that sharkskin look to it, don't you think?" said Matt.

"How's that?"

"Well, in the sunshine, the paint looks like it's got some yella' and some red an' blue in there, but here in the shade, it's got a green-like tint to it. It's kinda' like a lookin' at a sharkskin suit from different angles, ain't it," he said with a yellow-toothed grin.

B.J. egged him on, "Yeah, colorful… light kind of hits it like an oil slick, doesn't it?"

"It's really pearl gray," Mark responded matter-of-factly. "By the way," he added, trying to get even with B.J.'s waitress maneuver at the Bakersfield restaurant, "Matt… let me ask you something. How do you feel about Jimmy Carter giving away the Panama Canal?"

"Dang. No one's asked me that before. I reckon I'm against it… how else we gonna' get over to the 'Lantic Ocean?"

Mark was happy to have his "no" vote, even if his reasoning was somewhat confused.

They left Matt, the attendant, pondering the Isthmus of Panama. Mark pulled out of the station and continued to the east. They stopped to look at their first roadside historical marker, just east of Barstow. It recounted on a sand-burnished metal plaque that millions in ore had been mined from the Calico Hills during the silver rush of the 1880's.

Before they could get any real highway momentum going, a few short miles later, Mark saw another sign indicating an historical marker and decided to stop a second time. This one described the "Early Man Archaeological Site at Calico," a scientific dig that discovered some of the earliest remains of human beings living in this hemisphere.

"Get used to it, Jackson. I plan on stopping at all these markers along the way."

"Why is it that I have the feeling I'm going to rue the day I see another sign that says, 'Historical Marker - One Mile

Ahead. You know, if you'd read all your history books back in Catholic school, you'd know all this stuff and we'd be able to save hours not stopping at every one.'"

Mark ignored him.

The cold "Ollies" tasted great. It was now 3:30 p.m. They'd been on the road now for some eight hours, less the down time in Bakersfield. The day turned out to be a rather warm one -- in the mid-70's -- a pleasant March day in the desert. They still had nearly three hours to cover before arriving at Las Vegas. Again, B.J. offered to drive, but even though Mark felt cramps in his abdomen he was okay behind the wheel -- it took his mind off the pain. In fact, he could feel the stress seeping out of his body with each mile. He was really enjoying his first long drive in his new car.

Mark had charted each day's travel with great attention to detail. Tonight was Las Vegas. On Wednesday night they'd catch a Cleveland Indians spring training game in Tucson, Arizona. Thursday night they'd be in San Antonio, Texas. On Friday night they'd check out the disco scene in Houston with Paul Rumbaugh, a former Capitol Hill staffer and an old friend of Mark's who moved back home to Texas. The only thing Mark had asked B.J. to do -- in terms of planning for the trip -- was to call ahead and make plans for Saturday night in New Orleans, a city where Mark had no connections whatsoever. After bugging him about it several times, B.J. told him not to worry, a fellow named "Big Bart" would be seeing to their entertainment while in the Crescent City. Finally, Mark arranged for the two of them to have a nice home-cooked dinner on Easter Sunday evening, six days hence, in the Atlanta community of Buckhead, with his married friends, Doctor John and Katie Trask -- a couple he'd known since college days.

There were very few cars on I-15. Aptly, after the crash at the Air Force Base, the only radio station they could find that was playing any music at all, was a Barstow AM station airing John Williams' "Theme From Close Encounters Of The Third Kind." Mark pointed to the radio and staged a freak-out for B.J.'s benefit. Mark whispered, "They know we're here." The warning was met with silence from the passenger's seat.

The 109-mile stretch of road between Barstow and the Nevada State Line lies just south of Death Valley. It's uninhabitable country known as the Mojave National Preserve. It was, however, home to spectacular desert landscapes, with sand dunes and cacti for miles around.

"Stanton, this really is like Death Valley. Man there isn't a single animal living out here, is there?" B.J. muttered.

"I wouldn't say that. There are snakes and lizards and horny toads living out there..."

"You mean horned frogs, don't you," B.J. interrupted.

"Horny toads... horny frogs, what's the difference?" Mark paused. "You know why they call them 'horny,' don't you? Because it's a long, long way between toads out here... that's why they're so damned horny," he added, quite pleased with his ad-lib.

B.J. gave Mark a sideways glance. "Tsk, tsk... the toads are horny? *You're* the one who couldn't get laid in all of California... so look at who's calling the pink goose maroon..."

"Fantasy," by Earth, Wind and Fire was playing on the radio.

## Devil's Playground.

"HEY, EAGLE EYE, have you looked in the rearview mirror lately?" B.J. asked.

It was just about 4:30 p.m., and they were nearing the town of Baker, some 50 miles before entering Nevada. They hadn't passed a car, going either way, in a half-hour. Now that they were nearing the only town on this expanse of road, Mark thought that perhaps a county Mountie patrol car had pulled out of the sagebrush to chase the shiny new sports car, now clipping along at 80 mph. Cops, like neighborhood dogs, will do that from time to time, simply for the fun of it. But he didn't see a thing on the road behind them.

"No. I don't see anyone," Mark responded. "What do you mean?"

"The sky, Chicken Little," he said pointing through the sunroof. "Look at the *sky* behind us."

An ominous-looking black storm cloud was building up just over their shoulders. Amazing. The broad sky in front of them was bright and sunny. But looking straight up, through the open sunroof, Mark could begin to see the first inky wisps of the storm cloud quickly overtaking them.

"It can't be rain," Mark said. "We're smack dab in the middle of the biggest desert in North America. I'd bet that it hasn't rained here in a hundred years!" Mark yelled.

Just then they heard a violent clap of thunder behind them. B.J. had a bemused look on his face.

"I just felt a raindrop," B.J. said with his arm stretched out the side window. "Keep the faith and pair-off the critters, Noah. I believe it's starting to rain!"

Before Mark could slow down and find what looked like a solid stretch of road shoulder where he could pull over without fear of sinking into a sand pit, a fast-moving gust of wind hit them from behind. First there was just a drop, then another. Suddenly, it was raining like hell.

The Porsche's sunroof hatch was totally detachable. Mark had stowed it that morning in the all-glass hatchback. Once Mark pulled the car off the road; he jumped out of the driver's seat, only to be hit by a wall of pelting raindrops. Almost immediately, he was soaked. He raced to the back of the car and opened the hatchback. The rain was beating on his back like someone had turned a fire hose on him. Swearing profusely, much to B.J.'s enjoyment, Mark dug through all the things jammed into the small trunk space. He could feel his pants pockets filling up with water. Finally, he was able to get his hands on the sunroof hatch cover. He raced back to the open driver's-side door, in the streaming rain, jumped up on the running board and dropped the hatch cover in place on the just the second try.

B.J. was screaming at him, "Hurry up, I'm drowning... I'm going down for the third time!"

That wasn't far from the truth.

Mark jumped behind the wheel, pulled the car door closed and tried to latch the sunroof tight from the inside. But it was like trying to secure an open hatch on a submarine in the midst of an emergency dive. Water was pouring into the car on all four sides of the sunroof. After what seemed like an eternity and gallons of water, the sunroof hatch locked into place.

"Whew... nobody will ever believe it when we tell them," Mark said, wiping water out of his eyes.

"Believe it! This is nuts! It's monsoon season in the Mojave!" B.J., who'd never left the passenger seat, was drenched. Nearly an inch of water sloshed around on the front floor mats.

Mark turned on the windshield wipers. The scene before them was wholly ludicrous. The desert highway was gone, covered by a river of rainwater. They couldn't see more than a few yards down the road, but what little of the countryside they could see, was totally awash. They laughed; it was all they could do. There were no words to express one's reaction to being swept away by a torrent of water in the middle of the Mojave Desert.

Mark pointed to the map. "Jackson, I kid you not. Look at what it says on the map, right here, where we are..."

"'Devil's Playground,'" B.J. read aloud. "That's what Rand McNally has printed right where we are."

They looked at each other.

"Jackson," Mark whispered, "they know we're here, and now I think they're really pissed."

"Maybe it's your driving... how 'bout giving me a shot behind the wheel?"

No reaction from Mark.

The two waited a full twenty minutes before Mark even considered getting back on the highway. B.J. was still jabbering about being soaked. After discarding several damp butts from the pack, Mark finally found a dry cigarette and lit up.

The thunder squall ended as abruptly as it struck. Within twenty minutes the porous soil absorbed the gully-washer. The sun reappeared behind them and the dark clouds quickly vanished to the east. The car's windshield started to steam-up, so Mark rolled down his window.

Just then a semi-tractor trailer blew past them headed east, spewing off rainwater in every direction. Before Mark could react, his left side was drenched again and the truck-wash extinguished his freshly lit cigarette. He looked over at B.J. with a limp brown butt hanging from his lower lip.

B.J. was really enjoying this. "Hey sweetie, your fag's all wet," he said.

The offending truck went over the next rise and disappeared.

For the next ten miles Mark and B.J. witnessed a truly unique occurrence. The whole desert came alive in a kaleidoscope of blooms and flowers. It seemed that each cactus, every bush and plant blossomed into a floral rainbow. The clean, fresh smell that followed the usual urban rainstorm was very different in the low desert after a cloudburst. Every whiff they breathed was scented with the fragrance of nectar from some sweet flower that probably bloomed but once or twice a year. The desert birds and other animals came alive after the downpour. You could hear the birds singing and clucking and chirping their asses off.

"I think we ought to pretend like all that didn't happen," Mark said.

"Like what didn't happen..."

"You know, the storm," said Mark.

"What storm?"

"Okay, okay... I get it."

## Tonight's the Night.

THEY ENTERED NEVADA only an hour behind Mark's insistent schedule. Considering the bizarre circumstances of the last couple of hours -- the plane crash and the deluge in the desert -- Mark was content to finally be out of California.

Twenty minutes later dusk settled in. As I-15 gradually swung north, in the hazy distance they could begin to see the neon lights of Las Vegas. The radio was already locked on to a Las Vegas top-40 AM station. Bob Seger and the Silver Bullet Band were wailing out "Night Moves." B.J. had the volume all the way up and was alternately playing his harmonica and singing. He did his best impression of a back-up singer in a falsetto voice, as though he was a distant -- but never talked about -- member of Seger's "Silver *Bullet*" family. But Mark thought to himself, *B.J.'s singing wasn't of that caliber.*

The anticipation of a night on the town in Las Vegas for the two single thirty-year olds was exhilarating. Mark knew B.J. had night fever, but then again, B.J. always had night fever. And after almost twelve hours behind the wheel, Mark too was ready for some night moves of his own.

About 7:30 p.m., on the edge of town, they pulled into a gas station and Mark called Jerry Mulligan's home number from a pay phone. Mully's girlfriend Janet answered. "Mark, you don't know how great it is to hear your voice. Gosh, I hope you're still coming to town." When she realized that Mark was on the outskirts of Las Vegas she sounded very relieved.

"I'm sorry we're an hour later than I told you we'd be when I called last weekend," Mark said. "I'll explain what happened later. But we're here and we're ready to gamble and to bring a few casinos to their knees..."

"We've really been looking forward to your night in town. Jerry said after you check in at the Hacienda and get cleaned up, he'll pick you up at the hotel's main entrance at a quarter-to-nine."

"Where are you two going to take us?" Mark asked.

"Jerry's going to start you out at a country and western bar called the Country Rebel. I'll catch up with you later, after all the war stories."

"Should I wear my Stetson?"

"Wear whatever you want," she giggled.

Mully, using his hotel connections, had "comp'd" the twosome with a room for the night at a quiet place near the south end of The Strip. The Hacienda Hotel catered to an older crowd. The parking lot was full of Winnebagoes, but Mark and B.J. didn't care. The hotel room was free and they planned to be out most of the night anyway, hitting the hot spots.

It took a while to unload the car. Mark didn't want to leave anything valuable in the parking lot overnight, so they had quite a bit to haul into the hotel. Pushing a full luggage rack on wheels, the bellman wanted to know if they were staying for a whole week.

They showered up and were ready to ramble by 8:45 p.m.

As usual, B.J. wore denim, but the total effect of his stonewashed jacket and jeans was more of a Haight-Ashbury "hippie" look than the "Marlboro Man" look, but Mark didn't have the heart to tell him.

Mark wore his solitary pair of jeans and his only western-style shirt, a light blue one -- the kind with pointed black stitching and fake pearl snaps, instead of buttons, up the front and on the cuffs and pocket flap. The crowning piece of attire was his cocoa brown Stetson bedecked with a beautiful red-tailed hawk feather and Indian-beaded hatband. The band had been hand-made in front of him by an old American Indian woman in Sheridan, Wyoming. Mark bought the hat four years earlier on a trip he'd advanced for then-Secretary of the Interior, Rogers C.B. Morton. His tan Dingo boots completed his one and only country and western ensemble. Mark didn't own a real pair of cowboy boots; he couldn't bring himself to pay all that money to buy a pair he would hardly ever wear. The made-in-Australia Dingoes had a rounded boot toe, and he'd only worn them a few times. He'd bought the boots years ago in Ohio, trying to keep up with a fast-riding nurse who owned and raced quarter horses. That particular girl left him in the dust years ago, but the boots remained. Mark imagined himself as a sight for sore eyes for some poor cowgirl out there, roaming around Las Vegas.

For B.J.'s entertainment, Mark looked into the hotel room's full-length mirror and stared right in the eye of the young buck he saw. He pointed to himself and said in a stern voice, "Don't you ever get ugly."

"Come on, Tex, don't get your chaps in a knot," said B.J., laughing at Mark's audacity. "I'm sure your friend Jerry's waiting for us out front." This was the first time all day B.J. had worried about being on time. Apparently he couldn't wait to get to the roulette table.

Jerry Mulligan was standing under the neon-lit canopy talking with the doorman, a man he seemed to know quite well. "Mully," as Mark always called him, was wearing street clothes -- a starched white shirt, loose at the collar and a silver and black rep tie. He had his suit jacket slung over the shoulder and looked very crisp like he'd just come from an important meeting at his casino offices. But after not having seen him for more than a year, Mark had to admit he looked none the worse for wear.

"Mully, how the hell are you?" Mark and he greeted each other with a prolonged bear hug with the requisite two "guy" thumps on the back.

"Stanton, my main man... you, sir, have lost some serious weight..."

"Just a kind of a phase I'm going through these days..." Mark quickly changed the subject by introducing Mully to B.J. In turn, Mully introduced the twosome to the hotel's doorman, a smiling fellow named Early.

"Well, well and my, my, Early... it look's like that big cattle drive we've been hearing about has just hit town," Mully said, pointing a thumb at the "denim-ed duo." Early was looking over the two California cowboys, getting an eyeful of pseudo-western attire. Mully looked at the travelers sternly and warned, "Hope you boys don't plan on shooting up the town tonight. We got us a brand new sheriff in these-parts who insists that all firearms be checked before entering a saloon. So, sorry to disappoint, but there'll be no serious gunplay tonight in Clark County."

Early had to turn away to keep from laughing right at the tourists.

"Very funny, Mully... Janet already told us that you're taking us to a shit-kicking country and western bar, the Crazy Rebel. or whatever it is," Mark said defensively.

"Well, I'm sure you two dudes will do just fine with the dancin' girls there," said Mully. "But it's the guys I'm worried about. It can be a pretty tough place. In fact, if you want to go someplace else... that's fine with me."

"Hell, you're the one wearing the fancy suit," Mark said. "They'll probably take you for a tourist and lynch you with your own necktie."

"Don't worry about me, stranger. I'm well known in these-parts," he said in a mock western drawl.

"Jerry, we're all dressed up for a country and western adventure," said B.J., "so let's mount up and get it on... let's ride on over to the Crummy Rebel."

"That's the *Country Rebel*," Mully corrected.

Up until that point B.J. had been quiet, watching and listening to the verbal by-play between Mully and Mark. Now he seemed comfortable, better understanding the relationship, and he was ready to join in.

As Mully drove away from the Hacienda Hotel, Mark turned to him, "I notice you're sporting a little silver hair in that mustache and at the temples," he needled. "Don't know if we can be seen hanging around with an old guy like you who's going to have to start dyeing his hair any day now."

"Maybe I am getting a little gray," Mully answered, "but until tonight I didn't realize what a real western 'buckaroo' you'd become, living out there on the coast. I guess this California cow-puncher outfit you're wearing means you're going to be an advance man for Ronald Reagan in 1980."

"Not sure, Mully, but he's another old-timer, like you. I hear he might be dyeing his hair, too... getting ready to run for President," Mark said in a mock country drawl. "A reporter once asked him if he dyed his hair and you know what Reagan said?" Mark went into his Reagan impression, "Well... no... but I guess you could say that I'm just... prematurely *orange*.'"

"I guess I should ask if it's okay to call you 'Mully,'" B.J. inquired.

"That's fine with me."

"Then let me ask you something Mully..." B.J. added on a serious note, "Have you heard anything on radio or television this afternoon about a plane crash at Edwards Air Force Base?"

"No. Not a word."

"I think I'm going to call Perry Elam," said Mark, "You remember my reporter friend from Washington, don't you Mully?"

"Sure, Perry Elam... nice guy. He's that political reporter who loves to come out here every year to gamble. Remember that I fixed him up with a comp room last time, on your say-so. You should have seen him. He hit the Strip last year with a two thousand dollar bonus burning a hole in his pocket, and Las Vegas sent him back three days later, flat broke."

"That's Perry! He still works for the *Evening Star*. I'm going to call him up and put him onto this plane crash story. I know what we saw!"

"Tonight's The Night (Gonna Be Alright)" by Rod Stewart was playing on the radio as Mully pulled his Oldsmobile into the gravel parking lot of the Country Rebel, a more modern-looking structure than Mark and B.J. had expected. It was a one-story building with a red sideboard and white trim -- barnyard style -- decor. The parking lot had more pick-up trucks than cars in it.

## Rebel Without Applause.

AS THEY ENTERED Mark could see band members setting up on the small stage in the far right corner. It was rather dark and smoky inside, but he could make out about forty people in the place, most seated on stools around an oval racetrack bar.

No sooner had the three of them stepped into the place and Mully yelled out, loud enough so everyone in the place could hear, "These two guys from 'Cal-eee-forn-ya' say they can kick the shit out of any four sons-a-bitches in this place who want to fight for beers."

"Whoa, man," Mark lurched at him, grabbing Mully's up-reached arm, yanking it down. "What in the hell do you think you're doing," he whispered.

The place went silent – all you could hear was crickets. B.J. froze. The whites of his eyes grew to the size of silver dollars. The whole barroom crowd -- including the band – turned-as-one and gave the three newcomers a slow going over, top to bottom and side-to-side. Just as Mark was about to yell, "Just kidding," a loud voice from behind the bar bellowed: "Fuck 'em, Jerry! Let 'em *pay* for their drinks. We ain't fightin' tonight."

There was another quiet pause. Then the whole place erupted in a roar of raucous laughter. They'd been "had" by Mully. An anxious B.J. finally managed to exhale.

"Had you going there, Stanton," said Mully. "For a moment there, it was so quiet in here I thought I could hear you peeing down your pant leg."

"That wasn't Stanton, Mully, it was *me*," said B.J. with a relieved grin.

Apparently, reports of their cross-country trip and their impending arrival had been circulating at the "Rebel" for days. John Spacey, the bartender, and Mully cooked up the idea of a bar fight challenge when his California friends arrived. Mully had called from the hotel to say they would arrive around 9:00 p.m. While the threesome was riding over John the bartender clued-in the regulars as to what was up.

While the band continued to set-up the Country Rebel's jukebox played "We've Got Tonight" by Bob Seger and the Silver Bullet Band.

Mully walked Mark and B.J. around the bar and introduced them to virtually every person in the place, including two very attractive waitresses. Mark was impressed with one of them in particular.

Sally was a knock out, a sun-browned beauty with an athletic build. She wore her long ash blond hair pulled back in a ponytail. Mark sensed that she'd stop traffic on The Strip if she ever let down that hair. Also, she had a brilliant smile of white-white teeth, and a lithe body that even her country and western attire couldn't hide. Mark was mesmerized by the way she moved about. He couldn't quite place her accent, but she had a down-home, no-nonsense quality about her. It struck him that Sally wasn't a career waitress. Later, when he asked where she was from, she said she'd just graduated from college in Colorado and was spending a few months until summer visiting her girlfriend Cindy, the other waitress, here in Sin City.

*If Las Vegas was the big city*, Mark thought, *then she must be a country girl*. Knowing that Mark was Mully's good friend from California, she made a fuss over him. Mark let her. Her name was Sally Markham. He made it a point to remember.

Their grand entrance into The Country Rebel was a unique welcome -- and it sure broke the ice. Instantly, everyone knew who they were. That was Mully's plan all along. To a man they knew that Mark and B.J. were driving cross-country. Many of the patrons commented about how much they would love to do the same thing some day -- grab a case of beer and hit the open road.

Sally suggested, "You ought to keep a diary and write about the trip."

John Spacey shook their hands, and set up the first round of longnecks on the house. "Heard from Jerry what you guys are doing... driving cross-county. I'll bet that's got to be a great experience," he said with a genuine sense of envy.

Eventually the three men fell into a private discussion. Mully wanted to know about the trip thus far. B.J. explained what happened that afternoon; his perspective on the plane crash and the Mojave monsoon were entertaining. Mark finished the travelogue with his rendition of how he found B.J. that morning amid the piles of laundry in Laurie's driveway in Presidio Heights.

*Presidio Heights, that morning? God, it seemed like a week ago*, Mark shook his head.

Once the Rebel's house band cranked up, a little after 9:00 p.m., the crowd around the bar slowly began to grow in size. "No one around here really comes out until near midnight," said Mully. "That's just the way it is in Las Vegas."

"We're in no hurry tonight," said B.J. "I've been waiting for this... we're letting loose."

B.J. knocked back a few long necked beers and even danced a few times. Mark flirted with Sally Markham. He took advantage of every lull in the activity at the service bar to get better acquainted. But before he could work up enough nerve to ask for her phone number, B.J. -- who just couldn't wait to go gambling -- pulled him away from the bar. B.J. wanted to get to a casino now. Mark relented, figuring he could follow-up with Sally via Mully, if he ever had the opportunity to do so.

The threesome left the Rebel at 10:45 p.m. amid handshakes, hugs and kisses all-around. Mully's drinking buddies treated them as old friends. Mark and B.J. actually got lingering embraces and so-long pecks from the sensuous Sally and her friend, the scintillating Cindy -- as the two men had nicknamed them. As he waved good-bye, Mark noticed the two waitresses whispering something to Mully.

B.J. commented to Mark how welcome he felt in that place -- no fear and loathing in Las Vegas for these travelers. Mully hadn't let Mark down. That's the kind of friendship that picks up right where it left off. In actuality, Mark had felt more at home at the Rebel in the last two hours than he had at any bar in Palo Alto the last two years.

"Next stop, a casino, for B.J.'s benefit... we hope," Mully declared as they all piled into his spacious Olds. ABBA was on the car radio singing, "The Name Of The Game." Mully seemed in no particular hurry as he sidetracked them with a guided tour of The Strip. He pointed out huge holes in the desert sand where new hotels were scheduled to rise.

"How can Vegas keep growing like this?" Mark asked. "It's out-of-control. I remember the very first time I came out here in 1970, there were huge sandlots with tumbleweeds between the hotels. Look at it now, just eight years later."

"Where the hell does all this money come from?" B.J. asked.

"Las Vegas has gone legit," Mully said. "It's the hotel corporations that are putting up the money now, not the mob or the union pension funds. Why, in the near future, I'd bet that some of these places will be listed on the New York Stock Exchange."

The next stop, around 11:00 p.m., was the Royal Hotel, not a big-name casino, but a small off-the-Strip place with a pleasant and rather quiet oaken barroom. Again, Mully seemed to know everyone in the place. The female bartender, a striking brunette in a tuxedo shirt with a red bow tie, asked Mully, "Are these two cowboy characters your coast-to-coast guys?"

"Gee Stanton, see... our fame is spreading like a wildfire throughout Nevada," B.J. marveled.

"You bet," said Mully, loud enough for the bar crowd to hear, "direct from San Francisco and bound for Washington, D.C., where all your money goes. Mark and B.J., I want you to meet 'Juicy Lucy' and the 'gang that couldn't drink straight,'" he said motioning to all the regulars on stools.

"We're all drinkers who have a sleeping problem," said one.

The traveling twosome shook hands all around. Mully and Mark sat down at Lucy's bar and began catching up. Sensing that this reunion get-together between two old friends might take awhile, B.J. said he was off to try his fortune at the tables.

"His money will last a little longer in here," Mully smiled. "The odds on the slots at a friendly neighborhood place like this are a little better than on The Strip. In fact, I should have brought your reporter friend Perry Elam here when he came to town. This is a joint were locals come to drink and gamble a bit. I spend some of my free time down here."

When Lucy turned her attention to them, Mully jumped in and ordered two black coffees.

"Black coffee! In Las Vegas? What the hell are you trying to do, poison me," Mark protested.

"Well, I just thought you'd better pace yourself if you're going to stand-up for me later tonight," Mully said with a deadpan look on his face.

"Stand up for you?" Mark looked at him in bewilderment.

A slow grin grew on Jerry Mulligan's face, "What I'm trying to tell you, ol' pal, is that in one hour, the lovely Janet and I are going to get married... right here in this hotel. And since you're in town, I want you to stand up for me at the ceremony and be my best man."

"I'm in total shock. You could knock me over with a feather."

Things got quiet. *It shouldn't be such a surprise*, Mark thought. *Mully and Janet had lived together since '72. They had been together for six years now.* "Why tonight?" Mark asked.

"Why not? I've known you longer than I've known anyone in this town. When you first called two weeks ago, I started thinking about it... and then when we talked again this weekend, I was finally certain that you were coming. I figured this might be the perfect time to get hitched. So Janet and I got the license and the blood tests yesterday, and we're ready to go. The shindig starts at midnight. We thought we'd surprise you."

Mark stood up, gave Mully a bear hug and said, "Buddy boy, I'm honored!"

Relieved that his secret was finally out, Mully continued his explanation. "So, everything's set. I've got a judge, a ring, and a bride who's supposed to be here in an hour." Catching the still-stunned look on Mark's face, Mully said, "Now cowboy, drink your damned coffee."

It took a few more minutes to sink in -- Mark's good buddy since high school was getting married. Mark remembered every girl Mully ever dated back in school and had also known Mully's college sweetheart. Even though the two men went to different universities, Mark always knew what was going on in Mully's life. They'd kept in pretty close touch. *So tonight was the night*. Jerry Mulligan was getting on with his new life in Las Vegas. Well, good for him. He deserved the best, and Janet would see to that. And, the best part of it all, Mark was going to be there with a ringside view.

"Congratulations man, I just know you and Janet are right for each other," he said.

Forty minutes and two cups of coffee later, Mully and Mark roamed the hotel's small casino floor, looking for that big-time gambler, B.J. Jackson. They caught up with him at a roulette wheel. He was sitting at the foot of the long green-felt table surrounded by stacks and stacks of pretty pink chips. When B.J. spotted them approaching he held up two handfuls. He was beaming like a grandma at the county fair, holding the pie that won the blue ribbon.

B.J. must have had six hundred chips stacked in front of him. "Jackson," Mark said enthusiastically, slapping him on the back, "we're rich!"

"What do you mean *we're* rich, white man," B.J. said, doing his best Tonto impression.

"Don't get too excited, Stanton," Mully said poking Mark in the ribs, "big time B.J. is playing with twenty-five cent chips. But I'd guess he's sitting on $150 or so."

Going way back to their days at Dewey Beach, B.J. and Mark had always gotten a kick out of watching "Our Gang" comedies on hung-over Saturday mornings.  When things were going their way, there was a standing routine between the two of them that they had used many times before.  Mark started -- knowing B.J. would pick up on it, "Jackson, can you use the word 'isthmus' in a sentence?"

B.J. responded, on cue, just like the "Our Gang" character Buckwheat used to do:  "Isth-mus be my lucky day!"  The timing was perfect.  The handful of players around the table, the dealer and even the grizzled old pit boss, who'd probably heard 'em all before, cracked up.

"O-tay, Jackson," Mark said, "You'd better cash in them millions.  In about twenty minutes, we've got a wedding to go to..."

"A what?"

## Best Man in Blue Jeans.

JANET LOOKED LIKE the cover girl for a bridal magazine. Right at the stroke of midnight, accompanied by her younger sister as matron-of-honor, she swept into the hotel's richly paneled boardroom in a knee-length, peach-colored dress with lace ringing the neckline, carrying a nosegay of color-coordinated flowers.  She was a petite woman with delicate features and China doll skin, framed by a sculptured coif of tawny hair.

She spotted Mark and made a beeline for him.  "Oh Mark, don't you look lean and trim.  I can't tell you how happy I am that you decided to come through Las Vegas this week.  Your sense of timing is impeccable," she said, planting a big one right square on his lips.  "If you'd changed your plans at the last minute, I don't know what I would have done.  I'm not positive Jerry would have gone through with all this, without you standing here beside him."

Mark was flattered, and honored, and smeared with lipstick, all at the same time -- quite a feeling.  His only thought was how stupid he must look to everyone in his gawd-awful western garb.  *Thank God, it wasn't a black tie event,* he blushed to himself. He remembered what lonesome George Gobel used to say, "Did you ever feel like the whole world is a tuxedo, and you're a pair of brown shoes?" That's how he felt.

B.J. found a comfortable spot in a corner of the boardroom and just stood there with a totally bemused look on his face. Standing with him were John Spacey the bartender, Sally Markham and the scintillating Cindy from the Country Rebel as well as Juicy Lucy and several of her customers, people they'd met downstairs earlier. There were about two dozen others in attendance, local couples close to Janet and Mully. Still others, Mark learned from Janet's sister, would attend the reception later.

Mully looked dapper as a bridegroom in his charcoal-gray pinstriped suit, with the silver and black rep tie. Also, as a finishing touch, Janet had someone pin a peach-colored boutonniere on him just before the ceremony began. Fifteen minutes later, thanks to a very distinguished-looking judge, who was a regular golfing buddy of Mully's, Mark's friend from high school days was officially married to the love of his life. And after six years of waiting for her magical moment, the new Mrs. Mulligan was as genuinely happy as any woman Mark had ever laid eyes on. He was proud to be in attendance, and honored at having been tapped to play a small role in what he was sure would be an eternal romance. And, despite the strong coffee Mully had force-fed him, and all that caffeine, he'd handed the golden ring to the groom, right on cue during the ceremony, without getting jittery or dropping it -- the Best Man in blue jeans.

"Where are you two going for the honeymoon?" B.J. asked.

"First, we're going upstairs to the twelfth floor. The reception's in the Presidential Suite. I've got the place booked for the night," said Mully doing his best impression of Groucho Marx wielding an imaginary cigar. "Then, I've arranged to take Janet to New York City for a honeymoon shopping spree. But she wants to bring along about twenty friends. We'll have to see about that."

"We've been together so long, I'm embarrassed to call it a honeymoon," Janet reflected. Then suddenly she shouted out, "You're all invited to join us in New York. We'll be at the Waldorf for five nights." Hearty applause broke out. From the sound of it, Mark felt that quite a few of their friends were ready to take her up on the invitation to join them in New York.

It was quite a reception. Well more than one hundred people came through the hotel suite during the late evening. And Mark made it a point to apologize to each one for his casual attire explaining that the wedding had been a complete and total surprise to the Best Man.

## Happy Trails.

AT FOUR-THIRTY IN the morning Mark found himself on the twelfth floor balcony of the Presidential Suite with none other than the sensuous Sally Markham from the Country Rebel. The two were snuggled together on a chaise-lounge. They had been chatting, getting to know one another while looking out over the sea of neon lights on South Las Vegas Boulevard.

By now, Mark surmised that the newly wed couple was asleep next door in the presidential boudoir, adjacent to the spacious parlor room where the bridal reception had been held. As far as he could determine from the dearth of conversation coming from the parlor, everyone else had long since departed. The last time he'd seen B.J. and Cindy, the other waitress from The Rebel, the two were headed downstairs to gamble away B.J.'s roulette winnings.

The wedding reception had been a blast. Waves of people, as they got off from work, or as they headed for jobs on the graveyard shift, stopped by to congratulate Janet and Mully. It took two bartenders to keep up with the steady stream of well wishers. It seemed to Mark as though nearly everyone in this 24-hour a day town, but him and B.J., knew about the midnight nuptials.

Mully and Mark had always loved to surprise one another or to play practical jokes, going back to their high school days. But Mark had to admit to himself that this was Mully's biggest coup. Mark reflected that he had pulled-off a few good ones on Mulligan over the years. Like the time back in high school, Mully used to brag about how much he made in tips at the local grocery store's loading zone. Housewives would hand him tips for lugging grocery bags. One Saturday before Christmas Mully had mentioned in passing that he'd pulled in an extra $160 in holiday tips. A few months later Mark had Mully convinced that an IRS agent had been nosing around asking about tip money and why Mully hadn't reported any tip income on his IRS 1040 tax form. Mully broke out in hives worrying about an IRS audit, and he'd damn near punched-out Mark when he discovered it was all a prank. *Now how I am going to "top" this? The Country Rebel "fight" scene and then a surprise wedding, all in one evening*, Mark thought.

Personally, the idea of getting married seemed a far-away proposition for Mark Stanton. But when ready, he imagined that he would prefer to do it as Mully and Janet had, quietly, avoiding all the unnecessary trappings. But reality settled in and he figured that any future bride of his, and her mother, would probably veto Mark's idea about how a wedding should be conducted.

In the wee hours, as the reception waned, Sally and Mark had settled into an interesting embrace out on the top floor balcony. They'd drifted out there to have a cigarette. The only place left to sit was on the lone chaise-lounge. With time, Sally and Mark had inched closer and closer as they talked and got acquainted. One thing led to another and before they realized it, they were lying next to each other, talking excitedly, teasing and laughing.

Sally encapsulated her life story for Mark. He did the same. He even went so far as to confess that he was now officially unemployed, noting that he'd just taken a leave from his job to move back east -- it was the first time he'd admitted that fact to anyone, other than B.J.

"I've heard a lot about you from Jerry," she confided. "He's really been looking forward to your visit. He's told us all kinds of stories about the two of you growing up and going to high school together in Ohio, and about you ending up in Washington and all about your political exploits, like working at The White House."

"Mully and I do go way back," Mark said. "We met sophomore year trying out for the junior varsity basketball team. Mully eventually made the team as a second-string forward. After a career-ending injury, I ended up as the team's manager," he explained, "more a less a glorified gopher. Anyway, Mully and I wound up sitting next to each other, at the far end of the bench, all season long. He was in uniform, constantly wringing a towel, and me, in my civvies, keeping the scoring stats book. We became fast friends."

Sally snuggled closer and whispered, "Before I even knew your name, I knew all about Jerry's buddy who worked for the President of the United States. He's very proud of you."

Mark was a bit taken-aback. It always amazed him how friends talk, on and on, about their buddies. After fifteen years, Mark may have underestimated how closely Mully felt to him. Sure, Mark felt very close to Mully, despite the distance the friendship had to overcome. But Mark never really thought about it from Mully's perspective. Being asked to stand in as Best Man had been a re-awakening about what friendship truly means -- and to Mark, it meant a great deal.

No one can select family members, but one can take great pride in accumulating a world-class collection of good friends. Mark often found himself talking about friends -- what they were doing, their successes, or about how funny they were. Hell, he'd been telling B.J. for weeks how Mully would take great care of them when they got to Las Vegas. And now he had. Yet, Mark felt a bit off-balance when he learned that Mully had talked to Sally and others about him.

Sally interrupted his musings, "I kind of expected you to be a little different than you are."

"How so?"

"Well, after listening to Jerry... your traveling around with the President and all... I kind of expected you to roll in here wearing a James Bond tuxedo, or at least a three-piece suit."

"Disappointed in my lousy Hop-a-long Cassidy costume?"

"Well, let's just say, you shouldn't try to be someone you're not. And you're definitely not a cowboy. You know, people might think you're trying to make fun of westerners. We don't see our clothes as a costume. And we don't put on pin-striped suits and try to show off like easterners," she gently lectured.

"I'm not making fun. I just thought that in Las Vegas, hell, anything goes!"

"Well it really doesn't. Behind all the neon and glitter I've discovered there's a real town here, with real people in it, trying like hell to lead normal lives. People who live here avoid The Strip unless they work there. It's not considered a part of everyday life. Too many people come to Las Vegas trying to act crazy. Trying to be somebody they're not. I've seen it often since I've been here and it angers me."

"Well, does that mean you're mad at me for what I'm wearing?"

"Well, you sure look out-of-character. I'd rather see what you're like in your element some time, you know... wearing that three-piece suit... doing whatever it is that you do in Washington, D.C.," she paused. "And, by the way, I want you to know that I am a cowgirl, a real one. I grew up on a working ranch between Lander and Riverton, Wyoming. And I never in my entire life have seen such a drug store cowboy as you, or... I might add... a pair of boots that are as mule-assed ugly as those rounded toe numbers you're wearing tonight."

Sally stared at him and then giggled nervously, as though she might have gone too far. Mark feigned insult, then tickled her in mock revenge -- but then he had to stifle her screeches, lest she wake up the honeymooners. The lecture being over, the two snuggled closer. Finally, they kissed the kiss that Mark had anticipated for hours. *It was well worth the time he'd invested in waiting*, he thought. They quietly commenced the ages-old process of opening up to infatuation -- random attraction mutually magnetized. That bond established, they slipped off to dreamland together.

Mark awoke with a start. It was daybreak. The desert air had become quite chilly. From the morning sky he could tell the sun was about to rise behind them, on the other side of the building. The damned birds were already awake and chirping. He felt like hell, it must have been the combination of his testy gastrointestinal system, long necked beers, coffee at 11:00 p.m. and champagne. His budding headache made the damned birds sound even louder.

As he came to his senses, Mark realized that he had no sensation whatsoever in either his left arm or leg. Sally was pressed against him, asleep on the chaise. *Trying to extricate yourself from a sleeping embrace without waking your partner, has to be one of the more difficult tasks in all of love life*, he thought. Trying to do it while the left half of your body is effectively "Novocained" beyond feeling, is a challenge only surpassed by trying to eat spaghetti with a one-iron. Eventually, by slightly rocking the chaise from side-to-side, Mark managed to awaken Sally to at least a state of semi-consciousness.

"Hey cowboy, what do you think you're doing?  Are you trying to chew your arm off so you can run out on me?" she murmured quietly in sleepy-eyed wonder.

"Not really.  Just trying to shift a few pints of blood from my eyeballs down to the left side of my body, which is sound asleep," he said.  With her help he shifted his weight.  About then the "pins and needles" began their torture.

"What time is it?" she wanted to know.

"Almost six o'clock."

"We'd better tiptoe out of here," she whispered.  "There's a honeymoon taking place next door."  And that's exactly what they did.  The parlor room where the reception had taken place was a hotel maid's nightmare.  No one else was around.  The couple headed for the elevator and the lobby below.

Mark looked out front of the hotel, trying to spot a taxicab or a doorman on duty.  Sally's friend Cindy spied them and came over.  "Help!  We've been at the tables most of the night," she uttered with a roll of the eyes, "...and now B.J.'s 'down' a couple hundred bucks."

"Excuse me for a minute, ladies," said Mark.  "Allow me to gather up my friend so we can all get out of here."

Mark found an almost-lifelike crew of four at B.J.'s blackjack table, including a jaded-looking dealer and three very hung-over players, all with bloodshot eyes.  "Perhaps we can join hands and try to contact the living," he said trying to elicit a response.  No one even looked up from the cards.

"Well, Stanton," said B.J., "here's another fine mess you've gotten me into.  Get me out of here before I pawn my class ring.  I think this dealer is in the hunt for 'Employee-of-the-Month.'  He just can't wait to get that prime parking space right outside the front door of the casino."

Mark reached around his buddy and flipped two of B.J.'s remaining $5 chips to the dealer and said, "I'm sure you've earned this.  Thanks for baby sitting my friend, but he can't play with you any more, he's got to go home now."  The two departed the casino floor.  Sally and Cindy were waiting at the front door.

B.J. put his arm around Cindy and stepped into the morning air for a private conversation.

Mark turned to Sally, "I've got to go.  Jackson and I have to hit the road if we expect to get to Tucson tonight.  But before

I go, I would like your phone number. Once I get back east, I have a few unpleasant matters I have to attend to... but if all that goes well, I want to call you. Who knows maybe you'll receive an offer you can't refuse... a chance to visit Washington, D.C. and see me in my element. Are you willing to take a chance on a handsome guy in ugly boots?"

Sally was puzzled but silent about his reference to "unpleasant matters," but she wrote down her phone numbers in Las Vegas and at home in Wyoming. She said she had no idea how long she would be in Las Vegas visiting her friend Cindy.

Cindy drove the foursome back to the Hacienda. Coupled up, they said their last good-byes under the still-lit neon canopy.

"Mark, I really hope that whatever it is back east that you have to do... that when it's over you'll eventually get around to calling me."

"I hope so too. I believe I've found more than I bargained for in Las Vegas, but I'm pretty sure there's not much work here for a Washington lobbyist like me." Mark gave Sally a passionate kiss.

"Happy trails, cowboy," she said. With that she turned and departed.

Mark and B.J. got back to their sleeping room, or whatever you call the room where one stores their things while pulling an "all-nighter." B.J. called the hotel operator and asked for a 9:00 a.m. wake-up call. Each man fell face-first into his respective bed.

The phone rang -- it seemed to Mark like only ten minutes later. But it was already nine o'clock. Mark was exhausted.

The two dragged their asses out of bed and spent the next half-hour showering and getting cleaned up. Then they called for the bellman. *Thank God it was not the same fellow as the previous night,* Mark thought. While pushing the well-laden luggage cart to the entrance, the young man wanted to know if they'd enjoyed their week in Las Vegas.

# CHAPTER TWO

## Wednesday, March 22, 1978

### Extreme Unction.

THEY HEADED SOUTHEAST out of Las Vegas toward Arizona on U.S. 93. It was 9:45 a.m. Eric Clapton's "Lay Down Sally" clattered from "Stanley's" radio.

"Speaking of Eric Clapton... how was Miss Sally, last night?" B.J. asked, the devil in his tone.

"Why she's just fine. Thank you for asking. And when can I expect that the scintillating Miss Cindy and her hung-over, bloodshot boyfriend Goober-the-gambler will be getting together again?"

"None too soon," B.J. croaked. "She's not had much exposure to high rollers like me, and I don't think she suffers losers gladly."

"How much are you down?"

"I'm tired. I'm hurtin'. And I'm down a wallet full... I'm nearly busted."

"What? How much did you bring with you?"

"A couple of hundred..."

"Let me get this straight. You left San Francisco with just two hundred bucks and expected to make it all the way 'cross-country?"

"No. But as you no doubt recall, I left Laurie's place under, shall-we-say, less than agreeable circumstances. And due to the dire straits in which I found my ass yesterday morning, I didn't have the heart to ask her to pay my most recent home improvement invoice of $2,200. But I've got enough to buy us breakfast," he paused, "...we are going to stop for breakfast today, aren't we?"

"Isn't this exactly how we started out yesterday... with you whining about breakfast?"

B.J. winced. "They say gaggles of geese know when it's time to migrate by the low angle of the early morning sun. There may be something to the theory. This morning I figure from the angle of the sun on the windshield that we are already probably well behind schedule."

Mark stayed mum.

Then B.J. snatched the clipboard and closely eyed the itinerary sheet. "Hey Stanton, it says here we're only a half-hour late and there's a pit-stop scheduled at 10:30 this morning." He laughed. "I must have died and gone to heaven."

"Well, partner, I've been through Vegas before. And I know from first-hand experience how tough it is to get up after an all-nighter on The Strip, so I hedged a bit on today's starting time."

B.J. scribbled on the schedule sheet and stuck the clipboard back in its place.

While keeping one eye on traffic, Mark picked it up to see what he'd written. Next to "9:45 a.m. Depart Las Vegas," he'd added the words, "after Extreme Unction" -- a Catholic's last rites for the dying.

"Alright... alright... two stops this morning, first a hot meal and then a tour of the Hoover Dam," Mark declared.

"I thought it was the Boulder Dam."

"It was... until 'Herbert' heard about it."

B.J. sniffed the air, still not sure how the dam got its name. Without saying a word, B.J. reached around and grabbed Mark's brown Stetson from the hatchback area, slouched down in his bucket seat and pulled it down over his eyes. The straight-in-your-face morning sun was more than either of them wanted to bear. "Drive on, Stanton my man," he said. "And wake me when it's time for my ham and eggs."

Despite his condition Mark too had to admit that he was famished. Then it dawned on him that they hadn't had any dinner the night before.

Mark stepped on the gas pedal as Manfred Mann's Earth Band wailed "Blinded By The Light."

## John Snapper.

THEY SAVORED THE greasy steak and eggs like condemned men eating their last meal. They'd stopped at a local choke-and-puke at the Boulder City exit off Route 93. From the looks of the parking lot, only long-haul truckers frequented the place. As the two entered, the smells coming off the grill seemed encouraging. The mini-jukebox in their booth was cranking out "Jackie Blue" by the Ozark Mountain Daredevils.

B.J. seemed to be coming around a bit.

Mark noted that B.J. was beginning to form complete sentences -- but he smiled to himself figuring that despite his fancy Princeton education B.J. couldn't diagram a single sentence he was uttering this morning. Mark's prized Stetson remained atop B.J.'s throbbing head. Apparently B.J. liked the C&W look it gave him; and he used the hat as a prop, putting him in the unlikely character of a bad-assed country dude. And after the lecture Mark got from Sally last night on costumes, the Stetson could stay on B.J.'s head. Mark had lost all desire for the western look.

The two were unusually quiet as they ate; spending most of the time staring into the parking lot, watching the noisy semi-tractor trailers come and go.

After their second cup of black coffee, B.J. spoke up. "Stanton, you and Sally... something special going on there? You two seemed to really be in sync from the moment you met. You'd be a fool not to follow up with someone like that. But lately, you're not really practiced at fooling around, are you?"

"I'd like to see her again, in daylight. Up 'til now I've always had a policy about dating a woman I've met while drinking. I've got to see her once again in daylight before I officially ask her out on a date."

"Now what's that all about? For a guy with a shitty track record like yours in California, I'd have thought you'd be more than grateful that some woman... any woman... would be willing to spend more than five minutes with you in polite conversation."

"I have my reasons for exercising caution... way too many disappointing first dates a week later after meeting them due to blurred vision the week prior," Mark added. "In college,

I'd meet someone on Friday night over beers and then get all worked up that following week about the prospect of having a great-looking date for Saturday. I wouldn't be able to remember exactly what she looked like, that is until I picked her up. Then it would all come roaring back. The beauty mark I thought I remembered would actually be a hairy wart. At least I'm honest about it. My taste in food and women at 2:00 a.m. is probably not what it should be."

"Then I would advise you to go ugly early," B.J. offered.

"You're trying to put words in my mouth. That's downright rude... not to mention unsanitary."

"And who said your sense of taste in women at any other hour of the day is anything to brag about?" B.J. said. "Speaking of dating in college, what is the name of that all-guys school you went to? Cindy asked me last night where you went to college and I couldn't think of the name... wasn't it John Snapper College and Screen Door Company, or something like that?"

Mark grimaced. "I'll have you know that I am a graduate of *the* John Carroll University... as fine an establishment as there is in the nation. We only nicknamed it 'John Snapper' because, as students of a fine, upstanding Jesuit institution of higher learning, we weren't supposed to be eating meat on Fridays. We ate fish... *ergo*, the nickname John Snapper."

"So that's where the 'Snapper' came from..." B.J. recalled.

"Listen here my Ivy League Protestant friend. A famous scientist once said that for every action there is an opposite and equal reaction. And because we John Snapper students were mandated to eat fish every Friday, in return, we were rewarded with steak every Saturday night. In fact, as my fraternity brothers can attest, I came up with an ingenious scheme, known as the Stanton Plan that was guaranteed to get me and my fraternity brothers three steaks apiece every Saturday night.

"You see, exactly twenty-six miles on the odometer north of John Carroll University on the sandy shores of Lake Erie is the quiet hamlet of Painesville, Ohio, home to Lake Erie College for Women. We Carroll men used to refer to it affectionately as 'Lake College... for Eerie Women.'

B.J. delighted in the pun.

"The critical element to my three-steak plan was that John Carroll and Lake Erie College both had "Saga" the same cafeteria food-service company. Meal tickets from one school were honored at the other. So, if we timed things flawlessly on Saturday evenings, we could rustle-up three steaks for dinner. However, three important moves had to be made. First, we had to be in the John Carroll cafeteria line early and had to wolf down our first steak by no later than 6:30 p.m. Second, we had to pile into someone's car and negotiate the 26 miles to Painesville in less than 30 minutes, arriving just in the nick of time to catch the very end of Lake Erie College's dinner hour. And since the Lake Erie women rarely ate their allotment of Saturday night steaks, preferring salads and other low-fat items, the girls who worked the cafeteria line were always glad to hand out two steaks to any guy with a heartbeat who visited their male-starved campus on Saturday evenings. It worked like a military bonus for "re-upping." That's how the Stanton plan worked... three steaks every Saturday night of my senior year in college."

B.J. got into the moment. "So it's... 'stake' out a lonely girls' school and get a second and third steak. Maybe that's your very problem in dealing with California women, Stanton," B.J. added, "...too much red meat at a critically pubescent stage of development could lead to stalking."

Mark was afraid it actually led to something else.

## Eureka... It's the Hoover!

MARK AND B.J. eased out of the truck stop parking lot. Both were working their toothpicks like jackhammers. As for the long-awaited morning repast, Mark was not quite sure how he would describe it. Back in his hometown of Sandusky, Ohio, when people were fishing for something nice to say about a rather unpleasant feed, it would come out something like: "There was plenty of it, and it was plenty greasy enough, thank you very much."

Mark's stomach began rumbling before they reached the car. *Thankfully,* he thought, *they were scheduled to stop again soon.*

B.J. bought a Las Vegas morning paper at the checkout counter. He gave the headlines a quick going-over while Mark drove. There was no story about a plane crash at Edwards Air Force Base the day before. "Stanton, maybe we saw something we weren't supposed to," he said with a suspicious look.

"What's the headline?"

"No Movement In Carter-Begin Mideast Talks," answered B.J.

"What else is going on out there in the real world?"

"In other news... a French court has indicted the captain of the Amoco Cadiz, a super-tanker that crashed into a reef off Normandy last Friday. Hey, last Friday when it hit the reef was St. Patrick's Day. You don't suppose the Irish skipper was celebrating... do you, O'Stanton? Anyway, he was nailed for illegally discharging 700,000 barrels of crude oil along France's English Channel coastline."

"Discharge? Sounds like something an urologist should handle," Mark cringed.

"Let's see... for you Friday fish-eating mackerel-snappers there's this item, Pope Paul VI, is improving after a week of being down with the flu. It says the 80 year-old pontiff hopes to be able to celebrate Easter Mass this coming Sunday."

"The pope's on the ropes..."

B.J. shuffled the unwieldy pages in front of the windshield. "Another tidbit of news, spring began at 6:34 a.m. Monday, so that makes this the second official full day of spring. How 'bout that!"

"Hey... spring has sprung!"

"And lastly... for you reactionary Republican types... I regret to inform you that the Dow Jones industrial average plunged a perilous 11 points yesterday due to investor disappointment over Sears Roebuck's earnings report. The index wound up at 762.82. I'm sure your silk-stocking Republican buddies in New York are standing on building ledges all along Wall Street this morning."

"Thank you Jackson. So, let me summarize... the tanker's in the tank... the pope is on the ropes... spring has sprung... the brokers are going broke... sounds like a great day for getting away. What does it say in the paper about the weather in Phoenix?"

"Calls for a high of 85 today!"

"And, what's happening in sports?"

"Lemme see here... the San Diego Padres axed manager Alvin Dark yesterday and replaced him with pitching coach Roger Craig."

"Dark's totally in the dark..."

"On the tour... Nicklaus is still the number one money winner through the Tournament Players Championship, with $157,000 in the bank. My man, Tommy Watson, is second on the list with $103,000 so far this year, poor baby." B.J. paused for a moment, his eye catching an obscure point. "Hey, Stanton, catch this... comedian Redd Foxx had someone jump out of the audience onto the stage at his gig in Vegas last night. Foxx cold-cocked the guy, knocked him out. And then just went on with the rest of his act like nothing happened. Pretty cool, huh?"

"So, now we've got... the tanker's in the tank... the Pope's on the ropes... spring has sprung... the brokers are going broke... Dark's in the dark... Jack's in the black... and now it turns out that the joker's a poker."

"Enough already," B.J. threw up his hands.

*Spring has sprung.* That reminded Mark of a class skit he was in during kindergarten. He explained to B.J. how the teacher asked various kids in class to pretend to be trees or plants or flowers. Other kids were supposed to be bees a-buzzing, or chirping birds, or croaking frogs. When it came to him, she said, 'Mark, I want you to run all around, in and out of the plants and animals, just keep running around. Don't stop until I tell you.' While all the other kids were frozen in-place, Mark was running around like a nut, all over the stage. The teacher then told the entire school assembly that the name of the kindergarten skit was: "Spring is here and the *sap* is running." Mark never forgave her for that. He was known as the sap for years afterward.

"So, I guess you could say that in your kindergarten role as 'Sap' you were merely understudying for your future role in grown-up life as Slick the Slash, the guy *covered* in sap," B.J. sneered.

No response was forthcoming.

"That's Your Secret," by Sea Level was just finishing on the radio as Mark slowed and parked the car along side the roadway.

## Dams and Canals.

"HOOVER DAM WAS constructed between 1931 and 1935," said the matronly tour guide. "This National Historic Landmark was the first major dam on the Colorado River..."

Traffic has to cross the deep Colorado River gorge to get from Nevada into Arizona and U.S. Route 93 ran right across the top of the dam. So Mark's itinerary allowed time for a stop and a tour of the whole dam thing.

They followed the tour guide and small group of twenty or so who were being buffeted by winds swirling down the canyon walls. B.J., still sporting Mark's brown Stetson, had to hang on to the hat during strong gusts as they fell in behind the tourists.

"Behind us," she droned on, "is the 110-mile-long Lake Mead, with some 500 miles of shoreline. It was created by the Colorado River, and is the largest man-made reservoir in the United States. Thousands of bighorn sheep roam the canyons surrounding Lake Mead... yada, yada, yada."

It was quite a project. Children hear about projects like the Hoover Dam in school, but the immensity of the undertaking never hits a person until you're looking the damned thing right in the eye. Like kids with short attention-spans, Mark and B.J. were gawking and pointing -- paying very little heed to the tour guide who was trying to provide the group with a complete history in eight minutes or less.

"The roadway, where we stand, atop this arch dam, is exactly 726 feet above the bedrock base," she continued.

At this point, B.J. and Mark carefully leaned over the railing to get the full effect of the dizzying height. After what they drank Tuesday evening and what they'd just consumed for breakfast, neither wanted to look down for too long. When they did look back up, and glanced at one another, something was missing!

It was Mark's hand-made, Indian-crafted, red-tailed hawk feather and beaded hatband!

"Jackson... you ass!" Mark bellowed. The tour guide turned at the two of them and stared.

The hatband had popped off the Stetson when B.J. looked over the side of the dam. Quickly, Mark looked back down into the gorge and spotted it... drifting down into the canyon toward the Colorado River, which he'd just learned, was exactly 726 feet below. It was headed toward the massive hydroelectric plant situated tight against the canyon wall below, along the churning riverbed. Mark was pissed, and B.J. sensed it immediately.

"Stanton," he said with mock humility, holding the Stetson very much in a hat-in-hand pose, "the damn eagle feathers on the Stetson... has done flown... d'coop."

At which point the entire tour group except the tour guide turned to look at B.J. -- doing a double take on what he'd said. Some, Mark guessed, just wanted to see if they'd heard him right. If looks could kill, Jackson was a walking dead man. "It was made of rare hawk feathers, not eagle feathers," Mark said through clenched teeth.

The Park Service guide relentlessly pursued her script "...the dam provides huge amounts of electricity and water needed by Arizona, California and Nevada. Its construction set the stage for the phenomenal growth of the entire three-state region... yada, yada, yada."

Trying to change the subject, B.J. put his arm around Mark's shoulders, his arm making a sweeping gesture all across the dam, "Kind of impressive what big government can accomplish, huh?" he chortled.

For once, Mark didn't have a snappy response. But he had to admit to that it was a pretty impressive project, especially considering the fact that it was built in the 1930's with old-fashioned steam shovels and hand picks.

They hung around for a few more minutes of sightseeing, made a post-truck stop visit to the federally subsidized and publicly maintained rest room facilities. Upon their return, both of them walking just a little bit taller, they piled back into the Porsche.

Trying to settle into the front seat at the same time, Mark and B.J. realized how closely they were packed into "Stanley." With the back seat folded down and the entire hatchback loaded up, there was very little elbowroom for either one. Every square inch of front seat was taken-up. Mark commented that they were like two Project Gemini astronauts strapped in side-by-side for a long endurance mission. That was all B.J. needed -- he began parodying NASA terminology speaking to an imaginary Mission Control cap-com in Houston.

As they embarked on the 70-mile ride to Kingman, Arizona, B.J. chattered into his fist, as if he were holding a microphone, "Houston, this is Eagle-Feather-One! We have concluded EVA at coordinates Hoover, and are now ready for synchronized burn that will jettison us to coordinates Kingman, for rendezvous with Interstate 40. Over."

Then he imitated a NASA capsule communicator responding, "Eagle-Feather-One, this is Mission Control, Cap-Com-Houston! After reviewing the telemetry, we have determined that you are 'go' for burn and Kingman insertion. Godspeed, you two, your country is very proud of you..."

Mark squinted, stifling a smile, and tried not to react further. Sometimes, he figured, it's just best to let B.J. entertain himself in his own little imaginary dream world. Later on, B.J. fell asleep, Mark's Stetson, *sans* the expensive hatband, still shading his eyes.

With a little time to himself, Mark reflected on the trip thus far. He made a mental note to send Janet and Mully a wedding gift when he got to Washington, maybe a nice piece of Irish Waterford crystal. Looking back on last evening, he couldn't get Sally Markham off of his mind. God, he hoped he hadn't come off like a total jerk in the cowboy attire. Sally was a fine lady, the kind you could get real used to if she was around all the time. He dismissed further thoughts with a quick shake of his head. They'd be 2,500 miles apart and long distance romances never worked. No sense spending time thinking about that or anything else. He vowed to stay focused on what he had facing him next week at Johns Hopkins. The open road before them was smooth and Mark settled in for another long day behind "Stanley's" leather-wrapped steering wheel.

Mark was genuinely looking forward to catching a spring training baseball game in Tucson. The Tribe, as folks from northern Ohio called the team, wintered at Hi Corbett field in Tucson. He'd looked up the pre-season schedule and found that they were playing a game at Tucson on Wednesday, March 22. What a stroke of luck, he'd thought at the time.

At that very moment Mark saw a roadside marker flash-by that brought him back to reality. It also made him smile. The sign read "Sacramento Wash Canal" one-mile ahead. It set Mark to thinking some devilish thoughts. A half-mile later, he let the Porsche begin to coast, slowing it down gradually, trying not to awaken B.J. As they approached the canal overpass, Mark eased the car off the highway and rolled to a slow stop on the paved shoulder. He picked up the ever-present clipboard and a pen, and quietly stepped out of the driver's seat. Then he slammed the car door with a thud, harder than he needed to!

Without making eye contact with the startled B.J., he went right up to the green and white canal marker sign at the overpass and wrote down "Sacramento Wash Canal" on the itinerary sheets atop the clipboard. He spent a moment or two checking out the twenty-foot deep, mostly empty spillway -- only a trickle of water crept down the center of the concrete trough. Then Mark turned slowly, walked back to the car, got in, and immediately pulled out into the very light traffic.

Mark noticed, peripherally, that B.J.'s eyes had followed him the whole way, with rather keen interest.

Finally, B.J. bit. "What the hell was that all about?"

"All what?" said Mark nonchalantly.

"Why did we stop? The sign there... and all that."

"Oh, that. That was the famous Sacramento Wash Canal..."

"Yeah. So what's so great about that? Are we stopping at every *bridge* now?"

"So, I thought I'd stop and write down the name. After all, we're headed for Washington, D.C., right? It's my guess that President Carter doesn't even know about this Sacramento Wash Canal. And so, when we get to Washington, we'll find a way to tell him about it. And I'm sure when he finds out that we in the United States own another canal, he'll probably want to GIVE IT AWAY TO SOME TIN-HORN COUNTRY, just like he's doing with the Panama Canal!" Mark bellowed.

B.J. had a look of complete incredulity, as if in shock from the venomous bite of Mark's statement. Meanwhile, Mark licked his index finger and tallied one on the imaginary tote board. Score one for canal give-away opponents!

## Thumbin'.

WHEN THEY ARRIVED at Kingman, Arizona, the plan called for them to go east on Interstate-40 for some twenty-three miles, until U.S. Route 93 peeled off to the southeast toward Phoenix. That's where they were headed.

Kingman sits in a high basin, surrounded by mountain peaks. It has a history of being a crossroads, first for the Indians, then for the wagon trains, and finally, for the railroads. Mark made a quick stop at an historical marker that told the story of Conestoga wagon wheel grooves being etched into the volcanic rock. Sure enough, there were ruts worn into the red rock. Pretty damned exciting -- the kind of nitty-gritty history teachers never told you about.

When he got back in the car, B.J. wanted to know what the marker said. Mark told him, "Next time you've actually got to get out of the car and read about it yourself."

"Gee, Stanton," B.J. said sarcastically, "you move your lips when you read, but I never took lip-reading when I was a kid in school."

"They don't teach stuff like this to kids these days and they should. You see Jackson, the public schools just aren't hacking it any more, no matter what Teddy Kennedy says. He, like most of you limousine liberals, gives lip service to public schools and sends all his kids to private schools."

"There we go with the *lips* thing again," B.J. commented.

It was now about 12:45 p.m. and the radio was putting out "The Things We Do for Love" by 10 cc.

As the Porsche approached the I-40-East ramp they noticed a young, rather hefty, dark-skinned girl hitch-hiking. She held out a sign that read "Points East." As Mark and B.J. approached her and the highway on-ramp, she spotted the oncoming sports car and reacted. She stepped right out onto the road. With her right hand, she held her sign aloft. When she saw that the car had two male occupants, with her left hand, she jerked up the front of her gray sweatshirt, revealing what was without any doubt in Mark's mind the largest set of bare breasts he'd ever seen. As if that weren't enough, she began jumping up and down like cheerleader. Mark had to admit that those bouncing beauties certainly got one's attention.

B.J. screamed, "Stop the car! Stop the car! Stanton, stop the freakin' car, will you?"

Mark slowed down. He had no intention of picking up a hitchhiker. Hell, there was no room in the car, anyway -- let alone for a rather large woman.

As the car slowed, B.J. was stammering, "Pull-over. Let's give her a ride!"

"Listen to yourself, Jackson. You're being an ass... where in the hell are you going to put her? There's no room, unless *you* want to get out." The Porsche came to a half-hearted stop, half-on and half-off the highway.

"Hello sugar..." B.J. greeted her.

Having served their purpose by stopping the car, Mark noticed that the *Points East* were stored back in their original, upright, locked and undercover position. B.J. was engaged in conversation outside his passenger window, trying to figure out how to get her into the cramped confines of the car. Mark looked away, rather embarrassed. It was times like these that he was happy not to be considered a lady's man.

"How far you going?" B.J. asked her.

"Due east to Flagstaff," she said. "I go to school at Northern Arizona. Where are you two headed?"

"Southeast to Phoenix," Mark responded, hoping to burst B.J.'s ballooning bubble.

"Well, we can take you east on I-40 to where the Phoenix highway cuts off, can't we Stanton?" B.J. interjected. He turned his attention to the woman, "That is, if you don't mind sitting on my lap," he said with an inviting grin.

She never hesitated. She accepted the offer of a ride. It took three tries for B.J. and the woman to wedge themselves into their side of the front seat and still manage to swing the car door shut.

Three people, crammed into the two small bucket seats, looked like a Barnum & Bailey clown act. In every car that passed by, the drivers gawked at the three of them -- and every car that approached from behind blew past because Mark couldn't get the Porsche going much more than 60 mph.

She must have weighed close to 200 pounds. Nevertheless, B.J. seemed to be enjoying himself. Her name was Martha Mae. She was twenty and a senior at N.A.U., majoring in English. She was an American Indian and a resident of Kingman. She wanted to know about the California license plates. "Are you college guys?" she asked.

After B.J. explained that they were traveling cross-country, she began providing the two of them with a nickel tour of the area. "Those are the Hualapai Mountains," she said trying to free up a forearm to point. "The highest one is more than 8,000 feet." Martha Mae provided a running history of the whole Kingman area.

They learned that she'd been standing there at the interstate ramp all morning. No one had even slowed down for her. Finally, she'd worked up the nerve to try a stunt she'd heard about from a sorority sister. "Wait for a college guy to come along," she said. "A guy who's not traveling with a woman and then... basically, you flash him the goods," she giggled. "So that's what I did when I saw you two coming. And you know, it worked, didn't it?"

"Sure worked on me," said B.J. wiggling his eyebrows.

Twenty minutes and just 15 miles later, one could tell Martha Mae's presence was beginning to sink in with B.J. He found himself forced deeper and deeper into the bucket seat. Martha Mae's personality sort of grew on the two of them. She was an interesting kid, full of humor, and life -- chatting excitedly about getting back from Spring Break to her last semester of college. She looked forward to becoming a high school teacher and seemed to have her career all planned out. Mark was sure, despite the way they met, she would end up being a very positive influence on young people. She would certainly cut an imposing figure for most teen-aged boys.

It turned out to be a long twenty-three miles for B.J. By the time they dropped off Martha Mae at the I-40 and U.S. Route 93 interchange, B.J. was out of breath. As she was extricating herself from the front seat, Mark had to admit that he was glad they'd stopped for her. Although B.J. wanted to pick her up for all the wrong reasons, she didn't seem to care. But Mark did see B.J. stealing near-sighted glances at her mammoth chest when he thought she wouldn't notice. Martha Mae thanked Mark for stopping and wished them good luck on the remainder of cross-country trip.

Apparently, she knew all along that B.J. had been casting sidelong glances at her breasts. As she stepped out of the car, she said something that kind of became a catch phrase for Mark and B.J. "As for you..." she pointed straight at B.J. and said for Mark's benefit, "honey, there ain't no doubt in my mind, but... you'll be in trouble by midnight, tonight!"

With that, she purposefully gave B.J. a wink, lifted her sweatshirt and gave him a final flash of her bare breasts, smiled, and walked off, giggling to herself.

"Smart girl. She knew exactly what she was up to, didn't she?" Mark stated.

"I feel like a mouse that was sleeping with an elephant and the elephant rolled over on me. It'll take me a while to catch my wind, but it was worth it."

Without any further discussion from the breathless B.J., they turned southeast on Route 93, bound for Phoenix. "You Really Got Me," by Van Halen blared out of the radio. It was the last rock'n'roll song they expected they would hear for a while.

## Country Rebels.

THE 160-MILE STRETCH of road between I-40 and Phoenix looked like the remote set of every Western they'd ever seen, either in the movies or on television. As each mile passed Mark swore that he'd seen this mesa before, or that outcropping of rock, or, that landscape as the backdrop for some motion picture "oater." It would have come as no surprise had a troop of blue-shirted U.S. Cavalry suddenly appeared, led by John Wayne himself, singing "She Wore a Yellow Ribbon." And John Ford, a patch over one eye, would be cranking a wide-angle movie camera.

Twenty miles later the only stations the radio could pick up were all country and western. The twangy tunes all started to blend together into one big, on-going, country and western disaster. Based on what they were hearing, over and over, Mark decided what the pivotal elements of any successful C&W song were. A woman has to leave you. There has to be something wrong with your favorite form of transportation, preferably a truck of some kind or another. Whiskey, drugs, a dog or a train are optional accessories. Finally, it's best if someone has been cheatin' on somebody else.

"What's your favorite country song?" B.J. asked. "Hell, Stanton, you probably don't even have one."

"Yes I do. I'm not sure I've got the exact words of the title. But I think it's a real song. There's a line in it that goes: 'When She Left Me, There I Was, Lookin' Out the Window, Through the Pane.'"

"Not bad," said B.J. "How about this one, "I Love Women and I Love Jack Daniel's, And They Both Tried to Kill Me In 1956.' That's my favorite." A moment later he added, "You know, I'll bet we could write our own country and western song, right here and now..."

Mark thought about it. Somewhere a light bulb went on in the left side of his brain. "You know, Jackson, I think your lap-mate Martha Mae may have come up with a great country and western song title... 'I'll Be In Trouble By Midnight.'"

"Not bad. Maybe we could start right there, with that line." B.J. paused. "Now why would some cowboy say 'I'll be in trouble by midnight?'"

"Whoever it was... well, let's just say, he must have had mega-problems," Mark suggested.

B.J. grabbed the clipboard, set aside the itinerary sheets, tore a few pages off the yellow legal pad, and started jotting down ideas. "How does our song go?"

"Well, the chorus could go, 'Oh, I'll be in trouble by midnight. Oh, I'll be in trouble tonight.'"

After forty minutes, including several abortive attempts at differing rhyming schemes, two dozen balled up yellow sheets of paper on the floor mat at B.J.'s feet, and illegible Jackson scribbling all over the wrinkled legal pad, the duo came up with a first-cut at the opening verse. B.J. opened it with a harmonica prelude...

*I was a-drivin' home with Rover*
*A-sippin' a long neck'd beer*
*Damn train bore down upon me*
*So I threw 'er in higher gear*
*We got stuck up on the crossing*
*And what happened next - ain't clear.*

They were quite satisfied that this song was the start of a new career for both of them. Mark turned off the radio, trying to concentrate on coming up with the lyrics of the second verse.

It was a very warm March day in the mid-80's as they worked their way to the southeast toward Phoenix and Interstate-10. The two drove along a completely deserted highway. One signpost pointed to Signal, Arizona. Later, at the tiny village of Wikieup they stopped for cold six-pack; it was brain fuel for creative minds. A few more miles down the road, they passed a weathered road sign that led to a town called Bagdad, some 15 miles away. Not one car passed in either direction.

B.J. and Mark haggled back and forth about lyrics for the country and western song. Each tried to improve the other's lame lines, hammering them into the stilted meter of a new song.  About an hour and a half later, some 10 miles before Wickenburg, Arizona -- just north of the Merritt Pass -- they locked-in the second verse of song.  Then two grown men, singing at the top of their lungs, wailed out the newest verse:

*I was a-hearin' horns a-blarin'*
*When the train hit truck, whole-hog*
*I re-call my flyin' up*
*But my poor brain's all in-a fog*
*Now it's been an hour, since we hit*
*An' I still-ain't -- seen the dog.*

*Oh, I'll be in trouble by midnight*
*Oh, I'll be in trouble tonight*
*I'll be in trouble by midnight*
*That's midnight - midnight, tonight.*

Song writing, like everything else seems like a relatively easy thing to do until you have to actually sit down and write one.  They weren't great at it but they were having some fun and it sure helped to pass the time.  Until they started this mellifluous project, Mark thought B.J. was beginning to get a little bored with the sameness of the scenery.

The current terrain consisted of the vermilion and purple backdrop of the Harcuvar Mountains, which stood well off to their right.  Mark pondered the familiar crest line.

"Remember yesterday what I said about Laurie and the Grand Tetons?"

"Yeah," responded B.J.

"Well, after meeting your new friend Martha Mae, I may have to retract my earlier statement, about being the best West of the Tetons.  Jackson... I've only been with you two days in a row now.  And each day a well-endowed woman has, first unknowingly and now knowingly, revealed her boobs for me to see.  I've got to ask, is it like this for you everyday?"

"Some days are better than others," was all he said.

They pulled off the road near Wickenburg twice.  The first time, they stopped to get B.J. a bite to eat and to loosen their bones.  Mark skipped lunch, still feeling a little punk.

The second time, a few miles down the road, Mark stopped to read another roadside historical marker.  Even B.J. jumped out, jogged around a bit -- no doubt to work off the hotter-than-expected chili he'd downed. The marker described the history of the town: *Founded in 1863 by Henry Wickenburg, a Prussian immigrant who ended up discovering the state's richest gold and silver mine -- the Vulture Mine.* B.J. yawned.

Departing Wickenburg, they headed down a perfectly straight stretch of road that ran for more than fifty miles. The roadway descended in altitude and aimed due southeast into the Valley of the Sun and the heart of Phoenix.

Mark glanced at his watch; it was about 3:30 p.m. His thoughts turned to Tucson, still some three hours ahead, and his plans for attending a spring training game. "I'm really looking forward to baseball season..." he said. "...Even though the Tribe came in fifth place last year. It's been twenty-three years since we've seen the pennant, but I still follow them. I'm a diehard. I don't give up on them until they're mathematically eliminated."

"Cleveland Indians fans and Wiley-the-Coyote fans are gluttons for punishment," B.J. said. "Luckily, most seasons you only have to wait until *'Cinco de Mayo'* for the Tribe to be mathematically eliminated from contention."

"Yeah, some years that's true, but at least we have a team. Not like Washington, D.C. I guess I never really missed having Major League Baseball around until I lived in Washington. The damned Senators left town twice. The first time they left for Minnesota and the second time in 1971 for Texas. I remember being at the last game in RFK Stadium. Ted Williams was our manager. Frank Howard hit a home run. And before the game was over the fans took to the field. The Senators ended up having to forfeit the game. I recall getting Tim Cullen's autograph right before the game started."

"Washington got screwed by Bob Short, the owner. He just flat stole the team out of town," B.J. attested.

Mark agreed. Baseball still had a lot to learn about how to treat the fans. The minute either the owners or the players started taking the fan for granted, they did irreparable harm to the game. "My advice for the powers-that-be in baseball and those running the players union, is to stay true to the game and the money will follow. He who forgets this rule and starts thinking money first, will, in the long run, lose out on the money, honey."

B.J. could only nod in complete concurrence, for once.

Arizona's "Valley of the Sun" revealed itself before them in a warm afternoon glow. Mark had traveled to the area before, but had always arrived at the airport. Mark thought the Phoenix airport had the neatest name: Sky Harbor. The growth of the metro area was as pronounced as that of Las Vegas. Some twenty miles out of town they passed the first of many retirement communities, Sun City. As they approached a road sign designating the city limits of tiny Surprise, Arizona, they noticed saw a pair of coyotes crossing the highway. Their desert-tan fur coats camouflaged them effectively until they appeared against the black asphalt background of Route 93. The duo burst into view and trotted across the road, heads hung low, tongues dangling. Even at a distance they both cast a lean, hungry and dangerous look in the direction of the oncoming Porsche. Mark thought coyotes were nocturnal creatures, howling at the full moon. Perhaps these two were mad dogs, fevered and frothing, wandering about aimlessly in the noonday sun. Rabid coyotes? Now there was something he'd never have seen flying on an airplane or sitting behind a desk in the big city. "Hey Jackson, check out the canines," he said.

"Holy shit, those are real coyotes! For a minute there I thought you were talking about the two woofers in the Chevy," he said pointing to the two very sizable women packed into the car they were about to pass. It was the first car they'd seen in an hour's time.

Mark and B.J. continued down Route 93 through the bedroom communities of Peoria and Glendale, descending deeper into the valley. Thousands of Canadians and Midwesterners, fed up with winter weather, flocked to these sun-bleached suburbs each fall for the season or, maybe, for the rest of their lives. The collective impact of their migration on the valley was astounding. Squares of walled-off suburbia were being carved out, checker-boarding the desert landscape. Between beige stucco-walled and orange tile-roofed conclaves were patches of wild desert complete with sagebrush, cacti and critters.

Mark thought back to his first trip to Phoenix and to the barbecue steak dinner he'd enjoyed at Pinnacle Peak's patio, a rustic cowboy steak house up in the northern mountains overlooking the valley. He stared far to his left trying to pick out the unique rock formation, somewhat like a smokestack, that inspired the name, Pinnacle Peak. If an unwitting visitor happened to wander into the place wearing business attire, his necktie was summarily cut off, just below the knot, by the patio's prospector-look-alike greeter. It wound up being nailed to the rafters of the either the barroom or dining area. Mark had been amazed that there were literally thousands of gaudy half-cravats hanging there, many with business cards stapled to them. Pinnacle Peak's patio was definitely a tourist trap that even locals liked to visit on occasion, no doubt with pompous, over-dressed vacationing in-laws in tow.

"Knowing Me, Knowing You" by ABBA was playing on the radio.

## Eggs Agnew.

PERHAPS THE BEST-NAMED pile of rock in all America hails from the Phoenix suburbs, Camelback Mountain. Damn, but it looks like a giant camel just plunked down on its ass, somewhere northeast of Phoenix, between downtown and Scottsdale. Mark considered it the "easiest to identify" natural landmark in America.

On Mark's first visit to town, back in February of 1971, he'd stayed at Del Webb's Mountain Shadows Resort, on Lincoln Drive, on the north side of Camelback Mountain. He was doing political advance work for the Republican Party. Then-Vice President Spiro T. Agnew had been invited to Phoenix as the main speaker at a Lincoln Day fund-raising dinner. Agnew provided the conservative crowd with the usual Republican red meat, attacks on the liberal news media. But that evening's star attraction was none other than ol' "Blue Eyes" himself, who crooned after-dinner for the $1,000 per-plate fat cats.

Listening to Mark's set-up, B.J. settled in knowing another of Stanton's advance man war stories was coming.

"At the end of the evening, Sinatra invited some dignitaries, including the Vice-President, Republican National Chairman Senator Bob Dole and others to his hotel suite for a nightcap. As the advance man, in charge of the hotel set-up, I accompanied the Veep to the impromptu soiree, along with his ever-present Secret Service contingent. As a twenty-four year-old I was in heaven just getting a chance to meet a big Hollywood name let alone getting to have a drink in his suite."

"How many people are we talking about?" B.J. asked.

"Maybe twenty," said Mark. "Anyway, after forty minutes of chitchat in the suite, the big shot checks his watch, rises from the chair and says 'Look, 'I'll see you all at breakfast in the morning. There'll be a table under my name in the dining room... 8 o'clock tomorrow morning.' So we all took a hint, and left.

"Next morning at eight sharp, we walk into the dining room... the Veep, the secret service and two aides, including me. We waltz right past the nervous *maitre d'*, who's on his tiptoes, peering down the hall, on the lookout for the star entertainer. The poor fellow was so obsessed with the crooner that he didn't even recognize that the Vice-President of the United States of America, wearing casual attire, had just walked right past him!"

"No kidding?" said B.J. in mock horror, "was the *maitre d'* still wearing his wristwatch after Agnew walked by?

"No I am not kidding." Mark ignored B.J.'s taunt. "Then we seated ourselves at a long table. The waiters came around, started pouring coffee and juice, and begin taking breakfast orders.

"About half-way through the ordering process, in comes Frankie with his personal entourage. The star is being fawned over by the *maitre-d'* as he goes to the head of the table and is handed a tall leather-bound menu. While the big shot is thinking over his selection, a waiter is taking Agnew's order of eggs, over easy, with bacon, crisp. The impatient waiter, who is peering over the Veep's shoulder, has not a clue as to whom he is waiting on... just another tall fellow with slicked-back, silver hair. The *maitre d'*, the waiters, everyone's eyes are on the star. After the last order, which was being taken right in front of the celebrity, the *maitre-d'* comes to the head of the table. 'Mr. Sinatra, sir, what would *you* like for breakfast?' he asks.

"You know what the big shot says? Even after he's just watched a bunch of people, including the Vice-President of the United States, order their favorite breakfasts, he slams his big menu closed and says real loud, stirring one index finger around to indicate everyone, 'Wilbur... eggs Benedict all around.'"

"Man... what an ego," said B.J.

"Jackson... there was this momentary pause, and then everyone exhaled. And then we just... went along with it. Like, gee, why didn't I think of that?' Can you believe it? The *maitre d'* rushes off to the kitchen, probably to cancel a dozen orders. I looked over to Agnew, out of the corner of my eye, figuring that I might learn something here. The Veep is looking straight ahead at no one in particular, with a faint grin, the kind you wear while someone is explaining to you that your fly is open. Then I noticed that he sort of pursed his lips, as you might do when you've just realized that the meal you were looking forward to, the very one you'd just ordered, is now gone, to be replaced by someone else's idea of breakfast one-upsmanship. I'll never forget that moment."

"So what did *you* end up having for breakfast?"

"Cute. Real cute, Jackson. My stories are as pearls cast before swine."

"Oink.

Mark simply said, "Doo-bee... doo-bee... doo..."

## Don't Knock the Rock.

THEY GOT ON Interstate 10-East in the middle of downtown Phoenix. Just past 4:30 p.m., they passed the Sky Harbor Airport. It was a pleasant change, seeing other cars on the road -- the Phoenix rush hour was just beginning. As Mark glanced over at the airport, he thought about what a long, boring flight it was from here to Washington, D.C. It was an even longer drive, but, right now as he was tooling down the freeway, he figured he wouldn't trade places with any passenger in that building. He lit up another Salem and savored the moment.

"So what could your god-forsaken, always-in-last-place, Cleveland Indians possibly have going for them this season?" B.J. asked, trying to bone up for the game, probably his first dose of professional baseball in years.

"Well, based on ending up in fifth place last year, the aspirations of Indians' fans tend to be somewhat muted this season. But I would think, with a few breaks, we'll make a real race of it, for fourth place. Andre Thornton is our clean-up hitter. He managed to air out 28 fast balls last season. Buddy Bell's still playing the hot corner... he's okay. Rico Carty is the designated hitter. But what we lack in power, slugging, batting average and speed we more than make up for with a dearth of pitching talent. The front office traded Dennis Eckersley, who won some 13 or 14 games, to the Red Sox for someone I've never heard of, named Paxton. Middle of last season they bounced Frank Robinson as field manager and brought in the always-nebulous Jeff Torborg. That's about all I was able to glean this winter from the San Francisco papers, but it's probably more than you wanted, or needed, to know about the Cleveland Indians."

Mark had had a love-hate relationship with "the Tribe" since the 50's. As a kid, he listened to virtually all their games on his trusty transistor radio -- even the late-night West Coast games. He was as loyal as a fan gets by age twelve. He busted butt in school because, in Cleveland, if an elementary or high school student got Straight A's, the team rewarded a kid seven pairs of tickets to ho-hum games and Sunday double-headers. That was one major advantage of living on the shores of Lake Erie, no one but Jim Brown and the Cleveland Browns could fill up the 76,000-seat Municipal Stadium. So, the Tribe always had tickets to give away. Then in 1960, the Indians broke Mark's heart when they traded the team's only hero, Rocky Colavito, to the Detroit Tigers for Harvey Kuenn. Rocky had been the American League's home-run king the year before; Kuenn had been the batting champion. The season after the trade neither player did anything spectacular for their new team. It turned out to be a very bad deal all around.

As a superstitious baseball fan, Mark knew that the Red Sox had learned to live with a World Series curse known as the curse of the "Bambino." The Bosox had never won a World Series since trading away Babe Ruth to the Yankees, back in the mid-1920s. Now that was what he referred to as a big league curse. His Indians, he was afraid, had some type of a play-off curse called up on them, too, the curse of the "Rocco." The Tribe had never gotten to, let alone won, a World Series since trading Colavito away. It had been seventeen straight seasons now. This, too, was becoming a major league curse. "Don't Knock the Rock" had been a famous line around Cleveland when Rocky struck out. Like the Bambino, he would always come back. Mark could still recall a game on radio from Baltimore, where Rocky tied the Major League record by hitting four consecutive home runs in one game. Some things about baseball are just seared into a kid's brain.  Somehow, it's just not the same for kids today.  Now-a-days soccer is all the rage -- but no one remembers soccer games.  They don't even score four times in a weekend series in soccer.  Boring game.

Needing an excuse for a stretch of the legs around 5:30 p.m. Mark pulled off the highway at a rest area, an overlook which boasted a scenic vista.  The roadside park provided a view of Arizona's Picacho Peak.  From what one could read on the metal plaque, mounted securely on a granite boulder, a lava-flow formed the spectacular mountain before them.  The peak had served as a famous landmark, to the Spanish explorers and missionaries, to the Indians, and most recently to the westward-bound pioneers as they migrated through this territory.  This history stuff was really exciting -- kept one awake.

Some forty-five minutes later, with B.J. napping quietly, they entered the outskirts of Tucson.  "Sir Duke" by Stevie Wonder was on the Blaupunkt radio.

Mark was scanning the horizon looking for the tell-tale signs of a ballpark, the tall metal stanchions holding banks of brilliantly lit flood lights -- an easy sight to spot just an hour or so before dusk, but saw nothing on the Tucson horizon.  So he stopped at a Union-76 gas station to fill-up and ask directions.

"Some kind'a car you got there," said the pump attendant.  He was wearing a rather worn and oily baseball cap affixed with the Indian's Chief Wahoo logo on it.

"Thank you.  Just fill 'er up with high test, will you?"

Chief Wahoo, a red-faced grinning Indian in a pinstriped uniform, headband and feather, swinging a bat, had been the Cleveland Indians' cartoon mascot since 1914.  Now American Indian leaders were attempting to re-write the white man's history and geography books.  Everything from the names of mountains, like Squaw Peak, or Squaw Valley, to getting a ball club to drop the harmless and appealing happy Indian mascot, was part of the revisionist history process.  If the revisionists had an inkling as to what they were talking about, they would have known that the Cleveland Indians were called the "Indians" because of Louis "Chief" Sockalexis, a American Indian star performer from the previous team, the Cleveland Spiders.  So when Cleveland felt it needed to rename its American League franchise to draw more fans they chose "Indians," in honor of Sockalexis and two other Native Americans from the previous team. According to Mark, this was just another perfect example of why this know-nothing liberal obsession with re-writing American history, without a clue as to the real facts, was so asinine.

When Mark returned from the rest room, the attendant wanted to know what color the Porsche was.

"Pearl gray."

"Kind of has a blue tint to it, don't you think?"

"Blue? No, I don't think so." Trying to change the subject, Mark asked, "Can you give me directions to Hi Corbett Field?"

"Sure can. But there's no sense going over there. There's no Indians game tonight. It's rained out."

Mark cocked his head, slowly looked up at a perfectly clear early evening sky.

"Rained-out? You desert rats must be afraid of dew," said B.J.

The reference to rats drew a grin. "No, more of a swamp-out," the kid said. "Some lame-brain at the ballpark left the sprinkler system on last night, all night long, and the infield's a muddy mess. They 'bin talkin' about it on the radio all day. Next home game's tomorrow night."

"Are you absolutely sure about that?" asked Mark. "We've come a long way to see a game."

"Positive..."

Mark groped for a response to this devastating news. Over his shoulder he heard the sound of B.J. ripping up papers. Mark turned to see what he was doing. B.J. was tearing up Mark's day-by-day, hour-by-hour itinerary sheets -- the trip schedule he had worked on for days.

"Jackson, you Nimrod. What the hell do you think you're doing?"

"There's absolutely no use for this scheduling shit anymore," said B.J. tearing the carefully typewritten pages into bits of white confetti. "I've had it! I'm tired of hauling ass from one pit stop on the map to the next one, just to keep up with these piss-ant pieces of paper," he said with his voice rising in mock indignation. "And, I'm tired of riding shotgun on this runaway stagecoach," he said. "From here on out, this trip is no longer a whistle-stop tour. From where the sun stands in the sky, from this moment forward, we're going to drift back to Washington... if you catch my drift, Stanton. No more time checks and checkpoints. From now on... we're going to let loose. Besides, if the truth be known, you don't have to be in Washington for a job, you don't even have an interview set up yet."

The gas station attendant, who was the only audience for B.J.'s animated tirade, was grinning from ear to ear, just like ol' Wahoo on his cap. The kid took the confetti offered by B.J. into his baseball cap and emptied it with a flourish in the trash barrel.

"Thank you, Jackson. I wish you'd tell me how you really feel more often. I guess I just didn't realize the pent-up frustrations you accumulated sleeping through the better part of three states since yesterday morning."

"Sleep brings out a lot of demons," B.J. shook his finger at Mark.

Mark's carefully laid plans had called for the two of them to arrive in Tucson, check into any clean-looking motel near the ballpark and to catch the game, have a few hot dogs and beers, and overnight. Now he really didn't know what to do. Here it was 6:30 p.m. and the schedule was shot to hell. He turned to B.J.

"Jackson. This fellow swears there's no game tonight. And since you're into drifting, I'm asking you, right now, what exactly do you want to do?"

"Hey Moose, let loose..." was all he said as he turned away from Mark.

So Mark got directions and drove to Hi Corbett Field anyway. For him, there are few things in this world sadder than an empty ballpark. They parked, got out and nosed around. The lights were on, but the place was deserted, save for a few members of the ground crew trying to sop-up the muddy infield. Mark left B.J. leaning against the third base fence and went back to the car. He returned with two baseball mitts and a scuffed-up ball. They played catch in the bullpen along the left field foul line until their arms throbbed. The ground crew quietly went about their work listening to a Bonnie Tyler record blaring over the ballpark's public address system.

No one bothered them.  Mark and B.J. tossed the ball.  The ground crew raked the dirt.  All the while Bonnie wailed "It's A Heartache."

A short time later they got back on I-10-East leaving Tucson behind.  The town, which is surrounded on four sides by mountain ranges, was witnessing a breathtaking sunset that evening.  Mark kept one eye on the beautiful dusk in the rearview mirror.

B.J. reentered his orbital mode.  "Houston, this is Eagle-Feather-One.  We have encountered a minor technical glitch up here.  It seems our multi-synchronous orbital gyro is way off-line.  This will necessitate a major change to our flight plan and our pre-programmed rendezvous with coordinates Holiday Inn.  Due to unforeseen difficulties at Point Tucson, relating to the nocturnal venting of H-2-O, it is mandatory that we make an unscheduled burn and re-calculate our trajectory for a much wider orbit.  Over."

"Eagle-Feather-One.  This is Cap-Com-Houston.  Say again."

"Garble-garble-garble... Eagle-One... Unbelievable sun spot activity... Can't read your message... Severe pitching and yawing... Garble-garble.  Over."

"Eagle-Feather-One.  Boys, if you can hear this message, please know a grateful nation is holding its breath until we hear back from you. Over."

*B.J. really does live in a fantasy world*, Mark thought.  There is no way you would know that about him, unless you knew him well.  After rooming with him at Dewey Beach, Mark felt that behind those tinted granny glasses is one truly loose, very unusual, son-of-a-wild cur.

Some forty miles later they pulled off I-10-East at the Route 80 interchange.  The road leading south went to the famous frontier town of Tombstone.  They discussed driving the remaining twenty-six miles in the general direction of Mexico to visit the Old West town, but the sun was down and they didn't think they'd be able to see much of the Boot Hill Graveyard or the OK Corral.  So instead, the twosome opted for dinner at Martinez's truck stop dining room.  The aromas that wafted over the parking lot were awesome.  B.J. opted for the barbecued pork chop smothered in onions. Not being that hungry, Mark nursed a milk shake and nibbled on a grilled ham and cheese sandwich.

Mark found himself staring at the road map. After the soggy ballpark episode, he tried to recalculate where they could stop and spend the night. Meanwhile, B.J. kept checking-out the checkout girl.

B.J. knew he'd discouraged Mark by tearing up the itinerary and supposed he ought to offer a few alternatives. "You know what I'd like to do?" said B.J.

"Let me guess, Jackson?" Mark looked around then froze with his nose pointed toward the girl behind the cash register.

"Not bad, but that's not what I meant. I'd like to go all the way to El Paso tonight and then, first thing tomorrow morning, go over to see the Carlsbad Caverns in New Mexico."

"Well, let's see..." Mark sat up. "El Paso is about two-hundred and fifty miles away. We probably wouldn't get in there until after midnight. Carlsbad, which I must point out was never on the official itinerary, has got to be at least another 170 miles or so, east of El Paso. That would take us some three hours out of our way, plus another hour or so to tour the cave, right?"

"Who cares? What's with the obsession with time? We don't have any official reason to be in San Antonio Thursday night, do we? Answer me this. Do we have to meet anyone in particular? At any particular time? At any particular place?"

"No. Not really," Mark grudgingly admitted.

"Well, then I say we head for El Paso tonight and ride over to Carlsbad tomorrow." He paused. "Stanton, are we driftin' yet, or aren't we? What's the sense in racing across the country? You actually wanted to *see* the United States, didn't you?" he asked pointedly.

Mark thought about it. It was B.J.'s trip too. He answered, "Then I guess that we be *driftin'*."

"Don't Leave Me This Way," by Thelma Houston was thumping from the jukebox as Mark left the truck stop's restaurant.

### Chico... buddy, buddy.

AS MARK EXITED down the steps into the asphalt parking lot he noticed some activity where "Stanley" was parked.

When they'd arrived, there had been few cars in the parking lot. Now scores of souped-up, customized low-rider cars were parked all over the place. Under the glow of tall metal light poles, he could see a knot of teenagers sitting atop the cars, having an impromptu party. A smaller group had gathered around Mark's Porsche. At first, he wasn't sure if he should approach them. B.J. had gone to the carryout counter to see if he could find a cold six-pack to go. And, from the looks of the cashier girl, Mark was sure he had other business on his mind.

He walked around the outer ring of cars and teenagers, casually trying to sense what the gathering was all about. It didn't take long to figure it out. The main subject of conversation was the Porsche 924. From the snippets of conversation he heard, it seemed that most of the teens had never seen one. Mark figured that not many of the new Porsches had passed through this corner of the world. But from the tenor of the group, it seemed okay to step into the light in front of the circle of admirers and claim ownership.

"Hey, buddy, buddy," the group's ring leader asked as Mark approached, "wha' chew got in there?"

From the looks of the guy asking the question, Mark was not now, nor ever going to be, this guy's "buddy." "What do you mean?"

"Un'er the hood, man. Wha' chew got for an engine in thees here thin'?" asked the ringleader, a young Chicano wearing what used to be called a *dago* undershirt -- the kind with shoulder straps.

"Oh, I honestly don't know, I'm really not into engines and all that stuff," Mark said with a newfound sense of embarrassment. The statement brought on dismissive snickers from the motley crew. Hell, he'd never even asked a thing about the engine, its cubic inches, or its horsepower, when he bought the car. Right now it seemed pretty stupid not to know what type of engine was in the car he was driving.

"Hombre... why don' chew open 'er up and let us take a look in 'ere," said a second, much more menacing-looking fellow. This one was completely shirtless, a tattooed guy, with a toothpick dangling from his lower lip.

Ordinarily, Mark might open the hood and let an admirer take a look at the power plant. A Porsche engine was an impressive sight to see, all that equipment shoehorned under the hood, packed in without a square inch to spare – somewhat like a woman's suitcase.

*But was that all this mob wanted? A mere peek at the engine? Or were they about to jump him, steal the car and everything Mark and B.J. had stowed in it? Or, were they about to cut the car's ignition wires leaving them stranded out here in the middle of nowhere?*

Mark felt a growing sense of paranoia. Up until they'd asked him to open the hood, he thought he could handle this bunch. But now, he feared that opening the hood could make him and his partner very vulnerable.

*Where the hell was Jackson*? Probably trying to hustle that Chiquita behind the counter. He went to get the damned beer at least ten minutes ago, Mark steamed. Now here Mark was, outnumbered by Pancho Villa and his militia, twenty-to-one, feeling very surrounded. Mark's mind raced. Even if he managed to get into the car, he wasn't sure he could maneuver the Porsche out of the parking lot, what with all the low-rider cars parked helter-skelter. Besides, Mark couldn't leave anyway without B.J.

*Where in the hell was Jackson? And what did these punks want? What was he supposed to do?* Mark felt an intensifying pain in his stomach.

He took his sweet time getting over to the car door, stalling by patting his pockets, as if trying to locate the car keys. Maybe he could fake leaving the car keys inside the dining room, giving him a chance to return to the safety of the truck stop and to find B.J. But losing the keys and going back to the dining room would make him look really stupid, or really scared. Mark wasn't sure that would be the right thing to do in these circumstances. So, he quickly opened the car door and jumped in behind the wheel. With his left elbow, he surreptitiously pushed down on the door lock button. No one in the group seemed to notice. Now they were gathering around the front of the car, anticipating a view of the engine. Mark hesitated. First he screwed around in the glove compartment, shuffling maps -- stalling for time. Then there were catcalls, asking him to pop the hood. His suspicions were rising along with his blood pressure. Opening the hood was such a simple thing to do. But he was torn. *Was he walking right into a set-up?*

Mark's newest "buddy" in the strapped undershirt now began pounding on the hood with his open palms, as if it were a bongo drum. "Way to go Chico!" Mark heard another say. Then two other goons started rocking the car from side to side. The rest were egging them on. Mark's mood was now changing from fear to anger.

"What's the matter 'Parnelli?' Don't want to show these guys the giant gerbil on the treadmill you got under the hood generating all that Porsche power?"

*Jackson!*

B.J. stepped out of the shadows and into the circle of light. The crowd opened up. A shapely, dark-haired denim-clad woman accompanied B.J. His crack about the gerbil on a treadmill got a comical reaction from the mob. In one arm he carried a brown bag full of beer, and with the other arm he was squiring the beautiful dark skinned lass through the ring of teenagers. Upon closer inspection, she was the same girl who had, up until a minute ago, been working behind the truck stop's cash register.

"Consuelo, this is Mark Stanton. Stanton, say hello to Consuelo Martinez... and please turn on your lights and open the damn hood, will ya'... the suspense is killin' us?"

Consuelo was truly packed into her Wranglers. She seemed the perfect soul mate for B.J. Everyone seemed to know her. Mark began to relax a little. He opened the car window and pulled open the hood latch. The hood light went on revealing the engine. The "ahs" followed.

"These two are driving all the way cross-country," Consuelo announced to the group. "This one is William. I guess you already met Mark," she added.

"Neat-o," said the Chico buddy-buddy in the undershirt. "Where are you guys goin'?"

B.J. responded with, "To La-la-land-East, to Disneyland-on-the-Potomac, to Chocolate City, to Washington, D.C."

At that point the tattooed guy with the toothpick stuck his head in the car window. He wanted to see how high the speedometer went.

"It goes up to a hun'red and ceex-ty! Can you be-leef it?"

B.J. was standing by the right front bumper. He and Mark could see each other, but the upright hood blocked Mark's view of most of the group. They made eye contact. B.J. could sense that Mark had been worried. Mark's furrowed brow and stare also conveyed to B.J. that it was time to leave.

"Consuelo darlin', I must admit, you hang out with a very entertaining crowd. There's nothing Stanton and I would rather do than to sit around and drink beer all night with you guys, but we gotta' saddle up and get to El Paso tonight," said B.J., giving her shoulder a slight squeeze. "By the way, can any of you speed demons tell me if there are any cops between here and the New Mexico state line?" he added.

"No way, man. J'ees let 'er rip all the way!" Chico said. The rest of the group laughed a knowing laugh.

That told Mark all he needed to know. After good-byes and gimme-fives all around, the twosome departed. They turned east on the highway. "Thanks, Jackson," Mark said, "you came through at just the right time. It was just beginning to get a little bit hairy. I was getting pissed off."

"Well, Stanton my man, you can thank Consuelo for the dramatic sense of timing. While we were talking inside, she noticed the crowd gathering around the car. She suggested we walk out together to make sure no one got out of line. See, her daddy owns the truck stop and she knows most of that crowd pretty well... went to school with them."

"One of these days, Jackson, I'm going to figure out just how you do it. *'This one is William...'* he mimicked Consuelo's voice. "I think I would have barfed if she'd said 'sweet William.' Sweet William, the guy with a girl in every port," Mark added.

B.J. grabbed a bottle of beer and spoke into his makeshift Gemini microphone. "Houston, this is Eagle-Feather-One, we have just made incidental contact with an all-new alien lifeform, the *low-rider* people! After a close encounter of the sticky kind, we are fighting to get back on course. Please advise. Also, now that he has come down from his close encounter, we will be jettisoning Captain Stanton's soiled undergarments in hyper-space, en route to the planet, El Paso."

"Eagle-Feather-One. This is Mission Control, Cap-Com-Houston. Did you happen to get a photograph of the life form? Over."

"Negative, Houston. But we suggest that NASA check with the Cochise County, Arizona, Sheriff's Department for a possible photo match of life form named 'Chico, buddy-buddy.' Be on the lookout for a gold tooth and a tell-tale tattoo, which says, 'Just let 'er rip.' Over."

"Cochise County? Roger Eagle-One." B.J. smiled at his own creativity.

"I'm Gonna Take Care of Everything" by Rubicon came on the radio.

## Country Roads.

THIRTY MINUTES LATER, about 8:15 p.m. they stopped at a rest area to unload empties and to study the minutiae on a well-stationed roadside marker. Mark whipped out his trusty flashlight and homed in on the marker plaque. It noted that nearby Willcox, Arizona, was a major cattle shipping center on the railroad line. Also, the surrounding region was great apple-growing region sporting a crop of world-famous Granny Smiths. According to the plaque, there were more than one million apple trees growing within 30 miles of Willcox. B.J., as usual, remained in the front seat, unimpressed with the historical and agricultural information.

After they got back on the road Mark attempted to impart social studies on B.J. "Do you know any of the history of this real estate we're driving through?"

"Is this a test? What if I guess right? Tell us Don Pardoe what our guests win if they answer correctly..."

"Well, Jackson, my friend, you're taking this the wrong way. All I am saying is that we are riding around on a piece of history known as the Gadsden Purchase. The United States bought lower Arizona and New Mexico for $10 million, in 1853, from the Mexican government. The original idea was to have a non-mountainous right-of-way for the transcontinental railroad, even though they didn't get around to building the Southern Pacific through here until 1893. In fact, I believe that the Gadsden Purchase was the final boundary adjustment of the lower 48 states."

"Just amazing, Stanton. Maybe we ought to put a Smokey-bear hat on you and mount your over-educated head on one of these historical markers and let you answer questions all day. How the hell do you remember all this geographical trivia?"

"First of all, Jackson, eight years of Jesuit education comes in handy – four in high school and four more in college. Second, you should remember that I taught high school history, geography and social studies for two years, in '69 and '70, waiting to see if my Selective Service lottery number came up for a free, all-expenses paid, two-year visit to Vietnam.'"

As Mark was speaking, a good half-mile ahead in the distance, he saw a police car's distinctive red and blue rotator lights flicker, going around just once. The light snapped off as quickly as it appeared. Then it was pitch-black again.

Without being asked, B.J. said, "I saw it too."

They were doing better than 90 mph and the speed limit was just 55. Mark wanted to slow the car without hitting the brakes and flashing the telltale sign of speeding, bright red taillights. He shifted "Stanley" into neutral and they coasted. B.J. offered to help by sticking his arms out the window and cupping his hands in the wind stream. Mark ignored him and stared at the speedometer.

"Houston, this is Eagle-Feather-One. I am firing emergency retro rockets in order to keep 'Stanton' from getting a speeding ticket," B.J. whispered into his fist.

*Maybe the cop just bumped his light switch... well, you don't have to warn me twice,* Mark said to himself, easing onto the brakes. The speedometer now showed 60 mph.

"Houston," said B.J. "We are declaring an emergency. We are now deploying our heat shield and drogue shoot to slow us down even further, in order to re-enter earth's gravitational field..."

"Eagle-Feather-One. This is Mission Control, Houston... you may want to consider opening your outer doors to slow the capsule down even further... please advise."

"Jackson, quit screwing around... where's that cop car? Wasn't he right about here?" Mark said. They passed a point in the dark where both thought they'd seen the police car's rotating bubble gum lights.

"No, it can't be much farther..."

Just at that point, a huge white spotlight hit the left side of the Porsche -- obviously the very place where the police car was hidden in the underbrush. Again, Mark's eyes flashed to the speedometer; they were down to 55 mph. The officer waved the spotlight up and down at them, as they zipped by

-- a clear signal to slow it down.  Mark peered into the rear view mirror for several miles but no patrol car ever pulled out after them.

After two days on the open road, Mark and B.J. were so used to the feel of speed that 90 mph felt like nothing.  Even though the posted speed limits on Interstate highways had been 55 mph since the energy crisis of 1973-74, no one out west seemed constrained by them.

"What do you think that was all about?" Mark asked.

B.J. mulled the point for a moment and then said, "Stanton, you are one lucky son-of-a-bitch.  I think that one of two things might have just happened.  Either the cop had just settled into his secret radar trap-hiding place, and accidentally bumped the light-bar switch.  We saw his flash and slowed down enough before we passed him, so he just wanted us to know that it was his mistake that let us get away with speeding.  Or, that cop had just settled in with a couple of Big Macs or a bag of glazed jelly doughnuts, bumped the bubble gum light switch by accident, and then didn't want to spill hot coffee all over himself chasing us."

"Not a bad deduction, Sherlock."

"However Parnelli, if you keep up this pace, I guarantee that you'll be in trouble by midnight," said B.J.  With that, he pulled out his mouth organ and started singing the first two verses of their new Country and Western song.  The twosome sang at the top of their lungs, trying to etch the lyrics in their memory banks.

> *I was a-drivin' home with Rover*
> *A-sippin' a long neck'd beer*
> *Damn train bore down upon me*
> *So I threw 'er in higher gear*
> *We got stuck up on the crossing*
> *And what happened next - ain't clear.*
>
> *I was a-hearin' horns a-blarin'*
> *When the train hit truck, whole-hog*
> *I re-call my flyin' up*
> *But my poor brain's all in-a fog*
> *Now it's been an hour, since we hit*
> *And I still-ain't -- seen the dog.*

*Oh, I'll be in trouble by midnight*
*Oh, I'll be in trouble tonight*
*I'll be in trouble by midnight*
*That's midnight -- midnight, tonight.*

"Let's finish off this masterpiece," B.J. declared. With that, he grabbed Mark's clipboard and flashlight.

Over the next two hours, at 80 mph, as they crossed from Arizona into New Mexico, they were able, after much arguing and compromising, to hammer out the final two stanzas of their hit country song. B.J. even improvised a harmonica bridge between verses.

*So I'm a-sittin' here a-sippin'*
*And right now -- I feel no pain*
*But I breakout in goose flesh*
*When I jus' hear, or see, a train*
*And when some hound starts barkin'*
*Like my mind -- it goes insane.*

*Oh, I'll be in trouble by midnight*
*Oh, I'll be in trouble tonight*
*I'll be in trouble by midnight*
*That's midnight - midnight, tonight.*

*Each night I'm roamin' all 'round the town*
*And who-knows but what I'll see*
*One night I seen this la-dy*
*She's a-starin' straight back-at me*
*I went and sat beside her*
*And she whis-per'd, soft to me:*

*Oh, you'll be in trouble by midnight*
*Oh, you'll be in trouble tonight*
*You'll be in trouble by midnight*
*That's midnight - midnight, tonight.*

## I've Often Passed This Way Before.

THEY STOPPED IN Deming, New Mexico, for a stretch of the legs. It was a little after 11:15 p.m. when they got back on the road. A half-hour later, B.J. nodded off to sleep. Mark was becoming quite tired and fighting off more abdominal cramps, but they were just a few miles from Las Cruces and only had 42 more miles to go to El Paso. Mark surrendered to a giant yawn. A few miles later he saw a sign that read "Historical Marker - One Mile Ahead." He slowed down and eased the car into a dark roadside park. The headlight beams showed a couple of picnic tables and a 15-foot tall granite block with a large metal plaque affixed to it. He left the car running, grabbed his flashlight, and went over to read the plaque. There was a lot of text on the marker. It indicated that a few yards to the south, in the pitch-dark field before him, had been a way station for the famous Butterfield Overland Mail stagecoach line.

The night desert air was crisp and Mark could see his own breath vapor in the beam of the flashlight. It felt good to stand up and shake off the cramps.

B.J. awoke, stretched and popped his neck again. "What's it say?" he mumbled from the front seat while rolling down the window.

"It isn't *saying* anything! It's a rather inarticulate piece of granite. But, I have an idea! Why don't you get your lazy ass out here and come read it for yourself. It's too long for me to go back and re-read the whole thing again just for you."

Right in the middle of Mark's sarcastic assault on the hapless, sleepy B.J., another car veered into the small roadside park at a high rate of speed, hitting the gravel driveway with a crunch of noise and a cloud of dust. Mark jumped. The car's headlights blinded the two of them for a moment. Mark's flashlight beam picked up a cloud of dust and exhaust fumes.

"What's going on here?" a gruff voice from inside the car demanded.

"Nothing," Mark said, turning his flashlight toward the car, only to reveal that it was a state police cruiser.

"Then what are you fellows doing here?"

"Nothing much... just reading your historical marker here," Mark said pointing to the huge slab of granite.

Sensing a problem, B.J. got out of the Porsche and stood beside Mark. The officer stood on the far side of his car and aimed his flashlight beam at the two of them, looking them over from head to toe. Then he flashed his light at the

Porsche's license plates. He got back in his car and picked up his two-way radio, leaving Mark and B.J. there, whispering to each other.

"So what's your plan here, Kemo Sabe?" whispered B. J., doing his best "Tonto."

"I'm going to finish reading this marker," Mark said loud enough for the trooper to hear.

"Then what?"

"Then, we're out of here."

A moment later, the trooper climbed out of the cruiser and came around to where they were standing. "You two are a long way from home. Aren't ya'?"

"We're traveling cross-country," said B.J.

Mark noticed that B.J. did not use the "driftin'" word to describe their trip.

The cop wandered over to the Porsche. Peering into each window with his flashlight, he made his way around the sports car.

Mark hoped that B.J. had been hiding his empty bottles under the seat, like he had. B.J. was hoping the same thing about Mark's side of the car.

"What kind of car is this?" the officer wanted to know.

"A Porsche," Mark said.

"What color is this thing?"

"Pearl gray," he answered.

"Looks black to me," the trooper said matter-of-factly, staring at the Porsche symbol on the hood under the throw of his light. Then he turned his attention to the granite marker behind them. "So, this here historical marker... what's *it* say," the officer asked, shining his flashlight right at Mark's chin.

B.J. nudged Mark in the ribs and gave him a sideways glance, fully prepared for a typical Stanton sarcastic retort.

"What is this?" Mark whined. "A road side pop quiz? He pointed to B.J. "He just asked me the same thing. Officer, I've got a good idea... if you don't mind, why don't you pull your car up just a bit, and shine that big ol' spotlight you've got on this plaque. Then we can all read it together."

Surprisingly, the trooper hopped back in his cruiser. He moved it up a couple of feet and aimed his passenger side "alley spotlight" on the towering historical marker. The wash of light illuminated the monument and the entire desert behind it. All three of them could hear the night critters scurrying every which way to get out of the bright beam.

For the next five minutes, things were quiet – except for the background hum of highway traffic passing by at high speed. The three of them stood there, at 11:45 p.m., in the darkness, reading a lengthy roadside historical marker about the Butterfield Overland Mail stage line station.

When they finished Mark added from memory what he could to the marker's story. He noted that the Butterfield Overland Mail existed for only three years, from 1858 until 1861, before the onset of the Civil War. The mail came west from St. Louis through Ft. Smith, Arkansas, to El Paso and then went west of here, ending up in San Diego.

"Officer," said B.J., "I want you to know that traveling cross-country with a frickin' know-it-all like Stanton here is nothing short of a barrel of fun, let me tell you."

"I see what you mean..." the officer directed his aside to B.J. "But ain't that something. You know I must pass this little park about thirty or forty times a week... every week of my life for the last 11 years. I've never stopped, not even once, to read what it says. Who would've thought there was some real history along this sorry-assed stretch of road? Thanks a lot, fella'," he said to Mark, "I'm gonna' bring my two kids by here to learn all about this stagecoach stuff."

At that point there was a loud squawk and an announcement on the patrol car's radio. "Bravo one-niner. We find no warrants issued on a late model, black Porsche with California tags, Papa-Romeo-Sierra-5-1-4. Over."

"Well, gents, enjoy the rest of the ride. It sounds like something I would've liked doing at your age... driving all the way cross-country."

He advised the two of them to stick close to the speed limit through Las Cruces. "Those city limit 'Barneys' love to hassle out-of-towners," he warned. B.J. and Mark thanked him and wished him well on his rounds. As they pulled past him and waved a salute, B.J. could hear him say but four words into his two-way radio: "two sissies from California."

"Right Time of the Night" by Jennifer Warnes beamed down on them from a Las Cruces radio station.

## Talk is Cheap.

AS THEY PULLED out of the roadside park B.J. seemed to liven-up. "Houston, this is Eagle-Feather-One," he chirped out to no one in particular. "At this point in our mission, we are at one with the galaxy. We have seen the face of the ultimate lawgiver. All things are right and just. Over and out."

"Eagle-Feather-One. This is Mission Control, Cap-Com-Houston. We're going to log and store that last transmission. It's as if you've both just had a mutually religious-like experience. Hang in there, Eagle-Feather-One. Over."

B.J. continued to babble, "We're going to get in to El Paso too late for the news. I wonder what else we're missing on TV tonight."

"Look around. See if we still have that Las Vegas paper. See what it says. Maybe Merv Griffin has one of his famous 'theme shows' going tonight." Mark toggled on the car's dome light.

"Here we go... let's see... we're definitely missing some landmark television tonight. For example, there's the 'Life and Times of Grizzly Adams,' a 90-minute special about a guy, who walks around in the woods, rarely bathes and smells like a bear."

"No vast wasteland there!" Mark interjected.

"And now that you've mentioned it, ol' Merv does have a theme show of some sort going on tonight. His guests are, in order of appearance, Billy Graham, Charleton Heston and Mort Sahl. Now there's an eclectic mix. What would you call that?"

"That's an easy theme show. God, Moses, and the devil himself," Mark said, knowing B.J. would defend the liberal comedian.

B.J. shot Mark a dirty look. He read on...

"Our favorite girls, Charlie's Angels, are on tonight... hot...hot...hot."

"Jackson, the answer is Cheryl Ladd, on national television, with the whole world watching... what's the question?"

B.J. looked over but ignored Mark's obvious answer. "Stanton, you remind me of a consultant..."

"How so?"

"A consultant is the kind of guy who knows how to make love to a woman ninety-nine different ways... it's just that he doesn't know any women."

Mark rolled his eyes and turned away.

B.J. continued with the TV listings, "Perry Como has a special called Easter by the Sea."

"Now a show like that could put even a caffeine junkie to sleep. The dual sounds of Perry Como and the ocean... in the dark? That guy *is* a human tranquilizer."

"That's it for television tonight," said B.J., re-folding the paper.

"You know," said Mark, "I think ol' Merv might have something there with that talk show idea. That's the wave of the future. First you had Steve Allen. Then the Tonight Show with Jack Paar. Now it's Carson. On daytime TV, there's Mike Douglas in Cleveland... and then Phil Donahue in Dayton. There's this growing trend toward more and more talk shows. Maybe I should get into that line of work. Hell, I can talk. That's all I do is talk!"

"Speak for yourself," B.J. deadpanned.

They cruised past Las Cruces, New Mexico, and turned south toward El Paso. It was getting near midnight and they'd escaped trouble so far. Heeding the trooper's advice about speed until they passed Las Cruces, Mark finally stepped it up a bit.

When it came to broadcasting, Mark knew something about it. He'd gotten his college degree in radio and television broadcasting. It was a compromise after deciding to leave John Carroll's political science program. The Jesuits and lay professors who lectured in poly-sci were way too liberal for Mark, and they were partisan Democrats. It was the 60's and they didn't appreciate a student who supported Richard Nixon.

Mark advised B.J. that he was willing to stake his career on the future of the broadcast talk show -- not just political talk shows, but current event programs, women's programs, programs that sell things, programs for young people, even programs that average folks might not like much. They would run on network television, or, better yet, on some of these new cable channel systems that were being built around the country.

B.J. settled into an arms-crossed posture braced for what was, hopefully, Mark's last diatribe of the day.

Mark explained that he viewed TV as the old-fashioned circus sideshow updated by technology. The fast-growing cable industry could end up being the next wave for television, if those companies could afford to wire the entire nation. He had no doubt they would pay what it took to drag a copper wire up to everyone's front stoop. The problem would be what would they put on the air? Hell, there was even talk in the papers of starting up a 24-hour, all-news channel.

"I believe in the medium, but not in tedium," said B.J. "Twenty-four hours of all-news... that would be tedium with a capital T. B.J. added, "If I was the producer of an 24-hour, all-news network, I'd probably end up sending out hit-squads of people to stir up trouble, so I'd have some news for my on-air anchors to talk about."

Programming. That was the main problem in Mark's mind. From what he had read there would be scores of television broadcast as well as cable channels and maybe even world-wide TV signals bounced off satellites in the future. But there were too few good ideas about how to fill all that programming time. Lack of programming: that would be the death knell for the medium. Imagine thirty channels coming into every home in America, every night of the week, and then having viewers say to one another, "there's nothing good on tonight." What an insult to the whole industry that would be. Surely, heads would roll.

That's why Mark believed so strongly in talk shows. In his heart, that's what he wanted to do -- to get into creative programming. Invent a new format. Get away from all the monkey-see-monkey-do idiots in network programming. The ivory tower boys with their Ivy League credentials had no clue as to what the real world wanted. They never gave a thought to the men, women and children who lived west of the Hudson, beyond the Beltway, out here, where he and B.J. were driving. Places they only flew over. Those broadcasting bozos needed a breath of fresh air. They needed to get past the six varieties of canned-laughter sit-coms and really begin to educate viewers in an entertaining fashion.

It seemed, to Mark, that if one network came up with a sit-com about someone's pet dog, the very next season the other two competitors would premiere sit-coms about, respectively, a perky house cat and a talking goldfish that lives in the family aquarium. *Real reach-out and pluck-it-out-of-the-air creativity being demonstrated there*, Mark thought. Yes, that's what Mark wanted to do next – to overcome the ivory tower bozos and get into creative television programming.

"You know," B.J. said, "speaking of television, we're kind of like Martin Milner and George Maharis traveling on 'Route 66,' remember that one?"

"Sure I do. They were clean-cut, clean-shaven All-American types... like *me*."

"I can't help it if my hair is naturally curly..."

Now they were talking just to keep one another awake. It was midnight. B.J. brought out the flashlight and the mouth organ, and they wailed on it again.

*I was a-drivin' home with Rover*
*A-sippin' a longneck'd beer*
*Damn train bore down upon me*
*So I threw 'er in higher gear*
*We got stuck up on the crossing*
*And what happened next - ain't clear.*

*I was a-hearin' horns a-blarin'*
*When the train hit truck, whole-hog*
*I re-call my flyin' up*
*But my poor brain's all in-a fog*
*Now it's been an hour, since we hit*
*An' I still-ain't -- seen my dog.*

*Oh, I'll be in trouble by midnight*
*Oh, I'll be in trouble tonight*
*I'll be in trouble by midnight*
*That's midnight - midnight, tonight.*

*So I'm sittin' here a-sippin'*
*And right now -- I feel no pain*
*But I breakout in goose flesh*
*When I jus' hear, or see, a train*
*And when some hound starts barkin'*
*Like my mind -- it goes insane.*

*Oh, I'll be in trouble by midnight*
*Oh, I'll be in trouble tonight*
*I'll be in trouble by midnight*
*That's midnight - midnight, tonight.*

*Each night I'm roamin' all 'round the town*
*And who-knows but what I'll see*
*One night I seen this la-dy*
*She's a-starin' straight back-at me*
*I went and sat beside her*
*And she whis-per'd soft to me:*

*Oh, you'll be in trouble by midnight*
*Oh, you'll be in trouble tonight*
*You'll be in trouble by midnight*
*That's midnight - midnight, tonight.*

Following the advice of Dylan Thomas, they did "not go gentle into that good night."

Mark exited I-10 at the very first interchange inside the El Paso city limits. There was a decent-looking hotel with a flashing vacancy sign. B.J. was tired. Mark was debilitated. He had driven more than 700 miles since 9:45 that morning, and some thirteen hundred miles in the last two days. San Francisco and Las Vegas seemed like last year.

They toted armfuls of Mark's luggage and B.J.'s duffel bag up to the room. Mark did a half-gainer dive, facedown, into one of the sway-backed twin beds.

"Hey drifter, are we going to Carlsbad Caverns in the morning?"

"Sure, Jackson," Mark mumbled. "I'm just batty about the idea. Whatever you say." He was way too tired to quibble.

"Good." Said B.J. "I'll unpack my cowl and turn on the bat light... let them know I'm coming."

# CHAPTER THREE

## Thursday, March 23, 1978

### A River Seeps Through It.

MARK WAS A slut for sleep.  He was a bimbo for blankets.  He was a concubine for covers.  He just couldn't get enough shut-eye.  B.J. did everything short of defibrillators on his chest to get him out of bed at 8:30 a.m.  Mark had slept right where he'd fallen -- face first -- on top of the bed covers, in yesterday's clothes.

Even though the hotel room was on Mark's credit card, on his own initiative B.J. had gone ahead and ordered room service in hopes that the aroma of breakfast might get his friend's heart started.

As a world-weary traveler, Mark knew what to expect from room service in this caliber of motel, but the concept of a room service breakfast seemed a big treat for B.J.  So Mark continued clutching his pillow until the inevitable rap at the door; he was not ready for the prospect of motel food.

A thermos carafe of the inn's finest black coffee arrived with the oh-too-typical room service breakfast of mystery meat sausages, over-cooked scrambled eggs, and half-cooked hash browns enveloped with impregnable sheets of double-strength see-through plastic wrap.  A miniature Tabasco bottle sat on the tray; it was the first time Mark had seen one that small – and it was the best part of the morning's feast.  B.J. was overly impressed that the sleepy waiter had thought to deliver the morning paper; although the steward departed unimpressed with B.J.'s 75-cent tip.

B.J. was bustling with excitement.  The idea of touring Carlsbad Caverns certainly had him atwitter.  He showered and shampooed in less than 10 minutes. Then came the hair drying. He emerged from a steamy bathroom with his curly-perm exploded like Mark had never seen it before; Mark stared at Jackson's new-look hairdo. He looked like that wild guy with three-toned hair who used to be in every crowd shot at all the Monday Night Football games.

"I know... I know," said B.J. "Can't tell if it's due to the combination of shitty shampoo with hard water or just the shitty water."

"It looks like you've been teasing your hair with raw meat," Mark offered.

Mark was packed by the time B.J. was gagging down the last of the *huevos-'rancid'-oes*.

B.J. had chosen yet another ensemble from the Levi Straus collection. Today with just a tad-fewer silver studs than yesterday's western get up. The dark blue shirt he wore almost brought the whole outfit together, in Mark's opinion.

Mark was weak and way too tired to shave. The water pressure in the shower left something to be desired -- like pressure! He pondered Texas. Texans can sure brag about a lot of things, but rivers and water pressure sure aren't two of them. What Lone Star staters call a "river" wouldn't really make it all the way to the "stream" classification back in Ohio. In fact, a Texas river lies somewhere between an Ohio brook and a creek. In Ohio, if you can step over it, or jump over it, it's a rill or a brook. If it's a slow-moving body of water and you can wade through it while not dampening the family jewels, it's a creek. If it requires swimming, then it's a stream. If it requires a boat to traverse, like George Washington crossing the Delaware, then it's a river. River connoisseurs can save time and money by skipping Texas. He couldn't help but think that there is a direct correlation between the breadth and depth of rivers and the resulting water pressure. Also, those persons who like the shampoo to be completely rinsed out of their hair can avoid El Paso.

"Perhaps it should be called the *Rill-O'Grand* instead of the Rio Grande," Mark muttered stroking his facial stubble in the mirror.

The day before them promised to be a beauty -- the weather forecast on the radio was for the high 70's. At just after 9:00

a.m., the two departed the hotel parking lot in the already-hot morning sun and headed south into El Paso on U.S. Route 180. Andy Gibb's "(Love Is) Thicker Than Water" was flowing freely from "Stanley's" Blaupunkt.

Earlier, while B.J. was in the shower Mark picked up a local magazine lying on the dresser. There was a brief history of the area that impressed him. *El Paso del Norte,* the original name of the city -- the northern pass -- was a way stop founded in the 1530's on the old *Camino Real,* the Spanish missionaries' route through the surrounding Franklin Mountains en route from Mexico City to Santa Fe. El Paso is the largest city on the U.S.-Mexican border.

Also, since 1949 El Paso has been home to the U.S. Army's Fort Bliss, a huge tract of land north and east of downtown, out past the International Airport. While the fort has been a major troop-training center since World War I, these days it serves as the U.S. Army's Air Defense Center for guided missile research and combat training.

Eventually, B.J. and Mark turned and headed east-northeast on Montana Road, posted as U.S. Routes 62 & 180, toward Carlsbad, New Mexico. As was becoming the usual morning ritual, B.J. was trying to read the newspaper and shade his eyes from the strong morning sun coming head-on through the windshield.

"What's the good word today, Jackson?" Mark asked, lighting up his first Salem.

B.J. cringed at the aroma of the day's first smoke. He waved the paper like a fan. "First things first. I've been all through the paper. There still is nothing about a plane crash at Edwards Air Force Base."

"Cue the theme from *The Twilight Zone,*" Mark said. "What's the big headline?"

"Farewell," he said. "Headline reads, 'Carter Says Goodbye to Menachem Begin.' Subhead, 'Peace Still Seems Far Away.'"

"The old 'I'd love for you to stay and chat, but don't-let-the-door-hit-you-on-the-ass-on-the-way-out routine. Jimmy's making no new friends in the Middle East."

"Aha," B.J. responded, "but President Carter's good buddy, Mr. Bert Lance, has a new friend. It says here some president of an Arab-controlled bank paid off a $3.5 million loan for Lance, without so much as asking him to sign a note. It looks like he'll be in trouble by midnight."

"Shekels from Heaven. His mother never told him to beware of towel-heads bearing gift camels..."

B.J. continued, "On the southern front, six-term U.S. Senator James Eastland of Mississippi is calling it quits."

"My God, he's been in Congress since the Civil War."

"Searching... searching... Ouch! Stanton, my man, get hold of yourself. I'm afraid I have bad news. On the Caribbean front, I'm sorry to report that Karl Wallenda, 73, patriarch of the Flying Wallenda's circus act, met the Great Ringmaster in the sky yesterday when a gust of wind blew him off a tightrope, ten stories up, between the towers of the Condado Holiday Inn in San Juan, Puerto Rico."

"Well, Jackson, I guess it's down to just *you* now," said Mark, "...the only guy left on the planet working without a net."

"Try living out of a woman's residence while you're working on it and she's paying you to stay there, work there and 'perform' there, so to speak... after that... you can do anything without a net," B.J. said with much conviction. "Searching... searching... in the trivia department, publisher Larry Flynt who was shot on March 6th in Lawrenceville, GA, breathed for the first time without a respirator."

"Of all the people to come back from the dead... Larry Flynt," said Mark, "why not someone who cured a disease, instead of a carrier like Larry Flynt."

"And last, but not least, let me read you this one from back home in Washington. The Arlington County, Virginia, Board of Supervisors, after listening to three hours of testimony punctuated by laughter, applause and catcalls, deferred action on a law to prohibit smoking in a variety of public places."

Immediately Mark lit up a fresh Salem from the butt of his first one, in protest.

"Can you believe that?" B.J. exulted. "Finally, someone is trying to do something about smoking. Good for them."

"Never happen in America," Mark said. "In the land of the free, where we're entitled to life, liberty and the pursuit of happiness, and where metaphysical happiness is defined as a drag on a fag with morning coffee. Those rabid health freaks will never be able to ban smoking in public places... mark my words."

As B.J. was reviewing the sports pages, Mark's thoughts turned to old Karl Wallenda. *Why was he still doing the circus act at 73?* Most people that age couldn't get to the bathroom in the morning without tottering.

"You know, Jackson... I have to admit that I've always been traumatized by circus acts. As a kid, every time I went to a circus, something unfortunate happened. And every time something bad happens, do you know what they do?"

"Sure, they send in the clowns don't they?"

"How'd you know that?"

"Ivy League education. Easy now, Stanton, with all your babbling, it's beginning to sound as though you might need some professional clown therapy yourself..."

"I'm serious," said Mark, "when I was six, I saw a lion-tamer attacked in the cage. The house lights went out. A spotlight flashed on and out waltzed the clowns. Another time, when I was about twelve, I saw a guy fall from the high trapeze... he half-hit the edge of the safety net on the way down and flipped onto the floor. He didn't move. The band struck up and out marched the clowns. Still another time, when I was about eighteen and out with a date, there was this circus act with tall swaying poles. People shimmied up and slid down them, while they swayed. Then they started switching poles, a hundred feet above the floor. You guessed it. One guy missed the pole and fell to the floor. The house lights went out. The band started playing. And out came the clowns. To this day, I won't go to see a circus. I'm always a nervous wreck."

"That last act kind of gives a whole new meaning to the term 'pole-vaulting' doesn't it?"

Mark took a long drag on his cigarette and shivered away thoughts of the circus.

"Speaking of smoking," B.J said while waving the offending smoke away, "I was impressed that government is starting to do something about smoking. Personally, I'm tired of breathing someone else's smoke. It really pisses me off."

"If it pisses you off so much, maybe you should waddle around with your pants around your ankles... putting out people's cigarettes with your little pink fire extinguisher."

"Aw, piss on it."

## War and Remembrance.

MARK WAS HAVING trouble keeping his eyes open and it was only 9:30 a.m. After B.J. finished reading the paper, Mark finally broke down and asked B.J. if he wanted to drive for a little while.

"Me-e-e-e?" Jackson couldn't wait.

Mark was hoping to get some more sleep. Before making the monumental decision of turning over his pride and joy to B.J., he'd looked over the West Texas map. The road for the next 100 miles was absolutely straight as an arrow -- due east. *Even B.J. could handle this kind of driving*, Mark thought. He warned Jackson about keeping "Stanley" under 75 mph and not getting anywhere near the red-line on the tachometer when shifting gears, because the car was new and was still being broken-in. Mark pulled over to the shoulder of the road and they switched seats.

Even ten years hence, in 1988, Mark was certain that tourists will still be able to see the burnt rubber marks B.J. laid getting the Porsche back on route 180-East. Also, Mark expected, there may be a historical marker denoting the spot. As those who live in West Texas can attest, the 120-foot long tire peel-out tracks are a local attraction; they are situated about nine miles east of the airport.

Mark was apoplectic. "Jcksn! Slow this damned thing down... or I swear... I'll kill you in your sleep, by midnight - tonight!"

B.J. laughed him off. He knew Mark couldn't do anything without wrecking the car and killing them both. Mark was now experiencing his new car from a whole new perspective -- undergoing increasing 'G' forces, braced into the back of passenger's seat by something like twice the force of gravity. B.J. prided himself on being a skilled sports car driver. As a member of the privileged class, driving sports cars at high speeds was second nature to him. However, Mark thought, *rich people have a history of 'totaling' cars and then walking away from them, laughing*. "Stanley" was Mark's only car, his true pride and joy, not to mention his only transportation back east.

They took a rise in the road at 90 mph. They were airborne! Forget the 2-G's, Mark was now feeling a weightless sensation.

BAM! They returned to earth.

"Jackson, I mean it. Keep this up and you're a dead man. Dead. Dead. Dead. And after you're dead I'll hire people to spit on your grave. Slow it down," Mark yelled.

"I'm just blowing out all the carbon you've accumulated in the new engine, not to worry," B.J. yelled over the jet stream he was creating.

"(Your Love Has Lifted Me) Higher and Higher" by Rita Coolidge was rising from El Paso's only rock'n'roll station. B.J. howled and pointed at the radio.

They'd never seen such a straight road. As far as the eye could see, there were rises and dips, but the road, U.S. 62 & 180, shot straight ahead. It ran west to east on a kind of parallel track with the Texas-New Mexico boundary that was just twenty miles or so to their left. It was amazing to be able to see the road arc over the crest of each ridge for miles and miles in front of them. Being flat-landers from Ohio and Illinois, Mark and B.J. weren't used to that.

There was nothing but open land, spotted by cactus and sagebrush on either side of the road. A lone tree or a stand of brush near a water hole was a rare sight. Barbed wire fences portioned off the tracts of real estate, but there were few cattle in sight. Off to the left, the Cornudas Mountains, peaks of 6,000 to 7,000 feet stood between the road and New Mexico, to the north.

There hadn't been another car on the highway in either direction since the two departed the El Paso city limits. After Mark went hoarse yelling, B.J. finally settled in behind the wheel. Even Formula One-Indy car drivers eventually get into a rhythm and a groove.

B.J. finally eased up on the gas pedal and Mark slowly but inevitably succumbed to sleep. He awoke a half-hour later at the sound of the first car to pass them, going in the opposite direction. First thing he did was ogle the speedometer. B.J. was tooling along near 90 mph. It was 10:15 a.m. *So this was "letting loose!"* Mark thought.

Amid intense static, Jefferson Starship was playing "Count on Me" on the radio.

"Well there you are Stanton. See... you didn't wake up in either Heaven or hell. I'm still driving, and we're still in West Texas."

"How can I be sure this isn't *hell*?"

"Hell no. Right now I'm doing what I've always dreamed of doing... drifting around the country without a typewritten minute-by-minute itinerary and headed for a place I've always wanted to visit... the Carlsbad Caverns," B.J. said with a true sense of excitement in his voice. "When I was a kid in the sixth grade, back in Peoria, I recall doing a term paper about bats. I had this thing for bats... especially vampire bats. I read a book all about the bats that live in the Carlsbad Caverns. Well, I've been hooked on those nasty little varmints, ever since. And now I'm about to see something I've only dreamt of for years. In my book... that's damn exciting!"

"Well, B.J., far be it from me to stand in your way of fulfilling your childhood fantasy."

B.J. continued to aim the Porsche due east, in line with the perfectly straight road.

"So, Kemo Sabe, what did you read about as a kid, what did you want to do when you grew up?" B.J. asked.

Mark went into deep thought for a moment or two. "Like a lot of kids, I guess... at first, I wanted to grow up to be President of the United States. I was twelve years old when John Kennedy ran in 1960 and that was powerful stuff in the Catholic schools. The Irish nuns who taught us could hardly contain themselves. But I came from a Republican household, so I learned to keep my mouth shut. Still, I watched Kennedy closely and read everything about him that I could get my hands on. One day, JFK's motorcade came through my small hometown on its way from the Ohio Turnpike into Cleveland. It was a scene I'll never forget... I saw motorcycles, police cars and black limousines. I saw how the crowds were attracted to all this pomp and circumstance. I was hooked on politics and John Kennedy from that moment forward. Later on, that November, when I heard my parents say that they voted for Nixon, I couldn't bring myself to speak to them for days."

"So how the hell did you end up being a dyed-in-the-wool Republican, if you loved Kennedy so much?"

"Well, I continued to consider myself a Democrat well into high school at Cleveland's Jesuit-run St. Ignatius, although

I never said so to my parents. In fact, in 1964, I debated on behalf of Lyndon Johnson's election before my high school speech class."

"Let me get this straight," said B.J. "You, 'Marc-us Aurelius Stanton-us,' supported Lyndon Baines Johnson?"

"Yeah. But as you get older you're supposed to get wiser. For example, you learn there are two sides to every story... sometimes more than two sides. For me, the problem with Democrats came with Johnson's handling of the Vietnam War. LBJ let the damned thing get out of control. He and McNamara micro-managed us right into a national disaster. I guess they thought they were playing some kind of a Washington board game, but the pieces they were moving around were real soldiers."

"Whoa there... didn't your hero 'Tricky Dick' Nixon do the exact same thing?"

"A lot of people like you think so, but not in my opinion, and I was still a loyal Democrat when I made up my mind. To me, the Vietnam War was lost the very day Johnson said he wasn't going to run for President again, back ten years ago in March of 1968. As I saw it, Vietnam was never Nixon's war... by the time Nixon inherited it the whole mess was titled find-a-way-out with some respectable cover story. If you're not going to let the military win it the old fashioned way, then you'd better be trying to find a fast and graceful way to exit. Johnson and McNamara, in my opinion, did neither."

"Well, that's one man's opinion," B.J. responded skeptically.

"The kids who came after me, the guys born from 1948 through '51 and '52, the hippie generation, they were too young to understand Johnson's escalation of the war. They didn't grow up and wake up to national politics until early 1968 with Martin Luther King's assassination. Then during the '68 primaries they started listening to Eugene McCarthy and Bobby Kennedy. Then Bobby got shot in June, and then that November, Nixon won. When those hippie kids finally came around to what was going on in Southeast Asia, they saw Nixon in The White House, and so they saw the war as Nixon's... they had no depth of understanding. And then your buddy Teddy Kennedy, whose brother John probably started the whole mess in the first instance, had the balls to stand up in the Senate, in 1969... just months after Nixon took office... and referred to Vietnam as 'Nixon's war.' The hippie kids were too young to understand that their elected officials would use a war and real lives to demagogue an issue for political gain. The hippies never read about or understood the decisions that Johnson and McNamara had made that put us beyond the point of no return in '67 and early '68. But that's why I turned away from the Democrat party.

B.J. had had enough. "Hold on Stanton! That's a gnarly remembrance of things past. The hippies didn't wake up until Nixon was President? Hey, who do you think brought LBJ to his knees, fat-cat Republicans? From early 1965 on, *I* was marching in peace demonstrations, burning *my* draft card, pushing flowers up National Guard rifles. In 1968, we were young, but we didn't lose focus by whining... '*he* started it.' We just wanted to pick up our scuffed ball and go home. We swarmed to Clean Gene when he said he'd do just that... but the Richard Daley Democrats and the hard-hat union boys steam-rollered us at the polls. They still wanted to win the damn thing.

"Did we see it as 'Nixon's War?' Well, we didn't blame *him* for the first half, but the second half of the war, 1969 to 1973 remember, was fought and half the casualties notched after LBJ's sayonara. Excuse us if we thought five more years was too long for Commander-in-chief Nixon to find his promised, final solution."

"Jackson... by the time Nixon inherited it, the thing was so screwed up..."

"Hey, on Nixon's watch, kids were shot down at Kent State protesting his Cambodian incursion," B.J. countered. "Up to 12,000 protesters, including yours truly, were rounded up in D.C. and arrested by Nixon troops. Then there was massive carpet bombing of North Vietnam. Finally, the Congress spoke up and Nixon had to quit bombing the shit out of Cambodia.

"Tricky Dick, distracted by his Watergate woes, finally focused on ending it. He whisks the good guys off the roof of the Saigon embassy, leaving our Asian allies grabbing the air for departing helicopter struts. What a great photo-op ending to the whole travesty."

"Tragedy... not travesty," Mark interjected.

"From those halcyon days, I kept my long hair and my peaceable ways. What I don't understand, Stanton, is how you kept on being a Republican, and a Nixon apologist to boot."

The twosome rode in silence for many miles. Each had struck a raw nerve in the other. But they were close enough to understand that, so they had both better let it drop right there. Here it was, ten full years after the fact and good friends still found themselves arguing about Vietnam. Perhaps the lasting legacy of that sad war will be a lesson on how powerful leaders can manage to get a whole nation into a sucking quagmire but find themselves powerless to simply admit they made a mistake and lead us out.

Much farther down the road, trying to thaw the ice, Mark said, "So tell me Jackson, how do you *really* feel..."

"Up your nose with a rubber hose..."

## Roller Coaster Highway.

TRYING TO CHANGE the subject, a few minutes later B.J. asked, "So what do you think about the 1980 elections? Who's it going to be?"

Mark paused only a moment, "I think Carter's in some trouble," he said. "He's a nice enough guy. But he's an intellectual micro-manager. Staffers have to check with the President himself, to get a playing time on The White House tennis court."

"That depends on your definition of 'micro-management,'" B.J. countered.

"I'll tell you what my definition of micro-management is, it's trying to pick the *fly shit* out of the pepper... that's micro-management!"

There was a pause while B.J. pondered that well-seasoned thought.

Mark tried to temper his position. "Look, Jackson, I'll admit Carter's trying to do the right thing with the Panama Canal, he'll probably win the Nobel Peace Prize, but he's not being realistic. He's an apologist, trying to atone for America's imperialist sins going all the way back to the turn of the century. But what he isn't taking into account is that we're dealing with poor, corrupt Third World countries that wouldn't know what to do with a strategic asset like the Panama Canal. They'll screw it up. Just wait and see."

B.J., for his part, tried to return to the subject at hand. "So you think it'll be Ronald Reagan in The White House?"

"Sure. Jerry Ford's not making a comeback. In his wildest dreams, he never expected to be President in the first place. The only other guys out there for the Republicans are George Bush... a nice guy, but surrounded by way too many ivory towered Ivy Leaguers. Then you have Bob Dole... a guy who while he was Republican National Chairman during Nixon's first term, had to carry an awful lot of water for Nixon, Haldeman, Erlichman and Colson.

B.J. cringed at the mention of Nixon's "Murderers Row." "Reagan is a nice-guy, but a tool of the right-wing conservative crowd," B.J. opined. "He's just too connected to the big money boys for me. And, in my opinion, I don't think the guy's ever had an original thought."

"Well, you know what they say, Jackson... 'Money talks, but who can speak Arabic?' Sure, the fat cats like Reagan, but he can't help that. Republicans have always been connected to money... finding money... raising money... hiding money... not accounting for money, and so on. Republican scandals are always about *money*. Look at Watergate and Deep Throat, who always said 'follow the money.' On the other hand, Democrat scandals always involve *sex*. Look at JFK sleeping with some mobster's girlfriend, and John and Bobby with Marilyn Monroe... Wilbur Mills... Wayne Hays... it's always the broads who bring down the Democrat."

B.J. jumped to the defense of Democrats. "Well, Eisenhower and Nixon, Reagan and Bush... they just don't seem like the kind of guys you'd want to party with... no self-respecting women would hang around with those guys. No, there'll probably never be a Republican sex scandal," B.J. scoffed.

"On the other hand," Mark interjected, "someday one of your Democrats is going to be caught with dirty campaign money. Mark my words. It's just a matter of time. You know why?"

"Oh great political seer, sage, soothsayer... please tell me why?"

"Because Republicans already have the money. They don't have to jump through hoops to get it. And as the cost of television and campaigns escalate, some Democrat is going to take illegal money trying to keep up with the Republicans."

B.J. kept pressing Mark. "So after Carter, who do you see on the Democratic side?"

"Don't know... but you've got a fine crop of young, fuzzy-faced governors out there. One or two of them might surface. Governorships are the best breeding-grounds for the office of President, not the U.S. Senate... too many compromises on a daily basis there."

"Whatcha Gonna Do?" by Pablo Cruise was playing on Stanley's Blaupunkt.

B.J. was still behind the steering wheel and the Porsche 924 was climbing over another rise in the road, at what Mark gauged to be more than 90 mph. He braced himself. Again, he felt the sensation of weightlessness as the car jumped the crest.

"Holy sheeee-it!" Mark exclaimed. Mark's eyes opened to the size of silver dollars.

Arrayed a half-mile in front of them was a police roadblock bigger than any they'd ever seen on television -- or in the movies for that matter. It looked like every cop in West Texas was in the middle of their highway, just waiting for them. There were at least ten black and white patrol cars blocking the road, all with their red, white and blue wigwag reflector lights blinking. Uniformed officers with badges, shotguns and Smokey-the-bear hats swarmed all over the roadblock. The only thing between the police cars and the two of them was about 500 yards and a one-pump gas station at the gravel crossroads to Dell City.

Thinking quickly, B.J. pumped the brakes with a screech. The acrid smell of burning rubber swept past them. He swerved toward the tiny filling shack, sending cinders flying and a billowing smoke screen of dust into the air. An old fellow in overalls, who'd been asleep in a tattered wicker chair, sprang forward onto all fours at the sound of the Porsche hitting gravel. Mark thought that for sure they'd given the poor bastard a massive coronary, right on the spot.

B.J. held his breath -- for two reasons: First, he couldn't help but see swarms of police marshaling in front of them. And second, there was an old man lying prone on the ground beside the lone gas pump in the station.

"Do you think they're after *us*?" B.J. asked, jumping out of the driver's seat.

Mark snapped, "Daa-a-ah! Gee, Jackson, answer me this... have you seen another car on this road, going in our direction, since El Paso?"

"No, not really."

"Then they gotta' be after *us*, you ass!" Mark said with disgust, looking down the road at all the law enforcement hardware.

"Hey there good buddy, are you okay?" B.J. asked, helping the station attendant to his feet.

"You caught me nappin' there!" the old timer said with a toothless grin.

One whiff and B.J. could smell the liquor fumes on his breath.

"How long has that roadblock been set up over there," B.J. asked, pointing in the distance.

"What roadblock?"

"*That* roadblock over there!" B.J. now gestured more frantically. "You see... that one, there... the one with every cop in County... yeah, that one over there."

The old fellow tried to focus his bleary eyes a quarter-mile down the road. B.J.'s anxiety was growing. "Didn't see it... must'a gone up while I was dozin' off," the attendant said in pure amazement.

"See, Jackson, I told you, the cops must have just put it up. Who else would they be looking for but a flashy sports car, driven by an hippie in blue jeans, with an Afro hairdo, in a car with California tags, doing between 90 and 100 mph, and the only car headed east on this highway for the last hour or so? They've probably been tracking us on radar from a plane or a helicopter," Mark added.

Mark was growing angrier by the minute. He didn't want to go to Carlsbad in the first place. Then he got talked into it. He didn't want B.J. to do any driving, for this very reason. Then Mark got weak. He was exhausted. In his tiredness, he gave in. And now they were about to get arrested out in the middle of nowhere, because B.J. was driving like a maniac. On top of it all, B.J. didn't have a dollar on him. Mark had the sinking feeling that this arrest was going to take hours and lots of money -- in order to get his partner out of jail, and his car out of hock. He was super-pissed.

"If they're just after us," a puzzled B.J. asked aloud, "why are there so many? And why don't those cops just drive over here and arrest us? They can see us here as plain as day."

*It was true.* Mark stopped in his tracks and peered into the distance. The police at the roadblock could see every move they were making. While the officers moved back and forth, none of them looked ready to jump in a car to come to get them. *What gives? What were their options?* They could drive straight at the roadblock and throw themselves on the mercy of the court. They could turn around and go back to El Paso, about an hour and a half away -- probably being chased the whole way by a handful of police cruisers. Or, they could turn left or right at the gravel crossroads, but that option only offered north-south paths to nowhere. If they went straight to them, Mark expected that they were dead ducks. There was no getting around this roadblock. They'd situated the damned thing in the perfect place.

Still stalling for time, B.J. said, "Fill 'er up," to the old man.

"I ain't got but regular gas," the fellow said, correctly assuming that a fancy sports car like "Stanley" would take high-octane fuel.

"Forget it, Jackson," Mark said. "Forget the gasoline." He gave the old-timer a couple of bucks for his trouble. "B.J., I've thought about it, and I think it's best if we drive right up and face the music."

"That's easy for you to say, Kemo Sabe. But just like every other episode, Tonto here is certainly on his way to getting beat up and spending the night in an all-redneck hoosegow."

They got back in the car. Mark made sure he went around to the passenger's side seat. He wanted to make sure the guilty culprit, B.J., was behind the wheel.

"Got to Give It Up (Part One)" by Marvin Gaye came on the radio.

B.J. carefully edged the car back out onto U.S. 62 & 180-East. It *was* strange that no one on the barricade had come forward or made a move in their direction. B.J. eased the car toward the roadblock at 20 mph.

"Would you like a blindfold and a cigarette?" Mark asked B.J.

"Naw, Stanton," he said, "just shoot me and get it over with. But I want scallops and shrimp lightly dipped in Italian bread crumbs and sautéed in extra virgin olive oil with one clove of garlic, over linguini with marinara sauce, asparagus spears... very thin, broiled with blue cheese on top... and a crisp Pouilly-Fuisse... possibly a '76, for my last meal."

As they approached to within yards of the roadblock, it dawned on Mark.  These guys looked like UPS deliverymen, except that the shoulder patches on the brown uniforms said "U.S. Immigration and Naturalization Service."  They weren't looking for a speeding Porsche!  They were looking for wetbacks!

"May I see some form of identification for each of you... a driver's license will do... and the registration for the car," the stern-looking officer asked, stifling a grin by biting on his lip.  He stared down at the two of them through mirrored sunglasses.

"It's *his* car," B.J. pointed at Mark.  Then he turned, so the officer couldn't see, and made a wild face, eyes wide open and mouth agape, at Mark.  At that point B.J. too realized these guys were not looking for speeders.  He'd gotten away with it!  Both fished out their licenses and Mark retrieved the registration papers from the glove compartment.

"A long way from home fellows... where you headed?" the officer asked.

"Cross-country to Washington, D.C... but first we're going to the Carlsbad Caverns... to see the bats!" said B.J., just like an excited little kid.

Another trooper worked his way around the car peering at their luggage through the glass hatch back.  Then he came to Mark's side of the car.  He had what looked like a snow shovel on wheels, with a big mirror on it.  He rolled it under the car and peered into the reflection – no doubt, looking for some poor, unfortunate Mexican soul who could have been hiding under there, duct-taped to the exhaust pipe for the last two hours.

"Would you open up the glass hatch back for us?" the trooper asked.

When Mark said "sure" the officers surprisingly demurred.  They guessed that there wasn't room enough to hide anyone they couldn't see. *But how they could they let the hatch back go unsearched*, Mark wondered, *and yet still expect that some-*

*one could be hiding under the car, with a ground clearance of less than ten inches*?

During the search process one officer in particular stood there staring at B.J. through intimidating reflective sunglasses. Eventually he said, "You are free to go. And oh, by the way, hair-*tree*," he said directly to B.J., emphasizing the last syllable, "see if you can keep *his* car under 90 will you? We could hear you guys coming at us long before you ski-jumped that last ridge."

"*Gracias, senor,*" said B.J., hitting the accelerator, peeling away.

"Jackson... you lead a charmed life," Mark said with a relieved sigh.

"Stanton, that's true. And sometimes, I amaze even myself."

"The Way You Do the Things You Do" by Rita Coolidge was playing.

### Handball High Jinks.

MARK FIRED UP a Salem and tried to relax. After the roadblock, he decided to lay back and enjoy being the passenger the rest of the way to Carlsbad. They passed Salt Flat, Texas, at 10:45 a.m. B.J. had the speed down to a modest 75 mph. Dry salt beds lay on either side of the road for miles. Mark took a close look at the map. The Sierra Diablo Mountains were off to the right and they wrapped around to due east. Ahead of them, he could make out the Delaware Mountain Range. A few miles up the road U.S. Routes 62 & 180 took their first real turn since El Paso, swinging north toward the village of Pine Springs. In the distance was Guadeloupe Peak; according to the map, at 8,749 feet, it was the tallest point in the entire Lone Star state. The Guadeloupe Mountains lie about 40 miles southwest of Carlsbad, New Mexico. Mark commented that these mountains like most in the west were remnants of a prehistoric reef beneath the waves of an ancient inland sea. The salt flats they'd just passed were testament to the geology. And, Mark noted for good measure, that all this land once belonged to the Mescalero Apache tribe.

"Those Irish nuns and Jesuits sure did a job on you didn't they Spanky! You're a true Renaissance man. Politics. History.

Geography... and now, geology. Damn, Stanton, but you ought to be a poster child for Catholic education."

"And Jackson, you ought to be on the recruiting poster for the Ivy League."

"Naw. I don't like tweed smoking jackets and pipes."

B.J.'s comment on Catholics did make Mark think back to grade school days. Those nuns *were* as tough as nails. Then his cheeks flushed; and he remembered exactly why.

"Jackson, you've got me to thinking..."

"Oh, not again. God help me, I've somehow managed to trigger another story."

"Seriously, when I was a kid, back in Catholic grade school, we had this nun... named Sister Thomas More. We all called her Tommy-gun More because she could grab your ear with her left hand and fire off twenty-five slaps-a-second across both sides of your face with her right hand. She used to swoop in so fast and hit you so hard, both forehand and backhand, it was like a machine gun got you. Most guys never knew what hit them, until they came to. That was Sister Tommy-gun More.'"

With a sideways glance over at the driver's seat Mark could tell B.J. was braced for another tale.

"Catholic schools in the 1950's didn't get 'diddley' in the way of financial support. In most of my classes, we had more than sixty kids. Other than a blackboard and a pointer, we had no equipment to speak of. There were no fancy slide-shows or projectors like they had in public schools. No filmstrips. No field trips. No movies in the auditorium. Hell, no auditorium. No air conditioning. No gymnasium. No cafeteria. Not a chance of hot food. No refrigeration for the little glass milk bottles with the cardboard pog tops. No sports equipment. No nothing.

"At recess, if we were lucky, six of us got a chance to play a game of handball up against a brick wall. The wall was marked off for three handball courts with whitewashed lines. The unwritten rule was that the first six guys who got to the courts played. The rest of the kids got into a challenger's line. The winners always stayed on the court. He who was next in the challenger's line played the next winner.

"If you wanted to play you had to be ready when the recess bell rang. You dropped everything, and raced out of class, down the stairs, out the doors, and then you had to sprint the final hundred yards to get to the brick wall.

"I had this friend in 5th grade. He was a little guy named Boudreau, who ran out there every day as fast as he could, but always ended up way back in the challenger's line. He rarely got to play handball because recess period usually ended before he ever got to the front of the line.

"Then one day he shows up wearing new sneakers... the finest looking gym shoes I'd ever seen. He took off a shoe and held it up so we could see the tread design and the 'U.S. Keds' logo on the rubber sole. No one else in school had a pair like 'em. That day Boudreau whispers to me during class that he's going to be the first one to get to the handball courts. He said his new U.S. Keds sneakers were unbelievable, that he could corner like a rat.

"Five minutes before the recess bell rang Boudreau and I were in our 'starting blocks.' When it finally went off, we were out the door before the nun even heard it. I had a one-step lead until we turned the corner to go down the staircase. Then Boudreau took to the inside and went low on me at the first corner. It was a steep inside line, and I wasn't sure he could hold it, but he cut me off at the top step. Boudreau went down the staircase first. He was elbowing me back into second position, all the way down the steps. There were thirty or forty other guys thundering down the steps behind us. It sounded like a stampede on 'Rawhide.' Boudreau skipped the last two steps at the bottom of the stairs, made a dash for the outside doors.

"Now those heavy outside doors were both a challenge and an opportunity. They had release bars. And if you popped those release bars just right... the doors would spring open. When that happened, you were *golden*! But if you were off target... just a smidgen... when you hit those release bars the doors wouldn't budge. If that happened, you were shit-outta'-luck... you crashed right into the heavy doors. My friends lost many a front tooth on the bloody inside of those outside doors... all because their aim at the release bars was off just a hair."

Inside, B.J. was bursting at the seams.

"Now my man Boudreau had a two-step lead on me at the bottom of the staircase, and he's dashing for those heavy outside doors.  I'm running my little ass off.  Out of the corner of my eye, I saw Boudreau do one of those 'skip-steps' in the middle of his stride in order to time his hit on the release bars.  Then BAM!  He pops 'em perfectly!  On this day, he is truly golden!  The doors fly right open!  He's outside, headed for the playground when I hear... a dull *THUMP*!

"It seems that going down the outside steps, Boudreau had crashed right into a blessed nun!  And not just any nun, Jackson, but eighty-nine year-old Sister Mary Fatima.  She was the matriarch of the school's convent and a perennial candidate for sainthood, according to odds makers at The Vatican.  Anyway, it seems that the old nun had been gimping up the outside steps toward the heavy doors, with her cane in hand.  Apparently, Boudreau had blown through the doors and plowed right into her as she was coming up the steps.  He knocked her ass-over-elbows-'n'-rosary beads down to the bottom of the cement steps."

With a second sideways glance Mark could tell that B.J. was listening intently, still ready to explode.

"Let me tell you... it was not a pretty sight.  He had crashed into her squarely like a linebacker and knocked her straight back.  I was right behind him and I couldn't stop either, and so I tripped over her, rolling her over once on the ground.  And after me, three or four other dumb bastards, who were running behind us, ended up in a heap right on top of ol' Sister Mary Fatima.  It looked like a goal line pile-up.

"Well, no kid in his right mind wanted to hang around and take the credit for that hit, if you know what I mean."

B.J. just nodded, now biting his lip.

"At best, the nun was out cold.  Boudreau and I jumped up, quickly assessed the situation, looked at one another, dusted off, put our heads down and made the final sprint to the handball courts.  Several of the kids behind us, with some fancy footwork, had sidestepped the pile-up and had gone past us to take possession of the first two handball courts.  But Boudreau and I still managed to get to the third court ahead of the rest of the also-rans.  We started our game of handball, and never looked back."  Mark paused for dramatic effect.

"A few minutes later I hit a real *hummer* off the wall, so hot I thought the handball would knock Boudreau over, if he could even get to it. All of the sudden I heard a *THUNK*! The handball disappeared from mid-air!

"I looked up and there was a big fist suspended above me. That fist had just snatched the handball, probably going 100 mph, right out of the air! That fist with the ball disappeared into a lily-white nun's habit. And that habit belonged to none other than Sister Tommy-gun More! And, Jackson... let me tell you... she was as pissed as a nun is theologically allowed to get.

"She grabbed each of us by an ear and literally dragged us back to the schoolhouse steps. When we arrived at the scene of the crime, several nuns were already kneeling around the prone and still dazed Sister Mary Fatima. They were saying prayers for her recovery. The ancient nun had come-to, but she was still very groggy. We heard one nun say that she'd suffered a broken arm after being run-down by some *hooligans*. Two nuns were wrapping her arm in a splint made from a broken meter stick. Tommy-gun More shoved us before the eighty-nine-year-old nun for identification purposes. Basically, it was your two-kid line-up.

"Sister Thomas More said, 'Sister Mary Fatima, it has to be one of these two hooligans, who... according to everyone else... were the first two out the door.' The old nun looked up at the two of us through her Coke-bottle-thick eyeglasses and said she wasn't quite sure. I smiled. Tommy-gun More saw my smile and wiped it away with a burst of bitch-slaps that I've never forgotten... to this very day. My cheeks sting just thinking about it."

"Stanton, why would you do such a stupid thing... like smirk at the sight of a hurt old nun?" B.J. asked.

"Because, Jackson, when I looked down at poor old Sister Mary Fatima, I knew I was completely off-the-hook. It wouldn't take Sherlock Holmes to figure out what was truly a-foot. Right there, running up the front of her nuns' habit were the perfect outlines of sole prints from a brand-new pair of sneakers. Two dusty footprints were clearly outlined on her outfit as if Boudreau had stamped 'U.S. Keds... U.S. Keds... up the front of her lily-white habit. When I smiled, it had just dawned on me that it was just a matter of time before my buddy Boudreau, not me, was going up the river for this crime. I was smiling the same shit-eating grin that guilty murderers smile when a well-intentioned, but misguided jury pronounces them to be 'not guilty.'"

B.J. let go with his laugh.

"Boogie Shoes" by K.C. and The Sunshine Band was on the radio.

B.J. and Mark stopped briefly near the entrance to Guadeloupe Mountains National Park. They really didn't want to see another mountain range, they merely stopped to pick-up a six-pack, and some nibbles, while gassing up at a local filling station. The small village was Pine Springs, Texas. There were ruins of another Butterfield Overland Mail stagecoach station. A directional sign in the middle of town pointed northeast -- 65 miles to Carlsbad. The air was breezy, but rather balmy and clear.

"That's a beautiful car. What is it?" the woman behind the counter asked.

"It's a new Porsche 924," Mark responded.

"Well, it's a sleek looking car. I don't think I ever seen one before... and such a lovely shade of black, too.

"When I get it out in the sunlight, you'll see the color's actually a shade of gray."

"I don't think so," she said, rather sure of herself.

After several hours as the shotgun passenger, Mark was feeling a little better, rested and ready to drive again. After he paid for the gasoline, he jumped behind the wheel and started the car.

*The Porsche lurched out of control*!

Mark slammed on the brakes. "Stanley" nearly took out a whole display rack of oilcans. The lurch scared the hell out of Mark -- then it dawned on him. B.J. had left the car in first gear when he turned it off. "B.J., you ass, are you trying to kill me?" he yelled. "Don't ever leave this thing in gear when you turn it off. I never leave it in gear. Leave it in *neutral*, and put on the parking brake, for God's sake."

B.J. just hung his head in mock remorse.

## Cavemen.

A HALF-HOUR LATER Mark had to stop to relieve himself. The late-morning beers were taking their inevitable toll. They were miles from civilization and there was absolutely nothing around but the sparse Chihuahuan desert. No traffic was on the highway, so he eased the car onto the dusty shoulder of the road. He got out, walked a few feet, jumped a low wire fence, and ducked in behind a six-foot tall prickly cactus. As he leaped the fence, Mark asked B.J. to let him know if anyone was coming. Small lizards scattered in all directions as he landed.

No sooner was Mark in mid-stream than B.J. yelled, "Stanton... here comes a cop car!"

Mark frantically attempted to stop the irrepressible flow. Also, he tried to zip up and back out of the cactus patch, all at the same time. "Ow-w-w-w!" He'd turned and bumped his right knee into a rather nasty-looking, spiky little plant. The cactus needles were so sharp that, at first, Mark didn't even notice them sticking out of his knee -- that is, until he tried to jump back over the fence.

"Where's the police car?"

B.J. had a blank look on his face like the police car had disappeared in thin air.

"Damn it Jackson, you and your damned games... look here... I just punched my knee full of cactus needles because of your stupid high school prank."

"Sorry man, I just couldn't resist... as in, *'Let me know if anyone's coming,'*" he said mocking Mark's line. "Stanton, who the hell would be coming down this road, and what would they care if you were caught taking a leak behind a cactus?"

Mark carefully climbed in behind the wheel and showed B.J. the cactus needles protruding from the knee of his pants. He pulled out the long sharp spikes, making a dramatic grunt with the removal of each one. The barbed bristles had gotten a good half-inch or so below the skin.

"You ought to be helping me pull these things out," Mark said.

"As you know, I'm basically a pacifist... I can't stand to see pain and bloodshed... that's why I never watch a GOP convention on television."

"Some compassionate liberal you turned out to be. I hope they take your bleeding-heart ribbon away."

"Cold As Ice" by Foreigner was playing on the Blaupunkt as they entered the town of Whites City, New Mexico, home of B.J.'s big bat cave.

The puffiness in Mark's right knee was noticeable and it was becoming numb as well.

Following signs, they found the Visitors' Center of Carlsbad Caverns National Park without great difficulty. After all, it was the only cave in town. After parking, Mark took a seat on a park bench like some old-timer, rubbing his bum knee. B.J. waited in line to buy tickets with Mark's money. He returned all excited -- they couldn't move fast enough for B.J. to get on the next tour.

Five minutes later, a loosely knit group of forty or so badly attired tourists fell in behind a crisply uniformed, hard-charging, female U.S. National Park Service ranger. She marched the group down a long path toward the natural arch that formed the cave entrance. Everyone marched along, but Mark; he limped. The knee joint was painful to the touch, and getting worse fast. Now his whole right leg was beginning to go numb. Occasionally, while walking, there was an excruciating stab of pain, enough to remind him that he'd really screwed up running into that nasty little plant. His thoughts strayed to the ugly killer plant in "The Little Shop of Horrors."

The park ranger was well into her practiced spiel. She explained that the cavern entrance they were entering was formed when a portion of the original cave's roof fell in -- a confidence-inspiring thought as the group wandered downward beneath the remaining tons of roof ledge, some 200 feet above.

Mark lagged to the back of the pack while B.J., in his element, brown-nosed his way to the front of group, constantly asking questions of the ranger. When she talked about Indian drawings on the cave walls, there was B.J., right beside her, pointing them out to the group. The midday sunlight completely disappeared behind them. The band of explorers continued their slow but steady creep downward along the asphalt path. In just a few minutes they were surrounded by the dank, dark interior of the cavern. The always-descending, sometimes steep footpath was lit with small directional lights placed at ankle level, so the glare would not interfere with sightseeing. The footpath lights were located every fifty feet or so. Everywhere they went there was a disgusting musty odor. For B.J.'s sake, Mark gritted his teeth and limped on, downward, ever downward.

Because of the numbness, Mark couldn't really tell when his right knee was locked in place. He wasn't exactly sure when he could put his full weight on it. The knee joint felt quite wobbly, and the leg acted as though it was made of rubber. As the group passed an area of the cave known as "Devil's Spring" Mark's knee gave out completely. "Whoa, mama..." he bellowed. The words echoed throughout the cave. "WHOA, MAMA... Whoa, Mama... whoa, mama." He collapsed in a heap, with a muffled splat on the damp footpath.

With a collective gasp, the entire tour group of forty turned to Mark. Each was trying to figure out what had happened. Mark was sure from the muffled echoes that everyone could hear him muttering, but what they couldn't make out was the world-class string of cuss words he was whispering, under his breath, at B.J.

"Don't worry folks. He's all right. Just a trick knee," B.J. said, allaying fears that perhaps a giant wombat had attacked one of their number. His words "trick knee" echoed off the cave walls. He offered a boost to get Mark balanced back on his good leg.

"My damned knee just went out, Jackson. It's so puffed up and numb, I can't tell when I can put my weight on it," Mark whispered, massaging it. "I'm not sure when it's locked in place. I can't walk right now... how much farther do we have to go? Let's get out of here... it smells worse than cat-piss on an old mattress in here." "Cat-piss" echoed off the walls. All forty heard it.

"I'm not sure, Stanton, but the ranger did say that when we reach bottom, we can take an elevator back to the surface... if that makes you feel any better."

Just then a glob of something wet hit Mark in the face with a splat.

"It must be water from the roof of the cave," B.J. said, trying to divert Mark's attention from what he actually thought it might be, "What else could it be?"

"It better not be bat-crap!" "BAT CRAP... Bat Crap... bat crap..." echoed off the cave walls. The group heard it repeatedly. Mark wiped a handful of whatever off his forehead, bent down and held it at arm's length, under one of the footpath lights. He wanted to get a good look at it.

"It's hard to tell in here... I guess it's not bat-poop," Mark continued his rant. "BAT POOP" echoed off the walls. "What's a bat poop look like anyway? Do you think it's clear? You know I was hit by a sea gull once at Cedar Point, Ohio. It was a nasty experience, Jackson. I had to burn my shirt... bird shit is like nuclear waste... has a half-life of a thousand years... no way it would come out in the wash."

Totally grossed-out, the cave tour group murmured to one another then turned to give their undivided attention to the park ranger. Despite Mark's protestations to B.J. they continued the steep descent into the coal-black confines of the musty cave.

"A half-million Mexican free-tailed bats reside in the cave..." the park ranger noted. At that point they entered a large lit chamber with rather impressive stalactites and stalagmites. *"Tites" hanging on top of the clothesline and "Mites" crawling on the floor*, Mark reminded himself.

Despite the infirmity, Mark had to admit that the Carlsbad Caverns would be the perfect tour for a kid. A kid has the imagination to envision all kinds of things in the rock formations and shadows, not to mention the possibility of a boogieman lurking in the dark behind any rock. B.J.'s inner child was soaking it up.

Fifteen minutes later, they were still slip sliding away on the descending footpath. Walking downhill was difficult enough, but doing it on a slippery trail with a numb knee was damn near impossible. As the tour group was rounding a massive boulder known as Iceberg Rock, it happened again!

"Awwwh, shit!" Mark cried as he crashed to the footpath. The second fall was much less graceful and far more painful than the first. The "Awwwh, shit..." and the moist splat of his right side hitting the pathway echoed all over the underground chamber, "SHIT, SPLAT... Shit, Splat... shit, splat!"

This time the park ranger stopped in mid-sentence. The tourist group turned again to find Mark down on his right side, writhing in pain, rubbing his battered knee, muttering. For the second time B.J. moseyed his way over to Mark's assistance.

"Jackson," said Mark, "enough's enough... this whole scene is beginning to feel like the Passion of Christ. You know, Jesus falls the first time... then Jesus falls the second time, and all that..." his voice carried for all to hear.

"Maybe so," said B.J., "but I'll bet Jesus didn't cuss like you're doing. Stanton, quit all the sniveling and whining. Get your limp thing working again."

The group turned away, disgusted with Mark's display and repeated interruptions. *Thank God I'm not really hurt*, Mark thought. "Jackson, let's wrap up this outing. Find that elevator back to the surface." Pain was beginning to overtake the numbness in the knee.

B.J. spoke to the ranger. He came back to say they still had a little way to go to get to the elevator. So he helped Mark up on the good leg and stayed by his side, acting as a human crutch. They looked like Dustin Hoffman leaning on Jon Voight in "Midnight Cowboy," trying to get to the sickly Ratso Rizzo to Florida before he died.

Mark limped along for another half-mile through places with names like the Green Lake Room, the Kings Palace, the Queens Chamber, and the Papoose Room... it sounded like they were on The White House tour. After several hours underground, breathing the nauseous fumes, Mark was convinced that the guide could point to anything and call it the "Mona Lisa formation," and the tourists would nod and say, "of course, I see it."

At precisely the point when Mark's downhill limping was breaking through the so-called threshold of pain, the pathway started uphill. *We must have hit bottom*, Mark thought.

The park ranger continued her spiel. One staggering fact caught Mark's attention. "Ladies and gentlemen," she said, "we've just descended some 900 feet below the natural entrance of the cave. That's the equivalent of walking down the entire staircase of the Empire State Building, some ninety stories, from the observation deck to street level."

SMACK! Mark punched B.J. in the shoulder. "You ass! Did you hear that?"

The word describing the specific body part echoed throughout the cave, "ASS... Ass... ass..."

Their group, and several other unseen tour groups within earshot of the echo, broke up with laughter. "No one told me I had to haul my lame leg 900 feet underground." B.J. sat Mark on a rock to catch his breath. The group, tired of their antics no doubt, left them there.

"Give it a rest, Stanton, or you're going to be just six feet underground. We're getting closer and closer to that elevator."

When they caught up with the tour, the group was gazing at a mammoth smooth lime-green rock. The haystack-shaped formation was bathed in light from several white spotlights. This must be the centerpiece – what they'd come so far to see. Was it an eight-ton piece of jade, perhaps? Once they'd all gathered around, the ranger said, "This is a rare accumulation of petrified bat guano..."

*Bat guano*? Mark repeated the strange word softly to himself. At first he was not exactly sure what the Spanish word meant -- then he thought about it. What else could it be? "You mean petrified bat shit?" Mark said loud enough for the "excrementary" word to echo all over the cavern. "SHIT?... Shit?... shit?"

"Jackson! You mean to tell me... that you dragged me here, hours and hundreds of miles out of my way... almost a thousand feet underground... in this musty basement... me with a totally bum knee... to see what? A putrid pile of petrified bat shit! You've *got* to be kidding me! This can't be for real... this is the focal point of a National Park? Bat dung... this is a national treasure of some kind?" Mark's soliloquy reverberated.

"Stanton, what did you expect? Da-a-a. Does a bat crap in a cave? Of course it does."

After his temper tantrum, Mark turned and limped uphill past a formation known as the Bone yard. Finally, he saw a sign that pointed out the passageway to the lunchroom and elevators. He made a shambling beeline.

B.J. wanted to visit the souvenir shop to buy some postcards and stamps. Mark was sure B.J. had a black book full of women to keep posted on his cross-country progress -- like Laurie in San Francisco who thought they were headed for Seattle. *What would be her reaction to a postcard from Carlsbad when she thought they were headed for the Pacific Northwest*? Also, B.J. wanted to have lunch in the cave's underground dining room. But Mark drew a line in the guano and said he was headed for the surface as soon as he stopped by the men's room. Reluctantly, B.J. agreed to meet Mark at the elevators in a few minutes.

In the men's rest room, every urinal was in use, so Mark limped from door-to-door along the stalls. He finally found a stall that wasn't locked; he opened it to find a stalactite and a stalagmite joined into a solid pillar. No commode. Now that, thought Mark, is real "bat-room" humor.

Mark had had enough of being a caveman. Perhaps he had a touch of subterranean claustrophobia, because -- instinctively -- he knew it was time to get out of there. When he found enough overhead light to read his watch, he realized that they'd been underground for an hour and a half. It was 1:30 p.m.

The 755-foot elevator shaft had originally been dug to lower and raise guano buckets to and from the cave. Apparently some otherwise unemployable New Mexicans found regular work "mining" the bat dung for shipment to California's citrus groves. Now there's the American work ethic for you. When they finally surfaced, Mark wanted to kiss the ground, the *above* ground, like a guy who'd just landed in Miami after a bad flight through the Bermuda Triangle; and he would have, if his knee hadn't hurt so much. He sucked in a lung-full of fresh air.

The twosome bought hot dogs from an umbrella-stand vendor. They sat on a nearby log trying to keep the mustard, onions and relish off their clothes. Mark managed to eat only half a frank before he discarded it. B.J. jotted down quick greetings to several young lovelies on postcards and mailed them on-site. B.J. finished his gastronomic delight and they headed out of town. What with the knee and all, Mark had little choice but to let B.J. get back behind the steering wheel.

"Looks Like We Made It," by Barry Manilow was the first thing that came on "Stanley's" radio when B.J. started him up.

## Geared Up for Green Chili.

BY THREE O'CLOCK they were back in Texas, headed southeast on U.S. 285 toward Pecos. They'd lost an hour when they crossed the border back into the Lone Star State, moving from Mountain to Central Standard Time. Mark set his watch one-hour forward. B.J. continued to drive while Mark rested his throbbing knee. Off to their left, they passed Red Bluff Lake, source of the Pecos River, a *stream* that flowed southeast and eventually emptied into Mark's *Rill-O'Grand*. They passed cotton field after cotton field on the flat dusty plain. They were traveling west-of-the-Pecos, a spin-off of the now-famous quote about Judge Roy Bean who was, they said, "the only Law, west of the Pecos."

After an hour-long backdrop of "*Q-Tip"* farms, around 4:00 p.m. they stopped in the town of Pecos and took a stretch. They pulled up in front of an historical marker that noted the town had been settled in 1881 as a water stop on the Texas & Pacific Railroad. The town also bragged of being the site of the first official "rodeo" in the United States on July 4, 1883, when local ranchers came together for roping and riding contests.

They drove around, passing the railroad depot, the old sandstone Orient Hotel and the #11 Saloon until they discovered the Judge Roy Bean visitor center that is maintained by the Texas Highway Department. Back in 1881, Bean set up a tent saloon on this site and became the area's first justice of the peace the following year. Eventually he built a wooden structure that served as both his courtroom and as the Jersey Lilly Saloon. Fines for those found guilty often included a round of drinks for judge and jury. B.J. and Mark agreed, "Hizzoner" was their kind of guy. The two had Polaroid pictures taken standing behind the bars in Judge Roy's jailhouse.

Mark's knee slowly regained feeling. It had been three and one-half hours since the cactus had bitten him.

The next town on the map was Fort Stockton, Texas. It stood at the U.S. Route 285 interchange with Interstate 10. According to the map, the town was about an hour away. There were no other towns in between and for the next 45 minutes, as they drove southeast, they saw Fort Stockton in front of them, slightly off to the left -- at 11 o'clock on the dial as aviators would say. They were driving at 75 mph, but the damned town never seemed to get any closer -- yet it looked just a few miles away. After a while it got ridiculous. The other thing that got comical was the outdoor advertising situated along Route 285-South for a restaurant in Fort Stockton named Railsback's Diner. They must have passed ten billboards in ten minutes.

"Jackson, don't you think Fort Stockton was the perfect place to site a fort. The guy who built it here must have been first-in-his-class in fort-building at West Point."

B.J. yawned. "Why's that Kemo Sabe?"

"Well, because... you really can't sneak up on this place. We've been looking right at this town for the last forty minutes and we never seem to get any closer."

B.J. went into his Tonto impression again. "You're right about that masked man. I'll bet my red brothers quit trying to sneak up on it. The soldiers in the fort could see them coming for miles."

"Yeah, the look-outs could figure out just when the natives were going to attack... I can see them back in the old days, tacking up signs all over the fort, saying the big barn dance Saturday night is canceled... the Comanche war party should be here by then."

"No wonder my frustrated red brethren took it out on Custer. He had it coming anyway!"

It was a strange phenomenon. One would think that due to curvature-of-the-earth, if nothing else, that anyone approaching the fort wouldn't be able to see it from more than five or ten miles away. But anyone could see it from thirty or forty miles away – and conversely, those in the fort could see who was approaching from a long way off.

While the two of them mulled the mystery of Fort Stockton-on-the-horizon, they continued seeing the wacky billboards along the side of the road that read: "When in Fort Stockton -- Visit Railsback's Diner -- Try Our Famous Green Chili." Each outdoor ad was slightly different, but all mentioned the green chili to be had at Railsback's.

B.J. and Mark finally snuck up on Fort Stockton around 5:00 p.m., about an hour after they first saw it. B.J. crossed over Interstate 10 and pulled into the first filling station. Mark noticed an historical marker right across the street. So he got out and went for a walk to loosen-up his puffy knee.

*No wonder you couldn't sneak up on Fort Stockton*, Mark smiled. The plaque said that the town was built in 1858 atop a mesa, as a cavalry post. The town of the same name came along later in history. The place, originally called Comanche Springs, was a desert oasis at the crossroads of the Old San Antonio Trail and the Comanche War Trail.

When Mark crossed back to the gas station, B.J. was in a conversation with the attendant.

"I've got directions to Railsback's Diner," said B.J. "The green chili's actually supposed to be good." The attendant nodded in total agreement.

"Then Railsback's it is," Mark responded.

As he drove to the diner, B.J. asked, "Remind me again... what's the color of the car?"

"It's pearl gray."

"Well... that guy at the Shell station thought it was a dark blue, just for the record."

"Thanks."

Fleetwood Mac was singing "Don't Stop (Thinking About Tomorrow)."

Although it was somewhat early for dinner, but both men were quite hungry, probably due to all the walking and gimping around in the underground cave. B.J. managed to find Railsback's not far from the highway interchange. The restaurant's parking lot was empty. At 5:15 p.m., they were the very first to arrive for dinner, so B.J. was able to park right up front. Before entering, they peered inside the huge picture windows. At first, it looked closed. But upon closer inspection they saw people moving around inside and realized that it was open for business. The decor looked fine, so in they went.

The restaurant was clean. And, as the only customers in the place, the service proved spectacular. One particular waitress, Mindy, couldn't keep her eyes off B.J. Mark ordered the chicken special but skipped the green onion-mashed potatoes and gravy. B.J. insisted on a bowl of Railsback's famous green chili as a starter, and for an entree, he found something healthier, but probably not as tasty as Mark's meal.

"No wonder Fort Stockton was never taken by the Comanche, Jackson," said Mark. "That historical marker I was reading back by the gas station said the town's built on a three-thousand foot-high mesa. That's why we've been able to see it on the horizon for the last hour. The road we were on climbed three thousand feet in altitude the last 45 minutes. Rolling along at 75 mph, you don't realize it I guess. But if you were walking, or riding a camel, I expect that a person would come to appreciate every foot of rise."

B.J. had a somewhat puzzled look on his face. "You know, I'm surprised we haven't run into many American Indians on this trip so far. That really amazes me."

"You mean except for Martha Mae from Kingman, lest you forget."

"Lest I forget... she made a real impression on me." B.J. continued to try to recall meeting another American Indian during the trip.

"Jackson, did you know that one of Ronald Reagan's favorite stories is about the *Bureau of Indian Affairs*."

"Why do I have the feeling I'm going to hear more slander against the Redman? Isn't your insulting Cleveland Indians logo enough?"

"You're going to hear it because it contains an important message about how government works," Mark continued unabated. "It seems that while he was Governor, Reagan had to go to Washington, D.C., to discuss various Indian issues regarding the California tribes. So he set up an appointment to meet the head of the U.S. Interior Department's Bureau of Indian Affairs. He flew all the way to Washington and found this big building on Constitution Avenue, with a sign out front, *Bureau of Indian Affairs*.

"Reagan and his aides went inside. On the first floor, all they saw was rows and rows of desks, and behind each desk sat a bureaucrat. Same thing on the second floor, and the third floor... rows and rows of desks... behind each desk sat a bureaucrat. Finally, Reagan walked down one of the rows until he reached the very last desk in the row. Sitting at that very last desk was a bureaucrat with his head down on the desktop, his arms folded. The man was sobbing... just crying his eyes out. He was obviously very upset, and Reagan didn't want to disturb him. So the Governor tapped the guy sitting in front of the fellow on the shoulder and asked him, 'What's wrong with this fellow back here?'"

"The bureaucrat answered, 'Oh, him? *His Indian died*.'"

B.J. did a spit-take with a piece of biscuit. "Ronny Reagan can tell a story. I'll give him that." Then, with a sly grin, B.J. added, "Of course all you right-thinking Republicans, with the possible exception of Barry Goldwater, still believe that the only good injun is, in fact, a dead one."

"*That*," responded Mark, "hasn't been a plank in the GOP platform since Little Big Horn."

As they enjoyed their meals, several families came into the restaurant. Most people who arrived seemed to know one another. Mark overheard more than a few references to the fancy sports car with California plates parked out in front. It was beginning to dawn on Mark that even though the Porsche 924 was far from being a really expensive sports car, and despite the fact that it was becoming a popular car on the West Coast, it was a still a rare sight throughout the middle of the country. The number of people who had never seen one genuinely surprised him. And from the sideways glances cast in their direction from the patrons of Railsback's, it wasn't too difficult for locals to figure out who in the establishment might be associated with the fancy car with California tags.

After a delicious dinner of down-home cooking, Mark paid the tab at the checkout counter and headed for the car. B.J. wandered off to the rest room. As Mark neared the Porsche, a teenager who was having dinner with his family pointed at him. The family was sitting at a table right in the front picture window.

Mark got in behind the steering wheel and lit up an after-dinner Salem. He started the car. With a roar the Porsche *leapt right over the curb*, smashed through a three-foot hedge, and hit the restaurant's floor-to-ceiling plate glass window with a sickening sound!

The family seated behind the front window dropped their silverware and bolted away from the table. Mark held his breath, waiting for the window to fracture and disintegrate into bits. The window, now sporting a major crack from top-to-bottom, continued to reverberate, but stayed in place. Mark kept waiting for the inevitable crash of glass, but it never came. The teenager who'd noticed him earlier was pointing at him again, this time with a scowl and an entirely different attitude.

*Damn that B.J.! He left the car in gear again!* Mark was embarrassed to death. Some hotshot sports car driver from California he was -- smashing into a damn diner -- damn near killing an innocent family. Mark quickly shifted into reverse and awkwardly backed the car away from the window and off the shrubbery. He turned off the ignition and rushed back inside to make sure everyone was okay. The startled family huddled around the manager. Now all of them were pointing in his direction.

"I am terribly, terribly sorry... I hope everyone is all right," Mark said.

"Well Mister, that was a mite close," said the manager with a drawl and stern scowl on his face. "You've done scared the 'be-jesus' out of the poor O'Malley family here."

"I am sure I did... and I'd like to make things right with you," Mark said. He turned to the manager, and added, "and with you, of course... for the window... and the shrubs."

"No one's injured, so no real harm done, Mister," said Mr. O'Malley, a proud gentleman with a ramrod demeanor. "But I'll tell you what young man, you pick up the tab on dessert for the wife and kids... and we'll call 'er even."

"Dessert nothing," said Mark. He turned to the manager, "Please give me the dinner bill for the whole family, and tell me what it'll take to replace that plate glass window."

At that point B.J. came around the corner. Seeing the impromptu gathering, he asked, "What's up?"

"Never mind, Jackson... just get in the car," Mark growled through his teeth. He was furious. "And don't dare get behind the wheel," he added with a snap.

"Geez... what a grouch," B.J. said as Ed Norton would to a Ralph Cramden tirade on the "Honeymooners." He left the restaurant.

Mark knew that B.J. was upset for dismissing him like that in front of others, but, at that point, he didn't much care.

"Well, Mister," said the diner's manager, "why don't we say the dinner bill's $35.00, that's what it usually is for the O'Malley's. Plus a tip of, shall we say... four or five dollars? And the last time I replaced a front window, after the twister of '71, I think it was about $85.00 for the glass, plus labor. Shall we say... a total of $120.00? I wouldn't worry about the hedge... it'll grow back. So, I reckon the whole kit'n'kaboodle would come to about $155.00. Does that sound fair to you?"

Mark had hidden two $100 bills, as a cross-country emergency fund, behind the auto insurance card in his wallet -- just in case of an accident. This definitely qualified as such. He fished the two bills out, handed them over and said, "Here... I'd like to make things right with all of you. Mr. Railsback, get your window and your hedge plants fixed. Buy the whole O'Malley family dinner and dessert tonight, and if anything's left over, do it again next week. I'm really sorry to have messed up your Thursday evening. My buddy and I enjoyed our meal here."

"It's a fine thing you're doing young fella'..." were the manager's parting words.

Mark returned to the car.

B.J. must have gotten the picture, sitting there in the passenger's seat surveying the crushed hedgerow, a large picture window with a massive crack in it, and a scrape on "Stanley's" front bumper. All this havoc because he forgot what Mark had said about not leaving the car in gear when parking it. B.J. must have put two-and-two together and realized that leaving the car in gear had caused the mishap.

As they departed Ft. Stockton, neither said a word for thirty minutes. Finally, B.J. mumbled, "I'm sorry, Stanton. What did all that it cost? I'll make it up to you."

"It's not the money, Jackson... I'm angry that you didn't listen to me... I'm pissed that you didn't park it in neutral... I'm embarrassed about hitting the window... and I'm hacked off that I had to shell out $200.00."

"I'll even up with you in New Orleans. Big Bart will cash a check for me and I'll make it up to you. I promise."

"It's really not about the money... next time, Jackson, just listen to me, will you? That's all I want."

B.J. wanted to say *Listen to you? That's all I've done for three days.* But he bit his tongue. Knowing he was in trouble, B.J. tried to get Mark laughing. "Houston," B.J. intoned, "This is Eagle-Feather-One. I regret to inform you that the co-pilot, in his ineptitude, left an important toggle switch in the wrong position during the last EVA. This mindless glitch caused our belov'd capsule pilot, Captain Stanton, to inadvertently ram an alien object. I fully expect to be court-martialed upon re-entry for this bone-headed misadventure. Over and out."

"Eagle-Feather-One. This is Mission Control. Cap-Com-Houston. We concur with your bonehead description. You are hereby demoted to Ensign. Out."

Mark realized B.J. was sorry and it was forgotten, as far as he was concerned.

Aptly, on the radio, the Climax Blues Band was singing "Couldn't Get It Right."

## On the Fly.

IT WAS SIX o'clock when they departed Fort Stockton. By Mark's calculations, they still had another four hours of driving to reach San Antonio. The side trip to Carlsbad had thrown them off course a bit, but Mark figured they could get back on his original itinerary if he really stepped on it tonight. And secretly that's what he was planning to do. He wanted to spend the night in San Antonio, at the Davy Crockett Hotel where he'd made reservations, soaking his sore knee in a hot bath.

Owing to B.J.'s continuing silence, Mark felt somewhat uncomfortable so he attempted to come up with an innocuous subject that he and B.J. could discuss without raising blood pressures, something they might even agree on. But he couldn't think of one issue where their opinions converged. Then it hit him. *This "Big Bart" in New Orleans -- who was he? And what was that all about?*

"Jackson, let me ask you, who's Big Bart... the fellow we're going to hook up with in New Orleans?"

"Well, Stanton... you should remember the name Bart Franklin. He was a morning drive-time deejay in Washington."

"Vaguely. That's Big Bart? Bart Franklin. He left D.C. without a lot of fanfare. How'd he end up in New Orleans?"

"He's got another radio talk show. He claims he's the only black man on the top-rated radio station in town. Even local rednecks love to listen to him. According to Bart, the Cajun crowd calls-in to his program more than his brothers in the city do.'"

"Well, I'll be damned..." thought Mark. The more he thought about it, he recalled the deep voice of Bart Franklin on the radio from their days in Washington."

"Things were going well for him in D.C.," said B.J. "Then, all of the sudden he dropped off the air and left town. I kept in touch. Bart even came out to visit in San Francisco last year and looked me up."

"You know, Jackson... it's nothing short of amazing how we've both managed to keep up with friends from Dewey Beach days, despite the fact that we've been living on the West Coast. Those years at the beach were interesting times... young people from all over the country came to Washington in the sixties and seventies to jump-start their political careers.

A mere handful fell in love with Washington and stayed... some went back home to make their fortunes and raise a family. Only a precious few kept the political torch alive and went home to run for office... hell, that's what we all had planned on, right out of college."

"Like you, I've kept up with quite a few folks, but unlike you, most of them are women," said B.J. with a glint in his eye, "and a few guys, like Bart."

They blew by Ozona, Texas, the county seat of Crockett County, and home of the Davy Crockett Monument. During daylight hours, Mark would have loved to stop and see the memorial, but they were "truckin." Dusk was falling fast as they sped east at 80 mph. There was a heap-plenty of Texas between them and San Antonio.

"I've made it a point to keep in touch by phone with many in our old beach house crowd," said Mark. "I didn't know how long I would live on the West Coast and I wanted to stay in touch because I was commuting back and forth during the Congressional sessions. Also, as I said the other day, I had a lot of time on my hands in California."

"I'll stay in D.C. until someone we know throws a Welcome Home party for us. You know, a Butch Cassidy and the Sundance Kid have returned, type-thing. We'll make sure everyone from the old days is invited."

*Thank God,* Mark thought, the Railsback's Diner incident was forgotten.

"I Go Crazy" by Paul Davis was on the air.

At 8:45 p.m. they whizzed by Junction, Texas. Even though it was dark, one could still see that the terrain was changing. They were entering LBJ's stomping grounds, the Texas Hill Country. Falling behind them was the flat desert with its red rocks, sagebrush and cacti. Lying ahead were rolling hills with fields of prairie grass, mesquite trees and natural lakes. *The rivers here were so wide and so deep that they might officially be classified as creeks in Ohio*, Mark thought.

A little after 9:00p.m., flashlight in hand, Mark pulled over near the U.S. Route 290 interchange to read an historical marker which noted that just to the south were the ruins of old Fort Lancaster, built in 1855 to protect travelers along the San Antonio to El Paso trail. B.J. took another pass on getting out to read a roadside marker.

Upon his return to the driver's seat, "Jackson," he said, "I believe I learned more about human nature spending three or four summers at the beach, than I did during my first 26 years on the planet, including high school and college. At the beach, with all those different personalities, we learned how deal with people, you know, how to kid one another... how to criticize without hurting feelings."

"Well, at least you've mastered that with *half* the population."

## "Nothing but the FAX."

IT WAS AFTER ten o'clock. They were four hours away from Fort Stockton and San Antonio was just a few miles ahead. A sign for the Hildebrand Avenue exit was ahead in the distance so Mark got ready to ease the car into the far right traffic lane. He looked in the rear view mirror and found a black and white police patrol car right behind them. He was glad he'd used the turn signal to change lanes. The cops had snuck right up on him. *It must be the out-of-state license plates, they seemed to attract police.* For the next couple of minutes the patrol car was right on their rear bumper. Mark made sure he was doing no more than the speed limit. Then he glimpsed a ramp sign for Fredricksburg Road and Brackenridge Park and decided to take it, just to lose the police escort. The very instant his turn signal went on, the multi-colored rotator lights atop the cruiser went on. They were now officially in trouble, and it was well before midnight.

"If there are any beer bottles lying around on the floor mat, you'd better kick them under the seat, pronto," Mark said firmly. "We've got uniformed company."

"Umm, Kemo Sabe, I'm hiding the firewater as we speak."

The Porsche crept along the highway exit ramp, with the black and white patrol car right on its tail. B.J. tidied up. When there was enough room for other cars and trucks to pass by on the left, Mark pulled over and stopped. The police car came to a stop right behind them and turned a blinding "take down" spotlight on the back of the Porsche. The area was lit up like a movie set. After what seemed an eternity, two officers slowly emerged from the cruiser. The driver of the police car stepped up to Mark's side, while the second officer headed for B.J.'s door. Ordinarily Mark would have taken this for a routine traffic stop, but as he watched the trooper approach, in the side view mirror, he saw the cop unsnap his holster flap.

"No screwing around," he whispered to B.J. "These guys are serious about something."

"May I see your license and registration?" the trooper asked.

The second officer knocked on B.J.'s window and asked him to roll it down. Surprisingly, B.J. compiled without a wise crack.

"Here you go," Mark handed the officer his license. B.J. was looking around in the glove compartment for the registration. He couldn't find it.

Tension building in his gut, Mark snapped at him. "Jackson, we just had it this morning for the I.N.S. guys, remember? Keep looking!"

B.J. rummaged through the glove box. Sure enough, he found it.

"May I ask what you two Californians are doing in San Antonio?"

"Just passing through..."

"Have you stopped anywhere here in town in the last hour or two?"

"No sir. We just got into town. We've driven straight through from Fort Stockton along I-10."

With that he took Mark's license and registration and returned to the cruiser. Meanwhile the second officer just kept an eye on them from B.J.'s window. The wait seemed like another ten minutes. At that point a second police car pulled up. The word *Captain* was printed on the door. Then a third cruiser pulled up; then another. Finally there were four police cars, all with their bubble-gum-machine dome reflector lights flashing.

Trying not to move his lips while speaking, B.J. whispered an aside, "Were you speeding?"

"No," Mark whispered back. "I was following the flow of traffic. But with all these cops in a low hover... this has to be something more than a traffic violation. They think we're chain saw murderers or something... be very careful what you say."

After a huddle with the Captain, the first officer returned and asked Mark to step out of the car; he did. "Sir, would you mind coming back to the patrol car?" He complied. Mark noticed the second cop was escorting B.J. to another patrol car. *What was going on?* Mark knew they hadn't done whatever it was the police thought they did. And knowing that no policeman likes a smart-ass, he decided to keep cool. He hoped B.J. would do the same.

"Can you explain what this is all about?" Mark asked as politely and as firmly as possible under the circumstances.

"We've had an incident in the area and you and your friend fit the description perfectly... two white males... one tall with a beard... the driver of the car somewhat shorter. Even the car fits the description... a late model, black sports car, with out-of-state tags, headed east toward downtown on I-10. That fits you two, to a tee, doesn't it?"

"What are we supposed to have done... robbed a bank or something?"

"Two suspects got some poor fellow stinkin' drunk, rolled him, and then beat him up pretty good in a bar parking lot."

"Where?"

"A couple of miles north and west of here, in the Huebner Road area."

"Well, we drove past there coming in on the Interstate, but we never stopped."

"Where *have* you been?"

"Like I said... we woke up in El Paso... drove to Carlsbad Caverns... stopped in Pecos... drove over to Fort Stockton... ate dinner there... drove here. That's about it. That's a lot of territory to cover in one day, don't you think?"

"What time did you leave Fort Stockton," the officer asked.

"Let me think... it was early. We were the first people in there for dinner... I'd say we got there around 5:00 or 5:15. We ate, left about 6:00 and drove pretty much straight through..."

"What do you mean *pretty much* straight through?"

"I mean we stopped at a historical marker..."

"A what?"

"A roadside historical marker."

"Where? What time was that?"

"Excuse me, but am I on trial here, or something?" Mark was about to lose it. "It was a historical marker about a Fort... Fort Linkletter or Lancaster, or something like that. We must have stopped there somewhere around 9:00."

"Wait here," the officer said, slamming the car door as he left.

*Wait here? Where was Mark going to go?* He was locked into the back seat. First the officer went to the Captain's car and then to the squad car where they were questioning B.J. The scene was a bizarre one. There were still four police cruisers on the scene, all with wigwag signals flashing. A steady stream of cars coming off the I-10 ramp was at a crawl, each driver rubbernecking to see the two societal misfits who were getting their just desserts. It really was looking like a spectacle right out of a law enforcement drama. Mark listened to the constant squawking of the police radio coming from the front seat of the cruiser. It was apparent from the police radio traffic that he and B.J. were the one and only lead the police were pursuing on this beating incident. All the action, according to the dispatcher, was at the I-10 eastbound Fredricksburg Road off ramp. Sure as hell, that was Mark and B.J.

A few minutes later, the first officer, "Cranston," according to his name badge, returned. "Well, your story and your friend's don't exactly match up..." he said.

*Well, with all due respect*, Mark thought -- B.J. had to be telling the same story. That's exactly what the two of them did all day. *What's B.J. going to do, make up a complete lie?* And B.J. is smart enough to know that the police are asking Mark the very same questions. This Cranston guy had to be bluffing.

His stomach cramps had returned and his temper got the best of him, "Well that's a bunch of bullshit... and you know it. What I told you... that's exactly what we've been doing all day."

"Can you prove that?"

"Do I have to? I thought the burden of proof was on the accuser!"

"Well, we'll see to that soon enough, 'cause the guy who got beat up is on his way over here to eyeball you two."

"Are we being held? Don't I get a phone call to a lawyer or something?"

"You are being detained and questioned for identification purposes. We haven't heard back from California yet, about you, that car, and those plates."

With that, he left Mark alone in the patrol car again, locked in a caged back seat without door latches.

Soon the officer was helping some poor slob get out of still another patrol car. This must be the beating victim! Surely this guy could clear up the situation. After all, he'd been drinking with the bad guys for a while -- he must know what they looked like. But when Mark saw the poor sucker up close, he felt very sorry for the victim. The guy's face was a mess. The two assholes that beat him up did a hell of a number on him. The guy's right eye was so swollen it was closed. The other eye socket was puffy and bloodied -- and this poor slob was going to "eyeball" Mark and B.J. *God help us*, Mark thought. *We're as good as on the chain gang already*!

The police had the victim look at Mark through the cruiser's side window. The officers aimed flashlights at Mark's face and clothes. The badly bruised fellow got up real close to the window and tried to look Mark square in the eye. Mark kept thinking back to grade school days and the two-kid line-up for Sister Mary Fatima. Mark even tried to have a gentle look on his face. *What sort of look do you assume for a line-up of one*? For some goofy reason, Mark wanted to smile, but the mere thought of Sister Tommy-gun More and her slap sobered him up. Any hope that this episode would be over soon went out the window when Mark heard the pummeled victim say, "I'm not so sure."

"I'm not so sure... about what," Mark mumbled. *That we're the guys who beat him up? That we're guilty of assault and battery? What exactly isn't this guy too sure about?*

Mark's mind was racing. The burden of proof was shifting back to him and B.J.

*How could they prove they were innocent?* The last stop where anyone saw them was at Railsback's Diner. Certainly the people there would remember the two of them and the car, but not their names. Mark had no receipt. He'd paid for everything in cash -- including the $200 for damages. But earlier they'd stopped for gas! While Mark went to see the historical marker, B.J. paid for the gas. Maybe he had a receipt!

When Officer Cranston returned, Mark could tell he was more confused than before. Frankly, it looked like the man didn't know what to do with the two of them.

"Can I make a suggestion?" Mark spoke up.

"Like what?"

"My friend, B.J.... he might have a gasoline receipt from Ft. Stockton that could prove we couldn't have driven all the way here in time to get this fellow drunk and beat him up."

"Is that it? That's all you got?"

"Well, I hesitate to even mention it, but if you were to call Railsback's Diner in Fort Stockton, quickly, before it closes, I think they might remember B.J. and me... and they might remember that we left there around six o'clock. In fact, I'll bet you... if you described us over the telephone, and the car, they would remember us."

"Now why is that?"

"Because we smashed-in the restaurant's front picture window... that's why," Mark bowed his head, acting the part of one who had just "copped a plea" and confessed to a lesser charge.

Cranston looked at Mark sternly in the rearview mirror. The officer thought he had something now -- destruction of private property. Maybe he thought Mark was trying to plea bargain -- that the two would rather be held on breaking windows in Fort Stockton than for breaking bones in San Antonio. Mark had baited him. And the cop went for it. Cranston jumped out of the car and returned to the Captain's cruiser.

Mark had a feeling he would call Fort Stockton right away. Sure enough, a few moments later Mark heard the police radio dispatchers acknowledge an order to call the Fort Stockton police. The unheard, but acknowledged, radio call to the dispatch desk must have come from the Captain's patrol car.

The second trooper, who'd been babysitting B.J., walked up to Captain's car and whispered to Cranston.

When Cranston returned, all he said was, "Your friend says he has no receipt for the gas in Fort Stockton... too bad. All he's got a receipt for some postcards he bought at Carlsbad Caverns and a Polaroid picture of you two at Judge Roy Bean's in Pecos... but they could have been taken a week ago."

"But we're wearing the same clothes," Mark retorted. The officer kept mum.

It was now 10:45 p.m. This was beginning to be a nightmare.

Cranston stepped out of the cruiser once again. He and the other trooper talked for a minute and then he returned.

"What time did you say you were in Carlsbad?"

"Between Noon and 1:30 p.m.," Mark answered.

"That's eight and a half hours... that's still plenty of time to drive to San Antonio and beat this guy up."

"But that's nearly 500 miles of driving in there... plus a stop at Pecos and time for dinner," Mark said. Then it dawned on him. They'd lost an hour coming over the state line into Texas. Mark remembered changing his watch, *but did he set it ahead, or did he set it back an hour*? He was tired and confused, but his instincts screamed, an hour's time was lost! They lost an hour when they changed time zones. So they were actually on the road seven and a half hours, less the stop in Pecos, the stop for dinner, and the historical markers along the way. So, they traveled about 500 miles in less than seven hours.

Cranston left the car and walked over to the Captain's cruiser yet again. A few minutes later Mark heard the police radio dispatcher acknowledge a request for actual mileage between Carlsbad, New Mexico and Fort Stockton, and then Fort Stockton to San Antonio.

"Two-Victor-Twenty," it was the dispatcher. "Responding to your mileage request... Carlsbad to Fort Stockton is one-four-zero miles... and Fort Stockton to San Antonio is three-two-eight miles..."

That means 468 miles divided by six and one-half hours. Mark tried to concentrate. Seven goes into forty-six, six times with four left over, and a seven goes into forty-eight -- seven times! They'd averaged *at least* 67 mph while on the road, but it was probably more like 72 mph, times six and one-half hours, plus down time in Pecos and at Fort Stockton. Surely, that was proof he and B.J. couldn't have done it.

"Two-Victor-Twenty... Two-Victor-Twenty," the dispatcher called, "we've just received a telecopier transmission from Fort Stockton P.D. It confirms that your suspects departed *Rail-back* shortly after 1800 hours this evening. No charges for destruction of property. No warrants issued. Also, CHP has no outstanding warrants on a '78 black Porsche with tags Papa-Romeo-Sierra-five-one-four... Over."

They were off the hook! The receipt from B.J.'s stupid bat cave postcards and Mark's $200 "tip" had won the day. The police had to let them go. No way they could have left Fort Stockton at 6:00 o'clock, driven here, sat with some guy for an hour until he got drunk and then beat him up. No way. And, thank God for new technology -- a telecopier has saved their butts.

Cranston returned for the fourth or fifth time and politely handed Mark his driver's license and registration. "Are you two staying in this town tonight?"

"We've got a reservation downtown at the Crockett Hotel."

"The Crockett, huh? Can I ask you why you're staying there?"

"I heard it was a nice place, downtown, within walking distance of the Alamo. Why do you ask?"

"My wife works there... do you know how to get to the Crockett from here?"

"No, sir."

"Follow us. We'll escort you there. Sorry for the inconvenience, fellows, but you two and the car... it was a very close match to the descriptions we were looking for."

"I understand. You're just doing your job. No harm done... I just want to go to bed. It's been a long, long day. El Paso this morning? It seems like I was there a week ago."

B.J. and Mark were reunited. They looked blankly at one another, shrugged their shoulders, and piled into the car.

"Don't snap open any beer cans just yet, Jackson... we're supposed to follow these cops to our hotel."

"Wee... this is fun," said B.J., imitating a kid, "I know this is old-hat for you White House types, but I'm enjoying my first police-escorted motorcade. I could get used to this."

"Rumor Has It" by Donna Summer was playing on the radio when they pulled up in front of the Crockett Hotel.

That night, after they schlepped the luggage up to the room, the two men crashed and slept the peaceful sleep of the innocent.

# CHAPTER FOUR

## Friday, March 24, 1978

### A Hero Is More Than A Sandwich.

THERE WAS A pronounced knock on the hotel room door. A sleepy eyed Mark Stanton squinted at the nightstand clock; it was 7:30 a.m. "Room Ser-veece," an accented male voice said.

B.J. was still snoring. Mark didn't remember ordering room service, but he crawled out of his bed in boxer shorts and cracked the door open an inch or two. It wasn't your typical room service waiter with a black bow tie standing in the hallway. It was some prissy bastard in a suit, wearing a white carnation boutonniere and name badge.

"You must have the wrong room pal. We didn't order anything," Mark croaked.

"*Monsieur*, this is compliments of the Crockett Hotel and Sergeant Cranston of *zee* Police," said the dapper fellow. "*Ici*..." he handed Mark a telephone message slip through the opening in the still-chained door.

It was from Officer Cranston from last night. It read: "Caught the real perps just after midnight. The doughnuts and coffee are on me."

"So? May I bring *zis* in?" the fellow bearing the tray asked.

"Sure, why not?" Mark unchained the door. As the "suit" entered, he handed Mark a folded copy of the morning paper.

Mark stuck his head out into the hall and looked up and down the corridor to see if this was a "Candid Camera" set-up or some kind of Texas-style practical joke. The hallway was empty.

"I'm Pierre Rousseau, *fuud* and bev'rage manager, at your service..."

"Well," said Mark, "knock me over with a feather. You mean we have a hotel manager delivering room service, and now you're telling me the Police Department is springing for breakfast?"

"Well, not pre-*zise*-ly. But, shall we say... *zis* fine 'otel has very close relations *wiss* our friends downtown at headquarters... and it is my understanding..."

By now B.J. was sitting up in bed, listening, wide-eyed.

"That you had a... how shall I say it... an inauspicious entrance into San Antonio last evening. As a result... *zee* coffee and doughnuts are *on-zee-'ous.* You see, Officer Cranston's wife, Melody, works here at *zee* Crockett, in our sales office," he said with a broad gap-toothed grin.

"Thank you." Mark went to his wallet on the nightstand to find a buck for a tip.

Anticipating the move, Mr. Rousseau waved him off, "Zat will not be *nec-zee-sary*. Good morning to you bot'." By the time Mark turned, the fellow was out the door.

"Jackson, *zee* cops are buying us *zee* doughnuts. I wonder why?"

"You're welcome," B.J. mumbled.

"What's that supposed to mean?"

B.J. sat up and confessed. "Last night... sitting in the back of that police car, being interrogated like a common thug, I made some crack about cops and doughnuts," he revealed.

Mark stopped folding and packing clothes. "Oh, man... what'd you say?"

"Well, after the fourth cop car pulled up to take a look at us, I asked what they thought we did. I said something like... 'We must have knocked over the chief's favorite doughnut shop to get this kind of attention.' Anyway, Cranston's partner seemed to get a kick out of it."

"Well, they did hold the wrong guys for an hour last night. And, I don't think they want any trouble," said Mark, the wheels of his mind turning slowly. "Maybe it's just that Cranston fellow... he probably mentioned to his wife that we were staying here. He seemed a decent sort. When you think about it, I guess we're lucky to be eating doughnuts on the outside this morning, no special thanks to you."

"Hey, without my batty postcards and my leaving 'Stanley' in gear at Railsback's, we'd probably be in jail right now." B.J.'s face beamed thinking about the irony of the circumstances.

Mark threw the rolled-up newspaper at him, and then picked up a tempting glazed doughnut dipped in chocolate. Even though he knew his easily upset stomach would probably pay for it later, he devoured it in three quick bites.

B.J. reviewed the front page. "Let's see... exploring the Democratic side of the ledger... I'm sorry to report that twelve-term Michigan Congressman Charles Diggs was indicted yesterday for using more than $100,000 in government payroll money for private purposes."

"Good. It's about time we got rid of another thieving scoundrel in Congress. These are the kinds of things that happen after thirty-five years of one party control."

"Save it Stanton. I don't want to hear your right-wing guano. On the GOP side of the aisle, the fellow who most-closely reflects your personal political views..."

"Who? Bob Dole."

"No, Alf Landon... also of Kansas. Who, according to this story, rarely endorses candidates for office... a certain kiss of death with wet lips if history is any measure... has made an exception for a member of his own family, Nancy Landon Kassebaum, who is running for the U.S. Senate this fall."

"'Landslide Landon'... that endorsement should bring the Democrats to their knees."

"Yeah, what did he get? Two percent of the vote against FDR? Let's see... in other news the Amoco Cadiz, that beached tanker off Portsall, France, the one I've been reading about all week... well, its 223,000-ton oil slick threatens the English Channel islands and scenic places like Mont St. Michel."

"Is that the storybook-looking castle on the tidal island? They'll be serving up shellfish in sweet and sour crude for awhile."

"Sure. That's why they named them after a Republican... Oysters *Rockefeller*, 'cause of the oil." B.J. kept his eyes on the newspaper, "Scanning, scanning... hey, your silk-stocking Dow Jones industrial average slipped a point yesterday to close at 756.50. And tonight, while we're partying in Houston, we'll be missing Quincy on television... and of course, I'll have to miss my favorite Friday night program, the Donny and Marie Osmond Show."

"Poor baby..."

"But, Stanton... nowhere in the San Antonio *Express-News* does it say anything about a plane crash at Edwards Air Force Base this week. You know, it's gotten to the point where I'm not so sure I saw it myself. And so... *that's the way it is...*" B.J. finished, trying to imitate Walter Cronkite.

"If I could just get you to shave... and to process your kinky hair... and wear a tailored three-button suit... I believe I could make an anchor man out of you yet."

"Not a chance. I don't do interviews... on either side of the camera. So what's on the agenda for today?"

Mark reflected. "Today was supposed to be the easiest day of the trip. Before you so rudely tore up my itinerary, I'd planned a light day of driving... to break-up the week. This morning, I thought we would check out 'The Alamo.' Then try some good local Tex-Mex for lunch. And then drive the 200 miles over to Houston. We check in there and take a nap. Finally, we stay out late at the world-famous 'Élan' disco, with my ol' buddy Paul Rumbaugh. That's it... that's what *was* on the schedule for today... before it was unceremoniously shredded."

"That's close enough to driftin' for me. I guess I can go along with that."

They took their sweet time getting washed up and re-packed.

## The "Ears" of Texas Are Upon You...

MARK AND B.J. walked right past it, without even noticing. The Alamo. The most famous shrine in all of Texas. Hallowed ground. "Remember the Alamo!"

Both of them had grown up watching Fess Parker, as Davy Crockett on the Walt Disney television show, give up his life for the Alamo. Davy was supposed to have died in the thirteen-day siege that took place in March, 1836 -- one hundred forty-two years ago. If ever there was a historic landmark etched into an American kid's brain by the age of ten, it was "The Alamo." There wasn't a baby boomer kid born between 1945 and 1965 who couldn't sing the entire Davy Crockett theme song from memory.

Despite the countless times B.J. and Mark had seen the profile of that old mission, neither recognized it at first. They actually had to backtrack and take another look at the tourist map. Frankly, Mark had expected the Alamo to be sitting out in the middle of a very large park, like the Boston Common or something, or off on a secluded hill, like a capital building, or at least a county courthouse.

The old mission seemed jammed into a much-too-busy downtown city block. Commercialization was all around it. Neither Mark nor B.J. was prepared for that. They were somewhat disappointed in The Alamo's modern-day setting. After all, they'd heard and read about this place; both of them were "underwhelmed."

"This is it? The Alamo? I don't believe it. How many guys *died* for this? It's so small," B.J. said in mild disbelief.

Despite the disappointment, they took the 10:00 a.m. tour.

The costumed guide began with some history. "The original Spanish mission was built in 1718, as one of five missions along the San Antonio River. It was founded to educate and Christianize the local Indians. The current structure was finished in 1756 on the site of a prior church. The formal name of the Alamo is the Mission San Antonio de Valero."

The walls were massive with large, thick stone arches buttressing them.

"The Alamo compound includes the Shrine... the former mission church... the Long Barracks, and the mission priests' rectory," the guide continued.

Despite the mission's low-key location, Mark was fascinated by its rich history. This little church played a pivotal role in the development of the American southwest. Texas and the surrounding states might be part of a whole different country today had not this place surfaced in history.

"In early 1836, Colonel James Bowie was sent to San Antonio by General Sam Houston..." the guide went on. "The original orders were to destroy the Alamo. However, when Bowie arrived he found eighty Texans willing to stand and fight, so he changed his mind. On hearing the news that Bowie was preparing to take a stand at the Alamo, Colonel William B. Travis arrived in early February, followed the same week by Davy Crockett and more than a dozen Tennessee volunteers."

As they moved through the old mission, Mark tried to envision what it must have been like, to be facing Santa Ana's army of 5,000 regulars, knowing that if you stayed around to fight, the odds were that you were going to die here.

"On March 6th, at daybreak, the Mexican army assaulted the Alamo. The Texans repelled two onslaughts. But by early morning the third attack breached the north wall. It was all over for Bowie, Travis, Crockett and 186 others."

The guide also stated that the Mexican army had more than 600 casualties. "And one month later, Sam Houston defeated the Mexican Army at the Battle of San Jacinto, which secured Texas' independence," she said. "'Remember the Alamo' was the rallying cry that brought victory in that battle."

Mark read every plaque and historical flyer in the Alamo. He learned that after the revolution, the shrine was abandoned until the U.S. Army made a supply depot of it in 1849; by 1900 the place was a mess. The Driscoll family of Corpus Christi bought the property in 1903 for a mere $65,000. Later, the State of Texas purchased it. And today, the Daughters of the Republic of Texas run the shrine as a museum.

Around Noon Mark and B.J. departed the Alamo, still trying to mesh expectations with the reality.

"Jackson, after seeing that place, you know what I'm thinking?"

B.J. listened.

"I'm thinking that... with five thousand Mexican soldiers on the front lawn, if there had been a back door to the Alamo, there might not be a Texas today," Mark said.

"Better not say that too loudly, the *ears* of Texas are upon you..."

## The Makings of a Hero.

THE RIVER WALK in San Antonio is truly unique. Even though the river, so typical of Texas, is insignificant enough that one can spit across it in places, Mark thought it to be a neat place to visit. After wandering along the riverside pathway for what seemed like a mile up one side and down the other, B.J. ultimately selected a Mexican restaurant for lunch. It was Casa Something-or-Other, but the food was terrific. Mark ordered a simple grilled chicken salad for lunch. B.J. went for the *Rajas Poblanos*.

"Jackson, my man, I don't think I have the makings of a hero."

"A sandwich?"

"No a real hero... like at the Alamo," Mark said. "I don't think I could have made the ultimate sacrifice for the Alamo, especially if I was a volunteer from some other place, like Davy Crockett."

"I believe that most heroes are average people, just like you and me," B.J. said thoughtfully, "but they get frozen into totally foreign and very unusual circumstances, where they either suck-it-up and take a huge roll of the dice... or they lose face with others, running away screaming. Those who manage to survive the long odds stacked against them are the heroes. Those who don't... are the martyrs."

"Good call, Jackson. If I had been a 20 year-old at the beginning of World War I, I'm sure I would have enlisted as a doughboy. And if I'd been around at the time of Pearl Harbor, I just know that I would have signed up on the spot. And if I were a trooper with Custer at the Little Bighorn, I think I would have accepted the fact that there was no way out short of dying. But at the Alamo... up until that very last morning, any one of those guys could have left the place and lived to fight another day in a better circumstance. They chose to stay and die. That's a decision that I just don't understand and probably couldn't have made."

Rubbing his belly, B.J. said, "Stanton, don't sell yourself short. I just watched you shovel down a Tex-Mex lunch without blinking a tear from your eye. You never know what you're capable of until it's on the plate in front of you."

### Fan Mail.

BY ONE O'CLOCK they were back on the road again, burping out loud -- savoring the lunch a second time, as it were, and headed east on Interstate 10.

Dolly Parton was warbling "Two Doors Down" on a mid-Texas C&W station.

"So tell me, what's your buddy Rumbaugh do in Houston?" B.J. asked.

"By day, Paul's a sportswriter for the *Houston Chronicle*. By night he holds court at the Élan discotheque."

"And we're going to this Élan disco club tonight, right?"

"Yeah... it's a membership club. There's dining, good food and the place is supposed to be, according to Rumbaugh, Houston's hottest nightclub. It's where the wild and crazy people go to let off some steam. And, so that's where we'll find Paul, at 8:00 o'clock... we'll meet him there and he'll get us in. Hey, Jackson, I'm the advance man. I tell you, I've got it covered."

"Somehow I find it hard to believe that your idea of a swinging night club and my idea of a hot spot are anywhere on the same block, so to speak," B.J. said quite matter-of-factly.

About an hour east of San Antonio Mark saw a "Historical Marker - One Mile Ahead" sign, so he slowed down and took the turn-off. It was a bright sunny day, in the low 70's, but the wind was gusting a bit. The marker indicated that just south of this spot was the small town of Gonzales, the site of the very first battle of the fight for Texas independence, in 1835. Also, it noted that there was a memorial in the town's square dedicated to the 32 Gonzales volunteers who went to the Alamo and died for their cause.

After a quick jog around the roadside park to forcefully remove the last vaporous vestiges of lunch, B.J. settled into "Stanley's" passenger seat for the remaining two-hour drive to Houston. Mark was rested and feeling up to the drive.

"Lady Love" by Lou Rawls was wafting out of the Blaupunkt.

"Now Stanton, if I remember correctly, didn't you used to date a beautiful Texas belle named Kathy. I remember that she was a homecoming queen... or a prom queen, or a drag queen... something like that wasn't she? You brought her down to the house at Dewey Beach one weekend. A few months later, I asked you where she was, and you said she'd moved back to Texas. So, Casanova, why don't we stop and you can look her up while we're in town? She was beautiful. Maybe she could fix me up with a date for tonight."

"Good memory, Jackson, but a bad idea. First of all, she was from Dallas... not Houston. That's a mere 250 miles away. Her name is Kathy Blair, or, at least it was. And I'd guess that by now she's married to her old college sweetheart."

"Why didn't you follow-up on that after she left Washington? She was the BLT."

"The BLT?"

"Yeah Stanton, she was the Best-Looking-Thing I ever saw out with you..."

"Gee thanks. But all that's ancient history. That romance took place back in '73. Kathy and I were seeing each other pretty steadily in Washington, until she got a great job offer with a television station back in Dallas. She took the job. Who wouldn't have? We continued to keep in touch... but you know long distance romances just don't work out. I promised to come down and visit her. It took a couple of months, but I finally did.

"She'd landed a job as local anchor of the Noon news program. The news, weather and sports took up 15 minutes, and then she had a 15-minute guest interview slot each day right after the news and before the soap operas resumed at 12:30 p.m. She told me she had a totally female television audience. When I visited, she was still living at home with Momma and Daddy Blair. She hadn't had time to even look for an apartment.

"I learned that right after she returned to Dallas her ol' college beau sees her on television and tries to re-kindle the relationship. Well, let's just say that's what prompted my three-day visit, so to speak.

"So, there I was visiting Dallas, staying at her parents' home, spending most of my time with Momma Blair, because Kathy's got to work during the day. Having just started a new job at the station, she says she can't ask for any time-off. So, on the second day of my visit, Momma Blair and I are getting ready to have soup and sandwiches for lunch in front of the TV. We're all set to watch Kathy's noon news and interview show. Some baby doctor is booked to be on for that day's 15-minute interview. Just as we sit down to our lunch, the phone rings. It's Kathy, and she's in a total panic. The baby doctor has an emergency operation to take care of at the hospital. So, as a guest for that day, the doctor is toast. Kathy asks can Momma get Mark all dressed-up in a jacket and tie, and get him down to the studio in less than ten minutes.

"So you went on the show... *you* were the guest?" B.J. was becoming more interested in this story.

"You got that right... yours truly was the official substitute guest. The subject of my interview was supposed to be what it's like being an insider on The White House staff, as a former presidential advance man."

"So how'd it go, Kemo?"

"Well, Momma Blair's all in a panic! She's totally afraid her baby's going to get fired. Kathy's got no guest, except for this damned Yankee from Ohio who's come down to hassle her daughter. So I rush and get my blue blazer and a red rep tie and we race down to the station, Momma Blair driving like A.J. Foyt. We pull up at the front door of the TV station with a screech and I run in. They usher me right onto the set and wire-me-up with a microphone. It's 12:14 p.m. We've got one minute to interview time! I'm trying to comb my hair during the station break. Kathy races over to the interview set. She's just finished reading the news.

B.J. leaned back, arms folded.

"The red light on the camera goes on... we're on live, sitting eyeball-to-eyeball. During the intro, she builds me up to be a big shot Republican... a guy who did advance work for the President and Cabinet members... big Nixon and Ford Administration official. I was hoping that her college beau was watching the program that day. Anyway, she has to build me up, or she's got nobody as a guest, right? First question she asks, who is my favorite Cabinet member? I tell her it's Henry Kissinger, the former Secretary of State. She wants to know what he's really like. We've got fifteen minutes to kill, so I tell her the infamous Secret Service story..."

B.J. gave a puzzled look, "Have I heard this one?"

"I doubt it. Anyway, you know... the Secretary of State notices that his colleague, the Secretary of the Treasury, has more Secret Service agents than he does. I looked into the television camera with the red lights and said that everyone in Washington knows that the State Department, protocol-wise, outranks Treasury, but what few people realize is that the Secret Service is a subdivision of the Treasury Department. So I explained to her television audience that the Secretary of State lodged a formal complaint with the Secret Service. He ranted in his thick German accent that if kidnapped by the Soviets he had America's entire foreign policy strategy in his head, all these state secrets. And that, if captured and tortured, this valuable information could fall into enemy hands. The Secret Service honcho said he'd talk to his boss, the Secretary of the Treasury, to see what could be done about more comprehensive protection.

"Well, a month goes by and no additional Secret Service agents are added to the State Department detail. When the Secretary of State attends the next Cabinet meeting and notices, once again, the large Secret Service detail that protects the Secretary of the Treasury, he fumes. Later that day, he calls in the lead agent on his personal detail and barks at him, 'Vut's happened to my formal request for additional Secret Service agents?'

"'Not to worry, Mr. Secretary...' the lead agent says, 'we've discussed it at great length with the Department and we have been issued new protection guidelines for you in the event of a kidnapping. We've rotated several new men onto the detail who are crack shots. So you see... you really don't need any additional agents.'

'Vut are zee new guidelines?' the Secretary of State insisted to know.

"The lead Secret Service agent said, 'If we think anyone is trying to kidnap you, Mr. Secretary, our orders now are *that you're not to be taken alive.'*"

Mark paused for effect. B.J. doubled over in laughter.

"Well, as I finished telling that story, the whole crew in the TV studio cracks up, but Kathy doesn't react, she's still very much on-air. Somewhat embarrassed, she asks me a couple more innocuous questions. Near the tail end of the fifteen minutes, she has to stretch... you know, to kill some time. But I can tell she's fresh out of questions. So, in trying to drag it out, she ends up asking me three questions: 'Mr. Stanton, what's in store for you? Where do you go from here? What do you want to do next?' In the meantime, the stage manager is giving *me* the 15-seconds-left hurry-up signal, so I thought I'd be short and sweet with my answer. I said, 'I'm not exactly sure what Miss Blair... is next, but as for tonight, how about the two of us going out to dinner?' I said it right on the air. Kathy is stunned speechless. She has a dumbfounded look on her face... the 'I can't believe he hit-on-me, right on the air in front of my all-female audience' look. So she totally ignores my comment, turns to the camera and says good-afternoon and good-bye to the audience."

"She's really upset, right?" B.J. assumed, correctly.

"So pissed she won't even look at me. She's as serious as leprosy. Feeling the negative vibrations, I voluntarily cut short my visit to Dallas and left town the next day. Never did call her back. I wrote her mother a thank-you note and Momma Blair wrote back a few days later. She told me not to be too worried, that Kathy will eventually come around. And, oh, by the way, she writes, 'Kathy's fan mail is running 4 to 1 in your favor. Her viewers think that she should go to dinner with the nice young man who asked her out, on the air.'"

"You sort-of torched that bridge while still crossing it, huh?"

"I'm sure my tackiness... her expression for my type of behavior... drove her right into the arms of her old boyfriend."

Barry Manilow was singing "Can't Smile Without You" on the radio.

Around 3:00 p.m., feeling suddenly tired, Mark stopped for a quick look-see at the Stephen F. Austin State Historical Park, just off I-10. He learned that Austin, for whom the Lone Star state's capital city is named, brought the first settlers to colonize this area in 1824 under contract with the ruling Mexican government.

At Mark's request, B.J. took over the steering wheel. "Are you sure you're okay Stanton? You looked bushed."

"I'll be fine with a little rest," Mark said with a grimace. "Please... just drive."

## Houston Hotel Hassle.

ON THE HORIZON before them was the City of Houston, with its high-rise chrome and glass towers. It was 4:20 p.m., and the local radio station was airing "Southern Nights" by Glen Campbell. For the first time on the entire trip, Mark and B.J. were arriving in an overnight city refreshed, during daylight hours, *and* without a police escort. Mark had reserved a sleeping room at one of the national chain hotels just off the I-610 West Loop in a part of town known as The Galleria. When Mark called Paul Rumbaugh in Houston two weeks prior, Paul suggested that the cross-country travelers stay at a brand-new local hotel he knew about. Mark made a reservation; and thanks to Paul's directions, they found the newly opened hotel easily enough. It was a red brick building wedged in between two all-glass high-rise office towers. There was an indoor mall connecting all three buildings at the lobby level.

The hotel looked like it might be still under construction as they pulled into the parking lot; the entranceway was all torn up. Work crews were laying hot asphalt just outside the front door. There was a lot of background noise. All kinds of heavy equipment were on the site, dump trucks full of steaming asphalt, big heavy roller vehicles, and front-end loaders. The vast majority of the front parking lot was blocked off while crews painted parking stripes on the new asphalt surface. All the equipment seemed to be roaring, spewing black smoke or beeping while backing up.

The hotel's doorman, wearing a ridiculous white pith helmet with a red-plume sticking out of it, and an all-white uniform -- including shoes -- raced out to meet the Porsche. His first words were not "welcome gentlemen" or "good afternoon." He strongly suggested that the car -- sitting as it was near the front door -- was "*in the way*." He asked B.J. to please pull the car around back to a parking garage.

"But we'll just be a minute here... I have to check-in," Mark responded.

"Mister... it would be so much better if you would go around," the doorman said with a firm look.

Muttering to himself, B.J. drove around to the back of the hotel. The narrow driveway that led to the garage ran between buildings and along the left side of hotel. It was an obstacle course; orange traffic cones marked a treacherous path toward the rear of the building. It looked as though the work crews were getting ready to lay asphalt in this driveway next; men in hard-hats were spraying tar. A dozen manhole covers protruded a good two or three inches above the bumpy yet-to-be-surfaced driveway. B.J. inched along, between obstacles, afraid that one a false move would rip the muffler off the low-slung "Stanley."

Sure enough, the doorman was right; behind the hotel stood a four-story garage. They drove up the ramp. The first level, the green concourse, was completely filled with cars. The second inclined ramp led to the red concourse that was completely filled with cars. Also, the third level, the yellow concourse, was completely filled with cars. And, the fourth level -- the "open to the blue sky" concourse, which had no official color code -- was completely filled with cars. *Damn it*, B.J. fumed

Cursing the jerk in the sissified doorman's uniform, B.J. turned the car around and spiraled back down the concourses looking for a newly available space to park. They went past the yellow concourse, down to the red concourse. All full.

As they approached the green level, Mark noticed what he thought was a parking slot, right in the corner of the garage, between the first and second levels. "Over there... in the corner. Park in there."

"Stanton, I don't think that's a legitimate parking space, and it's a pretty tight fit. Besides, it's got hash-mark stripes painted across it like a 'fire lane,'" B.J. said, referring to a narrow pie-sliced slot at the end of a row of parked cars.

"The place is jammed full, just park it in there. 'Stanley' will be all right. Believe me. We can always move it later."

B.J. parked the car without further protest and they proceeded to unload. Mark's usual first load of baggage to be toted to the hotel room included the suitcases. There were three of them -- a large one gripped in his left hand, a smaller one under his left armpit, teetering on the one below, and a three-suiter gripped in his right hand. Also, Mark had a jacket tucked under his right arm. B.J. usually carried his duffel bag and two other canvas bags, containing prized possessions Mark did not want left overnight in the back of the car.

They were loaded down like a prospector's pack mules as the two of them headed for the hotel entrance. This arduous unloading process was the part of each day's routine that B.J. disliked the most. He felt they looked like "...gypsies moving in."

Mark eyed a sign on the garage wall with an arrow -- pointing to the right -- that read, "To Hotel Lobby;" to its immediate right was a rust-colored metal door. B.J. was as loaded down as Mark was, and he was trailing slightly behind. When Mark arrived at the heavy fire door, he juggled the suitcases -- setting down the large grip in his right hand, and grabbed a hold of the doorknob on the right side. Mark turned the knob and pulled the weighty door open. He managed to get the door open just enough to wedge his left shoe in the breach. Then, using the foothold as leverage, he pulled the fire door open so B.J. could follow, leaned his left shoulder into the breach, and went in -- *THUNK*!!!

Mark hit his head on something! He'd walked head-on into another rust-colored metal door! There were two heavy fire doors back-to-back, and they were just an inch or two apart. Mark damned near knocked himself out; he recoiled and staggered backward from the smashed-mouth impact on the second door.

B.J., who was just approaching the first door, saw Mark staggering backwards into the garage. "Ooopsy-Daisy," he said, "what's the problem Spanky?"

"There's two freakin' fire doors here, back-to-back... I've never seen anything like it. I'm glad there's not a real fire, or I'd have knocked my ass out cold. Remind me again to kill that doorman for sending us around... that is, if I live long enough to see him again," Mark said.

B.J. chuckled. "Here, Kemo, let me hold the first door open while you go to work on the second one." B.J. leaned hard against the first heavy metal fire door, keeping it wide open.

To confound things, the second fire door had its doorknob over on the left side, which necessitated that Mark shift all the luggage around so his left hand would be free to open this door. He repeated the initial effort; this time using his left hand to turn the knob, and wedging his right shoe into the opening. Then Mark leaned into the second door with his right shoulder. Moving quickly, the loaded-down B.J. wedged through the doorway right behind him.

Neither one of them ever saw the flight of stairs.

The twosome tumbled, ass over elbows, down the steps, into an office; they ended up sprawled out on a carpeted floor, covered by baggage -- three heavy suitcases, an overstuffed duffel bag, and two canvas travel bags. *Laurel and Hardy on vacation, that's what we look like,* Mark thought.

People came running at the sound of the crash, the moans, and the steady stream of colorful expletives emanating from Mark.

"Are we there yet?" B.J. asked, looking up at the concerned faces of a group of office workers who had gathered.

Mark picked himself up off the carpet, "I mean it Jackson! I'm going to *kill* that hotel doorman!"

"Are you *where* yet?" an office worker responded belatedly to B.J.

"Are we in the hotel?" B.J. asked.

"Close... but no cigar," said an older, balding man, looking down at them. He was shaking his head. "This is the last straw. This hotel sign bullshit is getting out of hand," he said to the assembled group.

"Then where the hell are we?" asked B.J.

"You're in the back office of an insurance company... in the office building next door to the hotel," said the bald guy, who was, apparently, the boss.

"Well, we would appreciate it if you could direct us to the hotel lobby, we're just trying to check in," Mark said with a great deal of resignation in his voice.

One of the women said, "Gather your luggage and follow me. I'll get you to the lobby..."

"Thanks Amy," said the boss. Then he turned to a second woman and said, "Jennifer, please get the hotel's general manager on the phone for me again. I want to give that guy a piece of my mind."

"So we're not the first strangers to drop into your office here..." B.J. deduced.

"In fact, you're the fourth group today. We've lost count the last couple days since someone put that hotel lobby sign out there on the garage wall," said Amy the office worker.

B.J. and Mark checked for broken bones, collected the luggage and tried to keep pace with the attractive Amy. She guided them through a rat's maze of cubicles and passageways. There were scores and scores of women of varying ages, sitting at rows of desks, equipped with either an electric typewriter or one of those fancy new Wang word processor machines. All were hammering out piles of what must have been insurance paperwork.

It was a female version of the opening scene of "The Apartment," where Jack Lemmon is one of a hundred or so worker drones slaving away at desks topped only with an adding machine and a phone.

Unfortunately, with the luggage, the entourage couldn't negotiate many of the narrow office passageways; desk chairs blocked the way. As they passed behind each desk the typist had to get up and roll her chair out of the way, so they could get through. Mark and B.J. must have inconvenienced sixty people trying to squeeze their luggage through the offices. It was embarrassing.

"Excuse me... pardon me... sorry... sorry for the inconvenience... pardon me... we'll be out of your way in a moment... sorry... excuse me... pardon us." B.J. and Mark were both repeating the same phrases over and over again; they sounded like a pair of babbling stewardesses apologizing to passengers disembarking following a particularly nasty flight.

The only solace to the whole humiliating experience was following Amy around. She got more attractive by the minute. She had an eye-catching sway in her walk and a lingering perfume scent that got both men to take notice as she ushered them to the agency's front door. *If B.J. wasn't going to hit on this one,* Mark thought, *he was. Neither one of us should let such a good-looking girl get away without at least a try*.

Along the way, Amy explained that the hotel's grand opening, held the previous week, had been a disaster. There had been a strike of construction workers, she said, so nothing had been ready on time. The front parking lot wasn't ready. Some of the rooms weren't ready. And last week there had been two days when the entire office complex had gone without water; it seems that the replacement workers broke a water main while digging. The *piece de resistance* of the hotel fiasco for her boss had been the incorrectly posted hotel lobby sign on the garage wall. Since the sign was posted hotel customers had been toppling into the back office for the last several days.

"Personally, I think it's a hoot," she said with a tilt of her head and a flip of her long black hair.

When the three of them finally arrived at the insurance agency's front door that opened onto a hallway, that led to the office building's lobby, which was tied into the hotel's lobby, B.J. made his move. "Amy, let me ask you something..." B.J. started, "have you ever heard of a nightclub called Élan's? Is it a happening place?" B.J. was still not sure that Mark's choice of a nightspot was really the "in" place.

"Sure. Everybody's heard of Élan... I've been there. It's the best place in town if you can afford it. Do you two need some directions to Élan... or can you Eagle scouts find your own way from here?"

"We can't even find the hotel's lobby," Mark said sheepishly.

"I know," she said, looking straight at him, stifling a grin.

"So Élan's is a good place to go, huh?" B.J. persisted. "We're sort of passing through and we've been invited to go there tonight, and I thought maybe we might see you there... buy you a drink to thank you for helping us out..."

"It depends..." she said, coyly, "maybe... I could end up there later on tonight, who knows?"

### Dauntless Doorman.

THEY MUST HAVE traipsed a quarter-mile from the insurance office to the hotel lobby. By the time Mark reached the front desk, his biceps were aching from toting the weighty suitcases.

The hotel lobby was an eye-catching and spacious atrium that rose to the skylight roof, some twenty stories up; but it was also empty and their footsteps on the brick floors echoed all about. The hotel doorman, the fussy guy in the all-white sissy suit who insisted they drive to the garage was conveniently out of sight.

Mark had just started talking with the frizzy-haired blonde behind the registration desk when her telephone rang. She cut him off in mid-sentence with an index finger in the air and answered the phone. Then she began a long, involved discussion with someone else and proceeded to ignore them for the next several minutes; Mark just stood there doing a slow burn. *Why is it that any jerk on the telephone is more important than someone in the flesh? I'd started conducting my business before the phone rang,* Mark thought to himself.

For some unexplained reason, when a phone rings, clerks -- all clerks -- invariably treat the person standing in front of them as a second-class citizen. The individual there, in-person always has to take a back seat to someone who's spent a whole dime on a phone call. After a few more minutes, a second clerk, a short redheaded lad, emerged from the back office and asked, "Are you being helped?"

"Does it look like I'm being helped?" Mark snapped. "Do I have that satisfied glow on my face? Or is there that certain edge in my voice indicating that you couldn't possibly pay enough attention to what I have to say right now... are you getting any of this?"

The young pimply faced clerk had the innocent look of a doe, chewing its cud, "No, sir, not really."

"I didn't think so."

The second clerk quickly looked for the name Stanton in the reservation file, and then reported that the reservations desk had never heard of him. "Oh boy," said the carrot-topped fellow, "there is a problem... I can't find a reservation for Stanton. Sir, could it be under any other name?"

"It should be... perhaps you should look under 'Sheraton,' or 'Hilton,' or 'Marriott'..."

The clerk didn't get it.

"Let me see what I can find for you," he said over his shoulder leaving the desk in a hurry. For nearly 2,000 years, those words have ripped at the heart of every traveler since Mary and Joseph, at Bethlehem.

The redheaded guy ran around for several minutes, looking frantically for either the lost reservation or an open room. In the meantime, the first clerk, the blonde who's hair had been through electro-shock therapy, was still ignoring Mark's pronounced glare, chattering with that really important person on the other end of the phone line. At least she'd dropped the index finger in-the-air routine.

After making B.J. and Mark wait even longer, "Red" stuck his head out of a door to tell them that the reservation had officially been lost. Mark started to say something, but the clerk beat him to it. "I'll be right back," he said over his shoulder, disappearing behind the door.

Meanwhile, the frizzy blonde hung up the phone. Wide-eyed, she looked up and asked, as though she'd never ever laid eyes on Mark and B.J. before, "Are you being helped?"

Mark pointed to his chest. "Are you talking to *me*?" In an exaggerated move, he slowly turned around to see if anyone else was in the registration line. Not only was no one else in line -- except B.J. -- but there was no one else in the lobby. "Why would you want to talk to a real person, like me, when you can talk to someone important on your telephone, right there?" Mark was working his up to a Jack Nicholson-style monologue in the diner scene in "Five Easy Pieces."

She didn't get it either; she rolled her eyes. "If you'll excuse me for just a moment, I'll get my manager," with that she turned and abandoned the desk.

The front desk manager, an older woman with straight black hair, tortoise-shell glasses and an all-business attitude, emerged from the wall paneling. By now Mark was certain word was getting around, and everyone in the back office wanted to come out to the front desk to see for themselves this customer-from-hell.

"Are we helping you?"

Mark tried a new tack. "I'm trying to get a room, but the other clerks... 'Mork and Mindy'... they seem to have lost my reservation... in fact, they seem somehow 'lost in space.'"

"Not to worry... I'm pretty sure we're wide open tonight," she said matter-of-factly. Hearing that, Mark turned, but B.J. refused to make eye contact with Mark knowing he was about to lose it.

Just then the Mork-the-Red returned waving a key fob. "I've managed to find you something on the sixth floor."

Mark threw up his hands. B.J. turned around to keep from laughing out loud. At last they got a room at the inn. The registrations form had a space for "City," Mark paused and then jotted in "Washington, DC." For automobile, he noted "Porsche."

A slightly moronic bellman with what must have been the noisiest luggage cart in all of Texas hauled their bags, amid an irritating symphony of squeaks, to the sixth floor room. They expected his name badge to read "Igor," but surprisingly, it simply said "Stevie."

"Have you stayed with us before?" Stevie asked.

"I thought you just opened for business this week?" B.J. responded, in wonderment.

"Yeah, we did... I guess not, then, huh?"

B.J. and Mark turned to one another; their eyes met in a squint.

During the elevator ride upstairs Stevie continued to give them the third degree: "Where were they from? Where were they going? Where they driving or flying? Had they been to Houston before? Was there anything they needed to know about the city?"

"We're from California, and if we live through the night in your hotel, we're headed for Washington, D.C.," said Mark, trying to minimize the conversation.

As Stevie rolled the noisy cart to the room, B.J. stated above the irritating din, "You ought to do something about that."

"We're out of oil," the bellman said.

"Now that's news," said B.J. "Did you hear that Stanton... Houston, Texas, is out of oil?"

No sooner had they unloaded their baggage and the nosy bellman with his squeaky cart had departed, than the telephone rang. It was Mark's favorite fellow, the hotel doorman -- the joker in the Good Humor ice cream outfit -- calling from the lobby. B.J. handed over the phone.

"Mr. Stanton, I'm sorry but you're going to have to move your Porsche. It's illegally parked in a fire lane. If it's not moved in five minutes, I will see that it is towed away... it's the law." Then he hung up!

*Damn*! Mark thought. He shouldn't have told B.J. to park "Stanley" in that half-assed parking slot. Mark slammed the phone down, grabbed the car keys from B.J., and headed downstairs to have it out with the doorman.

Seeing the look in his eyes, B.J. said, "I'm not even going to ask."

When Mark returned to the barren lobby, the doorman must have been hiding; he was nowhere in sight. *Probably out in the garage directing the high jacking of my car*, Mark thought.

He headed for the rear of the hotel, looking for the actual garage access door, the one they'd never found on the way in.

Mark couldn't find it on the second attempt either. After searching around and opening each unlocked door, he came to the conclusion that there was no door, at least on the lobby level, which connected the hotel with the garage. He stormed back to the lobby, his third trip through the cavernous Grand Central Station to ask for directions to the garage. Both Mork and Mindy were on the telephone now; no chance there. The doorman was still missing, and "Igor" the bellman was nowhere in sight.

Mark walked out the front door and turned right, headed toward the side driveway that led to the garage -- the way they'd driven in. But when he turned the corner, it was completely blocked off. Asphalt workers, spraying hot liquid tar, swarmed all over the place. No way in; no way out. *This place was insane!*

The only way Mark knew how to get back to the garage was through the office building next door, via the insurance agency on the second floor. So, after a fit of muttering to himself, that is where he headed. The insurance office staff seemed understanding about it. Mark retraced his earlier steps, and went to the back of the office, up the short flight of steps to the fire doors. This time he resisted his initial impulse to burst through the first fire door until he'd gotten a firm grip on the second door.

He made it back to the garage -- a real accomplishment, considering the obstacle course. Mark walked up the curving ramp until he found the Porsche parked in the corner quite peacefully. No one was around. No doorman. No bellman. No cop. No tow truck. From behind the car, looking at the way "Stanley" was parked -- it seemed like a legitimate parking space; the yellow lines crossing the pie-shaped space were out of sight, blocked by the car.

The garage was still full, so Mark waited beside the car a few minutes for someone to come along and yell at him, but no one came. He grabbed a few additional items out of the car and decided to wander about, looking for that still-elusive hotel lobby access door, this time searching from the garage side of the wall. He never saw it. He went up one level and saw two more signs, with arrows, pointing down-ramp, which read, "To Hotel Lobby." He tried several other metal doors along the way, but none led to the hotel.

Finally, Mark spiraled down the ramp to the ground level. He looked around the corner at the alleyway along side the hotel. The construction workers still had the driveway blocked. No way was a tow truck getting through that mess, so he headed back up-ramp to the second level, returning to the building complex the only way he knew how, back through the insurance agency. This time he navigated the two metal doors and the stairs without mishap. He tiptoed through the back office, hoping to avoid another run-in with the bald-headed boss.

Mark inched his way through the office aisles to the front door, excusing himself as he went. Few of the paper-pushers seemed to notice. Those who did look up from their work gave Mark a nod of acknowledgment with a puzzled look, trying to place the face they'd seen once before.

He saw good-looking Amy again; she seemed to be chairing a meeting of six or seven others in the glass-walled conference room. Amy happened to look up as he tiptoed by; Mark nodded to her with a smile. "See you tonight..." he said through the glass partition with a wave, hoping she could lipread. From the hesitant smile she returned, she was probably trying to figure out, *who is that guy*?

Mark crossed the desolate hotel lobby for the fourth time in less than twenty minutes. He stuck his head out the front door; the red-feathered doorman's helmet was still not in sight so he headed for the elevator and the sixth floor.

B.J. greeted him at the room door. "I just hung up with the doorman. He called again to say that the tow truck is here. I told him you were down there getting ready to move it."

"That dumb son-of-a-bitch." Mark left the room in a red-eyed, frothing-at-the-mouth rage.

On his fifth jaunt through the lobby, Mark finally spotted the doorman in the front window. The white helmet with the red plume bobbing around in the parking lot caught his eye. The elusive doorman was directing construction traffic. Mark burst outside to confront him. "Hey, you! Yeah, you in the milkman's outfit... come here!"

"Is there a problem, sir?" he asked, way too politely.

"There is if you just towed my Porsche. I'm Stanton," he said through his teeth.

"Hey buddy, I tried to warn you..."

"Listen here... I'm not your buddy, and I don't care what authority that red feather is supposed to give you. The number one rule in the hotel business is, you do not tow a guest's car away, is that clear? Now either you bring my car back here unscratched or you'll find that feather permanently attached to another part of your anatomy, do I make myself clear?"

The doorman stared at Mark, sizing him up, but then thought the better about arguing. "The tow truck is just leaving now..." he pointed behind Mark.

An old-fashioned service station tow truck was departing the parking lot. It was dragging a silver Porsche 914 behind it. Mark stopped in mid-howl. "That's not my car!" Mark realized that this was a case of mistaken car identity. "And if that isn't my car, why in hell do you keep calling up to my room?"

"Well, sir, when you checked in, you noted that you had a Porsche on the registration form. I told the front desk people that a Porsche was blocking the front door; I guess the clerks just assumed it was your Porsche! They're the ones who gave me your name and room number."

"It's amazing that either of those two blithering idiots at the desk ever took the phone out of their ear. As for you... when you called, you never said that the car was blocking the fire lane at hotel's *front* door... that might have helped, you see, because my car's parked around back in the garage, like you told us to do."

"Oh, well then, I'm sorry... never mind."

"Never mind?" Some poor bastard, a guest of this hotel, just got the shaft. The hotel was in the process of towing the poor fellow's car. In a minute, he's going to rush out here looking for his silver Porsche. Mark looked at the doorman. "You hotel people bring all this bullshit down on your own heads, because you don't have your act together!"

He traversed the vast lobby for the sixth time, eyes glaring. He marched up to the front desk and waited impatiently to see which of the two, Mork or Mindy, would hang up their telephone receiver first. When Mindy did, Mark demanded a private audience with the hotel's General Manager.

Sensing that this guest was about to blow a gasket, Mindy ushered Mark to a back-office waiting room. As Mark paced back and forth, he could hear a loud argument going on behind a closed door. A gruff voice could be heard, "...I'm sick and tired of 'touristas' tumbling into my office space. This shit has to stop before I wind up with a lawsuit. Either you deep-six those hotel garage signs today or I'll rip them down and shove them up your nose... got that?"

An office door opened, and slammed shut, the bald guy -- Amy's boss from the insurance agency -- stormed right past him.

"Hello, again," Mark said, with more of a smirk than a smile.

The insurance executive never saw Mark, or heard him.

A moment later, a rather meek-looking bearded gentleman in a pinstriped suit emerged from the same office and invited Mark in. "Yes sir, I am Henry Morrison, General Manager," he said, "What can I do for you?"

"First of all, my name is Mark Stanton, and I'm a registered guest. I've been here for less than an hour now... and I must say, I've become quite curious... and I need for you to answer a question," Mark said in measured tones. "Where *exactly* is the hotel's back door that connects with the garage?"

"What garage? Sir, we have no garage."

"You know... the garage behind the hotel... the one your doorman sent me to park in."

"Sir, that garage doesn't belong to the hotel. It belongs to the office building next door. So, as you might expect, the hotel has no back door leading to the garage."

"If that is so... then why, may I ask do you have all those signs in garage... the ones that read 'To Hotel Lobby.'' Which door are all those arrows pointing to?"

"Mr. Stanton, until... one minute ago... when I was rudely informed of such by one of our neighbors, I was totally unaware that there were directional signs posted in the garage."

"Where may I ask is a hotel guest supposed to park?"

"In the front parking lot, of course..."

"But no one can park in the front lot... because they're laying asphalt and painting white lines. It's all torn up."

"Sir, we've just opened this past week..."

"Mister Morrison, let me say, I've never run a hotel. And I'm sure it's quite a challenge... but I've traveled all my adult life... and I know when things are teetering out-of-control."

"Mr. Stanton, we're on a shake-down cruise..."

"This is no shake-down cruise, Mr. Morrison. This is the Titanic, the Lusitania and the Andrea Doria, all rolled up in one. This hotel is just begging for a *negative* five-star rating."

Mr. Morrison stood his ground, biting his lip.

"All people really expect from a hotel is a decent room, a bed, clean sheets, and a sliver of soap. Anything beyond that is pure ambiance. It's exceptionally difficult to screw up a customer's barest expectations. In fact, in these days of virtually nonexistent customer service you almost have to go out of your way to piss-off a guest. But in less than one hour your staff has made me very aware of a startling supply-side crisis in brains!"

"I see..."

"Mr. Morrison, your front desk staff approaches a guest like most people approach a tarantula. As a personal favor, I would appreciate it if you would relay to those two blockheads working at registration, that if they're talking to a real-live person, and someone else calls them on the phone, they should put the caller 'on hold,' and they should take care of the real-live person first."

"Will there be anything else?"

"Yes. Tell Igor to oil his luggage cart and then lose the stupid red quill sticking out of the doorman's helmet. He looks like a freakin' barker for a queer circus." Mark exited in a huff.

## Did "Disco" Well?

A SHORT NAP and a hot shower made Mark a new man. Thank God the hotel had hot water and water pressure, or B.J. expected that Mark would have walked down to the lobby, stark naked, covered with soap, and gone looking for Mr. Morrison again. B.J. listened to the radio while they were getting ready to go out on the town. "Hotel California" by the Eagles was on the local station. Later on, they strutted around the hotel room in stocking feet lip-synching "Hot Legs" by Rod Stewart, Mark in boxer shorts and B.J. in his briefs, as they donned dress shirts, slacks and ties. They were sprucing up for an evening at Élan's with Houston's main man-about-town, Paul Rumbaugh. Considering the disagreeable arrival, Mark felt that he'd managed to work himself into a rather festive mood by the time they hit the vacant lobby for the umpteenth time.

At that point Mark realized that he probably couldn't get "Stanley" out of the garage for awhile anyway as the construction workers were just finishing up in the side driveway. In order to avoid another confrontation with the hotel staff, he suggested that they take a cab to the nightclub. That way, he told B.J., if they were over-served by an unfamiliar "bartendress," a cab ride would be better than a car accident in a strange town.

After a brief tour of the Galleria district the taxi came upon a jammed St. James Place. A half-block down on the right was the famous Élan club. The porticoed driveway was crowded with limos and sports cars; the arrival line-up spilled into the street. The entire block looked like a used car lot on Rodeo Drive. An army of clean-cut valet parking attendants, in white Eisenhower jackets, darted in and out of the queue of luxury cars and cabs.

B.J. stretched, twirled his neck to a pop, and then nudged Mark in the ribs, motioning for him to take a gander at the car along side, to his left. Driving a red Mercedes convertible was a stunning young blonde, with a pixie hair cut. Her car radio was blaring a song Mark had not heard before; the chorus was "Hot Child In The City." And she was, too. After a few bars of that song and B.J. making goo-goo eyes at her, the traffic logjam broke and their cab pulled up to the club's front entrance. Having paused to pay the taxi fare, Mark followed B.J. up the driveway.

B.J. had raced ahead to open the door for the "hot child" from the Mercedes. She wore designer sunglasses, a black leather jacket with oh-so-tight matching slacks and steep see-through plastic heels. She had the longest legs Mark had ever seen. She tipped her shades at B.J. with a Marilyn Monroe smile and sauntered through the door. B.J., wearing his rather wrinkled blue blazer, nodded and switched on his best Sunday-go-to-meetin' grin.

Mark couldn't resist, "*now* you like my choice of night club?"

B.J. kept his grin, "I lik-ee."

Based on what they'd seen so far -- and they were still at the front door -- the Élan club was definitely the place to be on Friday night. It was everything Paul Rumbaugh had built it up to be. As Mark and B.J. entered the darkened interior, "Disco Inferno" by the Trammps was pumping throughout the club.

Paul had alerted the club desk that his guests were coming. *They've actually heard of us*, Mark thought. *It was so nice to be expected, for a change*. An attractive Asian hostess in a low-cut evening dress welcomed the twosome and pointed down the hallway, "I expect that you will find Mr. Rumbaugh at the far end of the curved bar... where he usually is."

The nightclub oozed with sex appeal and the atmosphere was electric with anticipation. Anticipation of what wasn't exactly sure. The dimly lit interior looked about half full, but it was still rather early in the evening. Every woman they laid eyes on was gorgeous and dressed to the nines. The sound system was like something out of "Star Wars." The clientele was surrounded with audio pulsation; the entire building seemed to throb to the beat of the disco music. By the time they reached the bar, the bubble gum group from Sweden, ABBA, was belting out "Dancing Queen."

"Stanton!" Mark heard a familiar voice. *I guess every person I know calls everyone else by their last names*, Mark thought.

Paul, who was holding court with a handful of people, waved them over.

"Rumbaugh!" said Mark, "it's great to see you!"

Paul interrupted his conversation and wrapped an arm around Mark. "Folks, this is Mark Stanton, my friend from California who's en route back east to Washington, D.C."

Mark introduced B.J. to Paul. "You may remember Bill Jackson from our days of youthful indiscretions at Dewey Beach..."

"You look very familiar, Bill... nice to see you again."

"Paul, I've heard Stanton here talk about you since we left California. By the way, everyone on earth with the exception of Stanton here, calls me B.J."

"Well then, B.J. it is. Welcome to Houston, B.J.," Paul introduced them to his knot of friends as "...this is the dynamic duo I was telling you about, the guys traveling cross-country."

"You were right on the money, Rumbaugh," Mark said. "This place is like Heaven. So far we haven't seen a runt in the litter."

"Wait 'til ten o'clock rolls around... in the meantime, I've reserved a table for dinner, so the three of us can visit for awhile before this place gets really distracting."

It was too late for B.J. He was already distracted. His "hot child in the city," in the slinky black leather outfit, slunk by while the three stood of them stood at the copper-topped bar. Mark saw her acknowledge B.J.'s nod with an alluring over-the-shoulder glance.

"You two go ahead and grab a seat in the dining room," said B.J. "I'll find you..." He went off in the direction of the disappearing blonde.

Paul and Mark walked up a half-flight of steps to the *maitre d's* lectern. The dining room was situated on a split-level tier, slightly above the bar and dance floor and slightly below the club's uppermost level. This nightclub was truly designed and built for the hunt. The tuxedoed *maitre d'* escorted them to a corner table overlooking the parquet dance floor. The couples below were spinning and strutting to "I'm Your Boogie Man" by K.C. and The Sunshine Band. Interestingly, the house disc jockey had mastered the ability to blend the downbeat of each fading song with the upbeat of the ensuing song. Thus, the auditory onslaught of disco music continued uninterrupted.

"So how's the long and winding road been treating you?" Paul asked.

"Well... let's see... we started out, bright and early on Tuesday morning in San Francisco. Since then, we've seen a plane crash. We almost drowned in the desert. In Las Vegas I was called on to be the Best Man at a wedding. On Wednesday we wrote a country and western song. Two days ago Jackson tore up my trip itinerary... and since then, we've sort of been drifting along. Oh, and we ran into a roadblock in West Texas... and toured the Carlsbad Caverns. Crashed the car into a restaurant, and were arrested in San Antonio last night. Boring stuff like that is happening every day. But, I must admit, I'm having the time of my life... really."

"Well, it's a unique opportunity, isn't it? I wish I were along for the ride. You know Mark, I've always told people you'd go places," Paul said with a smirk, "...and if you leave right now, you might get there."

Eventually B.J. joined them at the table, but his thoughts seemed elsewhere. Paul and B.J. enjoyed inch-thick New York strips; Mark selected the seafood special. The baked potatoes were the size of bricks -- with the works -- and they had a well kept bottle of Charles Krug Cabernet Sauvignon, 1974 -- Mark's choice. Selecting excellent California reds was one of the few lasting benefits of two years chasing California women who were "into" wine country.

For the next hour Mark and B.J. amused Paul with tales of the journey; he was intrigued by each episode. When they finished with that afternoon's hotel check-in story, he howled with laughter. As it turned out, the reason Paul had originally recommended the brand-new hotel was because he knew the General Manager quite well, a fellow named "Hank" Morrison. "In fact," Paul said, "Hank will probably stop by here, later tonight, when he gets off work... you'll have to meet him."

B.J. winced. He looked over at Mark and picked up his wine goblet, pretending he knew nothing. In Mark's running account of the day's check-in fiasco, he hadn't mentioned his testy meeting with Mr. Morrison, the hotel's GM.

In turn, Paul delighted the two of them with stories about the Houston Astros baseball team and their fortunes and foibles on the Astroturf. He'd just returned from spring training and was getting set for next week's home opener and another long season on the road.

Before dessert and coffee, B.J. politely excused himself from the table, "I've got to check on a little ol' widow lady I met on the way in..." with that he disappeared into the swelling dance floor crowd.

All through the meal, club patrons waved over at Paul, or stopped by briefly to say hello. Mark could tell that Paul was really enjoying being back home in Houston after more than a month at spring training in Kissimmee, Florida. It seemed as though everyone in the place knew him. "You're a sports celebrity here," Mark exclaimed. "It's nice to see a good friend in his element."

When Paul got around to asking what prompted the move back to Washington, Mark wished he had a better answer. "I have some personal things to attend to, Paul. I more or less gave up a great job, a good salary. But I'm just not a California kind of guy. Eventually, I hope to start over back east where I belong."

When the check arrived, Paul Rumbaugh made dinner his treat, surmising that Mark might not be working for a while. *Ah, friends,* Mark thought.

By ten o'clock the entire discotheque was surging with back beat music and humping hormones. Dancers could sense the musical reverberations from "More Than A Woman" by Tavares. The parquet floor below was jammed with couples doing dance steps Mark had never seen before. The never-ending vibrations of music seemed to keep the protoplasm in motion.

The disco scene was a definite phenomenon in Texas, all you had to do was look around in order to prove it. Mark hoped this trend was headed east, as he was. There was neither a cowboy boot nor a long necked bottle of beer in sight. This was not the Texas two-step crowd. This was the well-heeled, up-scale, cosmopolitan, call-brand drinking, high-life living, gold credit card elite clique.

As Paul and Mark rose from the dinner table, a dark-haired woman in a purple sequined dress swept Rumbaugh out onto the dance floor. He gave Mark a shrug and whispered, "I've been waiting for this one to come by all evening. You and B.J. are now officially on your own. Catch up with you later."

Mark returned to the curved copper-topped bar. B.J. was nowhere in sight.

"Jack Daniel's on the rocks with two splashes." He lit up a smoke and sat back trying to absorb the whole disco audio-visual experience. For the first time since they'd left the West Coast, Mark was completely relaxed. Being in Élan, he was like the new kid in the candy store. He didn't know where to look first. One couldn't help but be mesmerized by the spectacle -- the chic customers, the clothing, the non-stop disco music, the strobes, the light show, the fake smoke descending like a Scottish fog o'er the Brig O'Doon -- not to mention the remarkable food and wine.

### Tie One On.

"DID YOU TWO Eagle scouts ever find your hotel?"

Mark pivoted to his left on the barstool. At first, he wasn't sure that the woman, who was standing beside him, was talking to *him*. Then he did a double take. It was Amy, from the insurance office! She was trying to stifle a brilliant smile.

He smiled at the Boy Scout joke. "Hello again... I'm Mark Stanton... you know, the guy who 'fell' for you this afternoon."

"I know. I'm Amy... Amy Zimmerman. Nice to run into you again."

"The first time... this afternoon... it was more like we stumbled into you."

She giggled, and flashed that smile again.

Amy Zimmerman! So that was her name.

Amy had a whole different look about her. By day, Mark guessed, she did her best to hide her enticing side in order to be a buttoned-down, all-business insurance executive. But obviously, on Friday nights, she was a no-nonsense alluring beauty. And from the looks of her, her business tonight definitely had nothing to do with anything as boring as insurance.

"I heard he was missing..." she continued.

"Who's missing?"

"The doorman... at your hotel. You were on your way to *kill* him, remember?"

Mark finally caught on; she was still kidding around.

"I didn't recognize you at first. You look different... sitting up... instead of sprawled out on our office carpeting."

Mark blushed. He offered his barstool; she accepted. His eyes were drawn to her slender legs and the stylishly short skirt. He hadn't noticed her killer-legs this afternoon; but then again, she'd been wearing slacks.

"Mark, I see you smoke... could I ask you for a cigarette?"

"Sure. If you don't mind a menthol..."

"It doesn't make a difference what kind... I only smoke when I'm out on Friday night. It's not politically in, you know, for a woman to be smoking, let alone an insurance company employee." She lightly touched Mark's hand as he lit the cigarette and then took a short puff. "So, where's your partner... the taller scout... the one with the beard?"

"Oh, you mean Jackson. He was last seen drooling profusely, following around a blonde in tight leather slacks," Mark answered, trying to sabotage B.J.'s chances -- in case he returned to discover Amy -- while enhancing his own. *All's fair...*

"You two fellows were quite a sight this afternoon... lying there all over the floor. My boss got so mad about it that he went over and chewed out the hotel manager. But then we have had quite a few people barging into the back office this week."

"I know... I also met with the hotel manager... I was at his office and heard your boss yelling at him."

With that the couple settled into a comfortable conversation. They talked about where they were from, and how it was that they were in Houston. It turned out that Amy was originally from Abilene, but had recently accepted a company transfer to Houston in order to gain a promotion. She was very proud to be the first female vice president in her firm. Mark could tell that she was the type who had plans to get ahead in life and he could also sense that she was a small town girl quite enthralled about the new experience of living on her own in the big city.

After each awkward pause in the prolonged conversation, Mark fully expected Amy to excuse herself and wander off. He asked if he could buy her a drink. He offered it both as a way to keep her there, and to see if she would continue to get to know him.

Vodka with grapefruit juice... that's what the lady wanted, and that's what she got.

Mark wondered how old she was. She seemed rather young to be a vice president, maybe in her mid-to-late twenties. Amy was quite attractive. The perfume she was wearing was having its effect on Mark for the second time that day. Also, she was a "toucher" as she talked; she touched his arm, his hand and even patted his thigh to make a point during their conversation.

"Did I see you wandering around in my office late in the afternoon? Was that you waving at me through the conference room window?"

"Well, I'm kind of embarrassed to admit it... but yes. Most criminals return to the scene of the crime, don't they? Frankly, the only way I knew to get back to that damn garage was through your office. The outside alleyway was blocked."

"When I saw you again I thought for a minute that maybe you'd come back to introduce yourself. Maybe you were the shy type, especially around your partner," she said somewhat tongue-in-cheek.

"I'm not that shy. I was really lost... but it was awfully nice to see you again, even if for only a fleeting moment."

The club deejay was throttling down the heavy disco beat; he transitioned into a slower song, "How Deep Is Your Love" by the Bee Gees. The house lights dimmed and clouds of artificial smoke began to slowly billow across the parquet flooring.

"Well, Eagle scout, Mark Stanton... do you have a merit badge in ballroom dancing?" she asked.

"Well, I don't know all these disco steps, if that's what you mean..."

"Ah, there's nothing to it... it's just like a jitterbug, but to an up-tempo beat... come on..." she offered Mark her hand. "This one's pretty slow. You can dance to it. And don't worry, I'll show you what to do on the next one."

First he danced slowly; then he danced fast. Later he went stark raving mad and did the "Disco Rufus" by Stargard. By eleven o'clock, Mark Stanton was a dancing fool! Maybe it was the wine with dinner, or the Jack Daniel's, or the realization that he might never pass this way again, but in the anonymity of a strange city, he dropped his usual self-consciousness and danced like a sweaty frat rat on Homecoming weekend.

Amy was amused with Mark's antics. "I thought you might be a little bit stuffy," she said after they returned to the bar.

"Usually, I am, but hanging out with a younger woman like you does wonders for an older guy like me," he responded.

Mark didn't see Paul Rumbaugh again until midnight, and he hadn't laid eyes on B.J. since dinner. Rumbaugh was back at his usual haunt, at the far end of the curved bar. "Stanton... come on over," Paul hailed to him. "I want you to meet some people. This is Hank Morrison, the General Manager of the hotel you're staying at..." Mark quietly shook hands with Mr. Morrison for the second time that day. Also, Paul introduced his girlfriend, Sarah.

"Nice to see you again Mr. Morrison," Mark said before introducing Amy.

"Mr. Stanton and I met this afternoon, Paul," Morrison explained. "He was kind enough to drop by my office to offer some suggestions for our staff training."

Paul Rumbaugh did an exaggerated "spit-take" on his cocktail. "Stanton, these paw prints look oddly familiar... have you been using those White House advance man intimidation tactics, mauling my hotel friend here?"

"Well... let's just say that, after reflecting on my behavior, the only appropriate comment I had to make this afternoon was about a suggested change to the doorman's uniform... let's just leave it at that."

"Fair enough," said a very diplomatic Henry Morrison.

The group of five ended up talking at length about traveling and the hotel business. Mark learned that Hank Morrison, who -- by the way -- was quite an entertaining guy, had been around the hospitality industry for twelve years before becoming a general manager. The new Houston hotel was his first G.M. assignment.

Mark felt like a heel. He tried to make up for the afternoon's diatribe with a little humor. Hank Morrison seemed quite genial; so Mark told him several hotel horror stories from his days on the road, advancing for The White House. One involved a trip to the Soviet Union, where the White House Communications Agency had to search the hotel meeting rooms for KGB listening devices. Under an oriental rug in the Presidential holding room, the security agents detected a large metal plate cleverly set into the floor. A technician unscrewed the plate; underneath the plate they found electrical wiring and a metal canister fastened with a nut and bolt. Finally, after much struggling, the communications experts who were called in were able to remove the large bolt from the screw, probing for the KGB listening "bug" that surely must be connected to the wiring.

No sooner had they removed the bolt... than downstairs they heard a loud CRASH!

A Secret Service agent, posted downstairs, barked into his walkie-talkie that, without warning, "a huge crystal chandelier in the ballroom had fallen from the ceiling." It just missed him by a few inches!

Henry the hotelier enjoyed that one.

"If I Can't Have You" by Yvonne Elliman began playing. Amy wanted to dance again, so Mark used this exit from the bar as the opportunity to thank and say good-bye to Paul, Sarah and Hank. He and Paul Rumbaugh promised to keep in touch. And Mark vowed that their next dinner back in Washington was his treat.

Amy and Mark danced and continued their discussion on a slightly more intimate level. They gyrated through "Dancin' Fever" by Claudja Barry and "We Fell In Love While Dancing" by Bill Brandon. The hours with Amy went by all too swiftly; her outgoing personality, the obvious determination to make something of herself and her keen interest in Washington and politics impressed Mark. She was able to discuss the nuances of baseball with any man and could out-debate most people he knew on thorny political issues. For the first time in years, he'd listened to a woman more than he talked to one -- *now that was different*.

It was getting late and Mark was trying to figure out what was next. En route to the dance floor for the third time he peeked at his watch. It was almost 1:00 a.m. He was torn. Should he call it a night and let Amy slip away, or should he make a move? He wasn't sure; she was a difficult person to read. Hell, she knew Mark was just passing through town. *There was no future in a guy like me for a woman like her*, he thought. And yet, all night long, she hung in there beside him. When "You Make Me Feel Like Dancing" by Leo Sayer died down Mark carefully said *we* had better think about leaving, just to see what her reaction might be. She went for her purse.

Mark figured he would play it casually and just see what might develop.

Amy drove him back to Henry Morrison's pride and joy in her new Buick Skylark. As they pulled up to the front door, Mark threw his fate to the winds. He ignored the fact that she was a few years younger; also, he ignored the odds and he ignored his California run of luck with the opposite sex. What were the chances that lovely young, politically astute Amy would have fallen, head over heels, "in like" with him in the last three hours? But, people did meet and get involved on the first night. It happened all the time, all over the world, every night. It's just that it rarely, if ever, happened to Mark.

Amy parked at the curb, near the hotel's lobby entrance and turned off the engine. Without a word she opened her car door, Mark did the same. They squeezed into the same pie-shaped space in the revolving door entering the hotel. The lone reception clerk behind the desk was on the telephone. *Some things never change.* At the very least, he could say that Hank's front desk staff had achieved a certain air of consistency.

The tap of their footsteps echoed off the marble floor. They crossed the vacant lobby to the elevators -- his arm around her shoulders, her arm around his waist. All Mark could think of was maybe minor miracles do happen!

He rapped lightly on the hotel room door before entering, but he knew B.J. wouldn't be there. In they went.

His hand searched for, but never found, the light switch. As soon as the room door shut, Mark turned, and Amy was in his arms. She pressed hard against him. Caught off guard, he banged the back of his head on the door. She giggled at the "thud," and their lips brushed again. The rest came naturally. The couple lingered there in the entranceway, kissing in total darkness, locked in a tight embrace -- leaning back against the door, like two brooms in a closet. The initial kiss lasted for minutes. Perhaps it was the late hour, but Mark's mental focus narrowed down to just the two of them, to just that moment in time. He *was* Burt Lancaster on the beach in "From Here To Eternity." But he got carried away with himself, and Amy was trying to return the kisses while giggling at his increasingly stalwart approach. They finally came up for air, only momentarily, both trying awkwardly in the dark recesses of the vestibule to remove her trench coat.

That accomplished; they were back at it again, this time even more fervently. Slowly, both discerned the escalation toward critical mass. When she started gasping for air, Mark spun her around and they sprang into the first double bed.

The next few minutes were comedy and ecstasy. They were frantically undressing one another in the dark. She continued her high-pitched giggling. Mark was biting his tongue, totally focused on undoing buttons and hooks and flinging clothes over his shoulder. At long last, they settled into a naked, lusty clutch. She had a cool, smooth feel against his flushed skin. Their passion heightened, but their movements seemed to shift into slow motion; the concept of time became increasingly irrelevant, even to Mark. Unlike his quite infrequent California flings, this was a much more ardent, not meant to be swift, sexual encounter. Amy was "into" vigorous lovemaking. She was as impassioned on the mattress as she was enthusiastic on the dance floor. Hot breath and throaty moans accompanied her heightening sexual excitement.

The only thought that kept bouncing around in Mark's mind was, "I knew things like this could still happen to me!" It's just that things, like this, had not happened to him recently.

For no discernible reason, following their prolonged lovemaking, the intimate pillow talk was confined to whispers. After all those "what are you thinking right now" questions and answers, she slowly drifted off to sleep; it must have been those vodka-grapes. Mark laid wide-awake, trying to analyze, for some future frame of reference and meaning, what he'd managed to do right this evening. After some considerable thought, he determined that there was no particular rhyme or reason for this particular romantic fling. One could go insane trying to analyze the incalculable possibilities. Maybe it's just a chemical thing -- a random metabolic attraction that just happens at exactly the right moment. There's no way to steer it or control it.

*Perhaps the new-to-town Amy Zimmerman wanted to be with someone. Maybe his "passing through town" status was more of an attraction than a detriment for someone like her.*

The main difference between what had occurred that night and every other Friday night was that, with Amy, he'd simply let loose and let it happen. On any other night -- Mark being Mark -- he probably would have said "nice meeting you" and turned to leave, but tonight, he'd been totally natural, relaxed, and the rest was history.

He quietly searched around the unfamiliar hotel room in the dark and found his necktie. He tiptoed to the door; trying not to awaken Amy, and trying not to reveal his nakedness to anyone who might be passing in the hotel corridor. He reached out and looped the tie over the doorknob. "Ye olde necktie on the doorknob" – was the official, internationally recognized symbol that a man's roommate had a guest on the premises. It was a signal Mark hoped B.J. would notice before he came barging into the room.

# CHAPTER FIVE

## Saturday, March 25, 1978

**Missing in Action.**

WAS HE DREAMING? No he wasn't. Mark awoke to the lingering scent of Amy's exotic perfume on the pillow. He forced his eyelids to pop open; she was still there, snuggled up beside him. It was just past seven o'clock and getting light out. He knew that once awake, he'd never fall back to sleep, so he moved gingerly to extricate himself from the bedcovers.

Amy's deep steady breathing seemed to belie the point that she was a morning person; she slept like a child. Mark dialed room service, whispering into the telephone on the desk located in the far corner of the room. He found no room service menu so thought to himself, *eggs Benedict for everyone! Why not? Why hadn't I thought of that*! "Eggs Benedict for two, juice, an order of toast and a pot of coffee," he whispered into the receiver.

His next project was to scrounge around the carpeting in the semi-darkness, searching for the rest of his clothes. He reminded himself of B.J., Tuesday morning, gathering up his things in the driveway. Wearing nothing but his boxer shorts, Mark settled into the desk chair and lit up a Salem. He sat there in the half-light watching Amy sleep, reflecting on the wacky circumstances of their first meeting yesterday on her office floor and everything that had transpired since. Who would have ever guessed that yesterday, lying there in her office covered with baggage, that the two of them were destined to spend the evening together?

Two cigarettes and thirty-five minutes later he heard the clatter of the room service waiter tromping down the hallway toward the room. Before the waiter could knock, Mark met him at the door with a tip and took the hefty breakfast tray. The waiter looked at Mark as though he was from Mars. *Apparently no hotel guest in boxer shorts had ever taken a tray off his shoulder before*, Mark figured.

He poured a cup of steaming black coffee for Amy and set it on her nightstand. As he suspected it would, the distinctive aroma of strong hotel brew brought her around. A few minutes later she was awake and chattering like a sparrow. Amy was a very enthusiastic person; it carried over to morning. Also, he found her to be quite uninhibited; she was not the least bit uneasy about strolling around the room in the all-together. His eyes followed her every move. From her demeanor, Amy had no second thoughts about first-night passions; she was a totally up-front woman. Mark was the one beginning to have second thoughts and a slight guilt hangover. *How had all this happened so easily?*

Amy seemed impressed by eggs Benedict served-in-bed, but not by the truffles floating atop the hollandaise sauce. She removed the two black specks with her butter knife as if they were Egyptian scarabs; she went about it with the intensity of a brain surgeon and then scraped them onto Mark's plate. She finished her eggs and stole the untouched asparagus from his plate. He found himself gawking, trying to analyze her in every detail.

She broke the hiatus in conversation as well as Mark's trance. "Where will you be staying tonight?" she asked.

"Oh... we're supposed to be over in New Orleans... that is if my fellow scout Jackson finds his way back. I don't think he even knows the name of this hotel."

"So, Mr. Stanton, what do you think of Houston, Texas, this morning?"

"I'm thinking that Houston's fairer sex has a disturbing effect on virginal men from the West Coast..."

"We're like black widow spiders," she said waving a stalk of asparagus, "men rarely get away... alive."

They jousted verbally, making jokes back and forth. Amy managed to keep the discourse light, and talked around any "future" issues. Each avoided comments that might indicate that they expected any kind of future to this relationship. No awkward promises were asked for, and none were proffered.

She took her time getting made-up and dressed. Eventually though, she flipped her bulky purse over an arm, came over and gave Mark a long, tender good-bye kiss.

As they left the room together, she pointed to the necktie still wrapped around the doorknob. She started to say something but deferred as Mark tossed it back into the room, with a giggle she said, "That is *so* like you." They headed down the hall toward the elevators.

Arriving at the hotel's front door, they looked for her car along the curb, where she'd parked it last night; but it was gone. However, lo' and behold, Mark's decorous friend the Good Humor doorman was on duty.

"Good morning sir? How's the Porsche?"

"Just fine thank you. And how's your feather hanging this morning?"

No response.

"Say, speaking of cars... and knowing of your penchant for having cars towed, could you, by any chance, tell me where you might have had the lady's Buick taken? It was parked along the curb last night, right about... there," he pointed.

"You mean the '77 yellow Buick Skylark that was encroaching on the hotel's 'No Parking' fire lane?"

"Yes, that would be my Buick," Amy said without hesitation.

"First thing this morning, I had the tow truck take it around back to the first level of the garage."

"The garage? How'd you ever manage to shoehorn another car into that garage?"

"Why Mr. Stanton, today is Saturday! The garage is virtually empty. Besides, the hotel has a new policy... just put in place late yesterday by Mr. Morrison, our General Manager... we don't tow guests' cars off the premises. However, in lieu of that inconvenience, there will be a $35.00 towing fee charged to your room bill. Now what was that room number again... 626, right?"

"Right. Good work. It's nice to see that my new drinking buddy, Mr. Morrison is running a taut ship. I'll be glad to reference your good judgment on the Buick."

"Thank you, sir. Now let me get that Skylark for you."

Mark handed him Amy's car keys and a couple of bucks. The doorman ran around the corner to retrieve the car from the garage. Apparently, the asphalt on the side driveway was now ready for traffic.

Amy had a puzzled look on her face, trying to interpret Mark's very familiar dialogue with the doorman. She looked at him with a tilt of her head and a slight squint of her hazel eyes.

When the car arrived, she gave him a final hug and kiss. "Mark, I'm the only 'A. Zimmerman' listed with Houston telephone information," she whispered. "Good-bye... I hope you get back to Houston again soon, or perhaps I might end up in Washington... you never know."

He stood there on the curb with the doorman and watched until her yellow Buick disappeared from sight.

"Now that's one fine lookin' lady," the doorman said.

Mark could only nod in agreement.

## Your "Shake-up" Call.

THE SATURDAY MORNING *Houston Chronicle* newspaper had pages of stories about "recall moves in five states" for those U.S. Senators who had voted in favor of the first Panama Canal treaty agreement. He wished B.J. would return so he could rub his liberal nose in all the bad ink. The first Panama Canal treaty, requiring a two-thirds vote, had passed the Senate on Thursday, March 16th, by a vote of 68-32 – with only one vote to spare. Now treaty opponents, whipped into frenzy by chief opponent and Reagan ally, Senator Paul Laxalt of Nevada, were on the counter-attack. In Arizona, Louisiana, Montana, Tennessee and Wisconsin voters were livid with their lawmakers, demanding recall petitions. In a side bar story, the paper described how both U.S. Senators from Tennessee, Howard Baker and James Sasser, were in deep political trouble in the Volunteer State. In Arizona, Senator Dennis DeConcini had discovered that, much to his dismay, 84 percent of the voters in his state disagreed with his vote in favor of the first treaty. A final Senate vote, formally ratifying the two Panama Canal treaties, was still two weeks away, but the political fall-out was just starting to get interesting.

Meanwhile, in the Capital, President Carter was leaving The White House to spend the Easter weekend with his family at Camp David.

In other headline news, the beleaguered Amoco Cadiz oil tanker had finally broken in two, just off the French coast at Normandy, bringing that monumental ecological disaster to a head.

In the entertainment world, Mark read where Gunther Gebel-Williams, the famous lion-tamer with the Ringling Brothers' Circus, had been attacked by one of his leopards. The white-maned star had been in Knoxville, Tennessee, filming a commercial with the cats. *Gee!* First, Karl Wallenda falls to his death. And now, Gunther Gebel-Williams winds up in the hospital, on the critical list. No wonder he was traumatized by circus acts.

*Thank God the sports pages are not full of blood and guts*, he thought. The big news in the sports world was about O.J. Simpson, the charming fellow who held the NFL's single season rushing record of 2,003 yards. Apparently, O.J. had struck pay dirt in California. The San Francisco '49ers agreed to take over the final year of his three-year deal with the Buffalo Bills, who accepted his annual salary of $733,000, in return for five high draft choices. Way to go O.J.! A great deal for a really nice guy, now O.J. could finish his career in his hometown in front of family and friends. *O.J. Simpson... now here was a sport's hero with class that little kids could look up to, a guy with a real solid future in the business world after he retires from his athletic career*, Mark thought.

Also on the sports pages, Mark noticed the spring training box scores -- his Cleveland Indians had lost on Friday, 2-0, to the San Diego Padres. He scanned through every section of the paper. There was no mention anywhere of a plane crash earlier this week at Edwards Air Force Base. He looked at his watch. It was 9:30 a.m. and B.J. still had not shown up or called.

An idea came to mind. Mark dug through the luggage and found his little black address book. He picked up the phone and called long distance to Washington, D.C. It was 10:30 in the morning there; perhaps he could catch Perry Elam, his reporter friend who worked for the Washington *Evening Star*, before he headed out to "bust political chops," as Perry liked to say. Perry's motto, like that of all investigative reporters, was "to comfort the afflicted and to afflict the comfortable." Maybe with this call Mark could afflict some pointy-headed bureaucrat over at the Pentagon, who thought he had managed to cover-up a spy plane crash.

"Hell-oh..." said a dreary voice on the other end of the line.

"Rise and shine, shithead!" Mark barked. "This is your 'shake-up' call from Houston, Texas."

"Who in the *hell* is this?"

"My, my... Mr. Elam, how soon we forget our old friends... like that good-looking fellow from California... what's his name? Mark Stanton. That's it!"

"Stanton! Is that you? What in the world are you doing... waking me up on a Saturday morning, calling me from where? Texas, of all places. Are you in jail or something like that?"

"Good guess... but no tabloid story here, Scoop. Hasn't anyone told you that Bill Jackson and I are driving cross-country, en route to the Nation's Capital... and that we're coming there just to personally kick your Pulitzer prize-winning ass?"

"Oh, yeah... I guess I did hear some scuttlebutt about that. Well, hey, that's just great... in fact, if you two are back in town by Monday night, plan on coming over to the house. I'm having a bunch of people over for the NCAA basketball finals on TV! My boys from Duke are goin' all the way this year!"

"Okay, sounds great. We plan to be in D.C. Monday night and a party at your house sounds good to me... a hell of a better prospect than your Blue Devils making it to the final game. You're still living on Prospect Street, in Georgetown, aren't you?"

"Yeah. I've told people to come over between eight and eight-thirty. The game starts at nine. Can I tell people that you and B.J. will be here?"

"Sure, I'll see to it, even if I have to tie B.J. to the hood of the car like a downed deer..."

"Now tell me Stanton, what's going on in Texas? And to what do I owe the pleasure of this obscene wake-up call? It better be breaking news to get me out of bed this early on a Saturday morning."

"Perry, grab your pad and sharpen your crayon. Now listen, I don't want to sound like some kind of 'nut case' or anything..."

"Then *whatever* you say next will be quite a stretch for you, Stanton..."

"...but this past Tuesday, the twenty-first... late in the afternoon... Jackson and I were driving past Edwards Air Force Base, in California, out in the middle of the Mojave Desert. We heard and saw what we think was a plane crash... not a passenger plane... probably a military plane... or maybe a helicopter. Anyway, every day this week we've been looking through the newspapers in Las Vegas, El Paso, San Antonio and now Houston. There's been no mention of a plane crash... and that seems pretty odd to me. B.J. and I are suspicious. So we thought maybe you might be able to check it out. It could be that there's nothing to it at all. But maybe, just maybe, there's more to it than meets the eye. Perhaps you'd be interested in looking into it."

"Hey, Stanton... thanks a heap for such a white-hot tip. Hell, I'll just drop my four months of coverage of the United Mine Workers strike to check out a missing airplane for you. Things here on the strike are about to break and it'll be a front-page by-line for me when it's settled," he sounded tired. "But I'll tell you what... I promise that I'll call the Pentagon and see what they say. In the meantime, how's my buddy B.J. doing? Traveling all the way cross-country with B.J.... you two must be driving each other crazy by now. You're such frickin' opposites. And hey, did you say Las Vegas? We're you in Vegas? How's *our* buddy Jerry Mulligan?"

"Well, I'm not exactly holding a news conference here this morning... but to answer all your questions... the aforementioned Mr. Jackson is officially 'AWOL.' Last night he ran into some hot young blonde in a black leather pantsuit... and I haven't laid eyes on him the last twelve hours. But I've talked to the sheriff down here and he's all for rounding up a posse. And wait 'til you hear this... Mully got married on Tuesday while we were there in Vegas. I was his best man! He's in New York right now on his honeymoon, believe it or not. You ought to give him a surprise call or send them a fruit basket at The Waldorf."

"Married. Well, I'll be damned. That will cut back on our casino crawling next time I'm out there to visit him. But I'll tell him congratulations. And as for B.J., if and when you find him, tell him I said hello too. For now, I'll tell the editors to hold front-page space for your allegations of a plane crash...

and, oh... what's your middle initial, so I can identify the accuser precisely... the person saying there's a Pentagon cover-up going on."

"Whoa, I said '*we think*' it was a plane crash..."

"Don't worry dip-shit... I'll let you know what the Joint Chiefs' CYA 'bullshit' is. See you guys Monday night at eight, at my place..."

"Thanks, Perry... see you then."

"*C.Y.A.?*" *Oh yes -- Cover-Your-Ass. That was Pentagon "talk" all right.*

Mark placed a second call. It was to the office of Dr. Tom Roche, in Washington, DC. The receptionist on duty indicated that the doctor was on morning rounds at the hospital. When Mark asked if there were any messages for him, she said, "No, Mr. Stanton, the results of your second battery of tests have not arrived as yet, but they could be back from the lab by Noon when the office closes." She suggested that Mark call Doctor Roche at his home number this evening.

## Ready for Combat.

A HALF-HOUR AFTER Mark hung up the phone, B.J. hunched into the room looking like death warmed-over. He was no longer Missing-In-Action; but from the looks of him, his status could have been downgraded to Killed-In-Action. The only thing he said was, "I see from the room service tray in the hallway that we had breakfast for *two* in room 626 this morning... anyone I know?"

Mark begged the question. "Just talked to Perry Elam. He says hello and invited us to a party at his house in Georgetown on Monday night."

"Great... more drinking and carousing. Just what I need! Why's he having a party on a *Monday* night?"

"Well first, the NCAA basketball finals are on TV Monday night. Perry is sure his Duke Blue Devils will make the finals... and second, we're coming home!"

B.J. groaned. "I feel like I may be coming home like FDR, by train, in a casket. Tell my friends to wait along side the tracks, hats over hearts."

Mark sat in the room, waiting for B.J. to pull himself together so they could depart. He tilted-back in a chair, legs crossed, and heels resting atop the desk. He puffed on a Salem staring out the hotel window at the freeway below. His thoughts shifted back and forth -- between the call to his doctor's office this morning -- and what had happened the night before. He saw clips of over-heated disco'ers gyrating under blinking strobe lights. He felt the pulse of the music at the Élan club -- then the cool, smooth feel of Amy -- the contrast between the acrid smell of dance floor smoke and the alluring perfume Amy wore. It was surrealistic. But for some reason, he wasn't smiling; he found himself in deep meditation. Was all his fun coming to an end? Was this the last week he would ever enjoy himself like this?

B.J. went about his morning business in an unusually quiet manner. In the background, Mark heard the shower running. Minutes later, B.J. emerged from the bath in a cloud of steam. Without a word, he dressed and packed-up his duffel. A half-hour and a couple of smokes later for Mark, B.J. was standing at the ready, wearing his denim uniform of the day. Mark was prepared to upgrade B.J.'s status to "treated for wounds, ready for combat."

When B.J. jumped into the passenger seat he caught Mark staring out in space, deep in thought. "Stanton, are we on our way to New Orleans to see Big Bart? Or are you planning to stay here, riddled with self-guilt, until you feel you should rightly propose marriage to the girl you slept with last night?"

Mark snapped out of it, "We are headed out... next stop, Big Bart in the Big Easy." The thought of pulling out the little black address book and writing down the number for the only "A. Zimmerman" listed in Houston information crossed Mark's mind; but for several reasons, he set the thought aside. In stead of being on a high over his rare manifestation of passion the evening before, Mark found himself numb. Strangely, he felt that if he were to get through whatever fate he faced at Johns Hopkins in Baltimore that he would rather return to Las Vegas first and see Sally again before he would dial the only A. Zimmerman in the Houston phone book.

"Hey, big guy, are you all right?" the relationship-experienced B.J. slapped Mark on the shoulder, "get over it! You know the possibility even exists that *she* might have had a good time too. But knowing you, I wouldn't bet on it. Life will go on for both of you. I can almost guarantee it."

"I hope so," Mark snapped out of his daze. "Say, Jackson, catch this! When I went to the front desk to checkout there was no charge for our room on the bill... just the incidentals and a towing charge. Stapled to the bill was a note from Hank Morrison, apologizing for any inconveniences during our stay. He 'comp'ed' us the room! The note had been written at 7:30 p.m. last night. Maybe he didn't even know we were friends of Paul Rumbaugh when he did it. Class act... that Hank Morrison."

"Ditto," B.J. echoed.

## Weakened Warriors.

"SO WHAT ACTUALLY happened last night?" B.J. asked.

"Well, Mr. Sunshine, I could ask you the same question..."

"Yeah, Don Juan, but I asked *you* first."

*What could Mark tell him*? *What should he tell him*? He stalled for time to think and lit up yet another smoke.

"Undercover Angel" by Alan O'Day was on the local radio station.

They were headed due east on I-10 for New Orleans, some 350 miles away. They'd departed the hotel at 11:00 a.m., which meant they'd probably hit the Crescent City about four-thirty.

Mark took an exaggerated puff on the cigarette and carefully phrased an answer to B.J.'s hanging question, "Well, the short version is... I ran into Amy, that dazzling young thing who works for the insurance company... or should I say, she ran into me. Anyway, we kind of hit it off. Let's just say that I looped my necktie on the doorknob just in case you came home early."

"Oh yes, Amy. She's cute... not the classic lines of a Sally Markham, but cute."

"So, my leather freak friend, what's your alibi for missing breakfast?"

"Speaking of tying neckties, Stanton... I found myself sort of *tied-up* this morning as well," he said, but Mark sensed reluctance on B.J.'s part to add anything more.

Sharing conquest stories was not something the two of them often did. B.J. wasn't the type to "kiss and tell" and, usually, Mark had nothing to talk about, so he sort of eased back into the subject of last night by lightly poking fun, "Was that a genuine leather outfit I saw on the 'Hot Child in the City,' or was it some exotic skin, like nauga-hide?"

B.J. wiggled his eyebrows, stretched and shrugged his shoulders until his neck popped, smiled and leaned way back in the passenger seat. Then slowly laced his fingers together, wrapped them around the back of his neck, elbows wide. He said, "Stanton, last night was possibly the most incredible evening I've ever spent... I know I'll never live long enough to forget it. It was indescribable... and I'm embarrassed to tell you that I don't even know her name. She wouldn't tell me who she was... gave me the runaround all night."

"What *do* you know?"

"Either she's the daughter of some big shot Texas oil man, or she's married, probably to a much older man. Anyway, last night we had the entire mansion to ourselves, and we made the most of it."

"How many rooms can you use in one night?"

"Well, whatever the old record was, I believe we set a new one. Also, I think she was a Campfire Girl as a kid."

"Why is that, my faithful Indian companion?"

"Well, let's just say she likes to 'toast her marshmallows' in front of a roaring fire and she knows how to tie a mean knot. It took me damn near two hours to get freed-up this morning... I'm sure she still thinks I'm out back in the guest cottage, hog-tied to a brass headboard."

"You've got to be shitting me..." Mark's mouth was agape.

"Yeah. I am 'guano-ing' you..." B.J. said quickly, but not very convincingly.

The Atlanta Rhythm Section was singing "Imaginary Lover" on "Stanley's" radio.

About noon the twosome made a short stop at a roadside marker, just east of Beaumont, Texas. The metal plaque described the historical scene at the Lucas Well, the site of the first oil gusher in the region. That event led to the growth of Beaumont and to the development of the huge petrochemical industry complex that surrounds the city.

Mark and B.J. performed a few calisthenics -- jumping jacks and stretches -- to get the blood flowing and then hopped back into the car. It was a bright sunshiny day with a slight southerly breeze. The mid-morning temperature was already in the 70's.

They were experiencing the heaviest traffic thus far on the trip; up until now, the driving had been while most people were at work. This being a Saturday, they now were sharing the Interstate with lane weaving weekend warriors. It was a nightmare behind the wheel; every yahoo in Texas seemed to be on the road, tooling around in a pick-up truck.

"Jackson, there are so many idiots on the road these days we've got to come up with a way to warn folks when these crazies are approaching."

"So what do you suggest, Kemo?" B.J. asked sarcastically.

"I'm thinkin' that every driver, when they get their driver's license, should be issued a dart gun and a set of small darts with red flags attached. Then when you come across a complete asshole behind the wheel, like that guy in the next lane over there who's been weaving in and out of traffic, you just pull up alongside, and fire a dart into his rocker panel. That way, over time, an idiot's truck is going to get bedecked with lots and lots of tiny red flags. Then folks will be able to spot an asshole driver coming at them, a good mile away."

B.J. said, "Sounds like what *banderilleros* do to *El Toro*, sticking those colorful barbed spears into him..."

"Yeah, same principle... what do you think?"

"Hey, Stanton, far be it for me to get in the way of your gun-toting, NRA-inspired highway safety ideas! That sound's like a down-right Republican idea to me."

## Catch-up with Ketchup.

THEY KNEW THEY were in store for some fine dining in New Orleans; so B.J. agreed, just this once, to make an exception to his standing rule and he let Mark stop for a quick lunch at a fast-food restaurant. They pulled off the highway at the last I-10 exit ramp inside Texas, at the town of Orange. The only fast-food restaurant in sight had one of those new-fangled drive-through carryout windows. They ordered a couple of cheeseburgers and Cokes via the incomprehensible squawk-box speaker contraption; Mark couldn't understand a word the "Jackie" in the box uttered. Then they drove around to pick up the chow at a side window. However, another problem arose;

Mark and B.J. discovered that they were flat out of money. Mark had been so surprised at no charge for the room that he'd forgotten to cash a personal check that morning at the hotel. B.J. was tapped out; he'd used up the very last of his money this morning, no doubt paying for the taxi ride from the *'Marquise' d' Sade's* mansion back to the hotel.

They had less than two dollars between them; and the beefy woman in the carryout window wanted a total of $2.85! To make matters worse, they didn't accept a credit card for fast food and they were holding up a lunch time line of cars as they scrounged around the car, looking for loose change.

"Tell you what, ma'am," Mark said, "you hold on to that bag of food and I'll pull around to the front door, and I'll come inside to get it."

They just drove away; it was too embarrassing to pursue. Then they roamed around Orange, Texas, looking for a bank. The Holy Grail might have been easier to locate than a bank open on Saturday.

After stopping at a half dozen locations, all for naught, B.J.'s frustration came to the fore; "You know what this country needs?"

"Let me guess...a good stain remover for leather outfits?" Mark zinged, waiting for B.J. to react.

B.J. ignored him. "We need a vending machine for cash..."

"Oh boy, what a great suggestion... just what America needs, another place thugs can break into, any time, day or night, to find ready cash for drug buys. How long do you really think a cash vending machine would last in New York City?"

"Well... what if the machines were built like little brick shithouses."

Mark broke a smile. "So how would you get the money out? What would you do?"

"I don't know... I'm no banking expert. Maybe you could order a fifty dollar bill, and then they would put a $50 charge on your credit card account."

"Sounds complicated."

"You wait and see," B.J. said confidently, "These banks... they'll find a way to do business on weekends. They'll have to. Customers want and need cash on weekends... just look at us!"

They needed enough money for lunch and a full tank of gasoline, a total of twenty bucks or so. B.J. came up with an innovative solution to the problem; he convinced a country store entrepreneur to do business with the two suspicious-looking Californians. The deal was if they would agree to make a purchase of store merchandise equal to the amount of extra cash they needed, the store's owner said he'd take an out-of-state check. So, they bought twenty dollars worth of groceries and asked for another twenty dollars in cash. The purchase included a loaf of bread, a large package of bologna, a pack of sliced American cheese, two cold six packs of Lone Star beer and a handful of flashlight batteries, which brought them to the agreed-upon total. As they drove away with a crisp new twenty-dollar bill in Mark's pocket, B.J. was pressed into service as the sandwich maker.

"There's nothing like gnawing on a good ol' bologna and cheese sandwich instead of eating that fatty, empty-calorie, fast food," Mark said. "Where's the mustard?"

"Damn, all they put in the bag here is little ketchup packets," B.J. bristled at the thought of ketchup on bologna. You'll have to make do without mustard. Besides, Stanton... after what you pulled last night you should be eating crow... just three nights after falling head over heels for sensuous Sally in Vegas... you get sidetracked by the first good-looking Texas insurance agent that comes along... you ought to be ashamed of yourself."

"Hey, Jackson, really, as a friend... thanks for bringing that up. Just when I'm having second thoughts about last night, it's so nice to have my nose rubbed in it."

"Hey Casanova... what are friends for? Anyway, I'm rooting for Sally."

A few moments later it struck Mark. "You know, it's weird... what you said a minute ago... I hardly know Sally Markham, and yet this morning I kind of feel like a complete shit heel."

B.J. corrected him, "I believe the proper phraseology should be 'a total guano head.'"

Rod Stewart's "You're In My Heart (The Final Acclaim)" was booming out from the radio.

"Speaking of ketchup, did I ever tell you about my days working in the Stop N Shop super market with Mully back in Ohio?"

"Oh no, I've done it again," B.J. looked to the heavens. "How could I have activated a story about ketchup? What are the odds? Will this be a spicy story?" he wanted to know, tongue-in-cheek. "Don't worry," he added, "and when it's over, I won't make any nasty *condiments*."

Mark ignored him. "I'm in high school working at the grocery store. One Saturday morning Mickey, our store manager, gives my buddy Marvin and me a 15-minute break from packing bags. So we go through the back room headed upstairs to the Break Room for a smoke. We run into our co-worker Al who is being punished by Mickey for being late to work that morning. Al's sentence is that he has to unload a whole semi-tractor trailer of Heinz products… pickles, relish and ketchup… and stack the heavy cases of jars and bottles against the back wall before he goes home. It's an all-day job, and hot, strenuous and dirty work. You have to set up conveyor-rollers from the truck into the store and then load from the truck onto the rollers, unload from the rollers and stack these 30-pound boxes up high, way over your head. Al's been at it for hours and the job is about half finished. He's stacking the big cardboard cases about 20-feet high against the back wall of the storeroom.

"After our 15-minutes of R & R, Marvin and I head back downstairs through the back room en-route to the front of the store. As we reach the storeroom we're hit with a weird 'vinegary' smell. We look ahead and see that all the ketchup cases Al has been stacking against the back wall have fallen! We can't even get through the narrow corridor between shelves and storage pallets… a jumble of boxes, scores of cartons, all leaking ketchup, are in a pile-up, everywhere! A four-inch-deep ooze of ketchup is all over the floor and moving fast, down the corridor, toward us. We jumped up on the conveyor-rollers and started clearing a path through the huge stinking mess.

"Then I hear Marvin say, 'Oh, no!' He found Al lying underneath all these broken ketchup bottle cases… and Al's completely unconscious! He's covered with broken glass and just soaked in ketchup. I remember *hoping* it was ketchup and not blood. Marvin scraped ketchup off Al's face and we determined that Al was still alive but knocked out for sure, but with all the broken glass shards everywhere, we had to find out if he was bleeding to death. 'We need a hose,' Marvin said.

"I said, 'There's a hose in the bakery.' And off we went, Marvin had Al by the armpits and I had him by the heels."

"Now, in our particular Stop N Shop store we were famous for our fresh-baked-daily Italian bread. In the back of the store, there was a big picture window behind the meat counter where the bakers worked kneading their dough on a big wooden table and baked their loaves in huge ovens. The bakers usually waved and flirted with the housewives through the picture windows. The housewives waited out front, by the meat case, until they saw a fresh batch of bread come out of the ovens. Each woman wanted to bag the freshest loaf when the bakers wheeled their bread cart out into the back aisle of the store.

"Picture if you will the scene when Marvin and I come storming through the big metal bakery doors, in full view of the housewives, with an unconscious man covered in... take your pick: ketchup and/or blood. The frickin' bakers don't even offer to help... they're more worried about their dough. They pick up massive globs of it off the table in the middle of the room and hold them up in their arms, like precious babies. Marvin and I throw Al up on the big wooden table and "poof" this layer of fine powdered flour that is covering the table rises in a cloud. Now the out-cold Al is all covered head to toe in red *and* white.

"Out in front of the picture window, by the meat case, the first housewife faints in the back aisle and hits the terrazzo floor with a loud smack, followed closely by shrill screams and other hysterical goings-on. There's an emergency announcement, 'All packers in the back!'

"Meanwhile, back in the bakery, I find the water hose and turn it on full-force, aiming it at poor ol' Al. I washed him down pretty good until he started coming around with a sputter of obscenities. Believe it or not, Jackson, there was not a scratch on him, just a golf ball-sized lump on his noggin where the first case of falling ketchup must have hit him."

B.J. winced at the thought.

"Then the little Italian store manager, Mickey, barges into the bakery and starts screaming at Marvin and me, 'You fuckin' idiots,' he says, "if he ain't dead, he's gonna' be," and then he fires the three of us right on the spot... Al and Marvin and me.

I tried to protest saying that we were just trying to save a life, but the irate Mickey would have none of it.

"There I was... all wet, covered with ketchup and a sprinkling of flour, unemployed, and in my mind, very under-appreciated. As I left the store I noticed the scene in the back aisle where the housewives had been watching the whole incident. There were women lying all over the place, some out-cold, others crying or holding crying kids, the knocked-out ones were being tended to by store employees. Jackson, it looked like triage in a war-zone. They all stared at me as I walked by. What could I say?

"I went home. When I got there my mother was waiting for me at the side door. She knew what had happened. The assistant store manager had called her. She said, 'Mickey says you can have your job back if you change clothes and get back there by two o'clock.'

B.J. asked, "So what did you do?"

"I went back to work. I had no choice. I needed the money for college. *My* punishment was to clean up the back room. It took six hours with a snow shovel to catch-up with all that ketchup. And it took another month for the smell to go away."

"Quite a story, my friend, but you're a hero to me. Like they say, no good deed goes unpunished. Now... does that mean you want ketchup on your hero? Or not, baloney breath?"

## Alligator Shoes.

THEY ENTERED THE Pelican State of Louisiana at 1:00 p.m., crossing the Sabine River Bridge. Halfway across the gray-steel structure, a worn white sign with the state bird on it indicated that they were entering Calcasieu Parish.

"We're fixin' to enter Cajun country now," Mark said in a mock accent.

"*Laissez les bon temps roulez...*" B.J. stated with a surprisingly proper accent.

Mark chatted on about how he knew several people who lived in the Washington area who came from this part of the country. These Louisianans enjoyed kidding about their Cajun roots and friends. He recalled howling at some of their exaggerated stories, told in the marvelous Cajun accent and way of speaking. One tale in particular popped into Mark's mind.

"Jackson, have I ever told you the one about ol' Rene, the crazy Cajun, and his wife, Marie?"

"No, I don't think so, but I have that feelin' again... you know, like when static electricity builds up just before a lightning strike..."

"Hey, you'll love it."

"I'll be the judge of that..."

Mark did his best at imitating a Cajun accent. "Rrr-nay is this big, crazy Cajun who's married to the very lovely Mar-ree. They're two very poor people, who's livin' a way back out in the bayou, but they're very much in love. As their 15th wedding anniversary approaches, Rrr-nay keeps asking the lovely Mar-ree, what she wants as a gift. But she knows Rrr-nay can't afford an expensive present. But he jus' keeps pestering her. Does she want a fur coat? Mar-ree says... no. Does she want a string of pearls? No, she doesn't. Well then, says Rrr-nay, what does she want? Finally, just to shut him up, Mar-ree mentions that she's always wanted a nice pair of ally-gator shoes. Rrr-nay, he smiles.

"So, one day a week later, Rrr-nay's driving his 'pick-me-up-truck' along the levee road. He spots, a huge, big ally-gator crawlin' 'cross dat levee. Dat fat, big gator crossed the road right in front of him and slipped, real quiet-like, into the bayou. Rrr-nay, he thinks to his-self... this could be my best chance to get the lovely Mar-ree a pair of 'dem nice ally-gator shoes. So he slams on the brakes-down; he out of the 'pick-me-up-truck jumps. And after dat gator, he rushes. Rrr-nay tracks dat gator right into the swamp. Then he spots the fat, big gator, jus' sunnin' hisself. He sneaks up, and he jumps right on the ally-gator's back... and a drag out, knockdown, huge, big fight commences. Rrr-nay and dat gator... rollin' aroun' an' aroun'... in dat muddy, dark water. They thrash and thrash for an hour and a half... just feelin' each other out... seeing who will run out-of-gas first... Rrr-nay, or dat fat, big ally-gator. Dat mean ol' gator, he take Rrr-nay to the bottom of the bayou three-time... but Rrr-nay he hang wit'im. Rrr-nay, he's a Cajun on a mission for his lovely Mar-ree. Finally, Rrr-nay wears out dat huge, big gator; and he, back to the levee, drags his ally-gator ass. He pins down dat gator on the bank of the levee road. Rrr-nay is so tired and all soakin' wet... he's bloody and muddy... he's exhausted. But he gets a good grip on dat fat, big gator... and he goes to flip that reptilian bastard over on his back... and you know what Rrr-nay found?"

"What..." said B.J., trying to play along.

"He flips dat gator over... and oh Rrr-nay, he is the saddest Cajun in all Louisian'... can you believe it? After all dat fussin' an' fightin'... dat fat, big gator... he wasn't wearin' no ally-gator shoes."

B.J. hung his head. "Good gawd... have you no shame? A Cajun shaggy gator story? It's come to *this*?"

"It's my car, my story. If you want, I'll leave you off to slog through the bayous on your own."

"Great. Then maybe I can replace those dumb Dingo boots of yours with some nice ally-gator ones."

"Feels So Good" by trumpeter Chuck Mangione was blaring on the Blaupunkt.

## The Long and Short of It.

THEY PASSED LAKE Charles and Jennings, Louisiana, and entered Acadia Parish, headed for the town of Lafayette.

"I believe that Louisiana is the only state in the Union whose laws are based on the old Napoleonic Code..." said B.J.

"Then it's the only state in the Union that doesn't follow English common law."

"So what happens if you're caught speeding in Louisiana?"

"Well..." said Mark, casting a wary glance at "Stanley's" speedometer, "then we're going to have to *buy* a lawyer, a politician, as well as a priest."

"Stanton, I love this part of the country. I've always been impressed with Thomas Jefferson and the fact that he outsmarted Napoleon Bonaparte to land the Louisiana Purchase for a mere pittance... not to mention my great-great-great-great uncle, General Andy Jackson who won the Battle of New Orleans."

"You're kidding 'Jcksn'!" You're related to Old Hickory? I didn't know that..."

"I'm not exactly sure how, but my grandmother always insisted that we were related, so I believe it's true."

"Well, now I'm impressed by that... and I agree with you... the Louisiana Purchase was one hell of a good real estate deal!" said Mark. "Hey, I don't believe it. We're actually agreeing on something! Ol' Tom Jefferson was quite a guy too... and it ended up being one of the best land deals in all of history... with the possible exception of the Alaskan deal."

"Well, it doubled the size of the country in 1803... for a mere $11 million."

"Jackson, the thing I like most about what Jefferson did... it was a real presidential type move... the kind of leadership that gets your kisser chiseled into Mount Rushmore. Unlike your man, Jimbo Carter, who's trying to carve out a place on Mount *Gushmore* by giving up the Panama Canal... for absolutely nothing?"

"Hey, crawfish breath. Give it a rest, will you?"

Mark gave it a few minutes, and a few miles down the road. "You know, the Louisianan I've heard about most... up on Capitol Hill... was the 'Kingfish' himself, Huey Long. The guy who got away with murder... until they murdered him."

"Yeah," said B.J. "I never did figure out whether he was the champion of the little guy or one of the oppressors..."

"Some of both, I guess. This state has a colorful history as a capital of corruption. If the politicians down here had been honest, and if they'd taxed the big oil companies just a nickel for every barrel of oil taken out of this state, the roads here would be the best, and the schools here would be the best. But all the oil money ever did was line the pockets of the ward healers and political henchmen."

"You know how they used to lobby in Louisiana, don't ya'?" Mark asked.

"I doubt it."

"Well, you would take a politician to dinner and tell him what you wanted. Then you'd say 'Look Senator, I believe you dropped an envelope under the table.' And then the Senator would look down and say, 'Oh no, son, that's not mine... if it were mine it would be a much *thicker* envelope!'"

"I get it," B.J. grinned.

"When I worked on Capitol Hill, my friends from Louisiana loved to tell Huey Long stories. My personal favorite was the one about when he was Governor, back in 1929. During that legislative session, there was a real close vote coming up in the House. So Governor Long told his cronies to line up all the usual votes and to report on those legislators who were still undecided. It turned out that the nose count in the House was dead even, and they could find only one undecided vote... a legislator, from Shreveport... a freshman no one knew. So the Governor said, "Fine, boys, let's invite the young man over for lunch in the Governor's office, and I'll work on him... give 'im the political facts of life.'

"At high noon they ushered the young legislator into the Governor's private office. They had a fried chicken and potato salad lunch brought in. After they ate and had some casual chitchat, Huey lit up a cigar and offered one to the kid.

"Then Governor Long stood up, looked the young legislator straight in the eye and said... 'Son, this afternoon there's going to be a big vote in the House... and I need to know... can I count on your support?'

"Well, the young fellow summoned up all his courage... he looked the Kingfish right in the eye and said, 'Governor, when you're right, you're right. And I'm with you all the way. But when you're wrong, you're wrong. And I can't be with you. And on the vote this afternoon, Governor, you're dead wrong, and I can't be with you.'

"Huey Long was taken aback by the young man's effrontery. He puffed on his cigar a couple of times and thought about what he'd said. Then the Kingfish went over and put his arm around the young man and said, 'Son, I don't think you understand... you see, when I'm *right*... I don't need you!'"

B.J. laughed harder than he did at the story about Rene the Cajun.

"It Amazes Me" by John Denver was drifting from the radio.

## Old Mad River.

THEY PASSED LAFAYETTE, the unofficial capital of Cajun country and saw several billboards hailing the upcoming "*Festival International de Lousiane,*" an annual ethnic food and music festival held each April. It sounded so good; they almost wanted to wait around a week, just to taste the crawfish. Mark thought to himself, *I'd rather be here eating crawfish than where I'm going to be next week*.

The interstate along this stretch of road was built on stilts. The highway passed over the Atchafalaya Basin, an 800,000-acre wilderness of forests, swamps and bayous. The Basin was the area designed to absorb Mississippi River flood waters each spring, diverting them into back bayous, rather than having the deluge wash out the downstream Crescent City of New Orleans, which sits below sea level.

The two travelers crossed the mighty muddy Mississippi, at Baton Rouge on Interstate 10, shortly after 3:00 p.m.

"There it is, Jackson... old man river, or should I say old 'mad' river. We're halfway home." Mark lit up a Salem to distract from the pain again building up in his abdomen.

"Not exactly halfway, geographically speaking."

"Yes, but traditionally everything of importance in this country has been categorized with the caveat 'east' or 'west' of the Mississippi... like the tallest building west of the Mississippi, or the largest state east of the Mississippi."

"Well, Shazam, Stanton. What with you and Sally, and you and Amy, now you've been transformed into the biggest cheatin' heart *east* of the Mississippi, congratulations."

"Talk about giving it a rest!" The dig ruined Mark's Mississippi moment. After all, Houston had been the one and only notch in his headboard in months.

B.J. peered through the passing bridge struts. "It looks ominous down there."

Warming back, Mark said, "It is mad. It's the angriest, most unpredictable river in the world. And this is a real river... you're not in Texas any longer Toto."

"Alright, Kemo, why is it so pissed off?"

"Up in Minnesota, the river is shallow and a mile-and-a-half wide. But down here it's got half that width to move in. So it digs deep, 50 to 100 feet, and rampages from here to the Gulf, especially from now until June. Way back in 1927, it exploded over the levees and made a reservoir the size of the whole Northeast United States. It killed thousands and made a million people homeless. In the brouhaha that followed that flood, Huey Long was elected governor and an obscure flood rehabilitation guy caught the rising tide and rode it all the way to The White House."

"Who was that?"

"Herbert Hoover. Sound familiar?"

"Truly a heartless river," said B.J., "I feel a *depression* coming on."

Mark began to hum "Old Man River." B.J. whipped out his harmonica tried to drown him out with a few bars of "Your

Cheatin' Heart." Hank Williams he wasn't. Mark turned up the volume on the radio.

Off to the left, as they neared the eastern bank of the river, they could see the 34-story state capitol building towering above downtown; closer to the river was the old state capitol building. Once across the bridge, Mark stopped at the first historical marker. According to the bronze plaque, the French explorer, Iberville, named the city "Red Stick" after seeing a large tree trunk on the river's bank, reddened with the blood of animals sacrificed by local Indians. According to legend, the red stick stood as the local boundary marker between the territories of the Tunica and Choctaw tribes.

"There ought to be a 'Red Stick' boundary marker between all the chemical companies and oil refineries... that's the only thing you can see or smell on either side of the river all the way down to New Orleans," said B.J.

"Plants, refineries and L.S.U.," Mark responded, pointing out the campus and stadium, to the right of the highway.

"Aren't there supposed to be some beautiful old plantations down along the river," B.J. asked. "I'd really like to see one up close."

Ordinarily, Mark would have bitched about taking the time to tour a musty old mansion, but he reminded himself once again that B.J. and he were now "driftin'." "Well, since your great, great, great, great, thirteenth cousin... or what ever it is... Andy 'Jcksn' rescued this whole backwater swamp from the bloody British, I guess you're entitled to a look-see at a plantation."

Passing through Ascension Parish, B.J. came up with a rather interesting notion, to go with his previous brainstorm, cash vending machines. "You know," he said, "it's really too bad there aren't telephones in cars. If there were, we could call ahead to Big Bart... right here from the road... and set up a time and place to get together this evening."

"Hell, Jackson. There have been mobile radiophones in cars for years... they're like walkie-talkies. You've seen those 6-foot high antennas whipping around behind the cars. I had one in my car back in 1970, while working on a political campaign in Ohio."

"I know what you mean, but I'm thinking of a real telephone in the car, as standard equipment, just like we have heaters and radios in the car now. It's my bet that car telephones will be the next piece of optional equipment."

"Yeah, Jackson, and we'd all have one right now... except there's this little thing called 'no-such technology'... that is keeping it from happening."

"The technology will come. And when it does there will always be someone like you who will be against it."

"And then when a million cars a year are involved in crashes, because drivers tried to dial a ten-digit long distance phone number at 70 mph on the freeway, don't come around to sign me up. Who are you going to call from your car anyway? No one will buy it. It's just another way for the boss and the wife to maintain 24-hour surveillance."

In search of a plantation for B.J. to tour, they exited I-10 at U.S. route 61 and headed south toward Gramercy, Louisiana, and the "Great River Road" -- home to the *ante-bellum* mansions on the East bank of the river.

The last strains of "Telephone Line" by the Electric Light Orchestra were concluding.

At the foot of the highway exit ramp, Mark pulled into a service station with the same logo as his gasoline credit card, an important competitive factor now that they were strapped for cash. While Mark looked after the car, B.J. headed for the pay phone to call Big Bart with their remaining pocket change.

"Eh, Jack... I see where you guys are all the way from California," said the towheaded pump attendant.

"Yes sir-ree," Mark responded, wondering why the guy was calling him 'Jack.'

"Say, Jack... what kinda' car is this?"

"It's a Porsche..."

"I knew it... I just knew it had to be a 'Porch.'"

Mark was about to ask him about the "Jack" thing when the inevitable occurred...

"What color would you call this 'Porch'?"

"Gray... pearl gray... that's what the Germans call it..."

"Looks a mite reddish-purple to me..."

"Some people say that." Mark handed him the credit card and climbed back behind the wheel.

B.J. returned. "We're all set for tonight. We're going to meet Bart at the Commander's Palace restaurant for dinner, at seven-thirty. Let's roll Stanton. We've got to wedge in a quick plantation visit..."

"I'd love to leave, but 'Clyde' here hasn't returned with my credit card..."

Just then, the towheaded lad emerged from the front office.

"Hey, Jack..." he said, smiling, "You got a problem... I had to cut-up your credit card. You're on the hot list!"

"Listen here, pal, first of all my name's not 'Jack'. And second, my card number is not on your 'hot list'... I'm always current on that account. I pay my bills, and I made damn sure I paid my gas card down to zero before I left on this trip just five days ago."

"Well, tell it to the home office, Jack..." he paused, apparently beginning to realize the "Jack" thing was beginning to fray Mark's nerves, "...they're on the phone, and they want to talk to you." Mark felt a sudden twinge of pain deep in his gut.

Mark worked his way through three levels of oil company bureaucracy trying to convince the credit department that he really was who he said he was! The more he learned, the more it became apparent that "Clyde" was totally dyslectic. The poor bastard had inverted two of the credit card's numbers and ended up destroying a perfectly good charge card. And here Mark was, still three days from Washington, strapped for cash, and now he was traveling cross-country without a gasoline company card. The kid felt terrible about his mistake; but Mark didn't go out of his way to console him.

Mark continued talking with the oil company's clerk. "So how are you people going to make this right?" his voice rising by the moment.

"What do you expect us to do?"

"Well, listen here... what's your real name?"

"Mr. Jaspers..."

"And just where are you located?"

"In Houston, Texas."

"What's your phone number, in case we get cut off?"

Jaspers provided his number and extension.

"Well, Mr. Jaspers, consider my situation... I'm stuck somewhere ass-deep in a bayou. I'm halfway through a 3,600-mile, cross-country trip. I'm flat outta' cash... and I'm flat out of luck... and I got three more days of driving ahead of me. And now, one of your logo wearin' 'Clydes' has just destroyed my perfectly good credit card. When you're traveling, money comes in real handy 'cause it's hard to cash a check. And it would be so nice if I had some money, so I could pay the sixty-seven-point-nine cents per gallon to buy your gasoline the rest of the way, especially since I've got to use cash now that my credit card has been cut up into twenty guitar picks. So, Mr. Jaspers, what would you suggest, before I take this up with your boss?"

"Give me an address and I'll send you a replacement card."

"Now that's just swell! And it certainly helps me. It cuts right to the heart of my problem doesn't it, Mr. Jaspers? Look here, your local guy cut up a perfectly good credit card! So, Jaspers, you guys owe me... and if you don't come up with something more innovative and more responsive to my needs... pretty quickly... I'm going to call the president of your company. I'm going to explain to his secretary what happened. Then I'm going to tell her I'm stranded in Gramercy, Louisiana. And I'm going to say that a guy named Jaspers at your extension told me to 'take a hike' the rest of the way. Do I make myself clear?"

"Yes, sir."

After leaving the phone for a few long minutes to check with his supervisor, Jaspers returned to the line and said, "Here's what I've been authorized to do. We'll provide you with traveler's checks... probably a hundred dollars to get you through the rest of your trip. If you'll tell me where you're staying tonight, I'll get someone to deliver them to your hotel.

"Now you're talking Jaspers. Your boss is a smart fellow. I'll be staying at the Roosevelt Hotel tonight for just one night... that's in downtown New Orleans, Louisiana, on Baronne Street."

"You'll have your traveler's checks tonight, or no later than tomorrow morning. If there's a problem, call me. I'm terribly sorry about the misunderstanding."

"Yeah, okay, Jaspers." Without saying a word, Mark paid "Clyde" the twelve dollars for the gas, and returned to the car.

"Jcksn... you wanna drive?"

B.J. jumped in the driver's seat without a comment, but he suspected that something was wrong. Mark was giving up on the driving way too easily for the control freak that he was. He made a note to keep a closer eye on his friend. Something was up here.

It was 3:45 p.m. On the radio, The Sylvers were singing "Hot Line."

"Do we still have time to see a plantation?" B.J. asked.

"Sure. We're lettin' loose, aren't we?" Mark said, trying to relax and get more into the "driftin'" mood. Mark winced, closed his eyes and tried to think of anything other than the pain in his abdomen.

They decided on touring the San Francisco Plantation that lies some five miles south of the Veterans Memorial Bridge. B.J. favored that one because of its name. After all, that's where the two of them started their trip on Tuesday. When they arrived at the mansion a sign indicated that the last tour was at four o'clock, and that the plantation closed for the day at 5:00 p.m. They rushed up to the office, only to discover that there was a $5.00 per person admission charge.

"Man, I hadn't thought about an admission fee," said B.J.

"Neither had I."

"Tell you what, Stanton... give me what cash you've got left... and wait right here. Let me see what I can do." B.J. went inside. A few minutes later he reappeared with a real Southern belle, named Gigi, all dolled-up in hoop-skirted costume, no less, ready to give them a private tour.

"Ah un'erstan' you gentlemen are from the real San Francisco, out in Cal-eee-forn-ya', and y'all have but just a few minutes to tour *our* San Francisco. Mr. Jackson here tells me y'all are destined for N'Awlins this evenin'," she looked right at Mark. "And Mr. Jackson tells me of your deep interest in *antebellum* his'tree," she nodded at Mark.

Mark smiled stupidly. "Nice work," he whispered to B.J. as they headed for the mansion.

"My good looks... and the *fact* that I *am* the great, great, great grandnephew of General Andrew Jackson."

Gigi, the prim but handsome tour guide, gave them a thumbnail sketch of plantation life during the tour. One Edmond Bozonier Marmillion had finished the richly decorated main house in the mid-1850's; apparently he was a rather wealthy Creole planter and trader. Also, they learned that this particular mansion was somewhat smaller and less dramatic than her *ante-bellum* neighbors, up and down river; however, this house was well known for its unique frescoes, its louvered roof, and the eye-catching widow's walk atop the structure that commanded a sweeping panorama of the Mississippi. The plantation house, Gigi stated, was built according to the old Creole style, with the dining and service rooms located on the ground floor, and with the living quarters situated on the upper level. The San Francisco mansion had the detailing of a riverboat, all the way down to the exterior front porch staircases. Steamboat Gothic is how Gigi referred to the decor.

B.J. and Mark thanked her for the quick but informative tour and departed the plantation for their rendezvous with Big Bart in New Orleans.

As he started up "Stanley" for the ride to New Orleans, B.J. proudly produced a slip of paper with Gigi's address and phone number scribbled on it.

"Sweet Talkin' Woman" by the Electric Light Orchestra was on the airwaves.

You are one "Sweet Talkin' William," Mark smiled.

## Beltway Bandits.

THE FRENCH QUARTER came into view along the east side of Canal Street. They had exited I-10 and were headed south on the boulevard, which cuts through the heart of downtown New Orleans.

Green trolley cars busily worked their way up and down the median of Canal Street. Even though it was early evening, Mark could swear that he already heard the music and felt the excitement of the old *Vieux Carre*. B.J. turned right at Baronne Street, and unlike their experience in Houston, they found the Roosevelt Hotel without trouble.

Shortly after they arrived in the hotel room, the telephone rang. B.J. jumped on it, expecting it to be Big Bart. "It's for you," he handed Mark the receiver, "it's the doorman. We parked in a fire lane or something, and they're going to tow your car."

"Screw you, Jackson... real funny." He picked up the receiver.

"Mister Stan-tone?"

"Yes."

"I have an envelope for you at the concierge's desk. May I send it up to the room?"

Mark knew he didn't have any tip money for a messenger. He'd dodged the bellman coming into the hotel because he didn't have tip money. "No sir, I'm on my way downstairs, I'll stop by your desk." He headed out the door.

The envelope contained a message from the oil company and a whopping $300 in traveler's checks -- a pleasant surprise. Apparently, these oil company guys really were sorry about the credit card screw-up and didn't want to hear from any lawyers. Mark was vindicated; he felt important as a customer. He returned to the room to find B.J. already dressed in blazer and slacks and wearing one of Mark's favorite ties. Actually, B.J. looked rather civilized.

"You can find me downstairs in the Sazerac Lounge," he said on the way out. "While you were checking in, I noticed several attractive ladies refreshing themselves in the bar... so, ta-ta for now." He left. Now here was another first. B.J. was dressed and ready to go out on the town before Mark.

Mark hurriedly showered and dressed in a camel hair jacket. *Damn*! B.J. was wearing the tie he wanted, so Mark made do with a red rep even though it didn't exactly complement his brown slacks.

With B.J. already downstairs, he placed a call to Doctor Tom Roche's home in Potomac, Maryland. After a few pleasantries and one or two basic questions of the doctor, he cringed at what he heard and sat down. "Mark, I've looked at the second set of test results and I'm positive that we should stick to our surgical schedule for eleven a.m., March 29$^{th}$." The news made his skin crawl.

When Mark arrived in the lobby lounge B.J. was the only person sitting on a barstool, but he was engaged in an animated conversation with a group of five people at a nearby table. Three of them were young women.

"Stanton. These good folks are from Washington, D.C. And believe it or not they're down here on Easter weekend on business."

"We're here for an installation and training session," said one of the men, "the client wants it 'yesterday,' so here we are, stranded on Easter weekend."

"How nice... or should I say, how unfortunate, it being a special weekend and all that... but it could be worse, at least you're in the Big Easy." A preoccupied Mark gave a cursory wave to the group. There were two older men in dark suits, maybe in their fifties -- obviously "the bosses." The three women were probably in their late twenties -- and most likely mid-level managers. All three were wearing designer-crafted business suits, and they were fetching, each in their own way.

Mark slumped onto a barstool and with his elbows on the bar and his chin resting on his two fists he ordered a much needed and a much wanted Jack Daniel's on ice with two splashes of water. He was deep within himself and about ready to drown his troubles in good Tennessee whisky; he ignored the conversation behind him. The first sip went down like liquid silk.

The topic of conversation for all tourists in New Orleans' hotels, must be dictated by local ordinance. "Where did you eat last night?" "Where are you going to eat tonight?" And, "Where are you planning to go for brunch tomorrow morning?" B.J. was immersed in the thick of that inane conversation.

Mark half-listened over his shoulder for as long as he could stand it. Finally, he decided to join the fray and twirled his stool seat away from the bar.

"What sort of business are you-all in back in Washington?" He asked it without making eye contact with anyone in particular, thinking he'd break up the annoying "which restaurant-what dinner" blather.

"We're beltway bandits!" The most petite of the three women at the table said in a too-loud voice. "We market computer technology."

"I see."

"Beltway bandits," as they were known, were a relatively new phenomenon in the D.C. area. These new-age, high-tech consulting firms -- many in the burgeoning word processing and emerging computer field -- were located on both the Maryland and Virginia sides of the Potomac River, along the I-270-North corridor and I-495 Washington Beltway, respectively.

In Mark's Republican mindset, beltway bandits were lampreys -- federal government hangers-on -- sucking away at the financial largess of the Pentagon and other departments and agencies. Federal government, he believed, was fiscally out-of-control and most everyone knew it; and the uncontrolled spending and spillage was getting worse. The fiscally inept Carter Administration and the questionable legacy of thirty-five successive years of a Democrat-controlled Congress did not help the government's dire straits. Accepting government money for management consulting or for technology procurement was no special challenge. Every September, the conclusion of the federal fiscal year, departments and agencies literally threw bucks at any taker just to keep their predetermined slice-of-the-pie in next year's budget. Taking tax dollars from bumbling federal bureaucrats, who had little or no technical proficiency, was as easy as highway robbery. Hence the moniker, "beltway bandits."

"I'm Priscilla Griffin. My friends call me 'Cilla," said the petite one, hand extended, stepping up to the bar to talk directly with Mark.

"Mark Stanton, 'Cilla... nice to meet you."

"Your friend, William, is such a sweet guy," she said. Mark rolled his eyes at the phrase. "He was telling us about your cross-country trip." This woman had delicate, beautiful skin, and a mop of abundantly curly hair. Mark had to admit that he found her attractive, but there was something eerie about her that put him on his guard -- it was far too easy for everyone in the room to know her business. She had an "edge" about her, beyond talking a little too loudly for a public place. Maybe she was just a bit too aggressive. When she spoke, she emoted as though playing to some other audience – an audience no one but her could see.

"It's been an interesting five days so far," Mark said, speaking more softly than usual, a counter-mechanism to Cilla's piercing voice.

"When do you get to D.C.?"

"Monday night... in time for the final NCAA basketball game," he answered in a low whisper.

"What part of town are you from?"

"I'll be moving into a townhouse on Capitol Hill. I'm going to share it with a buddy of mine."

"I live out in 'condo canyon'... at the west end of Alexandria," she said.

As Mark ordered a second Jack Daniel's, he saw B.J. leave his barstool and take Cilla's open seat between the other two ladies. B.J.'s "game of love" had officially begun with the opening gambit. As of that moment, Mark was tactically locked-in to young Cilla; however, B.J., like a powerful chess piece, could now move in either direction. He had his choice of the other two. It was fun watching B.J., the undisputed master of his own universe, at work. B.J. had two; but Mark still had one. And Mark was still in better shape than the two older businessmen who, he figured, were just beginning to realize that the two remaining staffers were being mesmerized by B.J.

Mark grasped for something intelligent to say to Cilla. He focused on her strawberry blonde curls and the unusual hairdo. He knew he had to word his question carefully, lest it tumble out the wrong way. "I like what you've done with your hair... what do you call that?"

"Gosh, it's still wet. My friend Janie calls it that 'just screwed in the shower' look," she blurted out, bouncing an open palm off her curly locks. "I think it looks like a 'direct-hit.'"

"I see..." Mark choked a bit on his sour mash. Her "shower line" caught him in mid-sip and he'd swallowed way more Jack Daniel's than he'd bargained for.

She kept right on talking, not noticing the big gulp or his bulging eyes. "Where are you two having dinner?" she asked.

Now here they go again, playing that stupid New Orleans tourist game. "At the Commander's Palace," he managed to croak out.

"Us too!" she squealed, several decibels too loudly.

Mark winced at her shrillness.

"That's where we're going for dinner," she said, "...what a coincidence..."

"Yes. It really is... maybe we'll run into you later."

### Commanders-in-Chef.

THE COMMANDER'S PALACE restaurant is located in the beautiful Garden District of New Orleans, just west of downtown, accessible by the Charles Street trolley cars.

Big Bart Hampton met B.J. and Mark at 7:30 p.m. just out front of the restaurant, on the Washington Avenue sidewalk. B.J. gave him a big hug and several loud thumps on the back. It seemed that Bart remembered Mark much more clearly than Mark recalled him.

"Mark, it's good to see you," Bart said in his deep radio voice. "It's been quite a long time since we met at Dewey Beach back in '72."

Mark guessed that Bart's low pitched, resounding voice merely passed over his vocal cords, because Mark was sure that anything that deep must emanate from his hamstrings. He sounded a lot like the singer, Barry White, only maybe deeper.

"Yes it has," Mark said still trying to recall meeting such a large black fellow at Dewey Beach.

"Our table isn't quite ready yet, they've just seated a large group, but we can grab a drink at the back bar," Bart said.

The *maitre d'hôtel* ushered them into the restaurant, turning left through a dining room. Then they walked through a swinging door and went right into the restaurant's extremely humid kitchen. *Surely they must have made a wrong turn,* Mark thought. They dodged white-clad chefs in stiff puffy hats and bandanna'd kitchen help, humping around large trays of steaming platters. At the back of the kitchen, through still another swinging door, they entered a quiet, dark wood-paneled, air-conditioned saloon. The bar looked out on an open courtyard of garden tables with umbrellas. Farther back on the restaurant's lot was another building with still more diners looking out on the same courtyard from the opposite side. Behind the ancient mahogany bar were several picture windows, looking back into the kitchen. Each was filled with frenetic scenes of kitchen staff activity. To be sure, it was an unusual layout for such a fancy, well-known restaurant.

Mark enjoyed his third Tennessee sour mash whiskey of the evening. It was numbing his body as well as his mind, the exact effect he was hoping for. Meanwhile, B.J. and Bart were catching up on old times.

So this was Commander's Palace! The famed restaurant had always been on Mark's 'bucket list" of places to experience before he left this earth; he was prepared to thoroughly enjoy it. A bartender let them glance at menus while they waited;

Mark decided to sample the world-famous turtle soup with sherry as the appetizer, and to order the Tasso-stuffed shrimp for the entree, with the bread pudding soufflé as the finale.

When they were escorted to a table out in the courtyard, Mark noticed Cilla's "beltway bandit" group seated in the building at the rear of the courtyard. Apparently that is where larger business parties were wined and dined. Cilla waved and nudged her friend, Janie when she saw Mark and B.J. winding their way through the courtyard tables. Mark gave them an abbreviated John Wayne salute.

Big Bart noticed the wave and turned to see three of the five diners at Cilla's table waving back. The two dark-suited male *banditos* were oblivious.

"Old friends?"

"New friends... but same old story, boys meet girls," B.J. offered.

B.J. took over the discussion and recounted several stories about the cross-country trip for Bart before the threesome finished their *aperitifs*. However, he purposefully avoided stories that involved his glaring mistakes, such as -- he ignored his inauspicious start at Laurie's house involving the laundry; and he ignored the fact that he'd lost Mark's Stetson hatband; and he barely admitted leaving "Stanley" parked in the wrong gear at Fort Stockton.

After fifteen minutes of stories, Bart was grinning from ear to ear. "How would you guys like to be on my radio show... tonight," he asked.

B.J. feigned surprise, but somehow Mark sensed that B.J. knew all along that this was coming. "Be on your radio show? Tonight? What would we talk about?" B.J. babbled in an exaggerated way.

"You'd be doing me a favor," said Bart. "Right now I've got a local psychic lined up to do the show, but the more I listen to you two tell your war stories from the road... the more I think you'd make for a lot more interesting evening for my listeners. And it would sure be a lot more fun for me if you'd do it," said Bart.

B.J. pointed at Mark. "Stanton here is an expert at filling in on television and radio programs, aren't you? Tell Bart about your former girlfriend in Texas, Kathy Blair..."

"What would you want us to talk about Bart?" Mark asked, changing the subject and getting more serious.

"Your cross-country trip of course, and traveling the open road... two guys on the loose in a Porsche. It's a unique happening. Most people would love to do something like that while they're still young enough to enjoy it, but most never get the chance. Look... we're only on from ten 'til midnight tonight... two hours that go by real fast. How 'bout it?"

Mark looked at B.J., who blurted out, "We'll do it Bart... you wouldn't believe all the crazy things that have happened to us in the last four and a half days."

Now Mark was experiencing flashbacks to his television guest episode with Kathy Blair. B.J. and he were going to be radio show guests on an all-talk, late-night, AM radio station in New Orleans. Mark wondered how many people would actually be listening... ten, twelve, twenty-two?

As though Bart was reading Mark's mind, he bragged, "You're going to be on the top-rated program, on the top-ranked talk station in all of Louisiana, and parts of lower Mississippi and Alabama. I've got unreal audience demographics... I can't explain it to anyone, but these local honkies love to call in and mix it up with an uppity Afro-American... a college graduate... who knows how to use those multi-syllabic words in their proper context."

"Why all of the sudden am I not looking forward to this?" Mark muttered to himself.

"Stanton, how bad could you possibly be at this... all that is involved is... talking. That should be no sweat for you," B.J. countered, encouragingly. *B.J. couldn't believe that the one time on this trip that he actually wanted Stanton to tell stories -- the guy was beginning to clam up on him.*

Bart excused himself to call the station. "I've got to cancel that psychic. But then again, if she's any good, she probably already knows the score."

The Commander's Palace meal was outstanding. Bart was enjoying the local red fish and andouille sausage special. B.J. was working on Veal Christian. Mark's order of Tasso-stuffed shrimp was exquisite, but he wasn't feeling as hungry as he thought. Knowing they were going "on-the-air" in less than two hours, he did no more than just sip a light Italian white wine.

Halfway through dinner the tallest of the three female *banditos*, Janie, stopped by the table to visit B.J. *These three ladies were definitely on the prowl*, Mark thought. But he gave them the benefit of the doubt; they were probably just trying to dump their old fogey bosses for an evening on the town with people more their age. Janie invited the three men to join their group of five for a walk down Bourbon Street in the French Quarter, after dinner. B.J. was quick to explain that they were booked on a local radio talk show, later in the evening. He introduced Bart as the program's host. Janie was duly impressed.

"You and your friends are welcome to come over to the studio to watch and listen to the program," Bart offered. "Then I'll be glad to give you-all a personal tour of the Quarter. I know it well. I have a place there."

"Well, it sounds great to me... let me ask my friends," she said, retreating quickly.

She returned a few minutes later to say that she and her friends, Cilla and Patsy, would be happy join us at the studio; they could visit Bourbon Street tomorrow night. Apparently, their older male colleagues had other plans. Bart jotted down directions to the studio on the back of his business card. The radio station's studio was on the twelfth floor of a high-rise office building, downtown near the corner of Poydras and Camp Streets. "The show starts at 10:05 p.m., after the news, and ends right at midnight," Bart said.

Mark never expected the ladies to show; the thought of sitting for two hours, watching a talk radio show unfold, would likely bore anyone to death.

Fortified by the whiskey and wine, Mark bit the bullet and picked up the dinner tab. He paid for it out of the $300 windfall from his gasoline credit card caper. Also, he'd loaned $50, which he never expected to lay eyes on again, to B.J. After the tip, he was headed for broke again.

### Motor Mouths.

"WELCOME TO OUR show..." Bart crooned into his mammoth microphone, at precisely 10:05 p.m. "This is your host, Bart Hampton, inviting you to join us for a cross-country jaunt with Mr. William 'B.J.' Jackson and the Honorable Marcus Stanton. My guests are well known *bon-vivants*, world-travelers and dilettantes who reside on both coasts, and who are the authors of innumerable articles on travel and tourism in the United States... and around the globe..." There was a pause; and then the show's musical jingle came on.

*Honorable? World travelers? Dilettantes? Authors?* Mark's lower jaw went limp. Bart winked at him, and waved his hand in a dismissive way -- signaling him to relax. No doubt he was trying to reassure Mark that such biographical build-ups were just "hype" and no big thing in the radio biz.

B.J. and Mark were seated at separate microphones, situated across a large round console; they were wearing large headsets. Just outside the soundproof studio, through a double-paned picture window, sat the three *bandito* groupies, Cilla, Janie and Patsy. To Mark's amazement they appeared at the studio just as the show started, and to his surprise, they seemed to be enjoying themselves -- giggling at virtually everything said.

They returned from a commercial break. "William Jackson, you're half-way through this sojourn on the open road... tell me about your trip so far... what's the purpose of this particular cross-country journey?" Bart asked, crooning in his deep voice.

"Well, Bart... it's a trip Mark and I have been planning for some time. We wanted to tour the southwest, including Texas... working our way east toward the Nation's Capital. We've toured many of the historical sites along the way... and, ah, we've also been exploring country music too..."

*Exploring country music?* Mark was taken aback. Hell, they'd listened to the car radio and wrote a two-bit song. *Toured historic sites?* With the possible exception of the Alamo which they walked right past without seeing, and the Mississippi River plantation that afternoon, B.J. had stayed in the car at virtually every roadside historical marker.

"What kinds of historical sites have you visited, William? Anything out of the ordinary... or off the beaten track?"

Now B.J. turned to Mark for help, his "lying eyes" growing in size, looking for a way out; apparently, he just realized that he'd slept through most of the historical highlights. "Well, Bart... Mark Stanton here is our real historian, so I'll defer to him on the history lessons." Simultaneously, B.J. and Bart turned their attention to Mark.

Despite all the sippin' whisky, Mark dove in. "Jacks'... er... Mr. Jackson and I have visited several national parks on this trip. We explored the Hoover Dam, a most impressive structure on the Colorado River, at some 726 in height. It was the largest construction project ever built at the time it was finished. We walked the entire depth of the Carlsbad Caverns, more than nine hundred feet underground. That is... by the way... the equivalent of walking down the entire staircase of the Empire State Building in New York, from the observation deck to the first floor. Also, Bart, we saw colorful collections of petrified bat guano, while underground at Carlsbad. We've taken in some famous sites and shrines, like the Alamo, in San Antonio. Those are a few places that I would recommend be seen by the first-time cross-country tourist." No one responded, so Mark continued to spew minutiae, "But for my money, I'd rather spend my travel time studying remnants of the Old West... like the history of the Butterfield Overland Mail stagecoach line, or Judge Roy Bean's barroom and courthouse in Pecos, Texas. Those are the sites that mean more to someone with a background in history, like me." Finally Bart spoke up and asked B.J. a question.

*What in God's name am I blabbing about*, Mark asked himself? *What was it about a live microphone? Put a live "mic" in front of someone, with nothing but dead air between him and the audience, and a person will likely say just about anything.*

In D.C., they say that the most dangerous place in town is the space between a live microphone and a live politician; now Mark knew why. A person's motor mouth takes over; they feel as though they have to say something, anything, even a lie will do -- but getting away with a "whopper" is even better. Perhaps now Mark better understood why politicians lie so much; they're merely trying to fill airtime. The art of bullshitting on-air was highly contagious. Mark found that B.J. and he were as full of crap as Bart Hampton was!

*Why did I add those last two words, "like me," as though I was some kind of noted historian, he shook his head. Maybe, after all is said and done, I really do have the BS quotient needed for the makings of a talk show host.*

During the program, every time Mark looked over at the three beltway bandit ladies they were either headed to or returning from, the restroom. *Short-hitters*, he suspected.

Eventually, Bart took incoming phone calls and he was right on target about his listener base. As Bart had said, the program's audience was mainly white folks. Most asked obvious questions of the cross-country travelers, like "what towns on this trip have you enjoyed most?"

After Mark's lengthy description of the tour through Carlsbad Caverns in response to a caller's question, a female caller asked B.J., "What will William's next article or travel book be about, and would he consider writing about a trans-Canadian rail trip?" B.J. said he would be glad to share his sleeper car accommodations, if the sultry-voiced woman on the other end of the phone was willing to send him an address and photograph, care of Bart's radio station. They all chuckled at that one; even the female groupies outside the studio window enjoyed it. The caller promised she would write in to Bart.

The show continued to snowdrift with undiluted bullshit. *Who were they kidding?* Mark and B.J. weren't travel experts; they were entertainment, no more, no less. Little, if any, useable travel information was being doled out; but Bart seemed to be enjoying the ride. At one point he even had the gall to ask Mark, "As a road warrior and as a single man... have you ever run into romance on the road?" Bart seemed to enjoy putting Mark on the spot, especially in front of the groupies. *B.J. probably put him up to it*, Mark figured.

During his answer Mark turned to the studio window. The three women weren't in the waiting area. *Good*, he thought. Perhaps the program wasn't broadcast into the ladies room and they would miss this answer. "On rare occasions," Mark said straight-faced, "one might encounter a member of the opposite sex who is unaccompanied in her travels... and a romance could ensue. But, he said, such an experience... *in his experience...* was highly unusual. However," he added, trying to be cute, "the night in New Orleans is still young." He didn't even bother to turn and look again through the studio's picture window. He was sure that such a smug answer had sent the three *banditos*, screaming out the station's exit door.

It went on like that, more or less, for two quick hours. Inane questions from listeners were posed to the so-called visiting experts. In return, ludicrous answers were dumped on the unwary audience. In Mark's mind, the most amazing part of the evening was that the Federal Communications Commission had not pulled the station's license to operate. The threesome ended at midnight with a flourish, as Bart invited them to return when their next travel journal was out on the market. Mark and B.J. made a firm commitment. They would return, B.J. said, "just as soon as it was published."

## Big Bart's Bane.

THE GROUP OF six arrived at Bart's place on Chartres Street in the French Quarter a half-hour after the program went off the air. Mark drove the Porsche, accompanied by Cilla, who volunteered to ride along with him; they followed Bart's green Jaguar. B.J., Janie and Patsy, who seemed a little wobbly, accompanied Big Bart. The two-car motorcade passed the St. Louis Cathedral and Jackson Square, off to the left. To the right was Le Monde, purveyor of New Orleans' most famous powdered beignets -- confections that could sour one on mere doughnuts forever.

After turning left, they came to a stop in the middle of a dark and deserted block, at the east end of the Quarter. Bart whipped out a remote control garage door opener and aimed his fist out of the driver's side window. It didn't look much like a residential area to Mark, more like a warehouse district. Cilla chattered on, still talking too loudly, about the business dinner at Commander's Palace. The next thing Mark knew, a large gate on the left swung back, revealing a circular driveway and a well landscaped courtyard, illuminated by spotlights. There were palm trees planted in each corner of the yard and a small marble fountain splashed away at the center of the circle in the square. Mark followed Bart's car into the tight turnabout and noticed that surrounding the courtyard on three sides, like an open "C," was an elegant two-story residence. The open section faced the street. The first floor was overhung on all three sides by a second story balcony, open to the courtyard below. *This must be the best-kept secret in the Quarter*, he thought. No way would a casual passer-by on Chartres Street ever know that such a lovely home was hidden behind the old brick walls, the peeling paint and the plain gray gate. No windows on the first floor opened to the street. The group piled out of the cars and stood gawking at the beautiful home and garden.

Everyone, with the exception of Patsy, who was "blotto," was duly impressed with the home that surrounded them. While Bart provided the guided tour, Patsy immediately elected to stretch out on the living room sofa -- a rather presumptuous move, Mark thought.

Two things were readily apparent from the tour. Bart lived alone in this ideal bachelor's pad; and second, he had a real knack for interior design. He told them that he'd done-up the place himself. His impressive collection of African art, everything from wood and stone carvings to spears and shields, took up an entire twenty-foot wall. A white baby grand piano with a clear Plexiglas top took up a whole corner of the living room. Not a thing was out-of-place. Cilla and Janie loved the home and made numerous compliments.

By the time everyone returned downstairs, Patsy was sound asleep. B.J. pulled Mark aside. "These three *bandito* ladies must hang with a fast crowd in D.C...."

"What do you mean?"

"I think they're packing powder and I assume they've been into it while we were on the air. I'm just warning you... don't fall in-like with Cilla tonight, unless you love trouble."

"But it's already after midnight... so our new song doesn't apply," Mark said with a grin. This time B.J. wasn't smiling.

The three men settled in around Bart's bar, which was an oaken unit situated in what must have originally been the home's dining room. Bart had converted the room into a bar and billiards parlor. Cilla and Janie continued to roam about the house. Eventually, when the ladies joined them, the group took their drinks and settled into the living room area, trying to ignore the semi-comatose Patsy. In the background, just outside the casement windows, one could hear the steady gurgling of the courtyard fountain. B.J. remained on a programmatic high; he rehashed the entire radio show. What about this caller, or that one? What about our answer to the question! Bart, smiling, took it all in stride and tried to be complimentary, "Mark, I think you have a true talent for talk radio..."

"He sure has a face for radio," B.J. interjected. "Bart, I wish I would have remembered to tell the story about the roadblock we ran into out in West Texas," he added. Janie wanted to know all about it; Bart agreed. B.J. was coerced into relating the entire story of the run-in with the Immigration and Naturalization Service.

After hearing B.J.'s concerns about whether the women might be using drugs, Mark took a moment to size up the three of them. Upon close inspection, it was clear that the two still awake were overly elated about everything. B.J. was probably right; plainly, all three were feeling no pain. In no more than an hour, Mark guessed, the three men would have three out-of-control women on their hands. *The question is what to do*? Personally, Mark had no use for drugs; he'd gone through four years of college in Ohio during the late 60's without ever seeing drugs. In his mind, there was the beer crowd and the bong crowd, and never the twain did meet. Since college he'd run into pot at parties in Washington; and one couldn't live in California without at least being offered a joint at an after-hours party. But Mark had never been comfortable around people who used serious drugs, like cocaine. Maybe it was his Midwestern "sureness" that raised concerns. Mark wasn't entirely sure of B.J.'s experiences with drugs during the latter's halcyon years in the peace movement. From Dewey Beach days on, Mark had never seen B.J. ingest anything stronger than Southern Comfort on the rocks.

While B.J. continued the storytelling, Mark found Bart out in the kitchen rustling up some late-night cheese and crackers. He casually mentioned that the ladies looked a little "ripped" on something. Bart froze, poised before an open refrigerator door.

"Are they lit up on 'junk?'" he asked pointedly.

"Don't know for sure, but Jackson thinks they might be..."

"Well, then get the three of them the hell out of here! And I mean right now! I don't need trouble. I'm not going to tolerate that shit in my house. If those broads are ripped and carrying stuff... they're out of here, you understand? And you tell that to B.J. right now, you hear me?"

Bart was really pissed; Mark thought he was overreacting. From the kitchen doorway, Mark signaled B.J. who interrupted his storytelling and met Mark at the bar.

"What's up?" B.J. asked.

"If they're packing drugs... Bart wants 'em out of here... right now," Mark said.

"I'm not positive that they are... how can I be sure?"

"Ask if they have some. Give me a nod and I'll blow the whistle on the party."

"Where's Bart?" B.J. asked.

"He's pissed. Gone upstairs. I think we better handle this right now. After all, we're the ones who brought the three of them along."

B.J. went back to the living room and sat down beside Janie. Mark went looking for Cilla, who was nowhere to be found; when he returned, B.J. had his arm around Janie, whispering in her ear. They were engaged in an intimate conversation. Then B.J. looked Mark in the eye and nodded. That was all Mark needed; he went to the kitchen phone and called for a cab.

Two minutes later, Mark returned to the parlor. "Ladies and Jackson, listen up. Bart has had a long day and he's wandered off to bed. Also, Jackson and I have to get up at 'oh-dark-thirty' tomorrow morning and drive to Atlanta. And you three mavens of computer marketing certainly must have arranged a prior commitment to be at sunrise services on Easter Sunday morning. So I suggest that we call it a wrap and depart."

"What's wrong with you guys?" Janie asked, quite irritated.

"Nothing... we're leaving. I've called for a cab."

'Cilla and Janie both grumbled; they wanted to party on. B.J. had his hands full trying to convince them Mark was serious. Also, Mark tried to awaken Patsy, who was now sprawled in a not too lady-like repose, still taking up the entire sofa.

"What's the deal here?" 'Cilla yelped. "You guys invited us here, and now you want to get rid of us, just like that? Who the hell do you think you are? And who the hell do you think we are?"

Good questions. B.J. tried to be diplomatic. "Look 'Cilla, Patsy's out-cold, Janie's been sniffing junk and you're being way too loud for this time of the night."

"You righteous son of a bitch..." she tried to slap him. He ducked. That did it. These three were now officially out of control, Mark said to himself.

For the next few minutes the women unloaded verbally on Mark and B.J. Fortunately, a cab arrived quickly and honked its horn outside the gate. B.J. and Mark herded the three women outside. Mark handed the driver a $10 bill and told him to drop the ladies at the Roosevelt Hotel and instructed him that, despite any protestations, he was to drop them at the hotel, and not anywhere else. Also, he told him they'd be following in another car.

As they waited for the driveway gate to open, Mark noticed Bart standing on the upper balcony, looking down at the scene. Mark and B.J. waved a quiet good-bye. Bart motioned a quick salute, turned and disappeared.

The twosome trailed the taxi back to the hotel. The ladies disembarked, helping Patsy up the front stairs and into the lobby.

"Now what, Kemo Sabe?" asked B.J. in his annoying Tonto accent.

"If we were smart, we'd go inside and go to bed."

"Look," B.J. said, "it's well after midnight. And technically, we're not in trouble yet. We're still sober. We're in New Orleans. It's Saturday night. We won't be back soon. Let's do some damage!"

Shaking his head, Mark shifted "Stanley" into first gear, drove around the block and headed across Canal Street, back into the French Quarter.

## Bourbon On the Rocks.

"HEY, MISTER, I bet you a dollar I know where you got 'dem shoes..."

A young black kid, toting a wooden shoe shine box, pointed at B.J.'s loafers.

"No way you'd know where I got these, kiddo..."

"Show me a buck and I'll win it from ya'..."

Mark handed a dollar bill to B.J., who waved it in front of the kid.

"Okay, junior, go for it... tell me where I got these shoes..."

"You got 'dem on your feet!" he said, pointing right at Mark for confirmation." The kid snatched the bill out of B.J.'s hand.

"You little shits shouldn't be out this late... go home!" B.J. said, only half kidding.

There is no other place in the world like Bourbon Street especially on a Saturday night; it generates its own unique energy. The aroma that assaults your nose is sickeningly sweet -- a unique combination of beer, whiskey, urine and vomit. There is no one word that accurately describes it. It is a sensation that must be experienced.

The two men wandered down Bourbon Street, past open-door seafood cafes, a score of tee shirt shops, and seedy-looking barkers for the girlie shows and the boys-who-dress-like-girlies revues. The street was teeming with young people, mostly in their twenties; many looked to be just teenagers. The whole byway pulsed to the sound of live Dixieland jazz, emanating from saloons at every corner.

"I've read somewhere where there is more live music in New Orleans than any other city in the world," B.J. shouted over the din.

Mark just nodded, his eyes wandering over the scene before them.

At the east end of the street, where the throng dwindled a bit, B.J. spotted a quiet corner tavern. They entered and found two empty stools at the well-worn bar. After ordering, they turned to look back on the human spectacle surging up and down Bourbon Street; however the real spectacle was taking place at a table in the far corner of the bar. Two rather ugly-looking biker types were engaged in a total lip-lock. Upon closer inspection, it turned out that they were both guys!

"Thanks, Jackson... this is not how I envisioned my only evening in New Orleans. I just put three rather attractive, totally available women to bed, without so much as a pass, and now I'm face-to-face with spit-swapping bikers in a Bourbon Street gay bar. Thanks pal."

"You know, Stanton... with that desperate look on your face... it doesn't get much better than this, as far as I'm concerned."

"Jackson... ordinarily, I'd tell you to stick it in your ear. But in this joint I'm afraid someone might overhear us, come over, and actually want to join in."

The Dixieland group across the street eased into "Just A Closer Walk With Thee."

# CHAPTER SIX

## March 26, 1978
## (Easter Sunday)

### The Morning After the Night Before.

THE PHONE RANG. The clock radio on the hotel nightstand said it was 8:30 a.m. Mark had left a wake-up request for nine o'clock, but he grabbed the phone before it could jostle B.J. The voice on the other end was very deep -- some wake-up call. It was Bart Hampton, not the front desk.

"Is this Mark? Bart here. Hey, listen I'm really sorry about last night..."

"No need to explain man..." Mark responded with a 'froggy' voice, "B.J. and I totally understand. Those girls we invited along were out-of-hand and getting way out of line."

"Well... the reason I called... I wanted you and B.J. to know that I lost both a son and a marriage to cocaine. I've sworn never to give in to it. It's a personal thing that I've got to deal with, but I just can't let that stuff into my home. I hope you guys understand how strongly I feel..."

"Not only do we understand... we both agree with you. We should have picked up on it earlier..."

"Is B.J. around?"

"He's still sawing logs..."

"Well... listen, Mark, I'm on my way out for a morning jog... and I thought I'd call to explain. I wanted to catch you guys before you headed out of town. I thoroughly enjoyed having both of you on the show last night. I hope it'll give you something to talk about when you get back to Washington. Please tell all my friends back there that I'm okay... I'm reborn... alive and kickin' in N'Awlins', you hear me?"

"I hear you Bart... it was nice to get to know you. Thanks for giving me my first big break in talk radio... a real live guest shot on a number-one rated show. You've given me a whole new career to think about... and when you're pretty much out-of-work like I am right now, you've got to consider them all."

"Well, if you ever get your own talk show, I'll expect a reciprocal invitation."

"You've got it... so long Bart."

They were both hurting puppies. The twosome had stayed on Bourbon Street, wandering from bar to bar, drawn from place to place by the beat of live music until 3:00 a.m.

When the hotel's official wake-up call finally came, a half-hour after Bart's call, Mark let it go on ringing until B.J. cussed, rolled out of his bed, and picked it up.

B.J. threw a pillow across the room. "Stanton, get up!"

"I'm already awake."

"Where are we?"

"Still in New Orleans."

"Stanton, I had a dream last night... that a bunch of coke-snorting, biker broads with shoe-shine kits were chasing me around a fountain..."

"That wasn't a nightmare... we had a close call with disaster last night!"

B.J. got quiet again for a moment. Then he asked, "How many hours of driving do we have, to Atlanta?"

"Non-stop, I'd guess it's a good seven hours."

"When we leavin'?"

"Right now..."

"Good..." B.J. fell back onto his bed, pulled the covers over his head and went back to sleep. So did Mark, but an hour later, at 10:00 a.m., his body clock was screaming for him to get up.

The two of them looked like hell when they hit the lobby, running very late. Mark's gut was throbbing and he hadn't even bothered shaving; he didn't think that in his hung-over state of trepidation, that it was too brilliant an idea to be putting a sharp razor so close to his throat. As he headed for the garage, the concierge came over.

"Excuse me. But you are Mr. Stanton, right?" It was the fellow at the desk who'd handed him the envelope of traveler's checks the night before.

"Yes, it's me..."

"I was just about to call your room. I have another envelope for you..."

This time, Mark exchanged a dollar bill for the envelope of hotel stationery with his name scrawled on it. It was a note from Cilla. *"Mark: We were just being three wild and woolly girls who got a little carried away in the Big Easy last night. Please forgive -- and give me a call when you get to Washington. I'd love to see you again."* It was signed, "C," followed by a 703 area code Virginia phone number. *Kind of a schizophrenic response to last night*, he thought; and he tore up the note on the spot. He had a feeling that if he hadn't, some day he'd come to regret holding onto the damn thing.

By the time Mark checked out of the hotel and was ready to go, B.J. had finished loading and was already seated in the passenger seat -- a highly unusual state of affairs. As he was about to jump behind the wheel Mark saw a small Easter basket, with fake green cellophane grass, a big chocolate rabbit and bag full of jellybeans sitting there.

"What's this?"

"Happy Easter," said B.J., "...some furry, buck-toothed broad with big ears stopped by and asked me to make sure you got this."

Mark's $50 loan to B.J. was beginning to pay interest.

After two wrong turns in "Stanley," one of them up the wrong-end of a one way street, they found an entrance ramp to Interstate 10 east. Both of them were experiencing considerable mental cobwebs this Easter Sunday morning.

The only rock'n'roll station Mark could find on the dial was playing the theme from "Which Way Is Up" by Stargard. B.J. couldn't take it; so he punched a button and heard "Do You Know What It Means To Miss New Orleans," led by the incomparable trumpet of Al Hirt.

"Well, motor mouth, did you enjoy your talk radio debut last night?" B.J. asked.

"Terrific. You know, I think I could do that all day, every day... Bart must be having the time of his life." Then Mark paused for a moment, remembering something. "Oh, yeah... I meant to tell you... Bart called very early this morning..."

"When?"

"While you were still in REM sleep being chased around that fountain... he said he was sorry about last night. Then he said something I wasn't aware of. He said he'd lost both a marriage and a son to cocaine and that he just couldn't handle the thought of having drugs in his home."

"Well that explains a lot," B.J. with some amazement. "Bart told me that his teenage son died several years ago. And I knew that he and his wife, Evelyn, broke up soon after that... but he never offered an explanation why."

"He called to say good-bye. And he wants you to say hello to all his friends in Washington."

## Airing It Out.

IT WAS A crisp, foggy morning along Lake Pontchartrain. There was the promise of another warm day in the air, if the sun ever managed to burn through low-lying clouds. The surface of the vast lake, off to their left, was as smooth as glass. Mark pointed "Stanley" northeast toward Mississippi; they were nearing the City of Slidell. Although neither man could see it, both could smell the salty air of the Gulf of Mexico, lying somewhere over the dunes on the right side of the highway.

When the Dixieland music station faded out, Mark started searching for rock'n'roll. "You know... I really enjoyed being on the radio last night. It brought back memories of my college days when I worked on the campus radio station."

B.J. snapped, "At 'John Snapper' University!"

"Yes. Did you know that my degree is in radio and television broadcasting?"

"Well, with that lumpy body of yours, I knew it wasn't *phys-ed*," B.J. sported a shit-eating grin.

Mark ignored the slight about his less-than-toned body. "When I think of radio, I can still remember the very moment when I first discovered rock'n'roll. Up 'til then, musically, I was pretty much an oblivious butthead."

"My, but you've changed Bunky..." B.J. continued his early morning assault.

Mark plodded on. "I must have been eleven or twelve... visiting my cousins in Pittsburgh. They had a brand new transistor radio... carried it everywhere. When I heard the song "Sherry" by Frankie Valli of the Four Seasons for the very first time, it was the greatest sound I'd ever heard. Before that song came along, listening to the radio for me was strictly Cleveland Indian baseball games."

B. J. had deeper thoughts about the impact of radio. "During the 60's, when color television came out, rock'n'roll saved the radio business in my opinion," B.J. said. "Without FM rock, radios would have become antique doorstops by now."

"Jackson, while I was growing up in northern Ohio, rock'n'roll beamed down on us twenty-four hours a day, seven days a week, from a station up in Canada. The call letters were 'CKLW,' in Windsor, Ontario. It must have been a mega-watt station because it blew out all the frequencies on the American side of Lake Erie after dark and on weekends. On a clear summer night, the signal out of Canada was so freakin' strong you could pick it up on a ball of aluminum foil. The onslaught was non-stop... I'll never forget one summer evening sitting on the beach at Linwood Park in Vermilion, Ohio, listening to Barry McGuire, a Green Beret just back from Vietnam, belt out "The Eve Of Destruction" in his gravely voice. To this day, I love the sound of that song. Little did I know at the time it was the first Vietnam War protest song."

While listening to Mark drone on, B.J. opened his window, savoring humid and salty morning air.

"Mostly we just tuned-in to CKLW to listen to Motown... the tempting Temptations, the fabulous Four Tops, the scintillating Supremes, Martha and the vivacious Vandellas. It was prime time to be a teenager."

Chin resting on his arm and nose out the window like a hound dog, B.J. continued to listen and to stare toward the Gulf of Mexico as they moved along at 65 mph. He had sneaked one of Mark's cigarettes from the pack of Salem's; when Mark wasn't looking B.J. tossed it out the window. He watched in the side view mirror as it bounced on the pavement.

"After college, I would wake up to a radio program in Cleveland on WGAR called 'Imus in the Morning.' Imus was a sarcastic, irreverent disc jockey with a freaky hair-do, like yours, whose antics made Clevelanders laugh. This Imus guy and his cronies told people's fortunes over the phone by the way their voice sounded... pretty funny stuff. They called it "larynxology." After a while, Imus made it to the big time... which meant that he left Cleveland... like all the good ones did. There was very little show business in town in those days to keep the talented, whether you were a comedy writer, an athlete, or a disc jockey. That's how Cleveland lost Jack Riley and Tim Conway, who both ran off to Hollywood. I don't know what happened to Imus after he got to New York, but I just heard a rumor earlier this year that he was on his way back to Cleveland. Poor Imus had now come full cycle... from California to Cleveland, to New York, to Cleveland. *Too bad,* Mark thought, he always thought Imus had a real future in radio... like Casey Kasem."

B.J. stirred; he was coming alive. "Listening to you talk... you missed your calling... you're the one who should be motor mouthing full-time on the radio."

The Spinners were singing "The Rubberband Man."

## Pascagoula Pancakes.

AROUND ELEVEN THIRTY, after a good hour and a half on the road, they decided it was time to stop for breakfast. The two had already passed up opportunities to exit the interstate at Gulfport and Biloxi, Mississippi. On the outskirts of Pascagoula B.J. spotted a high-rise sign that read "waffles;" and he just couldn't resist his growling stomach any longer.

The small restaurant, which held fifty or so, was full; and, there were families, all decked out in their holiday finery, lined-up in anticipation of being seated. The good church-going folks of Pascagoula were set on having their Easter Sunday breakfast at this waffle establishment. The "chub-ette" hostess must have seen the two of them coming. Mark was sure the two of them looked like road warriors who'd been through fire and brimstone. Waving them past the queue of decent-looking townsfolk waiting for tables, she offered them immediate seating at counter stools. The men gladly accepted; neither wanted to stand for long in the coifed and perfumed Easter parade. Mark felt like a road-gritty, unshaven heathen in the midst of the brightly bedecked, church-going, Bible-thumpin' people.

After sizing up the place, it looked like it was going to take all morning to get served. There was only one short-order cook behind the counter. In addition to slinging hash for the whole crowd, he was the same person taking and serving up orders for the ten or so persons seated at the faded Formica counter.

The hunched-over, jug-eared cook was as busy as any man Mark had ever seen. But, as occupied as he was, the very instant the two of them sat down, he turned and asked, "A cup of brew?"

"Yes sir," Mark said.

The tag on his splattered apron read "Leon." Leon put on a mesmerizing act. In his left hand, he snatched up two saucers, balancing cups on top and quickly poured coffee from a large carafe in his right; he didn't spill a drop. Never setting down the carafe, with his left hand he slid the two full cups and saucers along the counter until they ended up right in front of Mark and B.J.

B.J., who was shielding his eyes from the diner's fluorescent lights by wearing dark sunglasses, said, "Stanton... this Leon fellow must be the hardest-working S.O.B. in Mississippi. He was as clearly in awe of the cook's talents behind the counter as Mark was.

Leon was a whirling dervish. He grilled sausages and bacon, and all the while he scrambled, fried and poached eggs. He grilled hash brown potatoes. He battered and poured waffles and flipped hot cakes. He toasted and buttered bread and bagels. In between, he dished out plates and set up garnishes of lettuce and sliced marinated apple rings.

The waffle shop customers, for the most part, were oblivious to Leon's Herculean feats, but B.J. and Mark did not miss a thing. They were totally captivated by his artistic moves; the man was a maestro. He was a Buddy Rich behind a set of Ludwigs -- a true master of his own universe. To make things even more challenging, no written orders were taken in the waffle shop. Every order Leon prepared, he did from memory. The waitresses, all four of them, yelled out each individual order. The atmosphere of the shop was sheer bedlam.

You would hear: "Give me two... slippery... patty cakes... a giant blue w' tubes..."

The maestro never even turned to face the waitresses or the customers. He kept his head down, shoulders hunched over the grill; he kept his mind on business, but you could tell he was listening.

Between orders, the waitresses, all older women in hideous hairnets, tended to stand around, socializing with customers. They eased Leon's hefty burden only slightly by pouring hot coffee and juice for customers seated in the booths. But when they needed to order, they just bellowed.

Poor ol' Leon didn't have time to write anything down. Mark watched him closely, trying to translate the orders, yelled in diner "shorthand." "Two sets slippery" seemed to be eggs over-easy. "Mixed-up" meant scrambled. "Flats" were bacon strips. "Tubes" must have been link sausages, and "patties" were sausage patties. "Yanks" stood for hash browns -- versus "rebs," which he supposed was grits.

When Leon looked over at Mark and B.J. to get their breakfast order, Mark just said the "Mississippi special," he didn't want to add to Leon's workload with a complicated order. B.J. must have been thinking along the same lines, because he added, "Make that two."

Then something quite extraordinary happened. An unusual quiet came over the waffle shop; it was no more than a momentary lull in the barrage of verbal orders from the waitresses. Leon made the most of it. He was a crazed conductor working toward some as yet unheard crescendo. There was a definite momentum and rhythm to his movements, and there were no wasted motions. He spun; he lunged and ducked like a back-up singer for a Motown group. B.J. was totally enveloped watching Leon work, counting no fewer than twenty-two empty platters lined up on the stainless steel rack. Leon slid pair after pair of fried eggs onto plates. He doled out rashers of bacon and sausages. He stacked pancakes dabbed with butter and slung potatoes and grits. He dealt out slices of toast like they were playing cards. He did all this to some inner rhythm. One minute all the platters were empty, except for the garnish. No more than a minute or two later, all twenty-two plates were filled with steaming eggs, breakfast meats, waffles, hot cakes, grits, potatoes and toast. However, all four waitresses continued to babble-on with their customers. Leon ended the lull; he clapped his hands loudly, twice. "Gals... cut the chatter... come and get 'em... this food's a-getting cold!" Then he slid Mark's and B.J.'s Mississippi specials in front of the hung-over pair. "Hope you boys enjoy your Easter breakfast," he said with a nod. Impressed with the show, B.J. and Mark broke out in spontaneous applause. Leon was a "phenom" as a short-order cook. Yet, not one person in the waffle shop seemed to understand why the unshaven heathens at the counter were clapping. The ovation did get Leon to turn and face the twosome.

"Leon, no one is better at this than you are," said B.J. with genuine sincerity.

"Ah, boys, this here ain't nothing..." said Leon, lighting up a smoke after having pulled off the filter and turned it around, smiling at Mark and B.J. through his tooth, "...you should see this roadhouse get four-star crazy when a coupla' mother-hunchin' tour buses pull in at the same time."

## Good-bye Interstate 10.

"HE'S A GENIUS at what he does, pure and simple," said B.J., still waxing poetic about Sir Leon of Pascagoula. At that point, they were twenty miles up the road, well into the State of Alabama.

"You're right," Mark agreed, "that guy deserves to be working someplace special... like The White House mess, where his talents could be appreciated."

Robert Palmer's "Every Kinda People" was playing.

B.J. had the look of mischief in his eye. "Houston, this is Eagle-Feather-One."

"This is Mission Control, Houston. Come in Eagle-Feather-One."

"We wish to formally lodge a complaint about the food up here in orbit. These toothpaste tubes full of baby-shit yellow paste just plain aren't cutting the mustard. We want to request that you freeze-dry two Mississippi breakfast specials from the Waffle Shop in Pascagoula, Mississippi and then send 'em up. Call and ask for Leon."

"Eagle-Feather-One, your food has been developed and prepared by the best nutritionists on earth..."

"If that's so, then make those geeks in the lab coats eat their own putrid meals, three times a day, for a solid week. Then take them over to Pascagoula and buy 'em a Leon breakfast special. That is all Houston."

"Roger, Eagle-One. Say, is there more than one Waffle Shop in Pascagoula? Hello? Come in Eagle-Feather-One?"

Mark spent the next five minutes trying to find his pack of cigarettes. Although B.J. knew what Mark was doing, he refused to help. When Mark did find the pack, it was empty, and he made a note to buy some at the next stop. As breakfast began to settle, Mark saw the first historical marker sign of the day. So he eased up on the gas pedal and pulled into a scenic roadside overlook.

They found themselves on the west bank of Mobile Bay, just south of downtown Mobile, looking east. The sun had finally reached its apex and the morning fog had evaporated. It turned out to be a beautiful day for an Easter Parade.

The nearly illegible brass plaque, eroded by the salt-air, went on and on about Mobile Bay's historical significance, all the way back to colonial days. The plaque described what an important shipping center Mobile had been for Confederate forces during the "Great War between the States." To the north of town it noted that the famed battleship, U.S.S. Alabama, which had served with distinction in World War II, was moored in retirement.

Mark and B.J. spent a few extra minutes with their faces pointed at the noonday sun; they sucked in the fresh Gulf air -- it would be their last of the trip. B.J. became so energized that he even jogged around the car a few times, until someone else pulled into the rest stop and began giving him strange looks.

"Do you mind driving Jackson? I'm a little woozy after that big breakfast."

B.J. quietly took the wheel.

A few minutes later, they reached a notable milestone on their cross-country journey. They departed good-old Interstate 10 for the last time, the main route of Mark's Southern strategy; it was the open road the two had traveled for more than 1,500 miles since Phoenix, Arizona. With the exception of the impromptu side-trip to Carlsbad, New Mexico, and Pecos, Texas, they'd been on this same superhighway for the better part of five days. Mark refolded the trip map for the first time since Wednesday.

I-10 intersected with Interstate-65 and so Mark and B.J. headed northeast toward the capital city of Montgomery, Alabama. There they would connect to I-85, headed toward another capital city, Atlanta, Georgia -- some four and one-half hours away -- and a home-cooked Easter dinner with Dr. John and Katie Trask.

Two weeks prior Mark had called John Trask and explained that he and a friend would arrive in Atlanta around 6:00 p.m. on Easter Sunday. John thought that such detail was funny.

"You're driving cross-country, Mark. No need to be that specific. Get here when you get here," he'd said on the phone. His wife, Katie, volunteered that she'd hold Easter dinner until six o'clock, but if they weren't there by six-thirty, the two travelers would be eating warmed-up leftovers.

So Mark made a bet with John. "Doc, I'll be knocking on your front door as the second hand of your Rolex sweeps past six o'clock on Easter," he said, "and you'd better have a Jack Daniel's and branch water on ice, ready to go!"

"You're on," John said, "but if you're not here at six, you and your pal are on K.P. duty."

"It's a deal." So Mark knew that he'd planned at least one good home-cooked meal during the trip.

"Carry On Wayward Son" by Kansas was pouring out of the radio as they started up I-65.

## Once Upon a Mattress.

"WHERE'S THAT PASCAGOULA newspaper you bought at the waffle shop?" B.J. demanded from behind the steering wheel. "What are this morning's headlines? Inquiring minds want to know..."

Mark dug around in the crowded back seat and found the paper. Then, trying to sound like a radio announcer, he started reading the news in a stilted radio voice, with one hand cupped behind his ear. "Our top story at this hour... it's the Kentucky Wildcats taking on the Duke Blue Devils in Monday Night's NCAA Men's Basketball Championship Finale. Our headline story out of the Nation's Capital is that the U.M.W.... I guess that's the United Mine Workers... have settled their 110-day old strike!"

"Oh, great, Perry Elam will be happy about Duke and a front-page by-line. He's been working on that strike story..."

Mark continued, "...on the weather front, a bizarre Easter weekend ice storm closed Chicago's busy O'Hare Airport yesterday for only the fourth time in its entire history. Also, massive power outages are wreaking havoc this morning in the Great Plains... at latest count, eight people died in ice storm-related incidents yesterday. *And, this just in!* We are receiving reports that the polar ice caps are melting... and giant cracks are beginning to form on the ocean floor. For complete details on these and other stories... stay tuned for the complete news on the hour and the half-hour."

"Say what?"

"Just trying to see if you're paying attention, Jackson. On a more positive note... for all devout mackerel-snappers out there, like me, who probably committed a mortal sin by missing church this Holy Day, Pope Paul was feeling good enough to say Mass on Easter Sunday in Rome. And that concludes our headline stories at this hour."

"Not bad, Stanton... for a poly-sci major... or whatever the hell you were in school. If I ever get a job in radio, you can always be my announcer... you're a real rip'n'read kind of news hound."

"Wrong, Marconi-breath! Actually, I majored in beer at college...

B.J. sat up behind the steering wheel, "Speaking of which..."

Mark grimaced. "Forget it. No beer is sold today. It's Sunday... Easter Sunday. And lest you forget, we're in Alabama... smack dab in the middle of The Bible Belt. There's no way we're going to find a stray beer today. So stop talking about beer... you'll just drive yourself crazy thinking about it."

Mark continued to look through the Sunday paper. "You know, there's still nothing in here about our Edwards Air Force Base plane crash. I always thought this cover-up stuff was bullshit, but now I'm beginning to wonder."

"Stanley" motored past the Monroeville exit headed toward Montgomery. Traffic volume had been picking up steadily since leaving Mobile. Easter Sunday drivers were out now, paying more attention to chitchat than to the fast-paced through traffic. Most were, likely, cruising over to Grandma's house for an early afternoon dinner.

Out of nowhere, in the rearview mirror, B.J. noticed a black leather-jacketed motorcyclist who darted into the fast lane, right behind them. He was hugging the Porsche's rear bumper, and it was beginning to annoy him. The cyclist flashed on his headlight and started weaving back and forth, signaling that he was anxious to pass. So B.J. moved over to the right lane and let him zip by on the left. He gave B.J. and Mark a dirty look -- a lingering glance.

"Nice of you to pull over," Mark said, "or he might have tried to jump right over us."

The biker must have been doing 95 mph. At the rate at which he blew by, B.J. thought they'd never lay eyes on him again. But about a mile or two down the road they caught up with him. The motorcyclist was stuck again behind slow traffic in the left lane. This time he was tailgating an old, exhaust-spewing flat bed truck, loaded down with well-worn furnishings.

Obviously, someone had chosen Easter Sunday as moving day. It looked as though they were trying to tote a full load of personal possessions from one residence to another. From what one could see, there was a heavy old Kelvinator refrigerator, a pine dresser, a couch, a dining table, desk, an ornate carved headboard, and various bentwood chairs all piled in the open bed of the truck. The wooden rails that were trying to hold the load in on all sides were tipped out wide, to more-than-full capacity. On top of the furniture heap sat a grungy old double-bed mattress.

As the motorcyclist agitated behind it, the overloaded truck was attempting to pass a big blue tour bus, which was spewing diesel exhaust and hogging the right lane. The problem for the motorcyclist was that the truck and the bus were side-by-side, both doing about 60 mph. At the unhurried rate these two behemoths were traveling, it was clear that the truck would eventually pass the bus -- but probably not until the year 1984.

The impatient motorcyclist was having a two-wheeled conniption; he was anxious to get past these two lumbering vehicles. At one point B.J. cringed, thinking the biker was going to try to slip between the two. B.J. was very uncomfortable with the way the scene was unfolding in front of them, with the overloaded truck tying up the left lane, and the motorcycle rider weaving back and forth, looking for an opening; there was nowhere to go. B.J. reached the conclusion that this situation was trouble waiting to happen, so he pulled "Stanley" over into the slower right lane, directly behind the bus, to wait it out.

After a few minutes, it seemed that the motorcyclist calmed down and resigned himself to following the old truck until it eventually passed the bus. The biker was still in the left lane just outside B.J.'s driver side window; he even looked over, recognized the two of them from a few miles back, and shrugged. Now, suddenly, they were "friends." A few minutes ago this guy was giving them dirty looks.

The four vehicles -- the loaded truck, the smelly bus, the anxious biker and "Stanley" -- continued on up the Interstate for several miles "in formation," not unlike the Blue Angels' flight team. Every time the old truck hit a bump or a dip in the road, the whole load of furniture, which was stacked way too haphazardly to suit B.J., bounced into the air.

*Finally, it happened!*

B.J.'s worst fears came true. The old truck hit a dip in the road and the load of furniture bounced; some of it went airborne. The yellowed mattress, which had topped the truck load, bounced high into air. It caught the slipstream at 60 mph and lifted right off the back of the truck. It flew backwards, bounced once on-end, on the highway pavement. The seedy-looking mattress poised vertically, on its end -- for just a split-second -- blocking the entire left lane of traffic. There was no way for the biker to stop in time.

B.J. gripped the steering wheel, anticipating a swerve. Mark held onto the dashboard and braced himself. Something ugly was bound to happen! "Holy Shit" was the most original thing Mark could utter, half in prayer and half in exasperation; he fully expected the rider to be knocked clean off the bike, or to completely loose control. In his mind's eye, he could just see the rider swerving, out of control, into the bus, and then into his Porsche.

By some miraculous twist of fate, the mattress teetered, and started to fall backward, toward the disappearing truck. Fast-approaching, the biker rose out of his seat and stood in the stirrups, braced like Evel Knevel going up the jump ramp. The motorcyclist hit the standing mattress head-on, like a big league fastball smacking into a catcher's mitt.

Somehow the big floppy thing flattened out and the motorcycle trundled right across it, doing at least 60 mph! The motorcycle rider held on for dear life; the bike wavered. B.J. saw a puff of smoke from his brakes. The rider bounced around in the seat of the speeding bike like a bronco rider whose glove hand was stuck in the reins. Twice Mark thought the rider had lost control.

Meanwhile, the old truck never slowed down. Its driver never even knew he'd lost the mattress.

Mark and B.J. could hardly believe the biker's luck. He managed to stay on and regained control, never slowing down more than a few miles-per-hour. B.J. looked over at the guy to see if he was okay. Then the rider looked right at the two of them with an ashen, blank look on his face, as if to say, "Did you see that?"

B.J. gave him the "thumbs up" sign.

The rider nodded and then began patting his chest with his right palm, signaling that his heart was pumping.

"That biker guy just saw his entire life pass before him..." Mark said.

B.J. agreed, "And based on his age, apparently that rerun didn't last very long."

"Who wants to go to hell because of a dirty old mattress?"

"Not me, that's for sure... if you'd been riding right behind him we might have run over the fellow."

"I was thinking the same thing," said Mark. "I'd like to die on a mattress, but not like that."

"Yeah," said B.J. "Kind of gives a whole new meaning to the expression 'roadbed' doesn't it?"

"Thanks for being in the right lane and not in the wrong lane, Jackson."

"Go Your Own Way" by Fleetwood Mac played on the radio.

The gut-wrenching experience of the motorcyclist hit Mark in the abdomen with jab of pain. He winced and realized that he'd broken out in a sweat.

## Cold Beer Sure Cuts the Taste of Maple Syrup.

AS THEY NEARED the Greenville exit off I-65, Mark asked B.J. to pull off the interstate into a service station right near the end of the ramp.

"Jackson, maybe I had too much of Leon's coffee." As Mark headed for the restroom, he said, "Fill it up with high-test," to the gas pump attendant.

B.J. jumped out of the passenger seat. "I'll see what I can do about a six-pack... you know a cold beer sure cuts the taste of maple syrup."

"Suit yourself, Jackson, but I wouldn't get my hopes up if I were you. Remember what I said about the Bible Belt."

Mark found the men's room around back. Thankfully, it was spotless. He knelt down before a commode and lost breakfast. It took awhile to gather himself and wash the perspiration off his face. He was seeing stars. As he returned the car he glanced into the convenience store window, B.J. was engaged in an animated conversation with the brown-shirted attendant. There was a large white tarpaulin covering the entire beer cooler; on it was printed in bold red letters: "ABSOLUTELY NO BEER OR WINE SALES ON SUNDAYS." That about said it; but B.J. was nothing if not persistent.

There were two other cars in the filling station. A kid, probably the owner's son, had the hood up on one car and was checking the oil.

As Mark entered the store to find a pack of Salems, B.J. was working over the attendant, "Look we'll be out of here in two minutes and you'll never see us again." He kept up the pressure. You could tell that the fellow in the brown shirt -- "Melvin" it said on his pocket flap – was just trying to be polite to a customer.

Then B.J. offered him fifteen dollars for two six-packs. Mark's $50 loan was sure going a long way, but the look on Melvin's face changed from a smile to a musing look. While B.J. awaited a response, Mark roamed around the small shop looking for something to settle his stomach until he ended up smack-dab in front of the cash register counter.

On the wall, behind the counter Mark noticed an official looking document in a plain black frame. At first it looked like a health certificate or something like that, but the official seal on it caught his eye. Upon closer inspection, it read: "State of Alabama, Butler County, Deputy Sheriff." There was a lot of smaller print, but what brought Mark's heart to a stop was the name, scripted in bold calligraphy, of one, "Melvin Calvin Anthony."

Immediately Mark had visions of leg irons, an orange jumpsuit with "County Prisoner" stenciled on the back, a dirty old former school bus with chicken-wire windows, guards with mirrored sunglasses and shotguns. He pictured himself on an Alabama road gang, swinging a grass cutter on a blistering hot day and yelling, "Takin' it off here, boss," like Cool Hand Luke. He shuddered at the thought of busting rocks for thirty days in some humid God-forsaken quarry.

And here was his cohort in crime, B.J., with his back to the certificate, trying to bribe the duly appointed Melvin Calvin Anthony, a deputy sheriff of Butler County, with the willful intent of violating the Sunday blue laws of Greenville, Alabama -- on holy Easter Sunday, no less. My God, there wouldn't be a *wet* eye in the courtroom when the two of them -- "drifters" from California as the local newspapers would likely describe them -- were sentenced to the county rock pile.

Mark interrupted and blurted out, "Jackson... just drop it or Melvin here will think you are serious!" He said in a loud, firm voice, "I don't want any beer, and neither do you! We gotta' go, and we gotta' go right now!"

B.J. turned and gave Mark a look as dirty as the motorcyclist had given him an hour before.

Mark stuck his head outside the store and asked the kid at the pump, "How much?"

"Twelve bucks," was all he said.

Mark fished out $13.00 and handed it over to Melvin. "This is for the gasoline and a pack of smokes," he said, not wanting the gesture of additional cash to be misinterpreted. A short-tempered Mark grabbed his partner's elbow and firmly ushered him out of the shop, but B.J. continued talking, over his shoulder, making additional points to Melvin. Once out the door, B.J., who was rather pissed-off at Mark at this point, shrugged away from Mark's grip and headed around back of the store, toward the men's room.

A car behind the Porsche was waiting for the gas pump, so Mark started up "Stanley" and pulled over, away from the pumps. He got in the passenger seat -- not feeling much like driving -- and waited for B.J. to return; but he kept one eye on the side view mirror, watching Melvin to see if he was pinning on his badge or strapping on his pistol holster.

B.J. returned a couple of minutes later and got into the driver's seat. Mark began to explain in earnest that Melvin was a duly appointed deputy sheriff. At which point Melvin rushed out the front door and headed for the car. Mark told B.J. to put "Stanley" in gear and to be ready to peel out.

"Hold on there fellows," said Melvin, carrying a bulky burlap sack. "Not so fast... you forgot something! He stuck his big head, baseball cap, and thick forearms into the car's passenger window. He pointed at B.J. and said, "Now before one of you opens a single beer, I want you to take your thumbnail and scratch off the Alabama tax stamps on each and every one of these cans... do you understand exactly what I'm saying?"

The two travelers nodded, like schoolboys, without saying a word.

"You understan'... if'in stopped by the law... you did not buy these here beers in the State of Ally-bama... is that crystal clear in both your minds?"

Mark and B.J. continued to nod like bobble-head dolls. Melvin dropped the burlap sack in Mark's lap; then he slapped the top of the car with a thud, and said out loud -- for the benefit of those standing on the pump island, "That's a good one! Now you boys be careful in that fancy black sports car... there's plenty a' troopers out there today just looking for out-of-state plates. Hell, with you two guys in this-here car and them California plates, they might pull you over just to see if you two are real gen-u-wine San Francisco queers." Melvin let out a roar at his own line.

As they re-entered the highway, Mark again tried to explain his actions inside the store. He told B.J. about the deputy sheriff certificate and Melvin's name on it; but B.J. was too busy driving to listen. So Mark went about the process of scratching off every Alabama tax stamp on the two six-packs; and he did them all before he snapped open the first one and handed it to B.J.

"Looks Like We Made It" by Barry Manilow was on the radio for their listening enjoyment.

## Groovin' on an (Easter) Sunday Afternoon.

THEY WERE MAKING good time. Upon arrival at Montgomery, Alabama, it was 2:00 p.m., Central Time. By Mark's calculations, Atlanta was only two and a half hours away with a one hour time zone change; and he still wanted to arrive at Dr. John Trask's home right at six o'clock in order to win the bet he'd made with the "Doc" two weeks ago. When they arrived in downtown Montgomery, B.J. pulled off the interstate and they drove around, giving the capital a quick once over. At B.J.'s suggestion, they stopped at the State Capitol building, and then went and peeked into the First White House of the Confederacy, where Jefferson Davis once lived, right across the street from the rotunda. The twosome spent a few minutes cruising around, trying not to let anyone see them sneaking sips of beer. Little chance; few people were downtown. And the few who were wandering about on the city's sidewalks on Easter Sunday afternoon had their own brand of brown paper-bagged refreshment.

Eventually Mark eyed a red-white-and-blue shield sign, and went up the interstate ramp. Now they were eastbound on I-85 toward "Hot-lanta," via the Martin Luther King Expressway.

"Downtown was completely deserted, wasn't it? I guess I keep forgetting that this is a Sunday," said B.J. "All this traveling... I've lost track of the days. We've been on the road for what... six days now? God, it seems like an eternity."

"San Francisco is a long way behind us. And, it's hard to believe we'll be in D.C. tomorrow night."

Both men grew quiet, thinking about the last few days.

Mark's quiet was more the result of gnawing anxiety; his sense of dread was increasing in geographic progression as he neared Washington, D.C. He'd offered his friends very little in the way of an explanation as to why he'd taken a leave from his job in California and decided to head back east. He considered telling Jackson the whole story, but perhaps now was not the best time.

After a noticeable lull in the conversation, B.J. spoke up. "Every year on Easter Sunday, back when I was growing up, we used to drive to my aunt's place in Peoria. My sister and I hated it. Aunt Mary always overcooked the goose, the turkey, the lamb, or whatever the hell animal Uncle Harry had killed on his annual hunting trip. She prepared every holiday meal down in the basement, in one of those old-fashioned electric steam ovens. Mom used to say that Aunt Mary didn't want to get her gas oven, upstairs in the kitchen, dirty. Easter dinner always was waterlogged. When it came time to eat, and Aunt Mary took 'it' out of the oven to be carved, most of the meat had already fallen off the carcass. Then Uncle Harry would yell at her and she'd slam the door and run upstairs, bawling her eyes out. Easter Sunday was always a traumatic holiday in our family."

Mark smiled. The thought of Easter Sunday as a kid brought back a particular memory.

"Jackson, just to let you know that your family was not the only one with trauma at Easter... I've got to tell you about my younger brother, Johnny. One Easter, when we were grade school kids my dad got my brothers and me some cute baby ducklings. We played with these tiny handfuls of fur all day. We named them Huey, Dewey and Louie, after Donald Duck's nephews in the comic books. That Easter was the greatest. We raised the ducks for several months until they were getting to be more of a burden than Mom wanted to assume. We just loved those ducks. My brothers and I could tell each one by the way it waddled. We cried big time when Mom said it was time they had to go.

"So a family meeting was called. The final verdict was that the ducks still had to go, but they would be offered to Farmer Dan, a nice guy who lived nearby. Farmer Dan had a rather large working farm with a real nice pond... the perfect place for three white Easter ducks. And the best part was that we kids would be able to look in on Huey, Dewey and Louie, from time to time. In fact, our school bus passed right by Farmer Dan's pond twice a day. For weeks and months we watched the ducks grow and float around in Farmer Dan's pond. On weekdays, we looked for them from the windows of the school bus. On weekends, we would walk a mile or so to visit the ducks. A year later, we could still tell which duck was which.

"On the Saturday after Easter, a year after we'd gotten the ducks, my youngest brother, Johnny, came into the house, crying. Between breathless sobs Mom was trying to find out what happened. It turned out that all week long, Johnny hadn't seen his duck, Louie, at the pond. So that Saturday he'd gone over to the farm to look-in on the ducks for himself. Huey was there, as was Dewey... but still no Louie. So Johnny goes up to Farmer Dan's house and knocks on the door. 'How's Louie, the duck?' he wants to know. 'Well,' says Mrs. Farmer Dan, apparently not a real bright lady, 'he was just delicious!' That satisfied my brother for a moment. But apparently, while walking home... that long, lonely mile... the demise of ol' Louie dawned on him. It was all over for Louie but the crying. So there, you see, your family wasn't the only one shedding tears... Easter can be a traumatic holiday for any family!"

The duo stopped in Tuskegee for a stretch of the muscles and to absorb still another historical marker. This one spelled out the history of the nearby Tuskegee Institute founded in 1881 by Booker T. Washington. According to the metal plaque, Washington almost single-handedly built the school from meager beginnings to have it become a world-renowned institution. Booker T. had envisioned a place of learning where blacks could gain the knowledge and skills to support themselves and their families following the abolition of slavery. The historical plaque also noted that the George Washington Carver Museum was located on the Institute's campus.

Mark, feeling better now, took over the steering wheel.

"Jackson, did you know that Carver invented several hundred industrial uses for the peanut?"

"Is this the start of another one of your Jimmy Carter peanut jokes?'"

"No, seriously..."

"And I thought they were just something that came with beer," B.J. said, popping open his last can of brew.

### Nixon's Nightmare.

THE WEATHER WAS changing; the sky was darkening.

Eruption was belting out "I Can't Stand The Rain" on "Stanley's" radio.

As they neared Georgia, some storm clouds threatened, but then moved off to the north.

"You know, Jackson... we've been pretty lucky with the weather this whole trip..."

"Yeah. So far the only serious rain we've seen was in the middle of the frickin' Mojave Desert!" They enjoyed a good laugh over that one.

At 4:15 p.m. the Porsche crossed into Georgia and into the Eastern Standard Time zone.

"Have you ever been to Atlanta?" B.J. asked.

"Oh, yeah... several times. The first time I passed through Atlanta was eight years ago, in 1970. I was on my way down to Fort Lauderdale in November... going to the beach for some sunshine, rest and relaxation. I was celebrating a campaign victory. Another guy and I took off from Cincinnati, Ohio, the morning after Election Day..."

"You really do enjoy this cross-country driving thing, don't you?"

"I guess I do. Anyway, one of my buddies couldn't leave that same morning so we arranged to meet his plane at the Atlanta airport the next evening. Now those were the days before Atlanta caught on as a major hub city for the airlines. In 1970, you could pull up and park your car at a meter right out in front of the Atlanta airport terminal building, and walk right into the gate. Now-a-days I hear the Atlanta airport is so overcrowded and screwed up that the city is building this huge new terminal complex, over on the other side of the runway. I've read where the new terminal facility is designed to expand to 145 gates! And guess what? It's going to have an underground railroad to get passengers out to the concourses."

"An 'underground railroad' in Atlanta? Is that ironic or what?" B.J. asked.

"What an unbelievable boondoggle! They'll never fill up 145 airplane gates -- not even if the city lands a national political convention, the damn Olympic Games, and a Mary Kay Cosmetics convention all on the same weekend. I don't think National and Dulles airports together have anywhere near 100 gates! Who are these Georgia politicians kidding? It's just a Democrat give-away, another keep 'em working public works project."

"Well," said B.J., "I've read that Atlanta's new airport is eventually going to surpass O'Hare as the busiest airport in the United States."

"No way. Atlanta's a nice city, but it's never going to amount to anything. You know what Atlanta's biggest problem is? It's surrounded by Georgia."

B.J. continued, "Stanton, I no longer make snide comments about places where people come from. And, you wanna' know why?"

Mark looked over, but said not a word.

"Right after I moved out to San Francisco, I heard somewhere that the State of California... if it was a separate nation... would be the seventh most powerful economic entity in the entire world. I was very impressed by that fact. So one day, a few months later, I'm defending California from verbal assault from some asshole from Fargo, North Dakota. This fellow is bellyaching about how California sucks... stuff like that. So I laid my economic fact about California's economy on the guy, figuring him to be some dumb dirt-buster with cow crap all over his boots. But the guy gets right in my face and says, 'big deal, if *North Dakota* was a separate country, it'd be the number two nuclear power in the world. Stanton, I had no come-back, so I stopped quoting articles right about that point in time."

"Smart move, plutonium breath," Mark said.

"Dust In The Wind" by Kansas was playing.

The stench hit them like a wet blanket. "Whew! Holy bat guano! What was that?" B.J. cried. They were grooving along at 75 mph. They drove through a fetid cloud of something that Mark had to admit smelled "gawd-awful."

B.J. turned, with an indignant look on his face he said, "I'd just like the record to show, that it didn't come from me."

"Are you sure? You've been drinking beer all afternoon, you know. Whew, man, that is a horrid odor... I'm afraid to ask what it could be."

"It's got to be either a cattle feed lot or a sewage plant... take your pick."

"What a choice. God, I don't know whether to open up the windows to let it out, or to close 'em up, to keep more of it from coming in."

"It's a sewage treatment plant. Look... over there," B.J. pointed.

"Remind me to call my friends at the Environmental Protection Agency when we get to Washington. Perhaps, they should come down here and give this plant a look-see. And speaking of Democrat construction projects, like the Atlanta airport, maybe we should ask Carter to rent a honey wagon and come back to Georgia to do something about this place."

Mark paused, "Say, Jackson, you remember when I worked at the E.P.A., don't you?"

"Sure, back around '74, wasn't it? I still find it hard to believe that you were once an environmentalist..."

"Most people probably wouldn't know this, but Richard Nixon is the guy who created the E.P.A. Back between 1971 and 1973, Nixon used to travel around the country cutting ribbons, opening new sewage plants. Nowadays, we don't call them sewer plants... they're wastewater treatment plants. Nixon used to make jokes that the news media would probably make sewer plants the only positive legacy of his Administration."

"You gotta' give the man credit... at least he was on target about that," said B.J. "His ultimate legacy did stink to high heaven! Now he *wishes* he could be remembered for building sewer plants."

"Anyway, as I was saying... we were trying to clean up the Great Lakes in those days, and we found that most of the pollution in Lake Erie was coming down from the Detroit River. So E.P.A. funded and built this big tertiary treatment plant just south of Detroit, Michigan. When it was finished, the water coming out of the plant was supposed to be much cleaner than the water already in the river. Anyway, Nixon and Russ Train, his E.P.A. Administrator, agreed to go to Detroit for the ribbon-cutting ceremony and the photo opportunity. I was the advance man on the trip.

"In those days, all the hard-hat construction workers loved Nixon, so they lined up by the hundreds to shake his hand. The construction firm's chief engineer gave us the plant tour. The White House press corps hung around, bored to death at touring their eleventh wastewater treatment plant in fifteen months. They were there just waiting for someone to fall into a vat of sewage.

"We toured phase one of the tertiary treatment plant, where the solids are separated out. The sarcastic press guys referred to this step as 'the turd hits the fan.' At that point of the tour, the odor in the plant was as bad as what we just drove through. Then we saw phase two, where the wastewater is aerated. The press called this process, 'the turd gets the shit beat out of it.' Then we visited phase three, where the effluent is chemically treated. The press named this process, 'brown bourbon and shit-water.' Well, by the time we finished the tour, I was laughing my ass off," Mark said. "At the very end, the chief engineer points to an effluent pipe that is dumping the treated water from the plant into the Detroit River. The engineer says, 'Mr. President, the water coming out of that pipe over there is so clean that you can actually drink it.' With that, one of the hard-hat construction guys stretches out a long telescoping pole with a cup fixed on the end of it and fills it up with water, coming right out of the effluent pipe. They pass the pole, with the cup, to the chief engineer, who, in turn, hands the cup of water to Nixon. Nixon peers into the cup with his nose all crinkled up. Secret Service agents were ready to knock it out of his hand, if he tried to put it to his lips.

"Nixon swirls the cup around and takes a whiff of it, as though it were vintage wine. Then he stands there holding it like cocktail he has no intention of drinking. Every television cameraman and every still photographer is poised, ready to take a shot of Nixon if he raises the cup above his tie clip. The Secret Service is praying that Nixon doesn't do it. Thinking quickly, Nixon hands the cup back and says, 'Thanks, anyway, but I never drink before lunch... but I've got my guy from E.P.A. here with me. Russ Train! Come here and give this a taste.'

"Now what's the head of the E.P.A. going to do... admit that he doesn't want to drink the clean water coming out of one of the new tertiary treatment plants his agency is regulating? Russ Train, a good sport, downed the brown bourbon and shit-water cocktail. Even the hale and hearty hard-hats that built the plant groaned and gagged when he did it. I almost "ralphed" myself just watching it happen. So whenever I come across a smell that bad, I think of poor ol' Russ Train having to down that cup of effluent water."

"Now there's a side of Nixon, I'd never heard about. That changes my whole impression of the man," B.J. said sarcastically. "So he wasn't a total shit, but rather a misunderstood shit kicker-outer."

Jimmy Buffett was singing "Margaritaville."

### Hot-lanta.

THE ORANGE AND white striped highway barrel, or at the very least, the orange traffic cone, should be a part of the coat of arms on the shield of the City of Atlanta. B.J. and Mark had never seen so much construction or so many orange obstacles as they saw the last ten miles of highway leading into the capital city. It seemed as though every lane of every road and overpass was being torn apart and replaced.

"I'd say that either Atlanta is growing like mad or your friend, President Carter, is spending all our tax dollars in his home state," Mark commented.

"Oh, it's probably just another one of those Democratic Party make-work, give-away programs you Republicans get so pissed off about."

The bumper-to-bumper weekend traffic slowed to a complete stop, every mile and a half. Finally, they hit the mother load, a thirty-minute crawling logjam. Traffic was beginning to grate on Mark's nerves; these were the worst tie-ups they had experienced on the entire cross-country trek.

"Well, I had hoped we could be at John and Katie's right at six o'clock for dinner."

"Relax... don't be so 'anal' about the time... we're driftin', remember? We'll just get there when we get there. I don't know why you're so hung up on *time*."

Finally, Mark squeezed the Porsche past the idiots who had been tying up interstate commerce for the last ten miles. Three lanes of traffic involving at least 3,000 cars were being funneled down into one lane. Why? So that two lazy jerks hanging off the back of a truck could pick up a never-ending row of orange highway cones without having to actually get off the truck and walk, as if doing some semblance of real work. It was maddening. Mark gave them a piece of his mind as they drove by; he slowed down and snapped a comment at one of the two nitwits hanging off the dump truck.

"My, my... but we get edgy when we're hungry, don't we?" needled B.J.

Mark looked and felt around the front seat in search of his elusive pack of cigarettes.

Eventually Mark found the exit off I-85 that led them to a neighborhood in North Atlanta, known as "Buckhead." The stately homes, on large, well-manicured lawns, framed by thousands of tall southern loblolly pines, were beautiful. B.J. grabbed the clipboard and read out loud the directions John Trask provided when Mark called to set up the trip. Mark still hoped to get there by six o'clock; he wanted to be right on-time, especially after Doctor John had been so skeptical. It was now five minutes before six.

"It says here if we stay on Powers Ferry Road, headed north, and get to the Red Barn Inn, we've gone a half-block too far," B.J. read.

Mark turned left onto a pleasant lane named Chastain Commons. "That must be the house... the gray house straight ahead at the end of the street, the one with the tall Palladian window." The Trasks lived in a French Normandy-style stucco home situated on a small cul-de-sac opposite the North Fulton golf course in Atlanta's Chastain Park. Mark slowed the car down as they neared the home. He planned to ring the doorbell right as the second-hand on his wristwatch swept past six o'clock.

B.J. pouted. "Don't you think you're carrying this timing thing a bit too far?"

"Maybe... but you're just going to have to deal with it," Mark said.

"Stanley" crept up the Trask's driveway. Then Mark tiptoed up the slate walk to the front door. He looked at his watch. It would be exactly six o'clock in eight, seven, six, five, four, three, two, one second! Mark rang the doorbell. The front door opened by a few inches. A man's hand emerged. It was holding a Waterford "rocks" glass; inside was Jack Daniel's and water, on ice!

"See..." Mark said to B.J., holding up his prize.

B.J. rolled his eyes. "Your friends only encourage your obsessive-compulsive behavior."

It was bear hugs and kisses in the front hall. Mark hadn't seen John and Katie Trask since a college reunion, four years earlier, in 1974. They looked great; obviously married life was agreeing with them both.

"Welcome, B.J.," John said. "Any friend of Mark's is a friend of ours. You poor devil... spending a whole week on the road with Mark. You are the true definition of a captive audience. By now you must be awfully tired of hearing Stanton tell stories. B.J., what you probably need most right now is a cold compress... and a dark, quiet room."

"It hasn't been quite that bad," B.J. answered with a knowing smile, "but he has kept me entertained most of the way. You're right though... he's got a story for every occasion, doesn't he? He even has stories about mustard and ketchup and stuff like that."

"Nothing about Mark has changed since college," Katie added, trying to throw Mark a bone, "and he still has that cute round baby face."

Mark groaned in mock protest. Then he introduced B.J. to everyone, remembering the children's names -- Adam and

Annie. He had always taken great pride in writing down the names and birth dates of the children in each family, in his address book, so he would remember to ask how they were doing whenever he called an old friend. It always surprised Mark's married friends that a bachelor, like him, would remember their kids' names and ages. A useful stratagem of the political trade learned from an elected official.

Mark was quite sure that neither of the kids remembered him. They were quite polite, still dressed up in their Easter finery. With the usual parental urgings, the kids shook hands with B.J. and Mark. The two travelers looked like hell; and they'd left New Orleans that morning without shaving. It was a wonder their looks hadn't scared the kids to death.

"Dinner's still a good twenty minutes off," Katie yelled from the kitchen. "You two must be tired. Go up stairs and freshen up... John show them up to the guest room!"

Mark shaved and jumped in the shower. B.J. changed into his last clean dress shirt, slacks and his seriously wrinkled blazer. When the call came up the steps from Annie, "Mommie says dinner is ready," they were set.

Katie had prepared a holiday feast of Waldorf salad, Virginia ham, candied sweet potatoes, broccoli and corn with country biscuits. B.J. and Mark complimented her throughout the meal, which included three generous helpings for B.J.

"This is misleading advertising," John explained to B.J., "I don't want you single guys to think we family men eat like this every day. Mark's being here is a special occasion for us."

"Oh, shush John," said Katie. "You'll scare these guys away from marriage permanently... turn them into hermits."

B.J. turned to the kids. "Does Mommy cook fancy meals like this for you every night?"

Both shook their heads with grins... no, apparently not.

"Sorry, Katie. They're the ultimate lie-detector."

"Well, that does it. The whole family's going on nothing but leftovers for the rest of the week," she said shaking her head in exaggerated disgust.

The kids hid behind their biscuits and giggled.

B.J. and Mark dominated the table conversation for the next hour, relating tales from the road, remembering to keep the language proper in front of the young ones. Both kids were old enough to understand most of it, and were hanging on every word of every tale. Of all the stories, the kids seemed most fascinated that they'd seen two coyotes walk right out of the desert while driving through Arizona.

"Wow, dad! Did you hear that! Wiley coyotes!"

After dinner the children went into the den to watch "The Love Boat" on television. B.J. and Mark helped Katie with the dishes until she shooed them out of the kitchen. John steered them into the living room and offered the travelers an after-dinner drink and a stout cigar from the Dominican Republic. He noted he couldn't join them in a drink because he was on duty that night, beginning at midnight.

"I understand from Stanton that you are a doctor, John, but what's your specialty?" B.J. asked.

"I'm a general surgeon, B.J., but I specialize in trauma and emergency medicine."

"Now I'll bet that's got to be interesting and challenging work..."

"If I worked at an inner-city hospital, I would probably agree with you. It would be a much more challenging situation. At least I'd get a chance to see a much wider range of trauma cases. But out where I work... in the far suburbs... it actually can get to be pretty boring," John said with some resignation in his voice.

"John's never happy unless someone's been stabbed or something... it's all so gory," said Katie, joining them in the living room.

Changing the subject from blood and guts, Katie wanted to know if Mark was "seeing anyone special" these days.

Before he could answer, B.J. chimed in, "Well if the last six days are any indicator, Stanton's been doing much better in that department. Let me see... there was Sally in Las Vegas... and Amy in Houston... and what was her name... Priscilla in New Orleans... not to mention that hitch-hiker Martha Mae..."

"You can't blame her on me, Jackson. If the truth be known, you're the one who insisted on picking up Martha Mae!"

"Sounds like some things never change," John said. "Say, Mark, when you're planning your next cross-country trip, why don't you think to give me a call..."

"Forget it John," Katie interrupted. "You're not going to be tooling around the countryside with Mark in that fancy foreign sports car, hitting on strange women.  Your toolin' days are long over."

"That's for sure."

The four adults shared memories back and forth for the next two hours.  There were stories about the trip, about what life was like in Atlanta for two transplanted Yankees from Ohio, about the children growing up, and about lifestyles in California.  Then suddenly it was 11:15 p.m.

John jumped up and said, "Fellows, I've got to get a move on... time for me to go to work."

"Let me take you," Mark said.

"What about the car?" John said, looking at Katie.  "How do I get home tomorrow morning?"

"Go with Mark," Katie said.  "I'll pick you up out front of the hospital at nine o'clock in the morning.  Go.  You two... just go.  It'll give you more time to catch up with one another."

## Living Vicariously.

JOHN'S HOSPITAL WAS out "in the sticks," well north of Atlanta's perimeter highway.

"This is some kind of car, Stanton!" John teased.  "I'll bet the chicks just love riding around in this thing.  What is it?"

"It's a Porsche 924 and I just got it.  It didn't help me much with the ladies in California... but I'm hoping my luck will improve once I get it to Washington."

The doctor chuckled.  "I'm happy that you called ahead and stopped by on your way through Atlanta.  We old married farts live vicariously through the exploits of you swinging singles."

"That's funny John... because, you see, we swingin' single guys see how nice it is to have a wonderful wife, a family, a home life.  You happily married ol' farts sort of give us hope... hope that there's a station wagon out there somewhere in the future with our plates on it."

"Oh, you'll settle down... I know it for sure.  And if you run into any problems finding a wife in Washington, just let me know, Katie has a sister she's trying to marry off."

The two old classmates drove in silence for a few minutes.

"We're from opposite poles, Mark... what with me getting married to my college sweetheart the week after graduation... and you, traveling all over the world with the president and all those dignitaries from Washington. But I'm damned glad we've stayed in touch over the years."

"Hey doc," said Mark, "that's what being friends is all about." He paused. "Let me ask you something my doctor friend, what do you know about colon cancer?"

"Like all cancers, it's a very serious thing... it can kill you... are you asking for yourself, or for someone else?"

"Unfortunately, it's for me. I've been diagnosed with it. In fact, I'm on my way to Johns Hopkins for surgery this coming Wednesday."

"I'm truly sorry to hear that, Mark. It's a relatively common occurrence. It eventually strikes 5 or 6 percent of the population, but not necessarily someone your age. You are not alone. Have they caught it early, in Stage I or II? Do you know?"

"It could be Stage II, they've done a lot of blood tests, and a biopsy, but think it might have spread through the wall of the colon... they believe it may be at the regional stage. They're going to open me up and see what they find."

"Mark, do not give up hope. We're doing wonderful things in medicine these days both in surgery and later with chemotherapy and radiation treatments if the cancer has gone beyond the local stage. Is there anything I can do for you?"

"Well, I might have my mother call you if she has any questions... just don't scare the hell out of her. Let's see what they find on Wednesday. Also, I might want you to talk to my doctors to see if you can glean anything out of all the medical mumbo-jumbo that I need to know."

"Who knows about this... how 'bout B.J.?"

"You're the first guy I've unloaded on..."

"Don't look at it that way. The people close to you need to know... they'll help you get through the worst of this. I've seen it a thousand times. People with a health problem do not want to be a burden. But they're never a burden to family and friends. We're all human and sooner or later we're going to need some outside support and help. I'm not sure how much pull I have with the 'chief-of-staff' in the sky but I promise the Trask family will be praying for you."

"Thanks doc. I'll keep you posted. It was really good seeing you, Katie and the kids. You're the luckiest fellow I know. Thanks for putting us up."

The two old friends parted ranks at the hospital's emergency room door.

Mark took his sweet time driving back to the Trask home. Purposely he drove past their exit and headed toward downtown Atlanta's well-lit skyline. He was savoring the last night of the trip. His mind gravitated back through a collage of scenes from the San Joaquin valley, to Las Vegas, El Paso, Carlsbad Caverns, through Fort Stockton, the Alamo, Élan's in Houston, and the French Quarter, last night. He shook his head at the thought of the plane crash at Edwards, of the deluge in the desert, of the broken window at Railsback's restaurant, and of the whole police scene upon arrival in San Antonio. He blushed at the thought of his behavior on Big Bart's radio show. He smiled thinking of Mully and Janet, probably still in New York City on their honeymoon. Then his thoughts turned to the remarkable Sally Markham; he dwelled on those for a few extra minutes. Also, he recalled the gruff cop at the roadside park out in the middle of the New Mexico desert; also, Rudy Cranston, the policeman who bought them doughnuts for breakfast. He thought of Amy Zimmerman in Houston and the poor bastard on the motorcycle who almost "bought it" from the mattress earlier today. He tried not to think about the upcoming week. After the entirety of the trip registered in his memory banks he u-turned away from downtown Atlanta and headed back up Peachtree Street to the Trasks' place in Buckhead.

*God, I am having a good time*, Mark thought. He really didn't want it to end; this was especially true as he faced the uncertainty of his visit to Johns Hopkins. Mark wasn't exactly sure yet what he wanted to do in life -- if and when he got through the next month or two -- but he knew was getting closer to making a final decision.

On his way back to the Trask residence, "I Like Dreamin'" by Kenny Nolan drifted out of "Stanley's" Blaupunkt.

# CHAPTER SEVEN

## Monday, March 27, 1978

### Reveille.

THE TRASK KIDS woke up B.J. and Mark with a "start-to-the-heart," at precisely six o'clock in the morning. Apparently they had gotten up early and turned on the television set in the downstairs den in search of cartoon shows. But they were too early and nothing was on yet but the test pattern. However, they had managed to turn the volume up all the way and left it there before wandering to the kitchen, in search of Cheerios. When the local television station came on the air at exactly 6:00 a.m., the thunderous reverberations of "The Star-spangled Banner" filled the house, the whole city block, and maybe the entire Buckhead community. The din was rather inspiring, as if the "President's Own" Marine Corps Band was in the next bed instead of B.J. Mark almost felt like jumping up and saluting.

B.J. popped up, coughing, as if trying to expectorate a hairball. "What the... what the hell is that?" he croaked.

Then, as quickly as the racket arose, there was complete silence.

"Sorry, guys..." Katie yelled up the stairs, "The kids were playing with the TV set again."

"Jackson," Mark said, "today represents the home stretch... I believe it's time we got a move on."

After a breakfast of cereal and sliced bananas with Katie and the kids, both men said their good-byes and tried to beat Atlanta's Monday morning rush hour. They didn't quite make it to the perimeter highway in time. The traffic on the north end of town, headed toward Interstate 85 was horrendous.

After sitting in bumper-to-bumper traffic and staring for five full minutes at an empty exit ramp with a convenience store at the far end of it, Mark pulled off the highway.

B.J. picked up a morning newspaper and two jumbo black coffees.

Two minutes later, they were back up the entrance ramp on the same highway, headed in the same direction, and three cars ahead of where we'd been, before they pulled off.

"What's in the paper, Mr. Jackson, on this fine Monday morning?"

"Remember when we were talking about the Atlanta airport yesterday?"

"Sure."

"Well, according to the Reuters wire service, it seems that yesterday there were some two thousand Japanese demonstrators, who felt strongly about a proposed expansion of the Tokyo airport. They worked themselves into a real Bonsai frenzy, and rampaged through the facility. The protesters stormed the port authority's control tower and took over operations for a while, until the police ousted them with fire hoses. Apparently, it was a real battle-royale at the Tokyo airport. In other news..."

He flipped through page after page of the Atlanta Constitution newspaper. "Nothing... nothing... nothing here... all advertising... nothing... nothing..."

"Looks like Easter was a very slow news day."

"In sports, Hubie Green captured the $225,000 Heritage Classic at Hilton Head Island yesterday, beating Hale Irwin on six of the last eight holes to get the winner's check of $45,000. Irwin went home with only $25,650. Too bad..."

"Twenty-five thousand for second place... for playing four days of golf? I'm in the wrong business. My family should have given me golf clubs as my First Communion present."

"Don't laugh," said B.J., "with what some of these athletes are getting paid, I wouldn't be the least bit surprised to see stage door dads appear... forcing basketballs, baseballs, tennis rackets and golf clubs into their kid's hands before they can even walk."

"Yeah. Stage dads who'll raise a kid who can score sixty points a game, or shoot a round of sixty, but who'll be wound so tight, that if they don't win the big one, they'll probably snap like Jimmy Piersall, and end up in the State Home for the Intensely Nervous. Anything else in the paper besides Hubie Green and the Japanese...?"

"Tonight's the big NCAA title basketball game... at nine o'clock... on NBC... Duke and Kentucky. My money's on Perry Elam's Blue Devils from Duke."

"I'll take ten bucks of your money on that," said Mark, realizing as soon as he said it, that technically, he would be winning back his own money... the very dollars he had loaned B.J. in New Orleans.

Finally, after an eternity inching toward the same highway interchange, they broke free of the traffic logjam. Today the truck-hanging morons were setting down the orange cones in a mile-long row. Despite relatively heavy traffic, Mark built up "Stanley's" speed to 65 mph.

Feeling more comfortable now that they were moving again, Mark started, "Speaking of the Japanese and airports... that reminds me of the..."

"You know, your buddy Doctor John was right... I'm going to need a cold compress and a dark, quiet padded cell when I get to Washington... just to get away from all your crazy-assed stories. How can anyone have a Japanese airport story filed away?"

"As I was saying, before I was so rudely interrupted... and, I might add that this is a *true* airport story... it happened in Hawaii."

B.J. groaned.

"Apparently, this 747 jumbo jet is coming in for a landing at the Honolulu airport on the new reef runway, the one that juts out into the ocean. It was built with fill-dirt or fill-lava, whatever they use over there. Anyway, this pilot calls into the Honolulu control tower and says... 'this is JAL-242-heavy, requesting permission to land.'"

"JAL?" B.J. asked himself, "Japanese Airlines, what else could it be?"

"Yeah. The tower answers back and gives the pilot permission to land. Then the tower guy says, 'JAL-242-heavy, after landing, contact ground control at such 'n' such a frequency, for taxi instructions. Good day.' The pilot lands the plane and calls into ground control... 'this is JAL-242-heavy, requesting taxi instructions.' The ground control guy says, 'JAL-242-

heavy, proceed down taxiway K, past the fuel storage tanks... then take a left at taxiway M, go all the way past the general aviation hangars, and then turn right on taxiway B and so on, and so on....'

"A few minutes go by. Then there is another call to the control tower, 'Ground control... this is JAL-242-heavy, could you run those taxi instructions by us once again... we're lost.' The ground control guy radios back, "JAL-242-heavy... you're lost? When was the last time you were in here?'

"There was a pause. Then you heard the Japanese pilot on the speaker box, 'Ground control... this is JAL-242-heavy, I was last here on December seventh, 1941. Made two passes... did not land."

B.J. laughed, stifling it as best he could, trying not to motivate another story. "Are you sure that's true?"

"Pretty sure."

## Like the Pimento in a Stuffed Olive.

THEY CONTINUED IN a northeasterly direction toward the South Carolina border. This was the final leg of the 3,600-mile seven-day marathon. The six hundred and thirty miles between Atlanta and Washington, D.C., were the busiest and toughest stretch of road they had to navigate. The driving was nerve-wracking and tedious. Semi-tractor trailers traveling in convoys of ten to twenty trucks held sway over the other traffic but a truck, in and of itself, was not a hazard. Over-the-road trucks were driven by professionals; Mark soon discovered that it was the small car drivers, weaving in and out between the huge trucks, constantly changing lanes, cutting the behemoths off that caused the closest calls.

After two hours of this type of driving, his arms ached from clenching his hands in a death grip on the steering wheel.

B.J. had conked out in the passenger seat about an hour north of Atlanta, despite the strong c-store coffee. He lay slumped against the window, snoring and drooling. Mark guessed that the Trask kids had gotten to him way too early this morning.

Mark spent what should have been a tranquil period concentrating heavily on his driving; and it was a good thing. Some fool, driving a beat-up, green Pinto, was darting in and out of the traffic, approaching them from behind. The overly aggressive driver would run up behind someone and then tailgate, flashing his headlights on and off until he forced a driver to pull over into the slower right lane. Glancing from time to time in the rearview mirror, Mark watched the Pinto driver intimidate his way past two trucks and three cars, until he was right on top of "Stanley's" rear bumper. Mark was doing 75 mph, keeping up with the flow of traffic.

Based on the way the Pinto driver was challenging people, Mark fully expected the fellow to give him a "rub" -- a bumper push -- just as they do in NASCAR races. His antics forced other drivers to go faster than they really wanted to. Mark was conjuring up what a redneck jerk this Pinto driver must be, wheeling around like Burt Reynolds, filming a sequel to "Smokey and the Bandit."

Up until now, the cross-country driving had been a pleasure. The first three days at the wheel had been long ones -- San Francisco to Las Vegas, Las Vegas to El Paso, and El Paso to San Antonio -- but the roads had been relatively empty. The rest of the trip had been short hops in moderate traffic between Houston, New Orleans and Atlanta. But the heavily traveled stretch of I-85 headed north out of Atlanta was becoming the "heartbreak hill" of this marathon. Mark made a mental note: *there would be no beers behind the wheel today*.

They passed another long convoy of trucks in the right lane. The wild ass in the green Pinto was still right behind the Porsche. With the slow-moving massive tractor-trailers in the right lane, there was nowhere for Mark to go. Despite the fact that he'd love to blow this Pinto driver right off the road, he worked to keep his temper under control. He hadn't come all this way just to let some irresponsible nut case, driving an olive drab Pinto no less, force him into a highway median or guard rail. After passing the lead truck in the convoy, the right lane opened up, so Mark slowed down, put on the blinker, and pulled over. The jerk in the dilapidated Pinto sped past; Mark couldn't help but look over at him. The Pinto driver didn't look like a redneck; instead, he looked more like a "greaser." He had long, stringy black hair, wore a sleeveless red shirt, and had a large tattoo on his upper part of his pale white arm. As he passed the Porsche, he sneered at Mark through his fly-eye sunglasses and flipped "the bird." To top off the entire ensemble to Mark's way of thinking, the car's license plates were from New Jersey.

*That figures*, thought Mark. After the greaser's car was well over the horizon, he managed to relax his knuckle-whitening grip on the steering wheel.

They entered South Carolina, and soon after, the northbound traffic lessened a bit. With B.J. still sound asleep, Mark enjoyed some additional quiet time to himself -- time to think. He re-ran the weeklong collage of cities, events and people that raced through his mind. California, Nevada, Arizona, New Mexico, Texas, Louisiana, Mississippi, Alabama, Georgia, South Carolina. They'd come through ten states, and still had North Carolina and Virginia to go. A dozen states in seven days, now that was "trippin'." In some ways it seemed like they just left San Francisco yesterday morning. But when it came to all the driving, it seemed more like they left the West Coast a month ago. Mark had to admit, that the cross-country trip had provided him with far more, in the way of interesting experiences, than he'd ever expected. Originally, he decided to drive back east and planned to return to Washington as quickly as possible, merely ferrying the new car east on the most direct route. However, by taking the more time-consuming, but certainly more interesting Southern strategy route -- and what with B.J.'s being along -- the trip had been a lot more fun and entertaining than Mark ever would have planned for himself. B.J.'s laid-back approach to all things, great and small, was a relaxing influence on Mark's Type-A intensity. Mark was certain that he wouldn't forget much about this weeklong trek. Every turn in the road, and every crazy episode, was etched into his brain. But he acknowledged that it probably wouldn't always be that way. With time, the turns and twists of the story were likely to fade a bit. *Maybe I ought to write about the trip – maybe a magazine article, he told himself. Why not... hell, I'm supposed to be a storyteller.*

Along the way, many people whom they'd met said that such a journey was an once-in-a-lifetime experience. After hearing the war stories of life on the road, several people, starting with good-looking Sally Markham in Las Vegas, had said, "You guys ought to write about the trip."

The jaunt had been more than a joyride or a lark; it had been a learning experience. Mark picked up an interesting perspective on the size, scale and scope of the country, as well as getting to better know its history and geography. But more than anything else, it was the people along the way who made traveling an educational experience. Ordinary, everyday people were what had made the trip interesting. The folks they'd met along the way had, for the most part, proven themselves to be decent people, friendly to two strangers from California. Maybe writing an article for *Washingtonian* magazine was the best way to memorialize the trek and to catalogue its lighter moments. The thought of writing about the trip led Mark to thinking about Jack Kerouac, the storyteller of the Beat Generation who'd penned "On The Road," the story of a cross-country bohemian odyssey that Mark first read as a high school freshman.

"Where are we?" B.J. asked. The sleeping bear was awake again.

"We just passed I-26, which goes down to Columbia, South Carolina. And my guess is that we're about a half-hour from the North Carolina line."

"I'm getting a little hungry here. Cereal with a hole in the middle of it only goes so far, you know..."

"I get the message. We'll stop somewhere along the line... soon."

There was an extensive amount of roadwork being done on the northbound lanes of I-85. There were construction zones every ten to twenty miles. Highway lanes shifted left and right to circumvent work projects. The omnipresent orange highway barrels and traffic cones grudgingly channeled the flow of vehicles. Inevitably, at every work site, there were scores of beer-bellied men in hard hats, muddy boots and flannel shirts, standing around, shootin' the shit, gawking at one fellow who was hip-deep in a hole, shoveling dirt. There were several dangerous slow-downs where two lanes of traffic were forced into one lane for miles at a time. Then there were rare open stretches of road, between the idle work gangs, where Mark actually got "Stanley" up above the 55 mph speed limit. But, a few miles later, there would be another construction zone and yet another annoying lane merge.

At one point near Gaffney, South Carolina, around 11:15 a.m., they were clipping along at 65 mph. Mark was in the left lane again -- which is supposed to be the fast lane. A temporary orange construction zone sign indicated that, once again, the left lane would end in one-half mile, and all the traffic was directed to merge into the lone right lane for the next five miles. The autos ahead and behind slowly began blending into the busy right lane. A forced lane merge was like shuffling two decks of cards; the only difference between cards and cars is that the cars are doing 60 mph. As they neared the final yards before the merge point, Mark double-checked the side view mirror for any stragglers in the fast-disappearing left lane. Mark settled in behind a large, slow-moving tractor-trailer, already yearning for another stretch of open road.

"Jackson, I was thinking, maybe we could stop at Kings Mountain for some lunch. It's about twenty minutes ahead..."

"Watch it...!" B.J. bellowed.

From out of nowhere, a car -- doing at least 90 mph – tried to dart in front of them from the left -- cutting in from the fast-disappearing and virtually non-existent left lane. The speeding car actually clipped the last two orange barrels that funneled the merge lane into theirs. Both barrels went flying. Debris and sand hit the windshield. Mark swerved to the right to avoid a crash with the interloper, but he had nowhere to go! He had to be careful to avoid the guardrails along the right shoulder of the roadway. Now there were two cars side-by-side fighting for space in one traffic lane. No sooner had the interloper cut them off, careening into their lane, than the other driver slammed on his brakes with a screech of tires to avoid hitting the rear end of the tractor-trailer in front.

"That idiot's going to kill us!" B.J. yelled, bracing himself against the dashboard and car door.

The Porsche 924 was half-on and half-off the highway. Mark's hands were locked tight onto the steering wheel. The two right tires were doing their best to cling to the highway's narrow right shoulder; and there wasn't much room between the encroaching green car and the right guardrails. Mark tried to slow down, but as soon as he touched the brakes, the truck behind him laid on his air horns -- trying to warn that his rig was traveling way too fast to stop suddenly. Mark was stuck between a complete asshole and the devil himself -- the interloper to his left, and a certain accident to the right. The Porsche fishtailed a bit on the sandy shoulder, but Mark continued to fight the wheel, slowly regaining control. Once the car seemed in check Mark shot his first glance toward the guy who'd cut them off. He wanted to memorize every detail of the fellow who was trying to send the two of them to hell. The driver was easy to identify; it was the red-shirted New Jersey greaser in the olive drab Pinto, the same son-of-a-bitch with the tattoo who'd flipped Mark off, just an hour ago. He was back!

The whole incident, which lasted just seconds, seemed to take longer to Mark because it took place in slow motion. In the rearview mirror, he noticed that the truck behind him had managed to back off a bit, making enough space for the Porsche to get back into the single lane of traffic behind the offending Pinto. What just took moments seemed like an eternity to Mark and B.J.

Mark was searching for an exit where he could stop. His heart was pumping a gallon of blood per beat; his stomach was tied in knots. His hands were still in a vice grip on the steering wheel and his arms were beginning to spasm. Finally, he spotted a flat wide spot on the right shoulder ahead without a guardrail; he braked the car and slid to a dusty stop. Traffic whizzed by on their left.

B.J. was raging mad. "Who's that fucking mad man? We gotta' call the cops on him. He's going to kill people between here and New Jersey. He must be on drugs or something."

Mark rested his sweaty forehead against the steering wheel. He exhaled, having no idea how long he'd just held his breath. It seemed like five minutes. He was muttering to himself: *After more than 3,000 miles of driving I've got to end up running into this same greaseball a second time.* He had no idea how the Pinto driver managed to get behind them, after passing them an hour before -- *maybe he'd pulled off the road for a few minutes to change the oil in his hair.* That irresponsible idiot had just tried to kill the two of them, cutting into their lane of traffic at full speed, past the last inch of the lane merge.

"Are you sure you're all right?" B.J. was worried. "I don't want you having the 'big one' behind the wheel," referring to a massive coronary attack.

"Don't worry, Jackson. I'll be all right. I'm just shaking off a case of the 'Grand Clong.'"

"The what?"

"The 'Grand Clong'..."

"What's that?"

"Medically, the 'Grand Clong' is defined as 'a sudden rush of shit to the heart.'"

B.J. relaxed; with that "guano" line he knew Mark was going to be okay.

Mark flexed his hands for a minute or two and shook the cobwebs out of his brain. A minute later, he found a gap in traffic and pulled back onto the highway.

B.J. and Mark were quiet for several miles. Both realized what could have happened.

The highway construction on I-85 continued throughout the rest of South Carolina right into the State of North Carolina. In fact, the closer they got to the city of Charlotte, the more orange highway barrels and cones they experienced. Mark decided to pass up his planned stop at Kings Mountain. He was keeping an eye out, looking ahead in traffic, for the Pinto driver, but once again the brazen fellow had disappeared over the horizon.

"Stanton, ol' boy. That was a great bit of driving back there," B.J. said with genuine appreciation. "You could have lost it... very easily. I just want you to know, I've come to admire your skills behind the wheel... and I have, since we set out six days ago. Believe it or not, I usually can't fall asleep in a car, unless I really trust the driver. And I want you to know that I trust your driving."

"Thanks, Jackson. Coming from you, a guy who's raced cars, I'll take that as a compliment."

"You kept your cool."

"Yeah... well... but if I ever lay eyes on that Pinto son-of-a-bitch again... I'm telling you, he's a dead man!"

"Now you're *losing* your cool..."

Somewhere between Gastonia and Charlotte, North Carolina, around high noon, their stomachs returned to their normal positions, and both men realized they were running on empty. They agreed to get off the interstate and see what they could find for lunch.

There was an exit just before the Catawba River Bridge. Mark took it, but there were no fast-food restaurants in sight, much to B.J.'s delight. Next to the only gas station was a brand new convenience store called a "Handy Pantry." Mark figured they could buy something to eat and then pull over to the gas station for a fill-up. "Stanley" wasn't right on empty, but a final tank-full would probably last them all the way to Washington. B.J. went inside the convenience store to scrounge around for something interesting to eat. Meanwhile, Mark's eye caught something interesting, parked next door in the gas station.

*It was the green Pinto*... the olive-green Pinto with New Jersey plates! It was just sitting there at the gas pump, with no one in it. Mark jumped out of the Porsche and headed across the small lawn that separated the two establishments. As he was nearing the gas station's pumps, the same greasy character, in the red sleeveless shirt, came sauntering out of the men's room. The driver ducked into the office, probably returning the washroom key; then he reemerged and headed for the Pinto, stopping momentarily to light a cigarette. It took him a second too long; that was his second mistake. He'd just gotten into the Pinto and had yet to start the car when Mark confronted him. The driver's side window was all the way down.

"You, scumbag," Mark said snarled through his teeth, "You are without a doubt, the biggest asshole on Interstate 85."

"Fuck off, faggot..." the Pinto driver flicked his lit cigarette at Mark.

With that, Mark reached into the open car window and grabbed the driver by his shirt with both hands and pulled the scrawny little shit right out of the car window; the greaseball popped out of the Pinto like the pimento from a stuffed olive. Mark threw the scrawny bastard against the side of the Pinto, and held him there with his left hand braced to the man's chest. Mark wanted the fellow to look him in the eyes, to know who he was. And he wanted the bastard to focus on the fact that he'd nearly killed two people back there. The greaser spit at Mark. That did it.

"This is for cutting us off and nearly killing me and my buddy back there..."

"I don't know what the fuck you're talking about... you're crazy, man..."

Mark hauled off and hit him square on the left side of the jaw with a right cross. The greaseball went down like a bag of bricks. "You miserable son-of-a-bitch... you coulda' killed us, you scumbag." Mark stood over him, raging profanities, to no avail; the guy was unconscious.

"Stanton, leave him be..." B.J. barked at him in a stern voice as he rushed up behind Mark. He grabbed the fuming Mark and spun him around.

An elderly station attendant came out of the office, "What's going on here?"

B.J. answered. "This little weasel cut us off on the freeway, damned near killed us both. He had it coming."

The station attendant immediately backed off. "I ain't got a dog in this fight," he said, "...besides that jerk didn't buy no gas from me... he just wanted to use the can."

The greaser, lying on the pavement, moaned and started to come around. B.J. was pulling Mark back. "Let's get out of here... and I mean, right now!"

B.J. pushed Mark across the lawn to the c-store parking lot. They jumped in the Porsche and departed the Handy Pantry rather hurriedly. In seconds they were back on the interstate.

"I hope that gas station guy didn't get a look at our license plates," B.J. said.

"No way! His eyeglasses were too thick. Besides, our car was parked too far away," Mark responded, staring straight ahead.

"I hope that asshole from New Jersey isn't a drug dealer, packing a rod. He might come looking for us."

"Naw, I saw him up close. He's just some pimpled little twerp. He'll hide for a half-hour before he gets back on the highway... the little shit," Mark continued to fume.

"Okay, Stanton," said B.J., "Relax... you've been edgy since we left New Orleans. Just cool your jets, man."

"Hell, Jackson, right now I feel a hell of a lot better than I have in some time. I believe I've actually relieved my pent-up frustration and stress."

"Oh, great... then let's go around beating the snot out of people... now there's a great way to get reduce stress and get in on this new fitness craze at the same time... why didn't I think of that?"

"Hey, speaking of stress reduction, where are my cigarettes? Have you seen my Salem's?"

B.J. was silent.

## Baseball Blues.

"JACKSON, THANK YOU for coming over to get me, back there. I lost it with that guy. I was so pissed, I might have killed him." It was a half-hour later. The twosome was passing Kannapolis, North Carolina.

"Hell, Stanton, you're a lover, not a fighter. You got off one lucky punch!"

"Lucky punch, my ass," Mark looked sideways toward B.J. "I nailed 'im."

B.J. was just trying to get Mark's goat. "I didn't come over to keep you from hitting him. I came over because I was afraid the punk might have a knife or a gun or something, so I was trying to keep him from killing *you,* Stanton."

Mark shot a sideways look.

B.J. recoiled, palms forward, to his corner of the front seat. Then he curled his right hand into a fist; then he whispered into it: "Houston... this is Eagle-Feather-One, come in. We've had an unruly incident here."

"Eagle-One. This is Mission Control, Houston. We read you, come in."

"I want you to note in the mission log that Captain Stanton has just returned from an EVA where I witnessed him interacting with an alien being."

"Are you kidding? You've made contact! Stanton's met an alien! An encounter of the third kind! This is just fabulous, Eagle One. What was the nature of the contact, Eagle-One?"

"Houston... I believe the first and only contact was an upper-cut..."

"An upper-cut?"

"It was a right cross," Mark interjected.

"Correction, Houston. Captain Stanton insists the mission's log be quite clear on this point. He has personally informed me that an earthling's first contact with an alien being was officially a right cross to the jaw-like area."

"You mean a right cross... like a blow struck?"

"Yeah, Houston. Except it was more than a cuff. I'd have to say it was a knock out punch. Do you copy that, Houston?"

"Roger that, Eagle-Feather One... Stanton cold-cocked the alien?"

"Roger that, Houston. We're headed home... it's been a long mission."

Thanks to B.J.'s shopping spree at the Handy Pantry, they ate roast beef and Muenster cheese hero sandwiches and Oreo cookies, washed down with cartons of cold milk. Mark enjoyed it; the cookies were a just dessert.

"B.J...."

B.J. knew something was up when Stanton started a sentence with "B.J."

"Yes, buddy, I know you have something you want to tell me don't you?"

"Yes. First of all, thank you for what you did back there at the last stop... I don't know what's got into me. I haven't been myself of late. I've been worried about my health... they tell me I have a cancer..."

B.J. froze, his eyes looking deep inside Mark.

"They're going to open me up at Johns Hopkins on Wednesday to see what I'm dealing with... I think it's about time I told you, but I didn't want to put a wet blanket on a great week traveling with you. If this was going to be my last week as a normal person, I couldn't have planned for a better time than I've had."

"Oh man, I'm truly sorry about the cancer... are they sure? What is the prognosis?"

"Until the surgery they won't know if it's moved out of my colon. If it has, it gets more and more complicated and far more serious. That's all I know or want to say about it now..."

"Okay, I can understand that... but I'm going with you Wednesday morning. The two men could not make eye contact at that moment.

Mark turned the car north near Durham, North Carolina. This northbound turn began the final leg of the trip up Interstate 95. They were poised at the top of the home stretch.

## Is That "U?"

TWENTY MINUTES LATER Mark broke the ice by asking, "Jackson, did I ever tell you about my fraternity brother from John Carroll University, a guy named Charlie Kapp? He grew up around here in Raleigh-Durham."

At this point B.J. was not about to give Mark any grief about another story. "I don't think you've mentioned his name..."

"Well, you and Charlie have a lot in common... you're both ladies' men."

"So, what's wrong with that?"

"Nothing... except that it tends to get you in trouble. Back in our senior year, Charlie was dating a lovely young thing, named Helen. She was a sophomore who still lived at home with her parents. The two of them had a real romance going, but Helen's father hated Charlie. I suppose he could see through Charlie's bullshit. Anyway, that year our fraternity had a spring formal affair... black tie and all that. Charlie picks up Helen in his beat-up, orange Volkswagen bug. Helen's father says she's got to be back home by one o'clock."

"I think I know where this is going..."

"Don't be so sure, Jackson... anyway, they have a great time at the formal. That night the weather was hot. The band was hot. And the music was hot. Everyone was sweating buckets. And everyone was drinking buckets of 'Wapatula.'"

"Wap-a-what?"

"Wapatula. Every college calls it something different, but it's the same basic lethal fruit punch. We made it up in 20-gallon batches in brand new plastic garbage cans... we added vodka, gin, grain alcohol and Southern Comfort and mixed it with every known fruit juice. Then we'd cut up grapefruits, oranges, lemons and limes and float them in there. The point was... the stuff was really potent... three glasses and you were seeing double. It kind of snuck up on you, it didn't taste like you were drinking a lot of booze. Well, Helen had a few too many that night, thinking that the Wapatula was mainly fruit juice."

"Now I *know* where this is going..."

"Not so fast Hawaiian Punch breath..."

"Charlie goes to take Helen home. It's already past one o'clock. When he drives up to Helen's house, the light in the living room is still on... meaning that her father is still awake and waiting up. But Helen is pretty much a semi-conscious mess, so Charlie decides to by-pass the house and wait-out her father. He doesn't want another confrontation with Helen's dad. He drives on past her house and parks a few houses down, on the opposite side of the street. Charlie keeps one eye on the living room lights at Helen's house through his side view mirror. He figures the old man will eventually give up and go to bed. Then he can sneak Helen into the house. In the meantime, Helen's moaning, 'Charlie, Charlie... I think I'm going to be sick.' So real-quick like, Charlie reaches over, and opens the door on her side of the Volkswagen. He holds on to the back of her outfit, by the nape of her neck, and lets her hang her head out the door. After a few minutes of horrid retching noises, he pulls her back into the front seat of the 'bug.'"

"Charlie looks into the side view mirror. The lights at Helen's house are still on. Dad-e-o is still waiting up. Helen is a gawd-awful mess. She smells like a 'Singapore Sling.' And now, after puking all over the curb, her hair is all tangled and the ends are stuck to the corners of her mouth. So Charlie goes through her purse trying to find her comb and some tissues. He cleans her up as best he can, and puts fresh lipstick on her. But he's a little smashed himself, so she looks like a complete tramp with an overdose of lipstick smeared all over her puss."

B.J. listened politely figuring this *could be* Mark's very last story of the week.

"Just then, in the VW's side view mirror, Charlie notices the living room lights are out at Helen's house. The old man has given up! He decides that now's the time to sneak Helen back into her house. He starts up the Volkswagen and turns on the headlights. No cars are coming in either direction. So he makes a sharp U-turn, and heads back up the street to Helen's house. Just as he finishes making the U-turn, he hears a sickening 'thunk.'"

"What 'thunk'?"

"The 'thunk' is the VW's passenger car door slamming shut. Helen is gone! She's not in the front seat any more. Then Charlie remembered... he'd never slammed her car door shut!

Somehow, during the U-turn, Helen was flung right out of the front seat into the street. Then after the turn, when he'd picked up speed, momentum had shut her car door.

"Charlie slammed on his brakes, waking up people all up and down Helen's street. In his rearview mirror, lying under the glow of a street light, was a pile of ass and elbows. Helen was out cold in the middle of the street where she lived. And she'd probably erased a couple of feet of the yellow dividing line skidding to a stop.

"Oh, no!" said B.J., his face in his hands.

"Yep. Charlie jumps out of the VW and runs back to her. At first, he thinks she's a 'gonner.' But then realizes that she's just unconscious. Finally, she moans and whimpers, 'What happened? What happened?' He picks her up and rushes back to the front seat of the bug. She's skinned her forehead, her nose, her elbows and her nylon hose are literally shredded at the knees. Her bruises and scrapes are starting to bleed. Charlie goes into her purse and finds a small compact case with face powder. He tries to stop the bleeding on her forehead and nose with caked powder, but it is kind of a losing battle. She keeps yelping, 'Charlie... Charlie, what happened?'

"Following the screech of brakes, front porch lights on houses up and down Helen's street go on, but luckily not at Helen's house."

"Oh, man, what a bloody mess," said B.J.

"Charlie patches up Helen as best she can. He brushes her hair. He re-does her lipstick. He blots up her scrapes with powder. But she's still half-whacked, moaning, 'What happened... Charlie?'

"Charlie quietly rolls the VW up in front of her house and leaves the engine idling. He lifts Helen out of the front seat and carries her up the steps, finds her house key and opens the door. He gives her a cursory kiss, opens the front door, and leans her up against the wooden banister at the foot of the staircase... just like a mop-stick handle. He says 'goodnight' and pulls the door closed and then breathes a deep sigh of relief. Then, as he heads back down the front steps, Charlie hears a muffled 'thud' inside the door."

"Oh, what did he do?"

"Well, now he was locked out and didn't want to wake the ol' man... so he departed."

"Some ladies' man... he ought to lose his union card."

"The next morning he's afraid to call Helen. He was relating this whole U-turn story to us, but wasn't sure how much really happened and how much was part of his nightmare. Just as he finished telling us the story, the fraternity house phone rings. It's Helen! And she wants to know... 'Charlie, what happened last night!' And so does her *father*!

"So much for Charlie and Helen I suppose..."

"Not so. Charlie and Helen got married two years later, the weekend after she graduated from college."

"I guess ladies' men do come through in the end," B.J. added. He was glad to see Mark back to his old self, so he continued... "Hell, speaking of real ladies men, I should tell you the one about my roommate at Princeton senior year, Vic "The Vapor" Thornton."

"Go ahead, lay it on me..."

"Vic Thornton was a real jock, you know, a man's man. And he had a crush on Princeton's head cheerleader, Annie Flanigan, for three years but never had the chance to even talk to her. Then, during the homecoming football game, senior year, Vic separated his shoulder. Everyone in the stadium could tell how badly Vic was hurting when they helped him off the field. The following Monday in class none other than head cheerleader and hot-body, Annie Flanigan, the recently-crowned homecoming queen, came up to Vic in the hallway and asked how he was doing... how was his shoulder? Vic was absolutely stunned to be on the receiving end of Annie's attention. He couldn't think of anything intelligent to say, so he asked her out on a date. Well, to make a long story short, Annie, no doubt feeling sorry for him, accepted."

"Good for Vic!" Mark said.

"That weekend they went out for dinner and a few beers. But as it turned out, Annie and Vic had very little to talk about. Conversation was at a premium all night and Vic sensed that she was bored to death. He knew he was blowing the best date he'd ever had. Even so he took her to the local 'Lover's Lane' and tried to put the moves on her. She put up with Vic's shenanigans for a few minutes and then told him, quite firmly, that she had an early class the next morning and had to get back to campus. Vic gave up without a fight. As he went to start the car he was so nervous that he dropped the car keys.

And, as he bent over to the left side of the car to retrieve the car keys, he let loose a wicked gust of break-wind right in Annie's direction. It was 'the fart heard 'round the campus,' the *very vapor* that earned him his nickname. Stanton, my man... as gas goes, this was a true knee-knocker... the kind where you're afraid to make eye contact with anyone who heard it.

"Upon the unfortunate and untimely release, Queen Annie jumped out of Vic's car and wouldn't return for a full half-hour. She rode back to her sorority house in the back seat... in complete silence. When they pulled up in front of the place, Vic sat there frozen behind the steering wheel, looking straight ahead. Annie asked him, 'Aren't you going to walk me to the door?' And Vic responded, 'Why bother? You're never going to go out with me again, are you?'"

"So that's how Vic "The Vapor" earned his nickname. Let me ask you something Jackson... did Vic end up marrying Annie?"

"Stanton... you guessed it. The two of them have been married eight years now, with three kids."

The Sanford/Townsend Band was playing "Smoke From A Distant Fire" on the radio.

## Home Stretch.

B.J. WAS LULLED to sleep again somewhere north of the tollbooth just outside of Richmond while Mark negotiated the drive up I-95. He didn't wake up for an hour and a half, until they were on Interstate-395, near Springfield, Virginia, at the confluence with the famous Washington "beltway." Thus, B.J. had managed to sleep through some of the most important battlefields of the Civil War and the very heart of tobacco country. But Mark didn't have the heart to tell him what he'd missed.

Again, with an ever-increasing sense of anxiety, Mark spent the quiet time contemplating his future. Trying to dismiss the overpowering fear of not getting his life back to normal, he finally decided that he had a rare opportunity in front of him, one that few people got. Mark had a chance to start his life and his career over again and he pledged to himself to make the most of it. Moving to Washington at his age as a single man was perfect for a fresh start.

*But looking beyond next week, what did he want to do with his life?* He loved Washington, D.C. -- the town, the people, the politics. But he also enjoyed traveling, seeing new places, and meeting new people. The real Mark Stanton was a people person. But there was more to him than politics and travel. Thanks in part to those blessed Jesuits he had a curious mind. Although far from being a true Renaissance man, he had a modicum of knowledge about a range of subjects; the downside was he was currently expert in none. His broad but unfocused scope was a direct consequence of a well-intentioned, but untargeted, liberal arts curriculum.

Mark was interested in biographies, history and geography; he knew the realities of politics and what it took to partake in that sport of fools. He was an avid reader of non-fiction, newspapers, and magazines and kept up with current events. He loved to tell stories and to hear an audience laugh; but suspected the number of job openings for troubadours and oral-historians was limited. Although he wasn't a bad writer, he had no intense motivation to sit down and write. And what was he going to write about anyway? He wasn't the modern-day Jack Kerouac.

*Who do I know who has their act together*, Mark asked himself. For some reason he thought of Mully, his lifelong friend, and of Janet, Mully's bride of six days. Mully was a lucky guy who'd found the right girl. *Who was the right girl for me? If I had to choose right now, who would it be?* Mark kept going back to that evening in Las Vegas, out on the hotel balcony. *Was there something special there? Is that why his mind kept going back to that evening?* He didn't know for sure; but he was already looking forward to a post-hospital visit back to Las Vegas for rest, recuperation and a second get-together with Sally.

"I haven't thought to ask, but where are we staying tonight?" a groggy B.J. interrupted Mark's pondering.

They were passing the world-famous profile of the Pentagon, on the left. Mark thought they were in Crystal City, a suburb-within-a-suburb of Arlington, Virginia, just across the river from the District of Columbia. But he saw new signs that read Pentagon City. "They must have changed the name of this place while we were on the West Coast," he said.

B.J. had more basic thoughts on his mind, "I'll bet that's not all that's changed in two years... hey, nimrod, like I asked, where are we stayin' tonight?"

"Well, my moving van won't be here for two or three days. So, I got a room downtown at the Statler Hilton. But after tonight, you're on your own, big guy!"

"Hey, that's putting real pressure on someone like me! You mean I've got to get a good-looking woman to fall desperately in love with me... a woman who owns her own place, a home that is in dire need of major repair, refurbishing, plumbing and rehabilitation. And, I have to find all this in less than 30 hours?"

"That's it."

"Man, I just hate working under pressure... Can you give me 48 hours?"

"Can you afford 48 hours? Not a chance, sweet William... not a chance."

"Then, because of you, Stanton, I may have to lower my standards or find a room at the YMCA, it's as simple as that."

"So be it... it's beginning to look as though the 'Re-hab Romeo' will finally hit the wall, so-to-speak. Only thirty hours to beat the clock."

As they crossed the low-slung 14th Street Bridge from Virginia into Washington, D.C., "We Are The Champions," by Queen, came on the radio.

Mark Stanton was home. The weeklong, 3,600-mile, cross-country journey was officially at an end. "We've been through so much, I kind of expected a brass band and some ticker-tape, or at the very least, governmental red tape, to cascade down on us at the District line," said B.J.

"Yeah, I know what you mean. This arrival... it's anti-climactic." B.J. couldn't resist, "Houston," he said into his fist, "...this is Eagle-Feather-One. Signal 'arrive-arrive.' We've survived the re-entry blackout and we're sittin' here floating around in the middle of the Tidal Basin with our rubber duckies. Where are all the rescue ships? Where is everybody?"

"Eagle-One. This here's Mission Control, Houston. I believe we've just had what you call a major technical glitch down here. Our new computer was just telling us that you guys were targeted to come down smack-dab in the middle of the Bahamas... and now you say you're where... in the Potomac River? Can you be more specific?"

"Well, Houston, this is a fine mess you've got us into... where the hell are we? I can't tell you our coordinates exactly... but we're surrounded by water and blossoming cherry trees, and I can see Thomas Jefferson looking down at me, you geeks!"

"Eagle-One. No need to panic. We just can't wait to see you guys. Please turn on your emergency radio beacon. We'll see if there's a satellite up there that can pick it up... and then we'll send a ship out to find you two."

"That does it, Mission Control. Fuck you, Houston. This is the last straw. Captain Stanton and I are gonna' put on our water wings and swim home the rest of the way. Explain to the American people that you couldn't find their two best astronauts. It just goes to show you... outta' sight, outta' mind. Good-riddance, Houston."

*It was a very good thing they were finished traveling*, Mark thought. He wasn't sure B.J. could stand another day; he sounded like he was coming down with "capsule fever."

"Well Jackson, you have to admit that 'Stanley' here did a fine job all the way cross-country without a hitch."

"Sure enough. *Now* I can ask you why you call the car 'Stanley.'"

"Sure, why not? My very first date in California was a blind date that one of the girls in the office set up for me. As it turned out, my date had an aversion to my fire engine red Cougar convertible with the white ragtop. Frankly, I believe she was embarrassed to be seen in it. Apparently, it wasn't California-looking enough. Also, she had some sort of a mental block on my name all evening. First she called me Stanton, then Stapleton, then Stockton. As you can tell, things were going along just swimmingly, and then she had too much to drink. Anyway, when it was time to take her home and say good night, she gave me a peck and then fractured my last name by saying thanks 'Stanley' for a wonderful evening, but if you plan to call me again, lose that convertible."

"I never saw her again, but when I traded in the Cougar, I thought it only appropriate that I call my new car 'Stanley.'"

"As usual, I'm so glad I asked. If I could have just held out asking that question for another five minutes, we'd be there," B.J. muttered to himself.

## Disneyland East.

IT WAS EARLY evening. They had plenty of time to check-in at the hotel before going over to Perry Elam's home in Georgetown.

The Washington weather was still somewhat brisk, normal for mid to late March. A steady wind out of the northwest kept all the American flags atop the government buildings outstretched. Mark drove up 14th Street, first past the Bureau of Printing and Engraving building, the birthplace of dollar bills, then past the red-bricked Auditors' Building and the ancient Agriculture Department buildings. As they crossed the open Mall, the west front of the Capitol building and the imposing dome looked radiant in the late yellow light -- at the left was the five hundred fifty-five foot high Washington Monument, its long evening shadow lying across the street in front of them. Next they passed the stately Commerce Department building on the left.

"Did you know that they used to call that building 'Hoover's Folly' when it was first built. Herbert was the Commerce Secretary in those days, and people said he would never need a building that big to house the Commerce Department's staff. Well, I read somewhere... recently... that not only is Hoover's Folly full, but the Commerce Department now has employees spread out in more than a dozen other buildings all over the Washington, D.C., area."

"Wouldn't doubt it for a minute, which sounds like government at its best," B.J. smiled.

They passed the bizarre "baroqueness" of the District of Columbia's City Hall, on the right. Across the square they saw the weathered turret of the "new" Willard Hotel, built in 1900. The previous Willard Hotel, which stood on the same spot, was once the temporary home of President-elect Lincoln and its lobby always teemed with opportunists hustling Congressmen. This ritual dance at the Willard added the word "lobbyist" to the American lexicon. Mark continued up 14th Street, zig-zagging through scores of colorful, battered gypsy taxicabs -- past the entrance to the National Press building, toward K

Street, where they turned left. Two blocks later, they arrived at the Statler Hilton hotel.

They unloaded all the baggage and Mark turned the car over to the valet parking attendant. He told the guy not to "bury" the car that they'd need it to go out, in just an hour or so. The two travelers entered the familiar lobby that Mark had passed through so many times before, when he worked down the street at The White House. He used to come to the Statler to get a haircut from Carmelo the barber, or to have his shoes spit-shined before really important meetings.

As they moved to the elevators, en route to the fifth floor room, the bellman asked, "Have you fellows been to Washington before?"

"Yes sir," Mark said, "been here before... and I'm just moving back from California."

"They say California is the land of fruits and nuts... that's what I hear," said the bellman, trying to be funny. "Welcome to Disneyland on the Potomac!"

It was great being back in the Capital! Mark had a growing sense of anticipation; he couldn't wait to see his old friends from Dewey beach at Perry Elam's party. He was elated at being an "East Coaster" again. Now that he'd lived both east and west, and traveled in between, this was where he felt most comfortable. Washington was his adopted hometown.

In the hotel room, Mark could hear the sounds of city traffic on 16th Street below -- impatient hacks tooting horns at meandering tourists, noisy buses pulling away from bus stops in choking clouds of diesel fumes -- sounds of a busy, no-nonsense city. "I'm not leaving this place again. This is where I belong..." Mark peeked through the sheer curtains at the street, "Jackson... my next move will be in the back of a hearse. I'm staying put."

Mark and B.J. showered and spruced up for the party, leaving the hotel room a humid mess, reeking of after-shave lotion -- Old Spice and Brut, respectively. The bathroom was a slippery swamp, with wet towels hung on every protruding edge. But the two of them looked like a million. Their facial tans, about to peel from a week of windburn and southern exposure, made them stand out in the midst of a city of pasty pale-faces who'd yet to experience the warming days of spring.

When Mark returned to the front door he gave the hotel doorman the valet parking receipt. "What kind of car is it?" he wanted to know.

"A Porsche 924..."

"What color?"

Mark hesitated for just a second, and then said with a resigned grin, "black."

"Black?" B.J. turned. "My... my... Mr. Stanton, but we've come a long way in a week... and I don't mean from California either."

Mark purposely took the long way to Perry Elam's house. They crept past The White House, which looked picture perfect in the early evening floodlights. The early-spring red and yellow tulips on the north front, surrounding the floodlit fountain, were in bloom. They drove up Pennsylvania Avenue, past 17th Street through the streetlight-lit corridor of nameless office buildings that house the capital's trade associations and law firms, passing the area known as Foggy Bottom, home to George Washington University and the State Department. They went halfway around Washington Circle, and Mark aimed the car toward the amber lights of Georgetown. Mark savored every city block.

"Right Back To Where We Started From" by Maxine Nightingale, was playing on "Stanley's" Blaupunkt

There wasn't a single parking spot remaining on Prospect Street near Georgetown University. Apparently, Perry Elam's basketball party had filled up the handful of parking spaces that normally could be found on the narrow brick lane. B.J. and Mark found it necessary to meander three blocks away before they found a dubious spot in a back alley near 35th and "O" Streets.

"How much time before the game starts?" B.J. asked.

"I'll be damned..."

"What's the matter?"

"My watch... I must have left it in the room," Mark said.

"This is officially too much for me to handle in one week... *you* forgot your watch, your timepiece... your reason for living? The world must be unraveling as we speak."

They strolled toward Paul's house on the uneven brick sidewalks, under the glow of antique street lamps, passing rows of aged, but well-kept federal-style townhouses. There was just a hint of chill in the evening air; spring had not yet fully sprung itself on Washington.

The seven-day journey had started out one brisk but sunny Tuesday morning in front of a well-kept Victorian home on Arguello Street, in San Francisco's Presidio Heights, three thousand six hundred miles away. Georgetown and Presidio Heights... same country, but definitely two worlds apart.

## Perry's Party.

PERRY'S HOUSE WAS packed. B.J. and Mark were welcomed by their friends, as though they were prodigal sons returned; at least some people cared that they'd made it all the way back.

They'd arrived before the NCAA championship game telecast began. But Mark could hear the television network announcers saying, "Welcome to St. Louis, Missouri..."

Their host, Perry Elam, who had positioned his favorite easy chair right in front of the TV, jumped up and greeted them warmly. He was surrounded by thirty guys, most of whom they knew, sitting all over the living room and dining room -- on chairs, the couch, the staircase and on the floor. The guys all booed and threw popcorn at the two as they entered, then the boos dissolved into cheers and jeers. Elam gave each a hearty handshake and a pat on the back. "Welcome back, world travelers," he said. "The food's in the kitchen. Beer's on the back patio. In the meantime, you two celebrities make nice with all the girls. The boys and I will catch up with you after the game." He turned and made a standing leap back into his overstuffed easy chair.

As they moved through the living room, B.J. and Mark shook hands like two politicians working the rope lines. At first they tried standing by the kitchen door, trying to answer questions from the women while keeping one eye on the ball game. But that didn't work too well; they kept getting "shushed" by the die-hard Duke fans, led by Elam, who were trying to concentrate on the pre-game show. So eventually, B.J. and Mark set up shop outdoors, on the back patio which overlooked the Potomac River and the Francis Scott Key Bridge into Roslyn, Virginia.

People kept arriving from eight-thirty on. There were warm reunions with old beach house friends, some of whom they

# THE BEST GOOD TIME

hadn't seen in years. After a while, Mark gave up trying to remove the smeared lipstick on his cheeks.

Some ninety minutes later, at halftime, someone yelled out the window that Kentucky was beating Duke, 45 to 38. Mark imagined that Perry was in no mood to party at this point, despite the fact that there were now fifty or sixty people in his home.

Mark must have told and retold various episodes of the cross-country trip a dozen times by ten-thirty. Everyone seemed genuinely fascinated by the journey. Mark could hear B.J. doing the same thing, eliciting squeals of laughter from the women gathered around him in the corner of the patio. Most said they would die for a chance to drive cross-country at a leisurely pace. Mark would start telling a particular story and people would crowd in to hear it; at one point, he found himself backed into another group's conversation with B.J.

Later on, in the midst of a story, Mark managed to back right into an old friend. It was Will Rathman -- the ol' redhead -- a drinking buddy from his days up on Capitol Hill; they shook hands. Mark quickly finished the story and then he caught up on what Will was doing, which was working for a trade association in the securities industry.

"I thought I heard your voice," Will said, "but I couldn't spot you. I was just about to light up when 'wham,' you backed right into me, Stanton. How 'bout a smoke?" He offered a cigarette. Instinctively, Mark started to reach for one, but they weren't menthols.

"Let me hold off on that for now..." he said.

Then it dawned on Mark. *Where are my cigarettes?* He didn't have a pack on him. In fact, he couldn't remember when he'd last seen his pack of Salem's. *Must have left them in the car. When did I have my last smoke? Was it today?* Mark couldn't remember. *Was it yesterday in Atlanta? No. Was it in New Orleans?* Yes, that was it. He remembered having a cigarette at Bart's place Saturday night. Could that have been his last one?

"Thanks anyway, Will, but I think *maybe* I just quit."

"What do you mean 'think?'"

"Not sure. But if I change my mind after a few drinks, I'll come looking for you."

Mark saw B.J. talking to some young lovely in a dark corner of the flagstone patio. He went over to see if he could mess up any shot B.J. had at an impromptu home improvement project.

B.J. saw Mark coming, "Stanton... meet Vicki Holmes."

"Vicki," B.J. said, "this is my cross-country chauffeur, Mark Stanton. The fellow I was telling you about."

"Nice to meet you Vicki," Mark turned to B.J. "Jackson, I quit smoking! Did you notice that? I don't think I've had a cigarette since late Saturday or early Sunday."

"Yeah, I knew that..."

"Why didn't you say something?"

"What... and remind you to light one up and blow smoke all over me? Hell, I've been sneaking cigarettes out of your pack, one at a time, and throwing them out the window, when you weren't looking, since our first day on the road."

"No wonder my pack was always empty when I went for one... I was so involved in the driving... I guess I didn't realize if I was smoking or not."

Just then all the folks out on the garden patio heard a collective grunt come from the living room. There was a smattering of applause in the house, but mostly groans. Mark assumed that the ball game was over. Then it was confirmed.

"Final score, Kentucky 94, Duke 88," someone yelled out the open kitchen window.

"Jackson," Mark yelled. "Where are you? You owe me ten dollars!" There was no response from the darkest corners of the patio.

A short time later the guys from the living room began piling out onto the patio deck. The storytelling about the trip began anew.

Perry emerged from the kitchen door to great murmur and applause. He was holding a huge flat cake. "Ladies and gentlemen," he said, "gather around. I want you all to grab a drink and join me in a toast."

Perry set the sheet cake on a redwood picnic table; the cake had an outline of the United States on it. Someone handed Perry a fresh beer. He snapped open the top and lifted the can.

"Here's a toast to our good friends, Stanton and Jackson, our own Lewis and Clark. They are two brave travelers who have returned to the Capital after exploring the Louisiana Purchase and other uncharted territories. Join me in welcoming back these wandering gypsies to our humble group."

"Here, here..."

"Speech, speech..." a chant went up.

Mark responded, "All I've done is talk... all the way cross country... and ever since I arrived here... I can't believe you really want to hear me say anything else... how 'bout you Jackson? Give them a speech."

The chant for a speech continued.

B.J. stepped before the assembled crowd. "I feel like Marc Antony when he stepped on Cleopatra's barge. I'm not here to *talk*." Then he went and sat down.

The crowd cheered the perfect speech.

Upon closer inspection Mark noticed that across the top the cake it read, "Continental Drifters."

"Thank you Perry, but you didn't have to go to all this trouble for us..."

"Hell, why not? You gave me a hot story, didn't you Stanton?"

"What story?"

"Obviously, you haven't seen the Evening Star?"

"No."

"Well, yesterday I called the Pentagon about your cockamamie plane crash story. A half-hour later a general called me back to inform me that he had no record that an aircraft had crashed at Edwards Air Force Base last Tuesday."

"So maybe B.J. and I are crazy..."

"Don't worry. I confirmed a crash with other sources out in California. Besides, when some 'Lieutenant Pissant' from public affairs calls me, I know nothing happened. But when a two-star general picks up the phone and returns a measly reporter's call with 'we have no record of'... when I have two semi-reliable eye witnesses, well, you know the rest of that tune." Perry grinned and wiggled his bushy eyebrows. "Welcome back, Stanton. And thanks for my obscene wake up call from Texas."

"Sorry about your Blue Devils, Perry."

"Ah, they were playing way over their heads anyway... it was a big deal for them, just to get this far. But I have to give it to that Kentucky player, Jack Givens. He scored 41 points against us. If you can't stop a guy like that... well you don't deserve to win it all."

Elam heard his doorbell. Excuse me... I'll be right back... I think I know who that is... and Stanton, stay right where you are." He rushed off somewhere. No sooner had Mark turned to look for B.J. then Perry was back again.

"Stanton, there are some people here with strange accents who say they know you. They want to come outside and say hello..."

A small group emerged from the kitchen door and stepped into the lighted area. It was Mully and Janet -- all the way from Las Vegas by way of New York City!

"What in the name of... what are you doing here in Washington?"

"We're still on our honeymoon, wise guy," said Mully. "Some best man you turned out to be... handed me the gold ring and then skipped town. What the hell do you think we're doing here in Washington? I took Janet to the Waldorf in New York for the honeymoon, and while we were there, we decided to come down here to Washington for your big arrival back home."

"That's great... but how'd you know we'd be here at Perry's?"

"I can still track your ass down... it only took one phone call to my old gambling buddy, Perry. Hey...," said Mully, "lest I forget... there's someone else here who wants to say hi."

Behind Mully and Janet, a vision stepped into the light. It was Sally Markham! Mark froze like a deer in headlights.

She wasn't dressed in blue jeans and cowboy boots tonight. She was dressed like a Miss America contestant wearing a slinky black dress and high heels. Mark was speechless. But he managed to give her a big hug and a wet one, right on the lips. She looked fabulous; every guy on the patio was staring.

Somewhere deep in the house, Perry Elam's stereo was playing Bob Seger and the Silver Bullet Band's "Still The Same."

"How do you like it?" she twirled around like a runway model, "I picked it up at Sak's Fifth Avenue, in New York."

"I like you in it... you're a sight for sore eyes... but how'd you get on this honeymoon trip too?"

"I and a dozen other people went along... I'd never been to New York City before. In fact, virtually the entire wedding party, *except you*, flew to New York on Thursday. We've been dragging Jerry and Janet all over, all weekend. We just got into Washington tonight on the shuttle out of LaGuardia. The rest of the group, including Cindy, went home to Las Vegas this afternoon. Jerry got a hold of Perry Elam and found out you were arriving tonight and coming over here to Perry's house. Janet and Jerry invited me to surprise you upon your triumphant return. I hope you don't mind, but being just a country girl from Wyoming... I've never been to Washington either! So I took them up on the offer."

"I'd love to show you around... what are you doing for the rest of your life?"

"You're on," she said over her shoulder, "on the condition that you wear one of your three-piece suits." Sally had spotted B.J. and was on her way over to give him a big hug and deliver a kiss on behalf of her absent friend, the Scintillating Cindy.

During the hug B.J. leaned to Sally's ear and whispered, "Sally, you are the perfect woman for that man." Then he pointed in Mark's direction, saying loudly enough for Mark to hear, "Sally... see that man over there... I'll bet you ten dollars he'll be in trouble by midnight, tonight."

"Hey... that reminds me, Jackson, you owe *me* ten dollars, pay up deadbeat."

Mully put an arm around Mark's shoulders, pulled him aside, and whispered, "Stanton, you did me a favor last Tuesday night... and as of tonight, I'd say we're even. And by the way, don't let Sally give you all that country girl stuff. She's got a master's degree in business administration from the University of Colorado at Boulder. And Cindy says her daddy's got a big ol' ranch up in Wyoming. Wise up, wisenheimer. This here's the real McCoy. And she's been driving us crazy, asking about you since last Tuesday night at the Country Rebel. I got her here. The rest is up to you. Janet and I already have intimate in-suite plans for two this evening at our fancy hotel, thanks to Perry. So you better get busy, buddy. Time's a-wastin'."

"Mully, it's times like this... now I know why we'll always be friends."

Mark found Sally and escorted her to a quiet corner. They sat and spoke quietly for several minutes. They kissed and returned to the middle of the party holding hands.

As the evening at Perry's wound down, Sally and Mark inched toward the door. Mark spotted B.J. surrounded by a laughing group of people. "Hey, Jackson, better call Mission Control in Houston and tell them I'm ready for blast-off."

B.J. smiled his winning smile, flashed the peace sign and yelled back, "Roger, Captain. All systems are 'go.' Godspeed. See you Wednesday morning... I'm driving you to Baltimore. Over and out."

Sally blew a kiss good-bye to B.J. "William Jackson, you're the sweetest thing..."

Sally and Mark stepped out of Perry's front door into the crisp East Coast night. *One giant step* -- he thought, as Sally gripped his arm. Mark shivered as Stage One jettisoned, and the two of them launched into the future.

# CHAPTER EIGHT

## EPILOG
## (Thirty-something years later.)

### "Stanley" Steals Away.

THREE SET OUT for Washington, D.C. in March of 1978: Mark, B.J., and "Stanley," the Porsche 924. One of them didn't quite survive the entire journey.

The evening of Perry Elam's party, when Mark Stanton and Sally Markham returned to the alleyway where he'd parked "Stanley," the pearl gray Porsche was nowhere to be found.

After a frantic search Mark came to the stark realization that he was definitely back in Washington, D.C. "Stanley" had been stolen for sure. By the time the police arrived to fill out the reports, Mark was sure his beloved sports car was on its way to a Baltimore chop shop -- but then, *so was he on Wednesday*.

The incident made for a very bittersweet ending to what had been a wonderful week. "Stanley" was gone; but Sally had reappeared in his life.

### Wednesday, March 29, 1978

B.J. borrowed Perry Elam's car and drove Mark to Johns Hopkins Hospital in Baltimore at 5:00 a.m. Sally Markham accompanied them. Later that morning Mully and Janet arrived at the hospital, having stayed over in Washington two extra days. Originally Mark had planned to tell Mully about the cancer, but when the wedding surprised him, he put it off not wanting to ruin the honeymoon.

Mark went into surgery at 11:00 a.m. and was on the table for more than four hours. According to Doctor Roche, it was a tough call. The cancer they found was in early Stage II. The surgeons removed a portion of Mark's colon and believed they had gotten the entire cancer. Later Mark received months of post-surgical treatments. The specialists told Mark that only time would tell.

## Easter Sunday, this year.

THIRTY-SOME YEARS AFTER the cross-country trip, "Sweet" William "B.J." Jackson is still not married, but perhaps he sowed the last of his wild oats on that cross-country trip. Today he is living with Laurie, the beautiful raven-haired lady from Presidio Heights in San Francisco. He moved back to "The City" three months after he arrived in Washington, D.C. Eventually, he finished installing Laurie's bathroom plumbing and they've been together ever since. They still share that same yellow and white Victorian house on Arguello Street in "the City."

The world is very different today than it was some four decades ago. International terrorism is perhaps the most dramatic change. Another one, thanks to Ronald Reagan, is that The Cold War ended and the good guys won. The world's economic system practically melted down in the wake of the Wall Street's "sub-prime" mortgage loan crisis of 2008. The Federal government debt problem now looms as almost insurmountable for the next generation.

But many of the life changes during the last four decades have been subtle ones.

One small example, Porsche doesn't make the "924" model anymore. First it was upgraded to the "944" series; then it was eventually discontinued.

Three weeks after B.J. and Mark arrived in Washington the Panama Canal treaties were ratified on April 18, 1978, in the U.S. Senate by a vote of 68-32.

That valley they drove through, outside of San Jose, despite Mark's prediction, is still called the "Silicon Valley." And he still thinks it's a stupid nickname.

B.J. was right about cigarette smoking, by the turn of the century it was pretty much banned from public buildings and places throughout the United States. In Washington, it's now impossible to find a restaurant table where one can smoke a cigarette, but in New York City and other major markets there are whole establishments -- cigar bars -- where you can light up and puff on a Churchill.  Go figure.

Two years after the cross-country trip, John Belushi and Dan Aykroyd, the Blues Brothers, did make a movie, as B.J. suggested they should.  Despite the untimely death of Belushi, the movie remains a cult hit.  Aykroyd and Belushi's younger brother, Jim, appeared in a sequel: *Blues Brothers 2000*.

It turns out that Mully was very insightful about the future of Las Vegas.  Many of the companies that now own Las Vegas casinos are listed on the New York Stock Exchange.  Today, Jerry and Janet Mulligan are still happily married and remain in Vegas.  Mully visits Washington, D.C. several times a year on business as a lobbyist for the gaming industry.

B.J. was wrong about 24-hours a day, seven days a week cable news networks.  They aren't boring.  Tens of millions of people watch them 'round the clock.

The country and western song lyrics to, "I'll Be In Trouble By Midnight" never went anywhere.  Mark sent it along to some friends in Nashville, but nothing ever came of it.  B.J. still has the original lyrics, written on a yellow pad -- jotted down at 70 mph -- stashed somewhere in a desk drawer.

B.J. was absolutely right about several things.  America did need a cash vending machine and a company out of Dayton, Ohio, the Diebold Company, introduced one after perfecting the debit card interface.  Today there are well more than 400,000 Automated Teller Machines (ATM) machines in the U.S. processing some ten billion transactions per year.  Also, B.J. was right about car telephones.  One year after the trip, in 1979, the first cellular telephone network was built.  The growth in cell phone use since 1985 has been nothing short of phenomenal.  Ten years after the turn of the century there were some 280 million cell phones in the United States facilitating more than 1.4 billion calls per day.

The oil company forgave the entire $300 in traveler's checks they provided Mark in New Orleans in return for cutting up his perfectly good credit card.  Had he known they were going to forgive the entire amount, he would have asked for a hell of a lot more money.

"Imus in the Morning," the czar of Cleveland drive time radio, survived a second stint in Mark's hometown and wound up back in the national limelight again with a nationally syndicated radio program aired out of New York City and New Mexico, and simulcast on cable television no less. The man has nine lives!

Mark Stanton was right about some things too. His faith, like that of millions of Indians fans, has been rewarded in recent years with two trips to the World Series in the '90's, but the Tribe's curse of the "Rocco" still lives on, they still haven't won the big one yet. Major League Baseball finally returned to Washington, D.C. However, they built a fancy new stadium in a very bad part of downtown and so far the team has had difficulty filling the ballpark with fans.

Last year Mark's alma mater, John Carroll University named its School of Communications after the late Timothy J. Russert, Class of 1972. Tim Russert was not only a great guy, a tremendous newsman for NBC, but was unquestionably the very best political reporter and analyst of his generation. Mark knew him well as a fraternity brother and friend. His untimely death was a sad loss for us all.

## Our Protagonist.

And what ever happened to Mark Stanton? You might have guessed...

More than thirty years after his colon cancer surgery Mark Stanton remains a cancer survivor. It was a close call, but he was quite fortunate. After recuperating from his surgery and the subsequent treatments, he went west again later that year, to Wyoming, where he found, courted and married the lovely, beautiful and remarkable Sally Markham.

Eventually, the couple settled down in Cleveland. Upon returning to his home state of Ohio, Mark looked up an old college friend who owned a radio station, and within a month, he became a local talk show host during the afternoon drive hours. The very first guest, by special invitation, on Mark's inaugural radio program, was none other than Bart Hampton of New Orleans. Who else but "Big Bart," the fellow with the very deep Barry White voice, the man who first introduced Mark to talk radio and was the first person to ever address him as "Honorable."

Three years later his same media friend bought a Cleveland television station and Mark hosted a local talk show. On the side, he managed to become a semi-successful Little League baseball coach.

Sally Markham Stanton became a broker and partner in a local real estate firm. Together, they raised three children, Marcus, who is starting out as an architect, Mary Ellen, a promising graphic artist, and Cindy, a freshman in college -- named after the scintillating "guess who."

After years of railing against the know-nothings in Congress while "on the air," in 1988, ten years after their cross-country trip, Mark Stanton ran for and was elected -- as part of the Bush-Quayle landslide -- to serve as a freshman Congressman from northern Ohio. Mark's being a local television broadcast personality didn't hurt his name recognition at the polls. Upon his election to the House of Representatives, Sally and he moved to the Washington area where they lived together for another twenty years.

There, in the U.S. House of Representatives -- of all places -- Mark met Congresswoman Amy Zimmerman-Wright, a second-term member from Houston, Texas. They remembered each other right away. Although details of their initial meeting, ten years previous, were never ever mentioned, they developed a friendly, close-working professional relationship. In Mark's mind, Amy remains a very intelligent, attractive and nice person, and her husband Vince turned out to be a great guy too. Having two years of seniority on Mark, she actually outranked him on the House Telecommunications Subcommittee -- small world department.

Sally and Mark and the kids truly loved the years he served in the Nation's Capital. Mark enjoyed showing Sally all the places she'd only heard about. He took her places where he'd gone as a young man, like the infamous Dewey Beach where Mark, B.J. and so many of their close friends had spent the summers of their youth.

With time, Sally grew fond of the Midwest and the East Coast even though Mark knew -- in her heart -- she was a girl of the Western plains. She made the most of life -- theirs and hers.

Tragically, Mark's beloved Sally died in an automobile accident, caused by a drunk driver in February, last year.

The event devastated Mark. He resigned from Congress in mid-term and took the rest of the year off. Before even thinking about the next phase of his life, he used the empty months to put thoughts on paper, to write a book -- after all, him writing a book was Sally's idea.

This Easter, at the urging of his three children, well more than thirty years after meeting Sally on that cross-country trip, Mark found a way to cheer himself up. He splurged and bought a new Porsche, a "Stanley-II", if you will. And he plans to drive cross-country again -- this time from Washington, D.C. to California. Again, B.J. will join him on the journey. They will end up in San Francisco and Mark will visit for a while with B.J. and Laurie. Once again the weeklong trip will give him time to think out loud with B.J. -- to put things in perspective and to decide what rightly should be next in life.

As B.J. can attest, Mark always did his best thinking behind the wheel, talking things through on the open road. This time B.J. said he couldn't wait to hear some new stories.

In his book manuscript about the 1978 cross-country trip with B.J., Mark Stanton dedicated the work to his children. He wrote:

*"For each of you, I hope you find joy in life. And that you give joy to others. I know I've been very fortunate. I've dodged a few bullets in my life. I've had many, many good times. And I hope there are a few more to come. But for me, 1978 will always stand out as a very good year. In fact, it was the best year of my life. And I will always cherish that marvelous week in March of that year. It was the week of the cross-country trip with B.J. It was the week I met Sally -- the true joy of my life. That week was, without a doubt, the best good time of my life."* Happy Easter, Love, Dad.

LaVergne, TN USA
04 August 2010
192162LV00001B/18/P